Sweet

Uzuri M. Wilkerson

Sweet
by Uzuri M. Wilkerson

Second Edition

Cover by ReBelle Design Studio

www.uzurimwilkerson.com
www.amazon.com/author/uzuriwilkerson

Other works by
Uzuri M. Wilkerson

Bitten:
Sour
Bitter

Sweet

One

THE DJ PUMPED hip-hop tonight. The bass literally rattled the walls, fueling the gyrating hips and shuffling feet. Sweat glistened on foreheads, pasted shirts to skin. A group of three guys showed off the latest dance moves—something involving jerky leg movements—all the while grinning from ear to ear from the attention.

The lights guy, feeling the groove of the evening, went a little overboard with the strobes. Celia tried to ignore the dull ache behind her eyes as patrons clamored around the bar, attempting to catch her attention while, at the same time, creating a different pain farther south. Celia pointed to a man with one of those douchebag, carefully constructed, messy bed-head hairstyles.

He reached across the bar, and took her wrist in his calloused hand. He used his finger to graze the sensitive skin of her inner wrist.

"Seven-and-seven, sweetheart," he called with a smarmy

smile, except, with his Revere accent that last word was more like "sweet-haht."

She refrained from rolling her eyes and slipped her hand from his grasp, all the while maintaining a friendly smile. Nothing to compromise tips. She was saving up for a trip with her boyfriend, Victor. Naturally, you would think that meant the sunny Caribbean or beautiful beaches of Miami. Nah. Sunshine was out of the question. He was talking Alaska or Washington and, needless to say, Celia was not all that enthused.

Turning to the back bar, she pulled down the Seagram's to make the man whom she now dubbed "Douchey" his drink.

"Can I have two Bud Lights?" someone called.

She topped off the Seagram's with 7-Up, nodded to the other man in acknowledgment, and then handed Douche Bag his drink. He left fifty cents and not so much as a second glance. Celia took two beers from the fridge and popped the tops. She slid the bottles across the bar.

"Ten bucks." He left her three dollars.

People lobbed drink orders at her left and right. That was the way it usually went on the weekends at Cage's Bar and Lounge. Weekdays were a lot slower-paced—well, *differently*-paced was more like it—since it was just the restaurant. Thursday through Saturday night, the tables and chairs were stored away at nine and Cage's became a nightclub, complete with ridiculous cover charge and steel cages for the dancers.

Sometimes there were issues with this process. For instance, if a table was lingering, taking their sweet time finishing up, the staff would have to clear around them. Once they realized that they were sitting in the middle of a dance floor, the table usually hauled ass. At times, stealthy dirty looks from the staff helped. You know, it wasn't like the guests weren't aware. There were ample signs posted, usually placed prominently next to the condiments, warning patrons that the tables were removed at nine and apologizing for the inconvenience. "Inconvenience" was spelled incorrectly because Bobby, Cage's owner and manager, hadn't notice.

Celia usually alternated days and nights. Bobby liked to have Celia work weekend nights because she was fast and efficient and it didn't hurt that she was pretty.

Celia was at the top of her game tonight. Guys decked out in Red Sox attire tried hard to capture her attention. They ordered often, each more googly-eyed than the last. She played along, an expert by now of *seeming* available.

Late in the night, a drunken chick complemented her necklace. She fingered it at the mention. A small heart on a glittery gold chain hung delicately in the hollow of her neck.

"It really is beautiful."

The smooth voice floated to her ears as easily as if he were standing beside her. A smile played at her lips. She didn't even have to look up to recognize the voice.

"It was a gift." She replied in a normal voice that no ordinary person would ever be able to hear in a noisy club. He did.

"A gift?"

"Yeah." She looked up into his gray eyes. One eyebrow was raised slightly in his amusement. "From this guy," she added casually.

"Well, he's a lucky man."

She laughed. A white light flashed across the bar. She noticed for the first time the pink in his cheeks and lips, how light his eyes were. Her laugh ceased almost immediately, her good mood slipping away.

She lowered her gaze to the bar in the guise of checking the bottles in her well. "I'll be off soon, Victor." Her voice was deflated, and she knew he could hear it, but she just couldn't hide her . . . what? Disappointment? Anger? She didn't know what she was feeling.

Victor's expression tightened. He nodded curtly and then disappeared so fast, it was as if he had not been there at all.

The DJ announced the last song five minutes before two. "Blame It" by Jamie Foxx. How appropriate. One of the many pluses that drew people inside Cage's glass doors was they played good music and played good music right up to one fifty-eight am.

The crowd was pretty calm by the time "Blame It" started to play so it wasn't too hard to clear the place out. Most of them even headed out of their own volition. Last Call was ten minutes ago. The bartenders were cleaning up and closing out tabs. There were already five abandoned credit cards.

"Hey, Seal." That was Trixie, Celia's friend. She was a dancer for the club. Go-go dancer, not stripper, though she often threatened to take it up. She would proclaim that she could make a shit-ton more money, especially as a twosome—wink, wink, nudge, nudge. Celia didn't even humor the idea. Along with strutting her stuff in steel cages, Trixie also worked tables as a cocktail waitress between sets.

Celia glanced over her shoulder. "Hey Trix. I'm almost done."

"Take your time," she said, flipping her thick black hair out of her face. Her lips were crimson red, her signature color when she was working. It blended nicely with her porcelain skin. Celia couldn't pull off red lipstick. Her skin was like coffee with three creams and no matter the shade, red lips didn't work on her.

Trixie turned for one of the booths to wait and count her tips but Bobby walked up behind her, startling her. Bobby was a solid man, in his forties, wearing gray slacks and a powder blue shirt. Tiny half-circles of sweat stained his underarms, a reminder of how hot a crowd of people could make a place. Now that it was empty, the AC actually gave Celia a chill.

"Stay close, Trixie," Bobby said. He raised his voice for everyone to hear him. There were twelve people in the area—the three bartenders, two bar backs, three dancers, and four custodians. “I need everyone’s attention.”

The girls behind the bar continued to clean while listening. Bobby put his hands in his pockets, trouble clouding his brown eyes. “There have been some issues at the front door,” he began.

Just then, the two head bouncers on tonight came down the stairs. They strode across the dance floor toward the bar: two massive meatheads who waddled more than walked since they could no longer lower their arms to their sides. Whatever stereotypical image that popped in your head about bouncers was exactly what Rick and Meat looked like.

“Rick tells me that our friends have been back.”

There was a collective groan. “Friends” was not a good word, even in jest. These “friends” were five guys who would periodically try to sell drugs in the club, or at least that was the common conception. They’d been threatened and beaten by the bouncers, as well as been arrested. Even so, they insisted on coming back. No one understood it. There were plenty of other clubs in the area; they were downtown after all. For whatever reason, these five guys kept showing up at Cage’s.

Celia had never seen any of them personally but she always heard about it later if there was an incident.

Bobby put his hand up to silence his employees. He’d been running Cage’s for eight years now. He was used to troublemakers.

“Be alert. Rick and Meat and the guys are good, but it helps to have the extra vigilance. If you see any of them, let one of us know. If you need reminding of what they look like, I still have their pictures up in the office. That’s all.”

Bobby strolled away with the bouncers. Trixie raised her eyebrows at Celia with a grin. She thought it was exciting.

After another thirty minutes, Celia and Trixie left out the front door for the night. Meat, having been charged with locking up after everyone left, smiled at them appreciatively. The light of the streetlamp above shone on his bald head.

"Night," Trixie called.

"It sure would be my night if you let me take you home," he called after them. Trixie giggled and waved over her shoulder as they continued down the street.

"You know Bobby doesn't like that," Celia chided, though she knew her friend meant no harm. Trixie stuck her tongue out at her.

It was sticky tonight, as it gets in August. The weathermen were predicting thunderstorms as cause of the humidity encasing the city. Celia felt the sweat building on her collarbone. She hated to sweat, which was probably why she seldom went to the gym. At least, that's what she told herself.

Taco's Tacos was a Mexican restaurant next door to the lounge. The owner allowed the club employees to park in his lot after hours, which was incredibly nice of him. Parking was scarce in Boston, even if you beat the nightclub crowd. Since public transportation stopped running at twelve-thirty and cabs could get expensive, you needed a ride.

Five cars were scattered in the concealed lot. The girls walked to Celia's black Honda Accord, their sneakers echoing on the cracked pavement. There was a slight movement to their right, a shift in the darkness. Trixie shrieked.

Celia rolled her eyes at Trixie's jumpiness. "Calm down, it's just Victor."

He emerged from the shadows across the lot. "That's so creepy," Trixie whispered to Celia. Celia tried not to smile because she knew Victor could hear her.

Victor looked all kinds of sexy in dark slacks and a slate gray shirt. The top two buttons were undone. The moonlight cast a shimmering spotlight as he made his way over. How was that possible?

"My apologies," he replied when he was closer to them. He bent to give Trixie a deep bow. "I didn't mean to startle you."

Trixie ran a hand through her hair, trying to compose herself. She gave him a tight smile. "I know you do that on purpose."

He shrugged as if to say *guilty*. Victor greeted Celia with a kiss on the lips and a squeeze of her waist. She didn't quite respond to the affection, letting him know she was still upset. They climbed into the car. The coconut-scented air freshener in her vents was suffocating in combination with the bottled-up humidity. They rolled down the windows for relief and Celia drove off.

Trixie rambled on about an upcoming date. She was having dinner on Sunday with a guy she had met at her day job with Verizon Wireless. Neither Celia nor Victor was listening. Celia dropped Trixie at her apartment she shared with her sister in Hyde Park. She lived in a brick building with bad lighting in the hallways, crappy plumbing, and paper-thin walls. The girls dealt with those lovely amenities because it was their own. Anything was better than living at home with their two brothers who, along with mooching off their parents, took great pleasure in tormenting their sisters between bong hits and video game tournaments.

Celia was about to put the car in drive when Victor placed his hand on hers, stalling her. His touch was warm. She groaned, and snatched her hand away.

"Do you want to talk about it?" he asked. His tone was patronizing.

She glowered at him. "You suck, you know that?"

There was a pause, Victor's face was motionless. Then he threw his head back and laughed. It was a hearty laugh and she could see his fangs were out. Celia fumed even more.

"Don't laugh at me!"

"Sorry," he said through his chuckling. "But, come on. That was funny."

It would've been funny to her if she weren't so fucking mad. Instead, she folded her arms at the chest and stared out the windshield. He moved so fast that she didn't even notice until his face was buried in her neck. His arms were around her, holding her in place because he knew she would try to push him away. It would be pointless, but she would try anyway.

He kissed her neck, inhaled her scent. "You smell like strawberries," he murmured.

"New shampoo," she grumbled. Her curly, auburn hair was pulled back and held in place by flower clips that kept it out of her face.

Her anger was making her heart pound and he was getting aroused. He licked her neck through his fangs to demonstrate. She moved as best she could, shrugging her shoulder up to conceal her throat. Seeing that she wasn't giving in, he leaned back, still holding on to her. He stared at her a moment. Her eyes were cold and unyielding. He sighed and let go.

"I give up! You know I have to feed—"

"I know!" she cried over him.

"So why do we have to go through this *every* time?"

He was livid now, which wasn't a good thing. He had a harder time controlling himself when he was angry. In fact, at that very moment, his hand was curled around the door handle. The metal issued a groan as his grip tightened.

She saw this and remembered how he had broken her armrest the last time they had argued. It still sat in her trunk, waiting to be replaced. He was supposed to fix that, if memory served her correctly.

Celia took a deep breath, forcing herself to calm down. She had to clear her mind in order to accomplish this task. He must've heard her heartbeat slow to its regular pace because he released the handle. It was thinner in the middle now, like it was wearing an invisible corset.

"Sorry," she said softly.

"I'm sorry, too." His fangs were gone now that he was calmer.

They sat in silence for a moment. She was imagining Victor with some girl in the lounge, maybe in the bathroom. In this particular vision, the girl was tall, rail-thin, with thick blonde hair that wasn't all her own and big, round . . . eyes.

It played out like a scene from a movie: He would pull her into an empty stall. Victor was very attractive, with soft, black hair, an angular chin, gray eyes, and a thin mouth. He didn't need to use the preternatural allure that vampires often utilized to capture humans in their control. The girl probably went willingly.

He would gently kiss her neck, not unlike how he'd nuzzled Celia a few moments ago. He would do this to soften the blow before he sank his teeth into her flesh. After, he would lave the wounds with his tongue. The marks would turn pink after thirty seconds, and then disappear after two minutes. That vampire mind-control would come in handy then, making her forget their encounter.

Her curiosity had been overwhelming, so one day she had asked. When Victor told her how it worked, Celia had been sick to her stomach. It didn't sit well with her that he erased himself from their memories, like some kind of supernatural roofie, only a helluva lot more effective and without the drowsiness and confusion later on. It was nauseating. What else could he do, though? Vampires were the stuff of legends and myths. If they didn't enthrall their catch, their secret would be out.

"Where do we go from here?" Victor asked. He always asked that when they had this argument.

She thought it over, as she always did. She liked Victor; he was sexy and fun and made her feel desirable. So, there were some things about him that were less than . . . savory. Everybody had their issues. Celia snored sometimes, for one.

She heaved a sigh and leaned across to press her lips against his. It was a deep kiss. He would know all was forgiven for the time being. She was happy his teeth were normal at the moment. It had taken her a while to get used to kissing him with his fangs, since they usually made an appearance when he was turned on. They were never put to use with her. Was there such a thing as blue fangs?

He rubbed her back, his fingers grazing her bra strap. Electricity passed through his fingers down to her bones, making her shiver.

She drew back to gaze into his face. Those beautiful eyes seemed even softer in the moonlight. She was sinking into those eyes, down inside him. She felt warm and tingly and light-headed. This feeling was so hypnotic; she found she could not look away.

He could do anything to her at the moment because she was his, all his. There was so much she wanted to do to him. She wanted to rip his clothes off with her bare hands like he could do, to pull his hair—in fact she raked a hand roughly through his dark mane. With her other hand, she cupped his crotch. She leaned forward and nipped his neck with a purr. Her breasts rubbed against his chest. She wanted to run her tongue over his body, nibble his nipples because he was one of the few guys actually finding pleasure in that sort of thing, kiss his navel, take him all in her mouth, in her—

"Stop it!" she shouted abruptly and the grip was released. She fell back into her seat as if he had been physically holding her. She had to close her eyes to make her head stop spinning. While she gathered her bearings, she realized she no longer yearned to rip his clothes off or have her way with him. Those urges vanished. There *was* one thing she wanted to do though and it was every bit her own sentiment.

When Celia opened her eyes, she punched him hard in his shoulder. She regretted that action instantly.

A jolt of pain shot up from her knuckles through her wrist. The ache was so excruciating and so sudden that all she could do was gasp. So, that's what it felt like to punch a brick wall. She held her aching hand to her chest as tears pooled in her eyes.

"Fuck, Seal, why'd you go and do that?"

"I told you about using that shit on me!" Her voice trembled, taking away from the indignation she was going for.

"Sorry, I can't help it sometimes when I'm . . . you know . . . Same with—" He held his right hand to his mouth, arched two fingers and jerked his wrist to indicate the fangs. She rolled her eyes, too achy to be annoyed.

He reached over and, as if she were no lighter than a doll, lifted her from the seat and into his lap. She had to duck her head so it didn't bang against the ceiling. Cradling her hand, he kissed each knuckle. It didn't help at all.

"Are you going to be okay?" he asked. She pouted in response. "Do you want me to take you to the hospital?"

She moved her fingers and, though her hand throbbed, it didn't feel like anything was broken. She needed her money to pay her bills, not a hospital's co-pay. "No, I think I'm okay."

He held her tighter, like he didn't want to let her go. She leaned into him. She was always surprised at how normal his body felt. Though he could break her fist with one punch, he still felt human, like someone with muscles from working out.

He smelled like evergreens and dirt tonight, which was weird. She wondered what he had been doing between dusk and appearing at the lounge.

Celia yawned. "Hmm," Victor said, his voice vibrating in his chest. "I guess it'll be an early night."

He shifted so that she was on the seat and he was behind the wheel. He put the car in drive and zoomed through the streets. She glared at him because she hated when he sped. He flashed a brilliant smile in response.

They reached Celia's house in no time. She lived in Dorchester, in a tiny one-bedroom apartment inside a brick building on a street lined with brick apartment buildings. She could only afford to live by herself because of a settlement with a major bus company. A driver for one of those Boston to New York express bus lines had been drinking on the job and rear-ended her on the Mass Pike, right outside of Newton.

She had volunteered to run some extra Baby's Breath to her uncle in Worcester. He was a florist, setting up an office Christmas party, and needed the flowers after one of his employees dropped a bouquet in a puddle. The Pike was quickest. The blustery cold that night had caused tiny circles of frost to form at the base of her back windows. Celia's heater had been on the fritz. She was shivering and cursing the fact she had to take the tolled road when the bus ran her off the road.

She was pretty set for a while with the settlement, plus the inheritance from her mother's life insurance that she never touched. She could've moved somewhere larger. She kept the small apartment because she loved it and didn't have any problems with her neighbors, like Trixie.

Victor found a spot and they climbed out. "Why is it that *you* can always get a spot right in front of the door?" Celia complained.

He kissed her forehead as they walked up the stairs to the apartment building. Inside, she turned the air conditioner on in the stuffy living room. The cooler air was the only way to ensure she'd be able to sleep. Forty minutes and the apartment would be a comfortable sixty-five degrees.

She stood in front of the AC, letting the bitingly cold air freeze her skin. Victor came up behind, wrapping his arms around her waist. Something cold and wet pressed against her skin. She looked down at the bag of frozen peas he held against her sore wrist.

"You're sweating."

Celia rolled her eyes. "Yeah, I do that sometimes," she said harshly.

"Are you going to be pissy with me for a while? I just want to be prepared."

She turned in his arms to face him. His voice had been joking but she could see he was troubled. She quickly told herself that she *had* agreed that all was forgiven and that she should chill the fuck out.

She smiled a little. "Let me just jump in the shower, then I'll be a happy camper."

He didn't release her—and the reason why pressed insistently into her hip. His eyes darkened as she watched, his expression shifting to a more serious one. He leaned down and their lips melted together.

"Ew," she murmured around his mouth. "I'm sweaty."

"I like when you're sweaty." He sounded slightly wistful. He was remembering when he used to sweat. She felt her heart break a little in sympathy. Victor didn't talk much about when he . . . came over, even when she let him know she was there for him.

There were times when she could tell he missed being human. She'd catch him staring at people as they walked down the street, smiling and oblivious. Yearning would blaze in his eyes, tensing his shoulders, something he couldn't hide. She never knew what to say to him during those moments. She usually held his hand or stroked his hair. Tonight, she flattened her body against his.

With nimble fingers, he removed her shirt and bra in three seconds flat, a new record. The air from the window unit chilled her sweat, causing goose bumps to erupt and her nipples to stand at attention. He kissed her lips, then her chin, then lowered her to the floor in front of the sofa.

Celia tossed the bag of peas aside; to hell with it. Giggles issued from her lips as his tongue flicked across her skin, running along her breasts and encircling her nipples. She interlocked her fingers behind her head as she watched his head bob on top of her.

He leaned back and pulled his shirt over his head, ruffling his hair. She took in his exquisite physique while biting her bottom lip in excitement. She tried not to be self-conscious in front of him, even now as nagging thoughts whispered in the back of her mind. He'd told her a million times he loved her body. She thought otherwise. It was negligible, but she had rolls on her stomach that only disappeared when she was lying flat as a board.

Victor took her black Chucks off one at a time and slowly eased her black jeans over her hips so he could take in a better view of her supple body. She ran her bare foot up his chest, prolonging him just a little more with a sexy smile.

He kissed her body, taking his time at her pressure points. He listened to her rhythm at her wrists, her chest, the back of her knees, and the crook of her neck. He parted her thighs and inhaled her scent. He used his fingers to taste her wetness first before lowering his face between her legs. Involuntary spasms made her shoulders twitch as his tongue stroked her middle. She held his head in place, tears streaming into her ears. She arched her back and moaned a string of profanity toward the ceiling.

She was nearly at her peak when he finally entered her, slowly stretching her until he fit. His fingers were rough as they raked through her hair. She winced at her poor little strands struggling to stay in her scalp.

"Too tight!" she warned, slapping his hand.

"Sorry." He loosened his grip. Hey, sometimes he forgot his

strength.

It only took two thrusts for the pain in her scalp to intensify his movements. Celia sank into his rhythm, bucking her body against his in a ravenous urge to feel more. She needed more of him, all of him. Victor tried to control himself but she felt damn good, she was all he needed to sate his urges. He buried himself deep within her, taking advantage of the pleasure and peace she provided. He let out a low primal growl and sank his face in her neck, to conceal that his fangs extended. Celia wrapped her legs around his waist to keep him in place as she murmured his name and scratched his back in a haze of ecstasy. Her nails dug deep but he could take it.

They came together; clinging to each other as stars exploded in front of them. A sizzle of energy sparked between them like an electric current. He gripped the rug and dug a hole into her shag carpet with his sharp nails. He pulled his face from her shoulder and panted with the exertion of not ripping her neck open. She glimpsed his fangs slowly recede after a moment.

"So," Victor replied, ten minutes later. Celia was curled against him, mostly naked, as he held the melting peas on her knuckle. The cold was making her hand numb but at least it wasn't aching at the moment. She had been slipping under the waves of bliss-induced sleep until his voice gently roused her. "Are we going to Alaska next month?"

She groaned. "I don't want to go to fucking Alaska. Who goes to fucking *Alaska* for vacation?"

"Someone who wants to actually spend time with her boyfriend."

"But I wanna suntan," she groused.

"Stop being a baby."

"I wanna shop for bikinis, not parkas!"

"Celia . . ."

"I wanna lounge on the beach and splash in the water and sip margaritas until I'm drunk out of my fucking mind and can't find my hotel room."

He sighed. They were both quiet for a moment. The air whooshed through the AC. A car horn beeped once from the street. Her freezer chugged to life in the kitchen.

"Maybe you should," he said softly. She stilled. "Go with Trixie. Go to Mexico or Hawaii and have fun."

Now, she felt like shit. She knew she shouldn't complain so much. They didn't get to vacation together. She propped herself up on her elbow and looked him in the eyes. They were so dark, they looked black. She ran a finger over his tense jaw, and then kissed his cheek.

"I hear Seattle's nice," she said.

His smile didn't quite reach his eyes but it still managed to relax his face. His eyes lightened, too, so she was happy. She kissed him again and rested her head on his shoulder.

She was out like a light.

Two

CELIA CUT TWO limes into small wedges and placed them into the plastic garnish trays. The slots for lemons were already filled. Personally, she preferred pinwheels for the fruit. Bobby had them do wedges, though, because he was neurotic like that and had to have a say in every minute detail.

Carson stood beside her, filling the sinks with ice. He was taller than Celia, who was only five-five, and he had a swimmer's build: broad shoulders and tiny waist, though his round gut put to rest any debate on his athleticism. His hair was brown and short, his blue eyes a little too small for his oval face.

He tried to catch her eye, and when she finally glanced up to look for the cherries, he smiled. She immediately darted him a look, warning him not to start.

"What?" he asked, feigning surprise at her gruffness. "I was just going to ask if you're ready for a fun night. Saturday's are awesome, don't you think? Especially when you're working with me." He jerked his thumbs to his chest, a smug grin on his face.

She rolled her eyes as she pulled the jar of maraschino cherries from the fridge. Her wrist was still a bit sore as she twisted the top of the jar. She had popped two aspirins at the start of her shift. She filled the trays, ignoring him. Next up, checking the cup supply.

"See, I was just trying to be nice."

She raised a single eyebrow, looking very much like one of those anime characters before they attacked.

"Carson."

"It's that time of the month or something? Where you can't even be *nice* to men?"

How original.

Going against her first instinct of punching the shit out of him, she closed her eyes to count aloud to ten. Carson snickered at "three" and left by "five." After counting, and making sure he was gone from her sight, she searched the bar for an extra wine key because she couldn't find her own.

Trixie flounced over to the bar where Celia was adjusting her outfit. The doors were going to open in a half an hour. It was strange that Mickey, tonight's DJ, hadn't started playing yet. The normal background music had been turned off five minutes ago, making every sound seem magnified in the quiet.

"Are you dancing tonight?" Celia asked.

She pouted. "No, I hurt my ankle this morning, running down the stairs. Bobby was mad." Celia peeked over the counter and saw the ice pack held to her ankle with saran wrap. Well, she could join the club.

"He'll get over it."

"Do I look okay?"

Celia looked her over. She was wearing a black mini-skirt that showed off her toned legs and a black tank top with sequins on the front that winked in the strobe lights. Her boobs were high and perky. Her hair was down over her shoulders and her lips blood red. A vixen to say the least.

"Teeth?"

Trixie bared her teeth. No lipstick stains. No remnants of her spinach salad.

"You look perfect. The guys are gonna be all over you." Trixie liked to hear those kinds of things.

She beamed. "Good. I need the tips."

Bobby emerged from his office to rush over to Mickey. "What the fuck?" he shouted. "What're you waiting for?"

The few patrons still munching hot wings and drinking beer glanced over at the outburst. Bobby's ears reddened when he noticed there were non-staff in the area. He ran a hand over the front of his pale pink shirt self-consciously before throwing an insolent glare at DJ Mickey.

"Sorry, B," Mickey called. "I was looking for my extra box."

"It's here!"

One of Mickey's entourage emerged from the back, holding a crate of records in his arms. Mickey looked relieved. He grinned at Bobby and flipped a switch. A Britney Spears song blared from the speakers. Trixie left with a wave, since conversation was no longer possible.

The music was like a cue. Carson and the other two bartenders came around the bar, taking up their stations. The doors were opened and people poured in like there was free chicken or something.

It was nearly midnight when Celia stepped out back. Beside the bar was the server's window to the kitchen. Before the window, a short hallway led to the kitchen and Bobby's office.

Celia pushed through the swinging door and entered the kitchen. She wasn't at all surprised to find it empty. Food service ended at eleven, which meant ten forty-five in the minds of the chefs. They usually checked out at eleven-fifteen, eleven twenty-five at the latest.

She crossed to the walk-in fridge for a bottle of water. She stood there, taking a long gulp while enjoying the cold washing over her.

She was making a semi-disgusted face at a pile of chicken wing packets when a crash on the other side of the door made her jump. She peeked outside, assuming she would be helping one of the bar backs clean up spilled beer.

The kitchen was small. There were only four chefs and they didn't need that much space. Three men struggled beside the silver table that served as a prep station in the center of the room. A rack was suspended from the ceiling above it, laden with silver pots and pans that quivered from the action below.

The men were grunting and panting. A blonde one with a denim jacket and black pants was holding a short man with dark hair and black clothes across the chest. The short man kicked the third one, who had fiery red hair and freckles and couldn't have been more than twenty years old. He hit the floor hard and kept sliding. Celia was mystified; the short man didn't look that strong.

When he broke free of the blonde's grasp, there was a cracking sound. The blonde yelped and held his forearm to his stomach. The short man punched him in the face. He fell against the table. Blood dripped from his nose like a leaky faucet.

Celia's jaw dropped. *Vampire*, she immediately thought.

The short man stood over him, looking triumphant. "Nice try," he said, being entirely too damn cocky for his own good. Even from her distance, she saw his fangs were out. He turned but the red head was quick. He ran into him with a grunt then jumped aside in case he attacked. A large, wooden stick was lodged in the vampire's chest.

He looked down, surprised. Blood spurted out around the stake, staining the table and floor and the red head's boots. A burning smell suddenly filled the space. The scent was so strong, Celia thought she would gag, but she couldn't look away. The exposed skin of the vampire's arms and face and neck turned black, like he was being charred by a fast moving, invisible flame. He looked to the ceiling, his mouth opened to emit one final scream. The sound never formed. The man crumbled into a pile of black dust or ash or something that tarnished the white floor.

Celia jumped back into the fridge and placed a hand on her chest. It felt like her heart was trying to shoot out and run from the room. While she waited for her pulse to settle, she realized something about the two humans. They looked so familiar yet, try as she might, she could not place them.

After a moment, she leaned her ear toward the door. She heard movement but couldn't tell what they were doing.

Her curiosity was winning out over caution. She pushed the door open slightly. The two men were crouched on the floor, one with a broom and dustpan, the other with a handful of cloth napkins.

"What's that, two tonight?" the blonde asked with a shake of his head. "They're growing."

They tossed the ashes into a black trash bag, along with the vampire's clothes and the stained napkins.

The blonde snatched up a napkin to wipe his face. He held his left hand to his chest, which must've been the cause of that snapping sound. They then headed out the door that led to the alleyway behind the lounge, their sneakers sounding heavy and official on the floor.

Celia stepped out of the fridge gingerly. She was shivering now and not just from the cold. She walked over to the side of the table where the fight had taken place. Only traces of the black ash remained. It could have been spilled pepper if you didn't look too closely.

Stooping down, she touched the smudges. She jerked her

hand away with a gasp. The ash was hot. She wiped the soot on her pants.

Footsteps sounded behind her. She glanced over her shoulder. Carson looked harassed.

“Celia!” he sighed. “There you are. Bobby’s furious.”

“Okay, okay. I’m coming.”

Celia was still thinking about the men in the kitchen as she waited for Joni to count out their tips. She was wondering if she should tell Bobby. Except there was no body and no real evidence of a fight. Plus, the men were gone. She could only imagine Bobby’s reaction to her telling him there had been a vampire in his club. She’d be on the next bus to the loony bin, complementary straight-jacket included.

The fight repeated itself in her head. The two men seemed to be experts; they knew how to kill the vampire. She figured at the very least she should warn Victor.

Oh, shit.

Victor.

That was what happened when a vampire died? Like, actually *died*?

As she tried to think of the right way to broach the subject, she hurried out the lounge, leaving Trixie to finish up whatever the hell was taking her so long. Celia debated in her head as she rounded the corner to the parking lot.

Victor appeared in front of her. She stopped short, her poor heart jumping into her throat. “Motherfucker!” she cried. She looked up at him and gulped.

Victor’s face was distorted in rage. He looked nothing like her handsome boyfriend anymore. She took a cautious step backward. He noticed that.

“What have you been up to?”

"Nothing. What do you mean?"

"You smell like death," he said coldly.

She frowned, confused. "Excuse me?"

He pointed to her thigh and she understood. "What happened?"

"These two guys killed someone in the kitchen tonight."

"When?"

"I don't know, around midnight maybe."

"What did the person look like?"

"He was short with dark, spiky hair. He was a . . . you know," she finished in a whisper. He grimaced.

"And you saw who did it?"

She nodded. "A blonde guy and a red-head." He was freaking her out, that's for sure. He was so angry that he wasn't making himself breathe; he didn't even blink. And his eyes were dark pools in his face, which was never a good thing. She tried not to look him in the eye because any little thing could set him off at this point.

He was going to say something, but then he stiffened even more, if that were possible.

"Trixie's coming. I'll talk to you later."

He was gone. Celia blinked a few times. He hadn't even stirred the air.

A moment later, Celia heard Trixie's heels on the concrete. She turned, arranging her face to appear natural. They climbed into the car.

"Come up with me," Trixie said when Celia slowed to a stop in front of her house.

"You making a pass at me?" she joked.

"I need your help picking out an outfit. For my date," she added at Celia's blank expression.

"Oh, right."

Trixie's apartment was stuffed with yard sale furniture—

mismatched sofa and loveseat that was so comfortable you could sleep for days, wooden coffee table with scrapes on the legs, worn bookshelves. The effect was cozy living. Her sister's door was closed. They kept their voices down. Celia followed behind Trixie into her bedroom.

Trixie immediately began pulling clothes out of the closet. She held up a brown sundress to her body and examined herself in front of one those wooden, stand mirrors. It would probably come apart if you tilted it too fast.

"Where are you guys going?" Celia asked as she leaned over to turn on the fan.

"A restaurant in the North End. They supposedly have the *best* raviolis." She giggled, apparently recalling her future date's description.

Someone pounded on the wall, the one Trixie's bed was pushed up against. Trixie and Celia both gave the invisible neighbor the finger without as much as a glance.

Trixie picked out a yellow, A-line dress with little white flowers along the hem. She held it up, and then dropped it on the bed beside Celia. Next was a pink, ribbed sleeveless sweater. She paired it with dark jeans, but shook her head.

She found a black mini-dress with green and white squiggly lines on the front. She looked at herself in the mirror and cocked her head to the side, considering. She smiled.

"Oh, yeah, baby."

She hung the dress on the closet door then dropped to her hands and knees to search through her shoes. A towering stack of shoeboxes sat on the floor beside her bed but most of the contents were tossed precariously on the floor of the closet.

Celia sucked her bottom lip, just to do something. She nodded her head to an unheard beat. She tapped her foot. She figured Trixie just wanted company for a little while, seeing as how she wasn't actually asking Celia for her opinion.

Trixie backed out of the closet holding strappy white sandals. She placed them on the floor below the dress. She sat Indian-style with a contented sigh before glancing down at her nails. "Are you working tomorrow?" she asked, sounding distracted.

"Yup."

Trixie stood and went to her dresser for nail polish. She sat on the floor again to touch up her toes.

"I guess Victor doesn't mind you working so much," she said.

"I don't work *all* the time," she said defensively. "We make time." Victor didn't like that she worked weekends so often because then they ended up only having two or three hours together.

"Mmm," Trixie replied with a smile. "I miss having a boyfriend or just someone to talk to all the time. Someone who makes me feel pretty and girly."

Celia smiled to herself. It was nice. Trixie fanned her toes. They were painted a soft pink color. Celia's mind drifted to Victor and where he went off to.

She faked a yawn and stretched. "Okay, Trix, I'm gonna call it a night."

"Aww!" She pouted, making her eyes all big and doe-like. Too bad that didn't work on Celia.

"Sorry, hon."

Celia stood. Trixie reluctantly walked her to the door. "Well, if you're meeting Victor, make sure he spends *extra* time working out your . . . kinks."

"Was that a black joke?"

Trixie gasped, aghast that she would take her words that way. Celia chuckled as she left. At home, the apartment was still, which was disappointing. She had been hoping Victor would be there. She took a quick shower, threw on cotton shorts and a t-shirt and curled up on the sofa. The lamp in the corner was on the dimmest setting, making the room glow yellow. She flicked on the television to review the shows she had recorded during the week.

The bad thing about summertime: the sun rose sooner. She liked working weekends, though. The time always flew by and she was able to bartend, which she really enjoyed. Besides, she and Victor had the week together.

She was pondering this because she was feeling guilty. Had she been neglectful? Now she wished more than anything that he were there.

She could have called for him, simply said his name with the right amount of urgency, and he would be there in a minute; something about their connection. He said it was strange because normally only people vampires had shared blood with could call that vampire. For whatever reason, it worked with Celia as well.

She looked at the time. It was after four. The sun was going to rise in less than two hours. She didn't want to bother him. Instead, she sighed miserably.

* * *

The white mini-mansion in Milton had two floors. The four pillars stood tall in the front, holding up a terrace. The front door was black, with beautiful ornate flowers and vines intricately carved into the wood, the doorknob a pewter color. The mansion showcased ten bedrooms and six bathrooms. It sat at the end of a cul-de-sac, nestled away from the street in an outgrowth of groomed trees.

Victor rushed into the house, inadvertently slamming the door behind him. He startled the four humans sitting in the living room, watching television. They frowned at the intrusion, then immediately averted their eyes and made their faces blank when they saw who it was. The strange part was that they were unsupervised. Cillian must've gone to his room.

Victor stalked past and up the stairs. He went to the last room on the left. He only paused long enough to knock once before pushing the door open.

Ramsey was perched on the foot of the bed, in the process of taking off his shoes. He'd already removed his shirt. He was tall and thick like a wrestler, with sandy-brown hair. He had the softest green eyes you have ever seen, like the color of the ocean in those enticing photographs of Bora Bora and other exotic places.

He wasn't alone in the room. The two human women with him, who had been kissing his chest and neck, were now staring hungrily at Victor, wanting him to join in.

"Victor," Ramsey drawled in his Georgia accent. He smiled, genuinely glad to see him. "How can I help you, buddy?"

"Have you seen Domino?" Victor said immediately.

He placed his black shoe on the floor. "Can't say that I have."

"He's dead."

The blonde female nuzzled Ramsey's neck and he petted her cheek. "Why do you say that?" he asked distantly.

"Someone saw him killed tonight."

"Mmm." He didn't sound interested. The blonde's hand had slid into his pants. "Your little pet, you mean?"

Victor clenched his fists. "Don't call her that."

Ramsey laughed, pleased he struck the nerve. "You're too easy."

"Ramsey, stop fucking around!" Victor bellowed. "Did you not just hear me say one of yours was staked tonight?"

He looked at Victor, his green eyes flashing angrily. In one swift movement that only Victor could follow, Ramsey was out of the bed and fully dressed. The two females looked around, confused.

Ramsey approached Victor at human speed. He liked Victor, very much so. In fact, he wanted him to join his nest. Victor never made any indication that he wanted a home. Ramsey didn't offer because he wasn't sure of the answer and he didn't like not knowing or worse, being rejected. No, that simply wouldn't do so he let Victor be . . . for the time being.

He clapped a hand on Victor's shoulder, and then smiled brightly, showing his fangs. "You worry too much," he said gently. "Domino's a drifter. He goes away sometimes, sometimes for years, but he always comes back."

"She smelled like him," he said, his voice tired. That gave Ramsey pause. He stared at Victor's face, thinking. Then his jaw tensed, his hands dropping to his sides as it sunk in.

"You know who did this, don't you?" Victor asked.

"I have my suspicions, yes."

"Domino was a friend. If there's anything I can do to help, please let me know."

Ramsey nodded once. He left the room in a flash. Victor turned to leave as well.

"Wait."

He glanced over his shoulder. The brunette smiled beguilingly as she crawled to the edge of the bed. They were both in underwear: lacy push-up bras, string bikini panties.

"You look a little pale," she replied. She brushed her fingers along her throat. He could hear her pulse, feel her heat. Instinctively, his top lip twitched, his mouth watering.

He hadn't fed tonight. His adventure earlier with the Monte Carlos ran over. They had been hunting grizzlies up in Maine. Just like the previous night, Victor was invited along for the journey. He liked the hunt but detested the taste of animals.

The blonde had sidled up next to the brunette at the foot of the bed, intrigued. She reached behind her back and unhooked her yellow bra. It was tossed to the floor at his feet. He looked at the yellow material and back at the ladies.

Letting his hunger direct him, he moved to the bed, removing his shirt in case of stains. He sat between them. The blonde lay across his lap with a welcoming smile. Her tits were fake, standing alert and unmoving on her chest. That was something he didn't particularly like, but hey, a throat was a throat. She rubbed his thigh, which he did like.

The brunette moved her hair aside. Her perfume was a vanilla musk. Victor grasped her neck and rubbed it with his thumb. His touch made her vein throb. Without further ado, he pulled her to him and bit her throat. She gasped excitedly. The blonde giggled below them. Runaway blood dribbled on her chest. She used a manicured finger to smear it across her peach skin. The heat from the brunette's blood filled every nook and cranny and Victor almost forgot himself as he moaned into her neck.

He pulled away before it was too late and lifted the blonde in his lap so that she was straddling him. He drank from her as she gripped his shoulders. He could taste the wine she had earlier. The brunette pressed her breasts to his back. He felt her skin, her rock-hard nipples; she had removed her red bra. He heard the girls kiss and moan beside his ear.

The only problem with feeding, especially when he was that hungry, was he usually became aroused, as if all the ingested blood went straight to his dick. A year ago, throwing both girls on the bed and ravaging their bodies at the same time, while filling his belly with their wine-tinted blood, wouldn't have given him pause.

Tonight, however, he cleaned their wounds and hurried downstairs. The four humans were still there, staring at the television. He glanced around until his eyes landed on a clock. Not that he really needed it; the pull of the sun was building. He had about an hour.

Celia's apartment was quiet and dark. He went to her bedroom, making no sounds as he undressed. Celia lay under her purple sheet. She was on her side, her curves making sexy hills under the cotton material.

Victor slid beneath the sheet and tucked himself behind her. She sighed in her sleep at the sudden presence. Victor kissed the back of her neck, kissed her shoulder. He gently pulled her shorts and panties off. She was stirring now. He gained entrance by lifting her leg and laying it on his thigh.

She gasped a little and he slid in between her tight folds. She began shifting her hips to meet his rhythm. Even half-asleep she knew his touch. He loved to make her moan, like she was doing now, only it was more like purring tonight. Trying to be quiet was the thing.

The headboard squeaked with their efforts. She put her hand against it, silencing the loose screws slightly. Victor ran his tongue along her neck, wanting so badly to bite her, to taste her. He refrained, as always, which took considerable willpower. Her neck was so perfect: not too long, not too short. The muscles under the skin were visible, taunting him.

He gripped her hips, bending her forward just a bit so he could slide deeper into her. He thrust faster to offset his yearning. He was running low on time. That being the case, Victor may have moved the teensiest bit faster than a human man would have. The sound of their skin slapping together replaced the squeaky headboard. Hey, it did the job. Celia was shuddering and leaking all over her sheets; he was satisfied.

Celia rolled onto her back to peer up into Victor's face. She smiled, her cheeks rosy, and gently caressed the side of his face. He took her hand to kiss her fingers.

He sighed. He hated to disrupt the moment, but he needed to leave. At least he had this image to take with him.

Celia's gaze dropped—she must've seen it in his expression. A couple of different emotions crossed her face. She then forced a smile and leaned forward. He met her halfway for a sweet kiss.

He disappeared before she opened her eyes.

Three

CELIA WAS DREAMING of the beach when an incessant ringing pulled her away. She groaned as she felt around the nightstand for the cordless phone. Her fingers located it and she unburied her face from the pillow.

"What?"

"Hi, Celia!" came a syrupy voice. It was her coworker, Tina, and Celia knew exactly what she was calling for.

"Shit."

"I'm so sorry, but I've called everyone!"

Celia groaned again, then looked at her alarm clock. It was five past eight. She would be late for the earlier shift at Cage's. "Switch or make up?"

"Switch."

"Fine," Celia huffed. Tina squealed.

"Thank you, thank you!"

Celia knew she had to move because she would fall right back asleep if she didn't. She forced her legs off the bed then went to shower. The hot water did help to wake her and she was giddy as she realized switching with Tina meant she'd have the night off. She would make Victor take her to a movie and dinner. Normal couple stuff.

When she got out the shower, she left a message on his cell phone telling him to come over as soon as he could and to bring his wallet. She bounced around the room as she dressed, picking up the trail of Victor's clothes from the floor. The staff was still obligated to wear black, even in the daytime. So, she pulled on capri pants and a quarter-length shirt.

Massachusetts' law stated that alcohol couldn't be served before noon on Sundays. Celia had to wait tables since Carson was already behind the bar and could handle the drink load. She was a decent server but she didn't like doing it. Therefore, she was more than a little ecstatic to get behind the bar at twelve for the brunch crowd.

When her shift ended at four, she decided to walk to Downtown Crossing, the little shopping hub of metro Boston, to run some errands. She stopped at CVS for toiletries, and then peeked in Aldo at pumps she shouldn't buy.

She arrived home at five-thirty. Goddamn summer. Victor wouldn't be around until after eight. She put her dry cleaning away and placed the chicken and broccoli pasta with garlic alfredo sauce she brought from work in the microwave.

The minutes seemed to tick by at a snail's pace. She flipped through channels, ate her very late lunch, did the dishes, and flipped through more channels.

To pass the time, she called her aunt. She had lived with her aunt and uncle until she was twenty, when she was rear-ended by the idiot bus driver.

"Celia, how are you?"

"I'm good, Aunt Meg. I was just calling to check in. I know it's been a little while."

"Yes, it has, but that's okay. I'm just glad to hear your voice." Celia winced. She hadn't seen her family in almost a month. Sundays were usually set aside for coffee and cake but lately she hadn't had the time or hadn't *made* the time.

"How's work?" her aunt asked.

"Same."

"And Victor?"

"He's good."

"Don't strain yourself with the details, Celia," she said in mock criticism.

Celia chuckled. "Sorry. All is well. No worries."

"Max is having a cookout. You two should come. I can show you off to the girls. They haven't seen you in ages." Her aunt and uncle knew all the people who lived in their area. During the warm months, the neighbors came together for block parties, and her uncle Max was always first to volunteer to man the grill.

"Just let me know when and I'll try to make it."

"Mm hmm," she said, obviously catching how noncommittal her words were. "How's that dancer friend of yours?"

"Trixie's fine. She has a date tonight she was all excited about. I hope it goes well."

"Is it with a customer?"

Celia rolled her eyes playfully. "What kind of bar do you think I work in?"

"Oh, I didn't mean it like that," Meg said with a hiss.

"I know. I don't know much about him. But she said he's cute."

"As long as her priorities are in order," she teased. Celia laughed. "Well, sweetie, I'm glad you called. I have some cake for you. Stop by to get some."

"Sure thing, Auntie," she said softly.

"You have a good rest of your night. I'll talk to you later."

"See you. Tell Uncle Max I said hello."

"Will do."

She hung up with a wistful sigh. A cool hand touched her cheek and she leaned into Victor's chest.

"Hey, you," she breathed.

He recoiled. "Celia!"

She gawked at him. "What?"

"You were eating *garlic?*" He said it like it was diseased fungus.

She gave him a look. "It was in the sauce," she replied dryly. "And screw you, okay? I happen to love garlic. It won't kill you if I eat it once in a while so shut it."

He put a hand over his nose and pointed to a door. She stared at him a moment longer before giving up. She trudged off to the bathroom with a groan to brush her teeth.

When she returned, Victor was by the window, staring out onto the street below. She knew he heard her but she still crept over to him. Standing on her toes, she blew in his ear.

"Better?" She made sure to blow her minty breath toward his nose.

He turned and kissed her. The kiss was meaningful and erotic, their tongues dancing together, leaving them on the bed spent and exhausted.

"Let's go out," Celia said a half hour later as they stared up at her ceiling. She had arranged those glow-in-the-dark star stickers on the ceiling to make it look like the night sky when the lights were out. They only glowed half-heartedly tonight, since she hadn't turned on her lamp.

He rubbed her thigh. "Why can't we just stay here? I like it here." His hand inched up.

"Because I want to go out," she said, ignoring his roaming. "And you're my boyfriend so you have to do what I want."

"Is that right?" She could hear the smile in his voice.

"Yup." She pecked his cheek then rolled off the bed before he could grab her. Of course, if he wanted to, he could've caught her.

Celia pulled on underwear, denim shorts, and a light green baby doll top. She crossed to the dresser and put on foundation and mascara and earrings. Her hair was being bushy today so she lobbed on the gel and brushed it back into a ponytail. It looked like a curly Afro puff.

"You're beautiful," Victor said, appearing behind her. He kissed the back of her neck, right on the gold chain.

"Un-uh," she said, wiggling from his grasp. "You're not getting out of this."

They held hands as they walked the two blocks to her car. Victor drove them to the movie theater where they saw a raunchy R-rated comedy. He kept squeezing her thigh suggestively and she kept ignoring him. She remembered that one time in the theater in Randolph when she'd felt especially frisky. Tiny shivers were circling her lower back as she imagined Dwayne Johnson knocking everything off his desk on screen, throwing her down, and somehow managing to get all of him inside her.

Celia had bitten her bottom lip and reached into Victor's lap. He had been lounging comfortably, his arm on the back of her seat. He turned to her with a raised eyebrow, waiting to see how far she would go. She accepted the challenge by unzipping his pants and laying her head in his lap. The theater hadn't been that crowded, but a couple of high school jocks had snickered and nudged each other when they were leaving, indicating that they hadn't been as covert as she had assumed.

Victor humored her by taking her to one of those chain restaurants just down the street from the cinema that was open late.

"Didn't you just eat?" he said as they strolled to the entrance.

"Yeah, like twenty hours ago."

He shook his head at her exaggeration, amused. "Maybe you're pregnant," he kidded.

"Oh, please don't joke like that." A sudden wave of panic hit her. She quickly counted the days since her last period in her head. Then she told herself to relax. She was on the pill—which made remembering her last period pointless since the birth control threw it off schedule. Besides, she didn't even think vampires could have kids.

"I'm only twenty-three. I can barely take care of my damn self."

His eyebrows were furrowed when he opened the door for her. "It wouldn't only be you."

Her expression was dubious. "Yeah, it would be. A father has to be around during the daytime, too, you know. For diapers and play dates and school recitals. Where's this coming from, anyways? I thought you fellas shoot blanks."

He halted. She could never hear when he was walking anyways, so she continued on to the hostess stand, unaware.

"Table for two, please," Celia replied. The hostess looked around, puzzled. Celia glanced to her left, then over her shoulder. *Uh-oh*, she thought when she saw the broody look on his face. She gave the hostess her name then walked back over to Victor.

Taking a deep breath, she apologized. "That was harsh."

"Bitchy even."

She slapped his arm—lightly though because she learned her lesson. "You've never said anything about kids before."

"Well, I think about it," he said gloomily. "I think about getting married and having children and grandchildren and growing old." He looked so sad. She rubbed his cheek, unsure of what to say. Those were all things she tried *not* to think about.

"Celia, party of two."

She gave him a small smile and took his hand. They were brought to a booth. Celia ordered a Cosmo. Victor, a glass of merlot. When the waiter returned with their drinks, he took a gulp.

"Yuck," he said, scrunching up his nose.

"Is the wine not to your liking?" the waiter asked immediately, concerned.

"It's fine," he grumbled. They ordered and the waiter left.

"Are you going to be alright?" Celia asked. He wasn't looking at her as he pulverized a napkin. She placed a hand on his. His skin was cold to the touch, meaning he had come straight to Celia's house.

To her surprise, he jerked his hand away.

"I don't know what you want me to say!" she exclaimed at his silence. "I can't change anything. This is the way things are."

"Yeah, well, it's still fucking annoying."

She scoffed. "I'm sorry to hear this relationship thing is so hard for you. It's no walk in the goddamn park for me sometimes," she snapped. She took a gulp of her drink. It was strong and warmed her chest but did nothing to squelch her anger. "And when you're imagining this life where you're old and wrinkly is it with me? Of course it's not," she said before he could speak, "because I won't be there."

The statement hung in the air between them.

She glared at him. He didn't know how to explain that yes, she was in his dream because she was in his life right now. He'd had this dream before; he just outlived the last person.

Victor figured she would go all womanly on him and get upset about it not necessarily being an original dream. Instead of explaining, he stewed in silence. Of course, that made her angrier.

The waiter came around with their meals. Celia's pasta was accompanied by garlic bread that she had neglected to tell him to hold. She picked up a piece and took a giant bite, chewing it slowly, deliberately.

The smell filled his nose. He stopped breathing. Even with that precaution, the garlic still irritated him, like an allergy. His nose became itchy and his throat was closing up. It was the second time tonight he was accosted by garlic because of Celia.

He didn't try to disguise his movements. One second Victor was sitting, then outside the booth the next, glaring at her reproachfully. He rushed out the restaurant.

Celia stared after him. She hadn't meant to make him leave, especially angry. She glanced around anxiously to see if anyone had noticed. A little boy with a button nose and a sprinkling of freckles stared at her with his mouth hanging open in surprise. His fork was in mid-air, on its way to his gullet.

"Timmy?" his mother said. She snapped her fingers in front of his face. "What's wrong, Timmy?"

Celia gulped, quickly calling the waiter over to wrap her food. She wasn't hungry anyways.

"Is this yours?"

She looked up. The waiter held a couple twenties in his hand. She couldn't help a smile as she took the money from him. It was more than enough to cover the meal and tip. Celia went right home, feeling miserable.

* * *

Victor roamed the streets, fuming. The garlic still irritated him, rendering his nose useless. But he could hear and feel the heartbeats all around him, pulsing in the baking heat of the night.

He was downtown, Faneuil Hall to be specific; a tourist magnet with its bars, shops and cobbled walkways. On any given warm day, you could find street performers banging away on plastic trashcans or break-dancing to the tune of blaring music and audience applause.

It was late Sunday night but people crowded the pubs like it was a Friday. He needed to soothe this aggression so he scoped out the possibilities.

There were two friends, stepping out of a side door to Quincy Market. Except they were orangey tanned, wearing tube tops and mini-skirts. Really? Who wore tube tops anymore? Not his type.

One guy was too burly. He wasn't looking for a struggle, even if he enthralled him. Men usually had more blood, meaning he could feed longer.

He rounded a corner and came across a lone man standing outside a pub, talking on his cell phone. He was a little shorter than Victor, maybe five-eight, lanky and wearing chinos and a light blue polo.

Victor's lips instinctually curled over his teeth, revealing his fangs. His nails grew from his fingers, sharp and hard like talons. He crouched a little, checking his surroundings. Seeing all was clear, he pounced. The guy didn't know what hit him. Victor had him around the throat, carrying him swiftly to the alley.

He slammed him up against the brick wall, little bits of cement crumbling onto his shoulders, and bit into his neck with no hesitation. The man's breath caught and his pulse raced when his brain finally recognized the danger. He tried to push Victor away. That wasn't happening.

Feeding was the only time Victor really made any pleasurable noises—as Celia could attest to. She often found it upsetting that he didn't make any sounds when they made love. It wasn't that he didn't enjoy sex but feeding made him feel human again, as strange as that sounded. The heat of the blood made his body warm, even to the touch. He could almost feel his heart thump in his chest. It was an illusion in his head of course, but the phantom pulse was a tantalizing sensation he welcomed.

At the same time, the experience was contradictory. When he was hungry like this, the animal inside of him forced its way to the surface, craving more and more. And the more he fed, the more . . . *humanness* he gained.

The man was going limp. Victor didn't stop, even when the warning bells sounded. After a short while, the man's head lolled to the side. Pretty soon, only Victor was holding him up, his hungry grunts filling the air.

His ears perked. There were footsteps on the main street, a good couple of yards away. Heels. The woman stopped and picked something up. Probably the cell phone Khakis had been using.

"Donny?" she said. Then a little louder: "Donny? Where are you?"

She was at the mouth of the alley now. Victor wanted more. The man in his arms was very much dry. Her heels stopped and she gasped. He released Donny, who slumped to the ground and turned on his next victim.

His eyes were as dark as coal. Blood dripped from his mouth, onto the collar of his shirt. Normally he was a lot neater than this, but he was gone. He stepped closer, arching his fingers. The woman stood paralyzed by fear. Her pounding heart echoed in the alley, exciting him even more.

He took another step.

The breeze shifted. What was that? Citrus? Like grapefruit? The garlic had worn off and he knew that smell. He still moved forward, concerning himself more with his hunger. This time she took a stumbling step backward into the pool of light from the lamp up above. The light shone down on the jet-black hair, the pale skin, the light blue eyes.

Trixie.

It took all his might to stop advancing. The bloodlust was powerful but he had to control himself, he had to reel in the animal. Knowing he could be in that alley no longer, he spun on his heel. He ran, since he was concentrating too hard on not attacking to use his normal teleporting. He scaled the building to the roof and ran as fast as he could, which was pretty damn fast.

Victor made it all the way to upstate New York before he felt the grip of his bloodlust peter out. He stood in a patch of woods, breathing heavily. Not from the exertion of running but from the effort to control himself. He walked around in circles for a little while to make sure he was actually calm, to make sure his hands and mouth were in order.

Without the bloodlust, guilt took over. He replayed what he had just done and what he had almost done. The trip back to Boston was much slower since he was beating himself up.

He walked through Celia's dark living room. He pushed the door to her bedroom open. She was lying on top of the covers in a white t-shirt and neon-pink panties. The stars on the ceiling barely glowed.

Victor went around to the side of the bed. He turned on the lamp and sat beside her, watching her sleep for a moment. Her expression was blank, as if nothing were troubling her at the moment. As if they never had that argument. As if she hadn't just killed a man.

Her chest rose and fell at an even tempo. He didn't want to disturb her but he shook her gently. She opened her eyes and squinted from the light.

"What?" she grumbled, closing her eyes again.

"Trixie saw me," he said tightly.

"Saw you what?"

"Feeding."

Her eyes popped open. She sprang up in the bed. The color drained from her face before his eyes. She stared into his eyes, unable to speak. Victor was clenching her comforter in his hands as he recalled that moment of complete weakness.

Celia rubbed his arm once she saw how troubled he was. He eventually released her comforter without leaving any marks. They sat like that for an hour before Celia lay back down.

She couldn't sleep though; she couldn't feel her arms. Victor lay beside her until five, when he disappeared.

* * *

Celia was terrified of what Trixie might do. Would she call

the cops? Would she hate her? Could Celia trust Trixie with the biggest secret she'd ever had?

She fretted until eight, when she got up to get ready for work. She had day shifts for the next two days, then Wednesday off, then nights Thursday through Saturday. She wouldn't see Trixie until Thursday.

She knew she shouldn't wait that long. But Monday became Monday night, which became Tuesday that became Tuesday night, and she still hadn't contacted Trixie. Her stomach was in knots, she was so nervous. She had a constant headache and all she ate were saltines and ginger ale because that was supposed to help with nausea.

"You're making yourself sick, Seal," Victor said, concerned. He rubbed her thigh. It was the best he could do since she was curled up in a ball in the crook of the sofa.

"I don't know what to say to her." Her voice was shaky like she'd been crying.

"Do you want me to talk to her?" he asked ominously. She immediately shook her head. "Why don't you call her now? While you're thinking about it."

She shook her head again. "I can't. Plus, she's at work."

He paused. "You're just going to lie like this all night again?"

"My stomach hurts!" she griped.

"Celia, come on. Maybe if you get out, get moving around . . ."

"No," she grumbled. He sighed and continued to rub her thigh.

Wednesday morning, she pulled herself out of bed at eleven with new, albeit reluctant, resolve. She couldn't put it off any longer. So she drove the fifteen minutes to the Cambridge mall. Trixie stood to the side of the store in her khakis and Verizon polo, showing a couple the newest Blackberry. Celia waited by the door with her hands in her pant pockets.

Trixie turned to lead them to the counter when she spotted Celia. You'd think she'd just seen an axe murderer, that's how petrified her expression became. The guy she was with even asked if everything was alright. Celia gulped.

Trixie was taking her time with the couple, stalling like crazy with ringing them up. Thirty minutes and two more customers later, Trixie stood awkwardly behind the desk. Celia sighed and walked over to her. Her hands were shaking so badly that she had to keep them in her pockets to control them.

"Can we talk?" she asked, surprised she could form words.

"Um, I'm working." She tried to sound curt but couldn't quite muster the attitude since it was Celia. Trixie's eyes darted from her face to the counter as she absentmindedly played with some Post-Its.

"Fine. Before you go to Cage's. I'll stop by."

She pursed her lips. Celia could tell she was trying to come up with an excuse. So she left.

Celia went to Trixie's house at six-thirty. Her sister, Suzie, was leaving as she came in. Suzie was a shorter version of Trixie, only gothy with the same jet-black hair, thick black eyeliner, and dark lips.

"Hey, Celia. Bye, Celia," she called cheerfully as she ran out the door.

Trixie was sitting in the living room, staring at the television. She had stiffened when Suzie spoke and she made no indication that she was going to acknowledge her. Celia lingered by the front door, anxious and fidgety. She didn't know how to start this conversation. She eventually walked up to her but didn't sit. The tension could choke a gorilla.

"What is he?" Trixie asked in a tiny voice. Her eyes were glued to the set.

Celia shifted from side to side. "Umm . . ." was all she came up with as she tugged on the hem of her top.

Trixie jumped up suddenly and began pacing the room. "This isn't real, right?" she rambled. "I'm dreaming, right?" She stopped and faced her, her skin paler than Celia had ever seen. "Donny's dead!"

"Donny?"

"My date!" Trixie shook her head, as if still finding it hard to believe. "We had dinner and then took a walk and we were at this bar in Faneuil Hall. Donny stepped out to take a phone call from his brother but he was taking so long so I went out to find him. His phone was on the ground.

"Victor did something to him. He had . . . blood on his face."

Celia's shoulders slumped at that. It had been a long time since Victor had killed someone, he had told her, and that time had been when he was incredibly angry. Now, she felt guilty because she had provoked him.

"Trix . . ." She trailed off.

"And then he ran up the building and was gone."

"Did you tell this to the police?" Celia asked cautiously.

"Do I look crazy to you?" she exclaimed, her eyes going all wide like a crazy person. "Who would believe that?"

"I do."

They stared at each other for a long moment. Trixie still looked scared. Celia bit her bottom lip fretfully. She didn't know what to say to ease her anxiety. Trixie picked up her manic pacing again.

"This doesn't make any sense," she said, more to herself. "That's why I never see him during the day? And why he never eats? And why he just . . . *appears*, like, out of thin air?"

She went into the kitchen, as if that had been a part of her pacing route. Celia heard the fridge open, then close. A beer bottle was opened with a fizz. She returned to the living room, chugging from the brown bottle. She then sat on the edge of the sofa. Celia sat beside her, looking at her face.

"What are you thinking?"

Trixie paused. "Does he have . . . fangs?"

"Yeah."

"Do they hurt?"

"I'm assuming so."

She looked at her. "He doesn't bite you?"

"No."

Trixie looked perplexed. "Why not?"

Celia shook her head. "I've heard that it's addictive or something."

"Heard from who?"

"Well, from Victor . . . and books and . . . I just don't want any part of that," she said hurriedly, feeling her cheeks warm.

Trixie gave a half snort of laughter. "But you can date him and kiss him and sleep with him. Oh, my God," she gasped. "You sleep with him?"

"Sure," she said lightly. He was her boyfriend after all.

"Doesn't that make you, like, a necrophiliac?"

Celia gasped, repulsed. "That's sick!"

"Well, he *is* dead, right?"

"Okay," she cried, jumping up from her seat and waving her hands in front of her. "Change of subject, please."

Trixie's gaze shifted to the floor, her mind still churning. "Can garlic kill him?"

"No, it just makes him sick."

"Does he turn into a bat? Is that why he appears and disappears?" This was intriguing to her now. Her posture had relaxed, which put Celia at ease as well.

"No, he doesn't turn into a bat. He can . . . appear . . . and disappear." That was the best she could do.

"Are there others like him?"

"Yeah."

Trixie sucked in air, not anticipating that answer. She wasn't really comfortable around Victor but she had never quite fully known why. Celia knew she was grateful they were never alone together, even if he was a nice guy and Celia liked him.

What if others like him weren't so nice?

She shivered. "Have you met others?" she whispered.

Celia had met Ramsey twice—both times he had come to the lounge looking for Victor. They were brief encounters so she didn't have a sense of him. Just that he was easy-going, always with a lazy smile. He had called her "brown eyes" each time.

Celia shrugged. "One other, but I don't know him."

"Do you think they come to the lounge?"

She had glanced at the clock. It was time for her to get ready for work. From the look on her face, Celia figured images filled her head of paper-white men with slicked back hair and pointy fangs that were too large to be concealed in their mouths, slithering in and out of the crowd at Cage's.

Celia walked over to her and placed a hand on her shoulder. She hoped it was comforting. "They're very low-key. They don't want to draw any attention to their kind. It's extremely important no one knows about them."

The warning was there, just below the surface. It took a minute for comprehension to light Trixie's face, but she eventually got it. And now she looked terrified all over again.

Celia rubbed her shoulder. "Don't worry."

"Easier said than done," she muttered.

Celia walked to the door. Trixie was still sitting on the sofa, staring at the floor. "Are you okay?" Celia asked.

Trixie looked at her and nodded. "Just a lot to wrap my head around."

"Well, give me a call if you need anything."

Celia left and went straight home. Victor showed up at eleven. "Where have you been?" she demanded.

He put his hands up as a shield from her verbal assault. "At

Ramsey's. He thinks he knows who staked Domino."

She paused. She'd almost forgotten about the vampire in the kitchen. "Was that his name?"

"Yes. He was one of Ramsey's."

She switched on the air conditioner because the apartment was getting too sticky. "Does that mean he turned him?"

"No. But he was a part of his nest."

"His nest. You said that's, like, his group?" Trixie's curiosity seemed to be rubbing off a little. "He protects them?"

Victor nodded. "He gives them shelter and guidance in exchange for their allegiance." He studied her for a moment. "You spoke with Trixie." It wasn't a question, and it made her wonder if he could smell her.

Creepy, she thought.

"She said you killed that guy." She hadn't intended for her tone to be so accusatory. He nodded, looking genuinely saddened. His lips pulled down and his eyes softened, like he was going to cry though he couldn't. The emotion was there.

"I lost my control."

He was guilty enough; she didn't want to add on to it. She walked up to him and wrapped her arms around him, rubbing his back to soothe him. After a while, his chest rose evenly with his breathing and he returned her embrace. When she looked up at him, his eyes were still pretty dark.

"Come on," she said, taking his hand. "Let's go to bed."

Four

RAMSEY CALLED HIS nest. All he had to do was think of them and they came; some ancient shit that had to do with vampire magic. As the leader, Ramsey had telepathic means of communication with his seethe. He had to call Victor's cell phone.

It was Monday night and they were gathered in the sitting room on the first floor of Ramsey's house. There were ten of them, male and female, and Victor, sitting on the two sofas and loveseat. Cillian, who stood in a corner next to the bar, was twirling what appeared to be a human finger on the marble counter of the bar.

Cillian was ancient, though he only looked thirty. He was an Irishman, with black hair and always in a spiffy suit. Tonight's get-up was navy blue and impeccably tailored. He wore a burgundy dress shirt and matching tie with little circles on it.

He'd lost his humanity a long time ago, well, except his sense of style, and because of that, was usually confined to the house. He wouldn't be able to blend since he didn't even try anymore. His "food" was brought to him and closely supervised so that he wouldn't mutilate or kill them, though it appeared some sap lost their pointing finger very recently.

Victor balanced on the arm of a chair with his arms crossed at the chest. Ramsey stood by the door with a grim expression.

"These hunters got some balls, eh?" said one of the vamps sitting on the loveseat. He had a thick Italian accent with dark hair that came to his ears and dark eyes under bushy eyebrows. His cheekbones were high, jutting from his face at sharp angles. When he spoke, you could see he was missing one of his incisors on the right side.

"How did they know where to find Domino?" asked another. He was a newer vampire, maybe five years old, named Trent. He sometimes had a hard time keeping his fangs in check. Every once in a while he'd sound like he was speaking around something in his mouth. At least his fangs didn't stand out. If anything, it looked like his canines were a tad bit long. Aw, baby fangs. It wasn't a normal thing, short fangs, but he learned to make due.

"They wouldn't be worth their salt if they didn't know how to track a vampire," Ramsey answered, his voice cold. "Especially one as reckless as Domino."

"I think it's because your nest is so large," Victor chimed. He had been quiet during Ramsey's speech earlier explaining Domino's disappearance. He had never encountered hunters before but he had heard stories.

All of their eyes swiveled to him now.

"They must have heard about you," Victor continued.

"They won't find the house though," the Italian said rather proudly. He was referring to the vampire hoodoo that protected the mansion. No human could locate it. The ones who came to the house were bespelled long before they were in the vicinity.

Like erasing memories when they fed, all vampires were equipped with the power to hide their resting places. This twofold magic secured their identities from humans, secured their homes.

It was the same enchantment that brought them back from the dead; that gave them strength that heightened their senses. A safeguard that lived in their blood.

"Plus, they are just idiot humans," the Italian went on. He looked to the others for support. "We can take them in our sleep."

Ramsey's mouth was a thin line as he contemplated.

"Yeah, Ramsey, I'm with Arturo." The one who spoke was a shorter, Asian vampire with an electric blue Mohawk and pierced lips: two silver balls, one just under his bottom lip, connected to the other at the top of that lip with a curved barbell.

"There's no way they can take us all out," he added.

"Don't underestimate hunters," Ramsey replied tersely. "They killed Domino, didn't they?"

"Hunters. Is that what they call themselves now?"

Only Victor and Ramsey looked to Cillian. His voice was raspy, as if it hadn't been put to use in a while.

"Yes," Ramsey said. He was watching him carefully. Cillian had attacked the other vampires a few times in the past. They learned not to turn their backs on him when he jumped Trent on the stairwell shortly after he joined the nest. He would try to sexually assault the vampire Annie, always Annie, if Ramsey wasn't near. He'd corner her in open rooms, murmuring about women he'd abused or violated. She rarely came to the mansion without her mate, Bryce, at her side. Cillian had bitten Bryce before, while he was watching a movie in the sitting room. Only Ramsey seemed able to control him. He and Elizabeth, one member of his seethe, argued often about the logic of keeping Cillian around. Ramsey always stood firm. When Ramsey wasn't home, Cillian had to stay in his room

Cillian smiled. The expression made him appear his human

age and he was actually quite good-looking, with his thick eyebrows and perfect teeth. Even his fangs were white and immaculately aligned. He enjoyed showing them when he spoke. Whether that meant he was hungry all the time or horny was your guess.

Too bad his mind was gone.

He stared at Ramsey, a supercilious look in his eyes, periwinkle blue eyes that were glazed over by a thin, milky film. A normal person would've surely cowered and fled the room at his piercing gaze.

"I loved the challenge," he said conversationally. "That village didn't stand a chance once I got their scent. I moved through there, under the cover of night. I moved from one house to the next, burning them to the ground. The screams were like a sonnet and I was the maestro. The people—" He broke off with a laugh. "They thought they could run."

His smile disappeared in a flash. His lips curved into a snarl directed at Trent, who jumped slightly at the sudden shift in his tone. Cillian finished with a growl. "But you can't outrun death."

This event was one of many during Cillian's reign of terror in Europe in the eighteen hundreds. The tiny village outside of Budapest was one of his last raids. Ramsey had been living in the capital. The stories of a crazed animal ravaging the poor villages made their way to his ears. Old tales resurfaced of hanging strings of garlic and crucifixes above the doors to ward off the monster whose eyes were as white as the moon. Many people were afraid to leave their houses at night.

Ramsey knew straightaway that it was no animal. Two puncture wounds were visible on what was left of the victims' necks, thighs, and wrists. Ramsey searched for the cause of these deaths, but was always a step behind, walking in on the wreckage. Dilapidated, burning huts, bodies strewn in the dirt, the few survivors struggling with what was left of their limbs.

He wouldn't catch the elusive Cillian until the next century. By then, Ramsey had an established seethe and was fully in control of the mental communication that came along with it. He crossed paths with Cillian one cool night in the back of a family-run restaurant in Seville, Spain. He was muttering to himself while digging through the garbage pails. When he heard Ramsey approach, he whipped around. A very large brown rat wiggled in his fist, its shrill squeaks echoing throughout the alley. He was dressed in black pants that were too big for him and a dingy white shirt that was buttoned incorrectly. His hair was in disarray. Dirt and dried blood darkened his temples, neck, and hands.

Ramsey was befuddled. Was this the silent monster destroying Europe?

The look in his milky-white eyes screamed lost soul. Ramsey didn't desire to destroy him. To his surprise, Cillian came willingly, settling the debate.

A tall, well-built vampire named Bryce rolled his eyes when Cillian spoke, clearly saying *not this shit again.* Cillian didn't seem to remember all the things he did in his life before Ramsey. Every once in a while, though, a memory would surface. Ramsey waited to see if there was more of this tale. Cillian gazed up at the ceiling, like something had just caught his attention. Ramsey continued.

"I know you all can handle yourselves. But I don't want a war. Just keep an eye out."

There was some shifting as the others glanced around. Victor kept his eyes on Ramsey. He was angry, Victor could tell. He didn't like having hunters on his grounds but Ramsey was more of a pacifist. He wouldn't feel right killing humans, even ones gunning for him and his. Since he was the leader of this seethe, the others had to do as he said.

Victor was at his side in an instant. "Do you know where

these hunters are? Or what they look like?" Victor whispered it, just for show. The other vampires busied themselves with conversation to give them the semblance of privacy even though they could hear every word.

"Andy and Bryce are on it."

Victor glanced over his shoulder. The spaces on the sofa that Bryce and the Mohawked Asian had occupied were empty.

Ramsey placed a hand on his shoulder and Victor faced him again. "You take care, too," he said gently. He caressed his cheek. "You should eat. You're pale."

Victor only nodded before vanishing.

* * *

Trixie was still hounding Celia with questions about vampires. Celia indulged her while trying not to seem annoyed by the constant rounds of inquiries. Like, did they all have special powers? Or was there a head vampire everyone had to follow? Those were questions she had never thought to ask Victor; her curiosity just hadn't run that course.

"How old is Victor?" Trixie asked Friday night, right before the doors were opened.

"Well, he was twenty-seven when it happened. But he's only about a hundred."

"Is it weird?"

"What?"

"Your relationship?"

"Because we're interracial?" she asked with false innocence. Trixie shot her a serious look, showing she wasn't amused. Celia chuckled. "I guess I'm used to it now," she said, answering her real question.

"So, wait, what is he? Where does he come from?"

"His father's Spanish and English and his mother's Italian. He lived in Italy when he was younger, then his family moved to England. That's when it . . . happened."

"How did it happen?" Her voice was a soft whisper, mingled with curiosity and fear.

Celia sighed, deflated. "He's never said."

Trixie shook her head, amazed. Celia watched her. It was nice being able to talk freely with her. Trixie was like her best friend. She felt lighter, like she could breathe easier now that she didn't have to keep this major part of her life from her.

"He doesn't sound like someone from the nineteen hundreds," Trixie was saying.

Celia agreed. "He's learned to adapt."

"I'll say. He's probably seen so much, traveled everywhere."

"Mm, yeah, I'm sure the pyramids are most beautiful at night."

"Oh!" she said, putting a hand to her mouth, embarrassed. Celia smiled then opened her mouth to tell her she was just fucking with her when they were interrupted—

"Pyramids?" They turned and Celia's smile evaporated real quick. Carson had sidled up to Celia behind the bar. He was holding two fresh bottles of gin for the wells. "Who's seen the pyramids?"

"Celia's boyfriend."

Carson's smile froze on his face. He tilted his head to the side, like he was trying to recall something. "Victor?" he asked with an uncertain frown.

"He hasn't seen the pyramids," Celia said briefly, choosing not to take the bait of his little act of forgetting Victor's name. She opened the fridge for a bottle of water. Trixie left to climb into her cage. Carson dropped off his gin, and then proceeded to drum a beat on the counter with his fingers. Luckily, Mickey turned the music on before Celia snapped at him to stop.

"There's this movie," Carson said, leaning close so she could hear. He smelled like licorice, which she thought was odd for cologne. "One of those blow-shit-up movies. Wanna see it tomorrow before work?"

She surveyed him a moment, confused by this request. Carson always found ways of pissing her off, which was typical of immature boys when they liked a girl. She just never once considered that that had been the case. She had assumed he only enjoyed pissing her off. This, however, was definitely upfront and sounded date-like.

"Only if Victor and Trixie come, too."

A cloud crossed his face. He fixed it quickly. "I wasn't trying anything."

"I think you were." She took a step away from him.

He tried to laugh it off. "Aw, come on, Celia," he said lightly. "I was talking about a friend thing. You *can* have friends, right?"

She didn't like his tone—sarcastic, a bit chiding. "Carson, stop being a dick."

"Ouch!" He clutched his chest like he had been stabbed. She did want to throw something at him. "I was just trying to be nice."

"Well, keep your nice to yourself." She glowered at him but he laughed. He thought it was cute when she was angry. He then shot finger guns at her like an ass and walked away to most likely lick his wounds in private.

Victor showed up around midnight, when Celia was getting ready to take her break. He saw Trixie at a table a few feet away, talking up three guys. She laughed, throwing her head back and grazing her fingers along the exposed skin of her neck flirtatiously. The muscles in her neck formed a perfect V at her clavicle. He raised a brow. He'd never noticed before, the porcelain skin, the toned muscles, the blood-red lips. Her citrusy scent wafted to his nose through the beer and vomit and blend of perfumes in the air. His gums trembled.

Trixie's eyes landed on Victor and she stiffened. He heard one of the guys ask if she was okay. She quickly looked away from

Victor and picked up her tray.

"So, that was three Jack-and-Cokes?" she asked hastily. The guys were confused. She rushed off, taking the long way to the bar to avoid Victor.

Well, that wasn't awkward at all.

A few minutes later, Celia slid through the crowd. He could smell her before he saw her. She slid her fingers around his waist, and then pressed against him. He smiled down at her.

"Hey," she mouthed.

"Hey," he mouthed back.

They danced provocatively. He had to stoop down to allow her to grind her ass in his crotch. He certainly didn't dance like someone from the nineteen hundreds. Good thing Bobby was in his office because he would have scolded her for behaving in such a way. Of course, dancing like she was sexing him up would only help to boost tips at the bar since men were horny and single-minded that late in the night.

When she returned to the bar, Carson gave her an appreciative once-over. She ignored him because punching him in the arm like she wanted to do would only serve to entice him further.

Suddenly, a scream rose above the noise of the club. It hung in the air for a second, before it was swallowed up again by the Flo Rida song. Celia's head jerked up at the sound. The dance floor was crowded but she could see the struggle. Four guys were fist-fighting next to the DJ booth. The green and red strobe lights bounced off their backs and heads.

People stumbled and pushed each other to get out of the way. As the crowd parted, Celia got a good look at one of the fighters: the blonde from the kitchen. He was sporting a blue cast around his wrist that he used to hit one of the others over the head.

Her eyes widened.

"Hey guys, come on, now," Mickey called over the PA. "Break it up."

They weren't listening. One of the men, who had to be a vampire, or at the very least, a linebacker, Celia thought, tossed another like he was a pillow. He crashed into spectators, bringing six people to the floor with him.

The blonde-haired guy laced his arm around the other vampire's neck and jerked his elbow twice, stabbing him in the back with something she couldn't see.

The vamp went down. Celia waited for him to turn crispy, thinking the blonde was being very reckless doing this in front of a crowd of people. But the vampire didn't go crispy. Instead, he sunk to his hands and knees, heaving. His blue Mohawk bobbed up and down, like he was trying hard to spit up a hairball.

The larger vampire whipped around to see his companion in trouble. He was about to attack when four security guards barreled through the crowd. They grabbed the fighters and took them outside through the kitchen, probably to rough them up a little for disturbing the peace. The vampires allowed themselves to be led away to avoid detection. The Asian one needed to be carried. His Jordans dragged along the floor.

Celia and Carson exchanged glances—his excited, hers nervous. She scanned the crowd for Victor but he was nowhere to be found. She didn't have time to really search. Now that the fight was over, the clubbers were back to yelling for her attention.

* * *

Victor stalked silently behind the bodyguards as they pushed the four outside, where they took a few minutes to knee and punch them in the alley. Victor slid around a corner as they reentered. The guards decided to lollygag by the door, snaking bread and leftover pasta from earlier. He had to wait five minutes for them to go back to where they were supposed to be.

He opened the back door, expecting the guys to be gone.

Surprisingly, they weren't. One of the vampires was dead; he could smell the ash. If it was examined, someone would probably find the silver barbell. There was another odor on the air, too, like rotting lettuce. He didn't know what that was.

The remaining vampire, Bryce, punched one of the humans in the gut and he went flying into the wall. He stayed there. The bricks held him in place.

The blonde human used his distraction. He pulled a stake from his back somewhere and ran at Bryce. Victor crouched for more leverage then jumped into the air. He landed in front of the blonde, some six or seven feet away, without a sound. The blonde stopped short, his eyes wide in surprise.

Victor snatched the stake from his grasp and rammed it into the blonde's chest. The sound of his sternum cracking bounced off the walls. The hunter coughed and groaned, stumbled on a chink in the pavement and fell backward.

Bryce spun around, stunned. "Victor," he said. The red geyser caught his attention and his bloodlust took over. He was all over the blonde. Victor stepped away because the delicious smell of blood was making him ache.

After a moment of greedy gobbling, Bryce looked over his shoulder. His lips were crimson. "Have some," he said.

Victor shook his head, declining. Bryce shrugged then went back to work. The blood spraying up from the chest wound slowed until there was no more. When he finished, Bryce scooped up the inert body and tossed it in the open dumpster. The cover shut with a bang. He was about to move on to the man in the wall but Victor stopped him.

"Ramsey will want to speak to him. If he can," he added dubiously. The man's heartbeat was threading and he was sure there was internal damage. You couldn't just walk it off after being literally thrown into a brick wall.

Victor tugged and the man slumped over his shoulder. Not

even a groan. They ran all the way to Ramsey's. The man died as they walked inside.

* * *

Jay had been following the hunters for most of the night. The youngest of the group looked to be about twenty. Jay first saw them meeting in a skanky diner around nine-thirty in the evening, talking too loudly about gathering wood to make stakes. Amateurs.

Though they were being real dumb, it sounded like they knew where vampires hung out.

Jay hailed from Texas. He was in town looking for a vamp that had escaped his grasp. He had happened upon the vamp feeding on a family of four like it was the Sizzler's. Apparently, he'd been keeping them alive, dragging out the torture for two weeks. He found that out from the oldest son—right before he died. Jay had tracked the vamp to Boston, and it appeared that another night of searching stretched out before him. He had walked into the greasy spoon diner, starving.

Lucky for him the five of them were there, announcing their business like a bunch of horses' asses.

The olive-skinned one, with his dark hair swept into a low ponytail and a stern expression, appeared to be the leader. He was in his late thirties with black eyes and long lashes. A discolored scar the length of his pinkie sat on the left side of his jaw, disrupting his beard. A matching one crossed his nose. He snapped at the others often to lower their voices. They called him Snipe. He dispatched the blonde guy, named Booth, and another named Teddy to Cage's.

Jay followed them to the lounge. Unfortunately, he lost track of them inside after spotting a vampire talking to a young girl. A vampire in the hand, right? Or . . . some shit like that. He veered off course. This one glowed brightly, making him look white as light.

That was Jay's . . . you could call it, ability. He could see vampires for what they were.

They were headed to the bathroom, the vampire and the girl. He wasn't one of Ramsey's so maybe he was a drifter from out of town. The girl couldn't have been more than eighteen with a shirt that was cut way too low. She was receiving the intended results. Many of the men around, including Jay, had a few peeks of her young, ample cleavage.

The men's room appeared empty when Jay opened the door. Lady Gaga was telling everyone to just dance on the other side of the wall. It was a really nice bathroom, with red walls and rows of flattering lights along the mirrors. The floor was covered with black tiles that were so shiny you'd probably have no trouble looking between that teenager's sexy, firm thighs.

Jay pulled out his stake from the holster at his hip that had, up until now, been concealed by his leather coat. Not an ideal coat for the summer but it covered his weapons.

A giggle floated from the handicap stall.

Jay kicked the door in without hesitation. The girl shrieked. The vampire hissed at the intrusion. Like Jay had suspected, he was a newbie. Newborns glow brighter than others. The vamp didn't know all his strengths yet. He could've easily jumped over the stall wall, or hell, he could've even gone *through* the stalls. Instead, he just snarled at Jay while attempting to use the girl as a shield.

Jay shoved the girl aside while simultaneously punching him in the face. The vamp's head jerked back and he fell against the toilet, releasing her in the process. The girl tripped in her haste to get out of the line of fire. She fell into Jay, who once again, pushed her aside.

The vampire hissed and howled. Jay wasn't impressed. He threw the stake across the stall. It stopped just to the left of the middle of his chest. The vampire looked stunned. He stared agape at the hunter. Jay lifted his knee and kicked the stake in farther.

The vampire's face froze; his mouth open, his eyes terrified. That noxious burning smell filled the stall. The vampire smoldered without a flame and collapsed into ash in and around the black toilet bowl.

The girl screamed again, clapping her hands to the sides of her face. She looked quickly from the clothes on the floor to Jay and back, as if she were viewing a particularly gruesome tennis match. Jay bent down to pick up the stake and returned it to his holster. The girl was screaming bloody murder. He glanced at her briefly before leaving the bathroom to continue his interrupted tail of the hunters.

"Yo, you saw that!" a guy next to him shouted over the music to his buddy. "I think he broke that guy's back. All he did was kick him!"

Jay looked around, and then headed toward the front entrance. Two bouncers were by the door, staring outside and talking. The woman behind the little desk took money from two women in mini-skirts.

No sign of the hunters. He turned back and moved along the edges of the crowd, hunting for another exit. He went down a short hallway and came into the empty kitchen. There was a door on the other side of the room. He bounded across and pushed it open.

The alley was deserted. The pile of ash didn't escape his notice—well, what was left after the wind got a hold of it. He saw the odd pattern in the brick wall across from him, and the small, dark puddle on the ground.

With tightness in his gut, he approached the red puddle. He stooped down for a better look. He knew before he leaned closer that it was blood. He sighed, and glanced around for a trail of some sort. Five or six small, red dots pointed to the two dumpsters lined up against the wall.

Jay straightened and headed over. Pushing the heavy cover upward, he peered into the filthy dumpster. The blonde hunter lay on top of black trash bags. His right leg was bent unnaturally behind him, and his head was craned to the side. His skin was already as white as paper. His impact must have broken one of the trash bags because lettuce and some kind of yellow substance stained his pant legs. The wooden stake protruded from his chest. Jay could see the white of his bones and the grayish-pink of his muscle. The only blood was drying on his shirt around the weapon. There were two puncture wounds on the left side of his pale neck.

Jay swore and let the top fall back into place. He certainly would have told the hunters that one of their men was dead behind the bar but, alas, he didn't know where they were.

Back inside, the club was still jumping all around him as they moved to "Single Ladies." He stood still, tense and annoyed as he took a moment to figure out his next move.

A pretty female with black hair and red lips came into his view. She had a nice body, he observed. She smirked at him, holding a silver rack full of test tubes of varying colors under his nose. He smelled licorice and bubble gum.

"Would you like a shot?" she asked. She was smiling but there was sadness in her eyes. He wondered fleetingly what that was about.

"No, thanks," he said.

She shrugged and moved on. Jay remembered the hunter and quickly left the club. He had to walk five blocks before coming across a payphone. He dialed 911, disguised his voice, and told them about the dead body. He then returned to the club. Instead of entering, he sat down on the stoop of the office building across the street.

Fifteen minutes later, a blue-and-white cop car double-parked in front of the club. The two officers climbed out. Rick and Meat were both outside, Meat smoking a cigarette. The bouncers seemed troubled to see the police. They spoke for a moment before Rick led them inside.

Jay watched the progression from his stair. Five minutes after disappearing inside, one of the officers appeared at the end of the street, having walked through the alley. He went to the car and produced yellow police tape from the trunk. He used it to block off the mouth of the alley.

Thirty minutes after that, an ambulance appeared with no lights or sirens. The EMTs disappeared down the alley. Another blue-and-white showed, then a white Crime Scene Unit van, a tan sedan of which the medical examiner stepped out, then two unmarked Crown Vics. The four male detectives looked stern. They spoke with the officer manning the alley before slipping under the tape like everyone else.

Cars slowed on the way past, the nosy drivers trying to see what was up. Three more squad cars sped down the street and came to a stop in front of the lounge, adding to the many cars clogging the block. Two of the uniformed officers stood at the entrance of Cage's, barring anyone from entering or exiting. No doubt, the police were beginning the arduous task of questioning everyone inside.

A news van arrived on the scene. A pretty black woman with bangs, a gray pencil skirt and a burgundy silk blouse hopped down from the passenger seat. She wasn't awkward in the least in the constricting skirt; she obviously perfected a method of getting out of the van gracefully.

A lanky man in jeans and a wrinkled white shirt, holding a video camera, emerged from the back. They both made their way to the officer. He told them something. They moved a few feet away to set up their shot.

The ambulance pulled off with the body around two-thirty, the medical examiner in tow. The CSU team left an hour after that. The officers cleared away the yellow tape. The news van packed it up just as the crowd began to swell from the entrance. The people hung around, staring at the cop cars.

Jay's eyes roamed, looking for more vampires in case some showed up for the buffet that was club let-out, even if it was later than usual. It was nearly four in the morning when the last of the club-goers finally stumbled into a cab that drove off toward the expressway.

He was about to call it a night when a tall man came around a corner, walking briskly to the door of the lounge. Jay stood up straight. There was something a little off about the man and not just because his shoulders and back were tense, his fists clenched like he wanted to rip somebody's head clean off their shoulders.

Jay narrowed his eyes, studying the man to decipher what had put him on alert. Then he realized. Yup, it was faint but there was a glow. It pulsed from his skin like a heartbeat. He must've been hungry.

Jay took a step toward the street. Just then, the front door opened. The dark-haired girl hawking shots stepped out between the officers. She waved to the burly bouncer holding the door for her. Her steps faltered when she saw the vampire. Fear crossed her face. Her right hand clutched her left elbow, shielding her body. That was enough confirmation for him. He checked the silver handcuffs clipped to the back of his pants. He could feel his fake badge in his pocket.

A second woman emerged from the depths of the lounge after her. She was laughing at something and it lit her from within. The beautiful face stalled him. Her curly hair flowed in the wind, accenting her full cheeks and brown skin. Honestly, it was like something out of a movie the way her hair danced in the wind, how the light shone on her.

He watched with a mixture of loathing and surprise as she stood on her toes in front of the vampire. She kissed his lips gently. She didn't look like a vampire groupie. No visible markings, no shakes or itching. The vamp rubbed her back at the greeting. His glow pulsed even more. She took his hand and the three of them walked down the street. The dark-haired girl slowed slightly to peek down the alley.

Jay was fully aware that the vampire had to know he was there. He would've heard his footsteps, his heartbeat. When he finally glanced over his shoulder, Jay had his head down, nodding to unheard music. He kept his pace steady and his posture casual, giving off a non-threatening appearance as it were.

The group continued on around a corner. Jay listened for a moment to make sure the coast was clear before sticking his head out. He peered into the parking lot of the taco joint and spotted them piling into a black Honda.

He hurried back to his own car: an old-fashioned but gleaming black Mustang. When he got behind the wheel, he saw an orange ticket under his wiper. The Honda passed and he pulled off. Twenty minutes later, she double-parked in front of a modest apartment building. The friend got out and rushed up the stairs. The Honda rolled on. Jay followed until she parked on a quiet street. He stopped his car at the corner and hit the lights so they wouldn't notice him.

They got out and walked hand-in-hand for a block back to one of the apartment buildings. The girl was talking about something serious, he could tell by the crinkle between her brows. The vampire was trying to look ordinary. It was no easy feat. He was hungry and possibly aware of their company.

After they went inside, Jay found a spot and turned the engine off. He had a clear line of sight of the building from his rear-view mirror.

A light came on in a window on the second floor. A silhouette appeared behind the thin curtain. He knew it was the girl because of her hair, all curly and flowy and sexy . . .

The guy's shadow came across the window next, interrupting Jay's reverie. He could tell he was kissing her.

Jay shuddered. He wondered if the girl knew what she had let into her house. The thing could rip her apart with his bare hands.

He checked the time. Quarter to five.

The vamp would need to leave within the hour to beat the sun. So, he waited, stake in hand. The lights went off in the apartment after twenty minutes. He watched the building and the street. Three cars passed him. A middle-aged man walked his Schnauzer.

Ten minutes to six, a shadow appeared at the front door. Jay perked, his hand going to the door handle. The man who came out was shorter and fatter with a bald spot on the top of his head. He was wearing a green track suit and headphones over his ears.

Jay groaned and relaxed back into his seat. Eventually, the sun streaked the sky orange and the birds came out of hiding.

He sighed, annoyed because that probably meant this vampire had powers that allowed him to move about without the use of doors. That was something he couldn't tell by looking at them. He climbed out the Mustang to pee behind a dumpster in an alley; not very dignifying but whatever. Going by the smells, this was a hot spot for lazy people in need of emptying their bladders.

He stretched by the car and looked up at the second floor window.

He could've just left, maybe come back at dusk to wait for the vampire to show again. But there was something about the girl that tugged at him. He felt he should warn her, protect her. Since she quite possibly wasn't a vamp groupie whore, she probably didn't realize the danger she was in. Vampires were unstable at best, according to what he had seen. They could snap and drain you in a heartbeat, like some kind of rabid animal you shouldn't turn your back on. He wouldn't be able to sleep if something was to happen to her and he could've prevented it.

That's what made him get back in his car, but it wasn't what made him perk up when he saw her descend the stairs with a skip at nine. She was wearing all black again. He followed her back to the lounge.

Five

"CELIA, YOU GOT a hottie at twenty-three," the hostess, Lynn, called into the kitchen at ten-thirty. Celia glanced up from the crossword puzzle she was attempting with Maria.

Maria grinned at her, happy that she wasn't given the first table. Celia stood, adjusted her black apron (they were short in the summertime), took a quick whiff under her arms to check the strength of her deodorant, and then headed out onto the floor.

She raised an eyebrow when she saw Jay sitting in one of the booths in her section. He was extremely handsome—was that mentioned? His light brown hair was short, in a crew cut. He had green eyes and morning stubble that added to the rugged look he was rocking so well. She could see the muscles trying hard to break free of his brown shirt. He watched her as she approached, making her shiver in a good way, which was . . . unexpected

"Hi," she said carefully, trying not to be a dork and having her voice crack. "I'm Celia. Have you been to Cage's before?"

“Not for food,” he replied and she noticed his slight southern twang.

“Well, our special today is grilled sea bass with a mango salsa. There’s also an Italian Wedding soup that’s not listed in the menu. Can I start you off with something to drink?”

He was still staring at her, examining her. His eyes skirted her neck and exposed forearms. She kept her face neutral, though she couldn’t help a creepy-crawly feeling on the back of her neck. His attention was focused, and was beginning to sketch her out. What the hell was he looking for?

“Just a Coke,” he finally said. She gave a small smile then walked away, hiding the fact that she wanted to bust out in a sprint. He may have been cute but he was being weird.

She returned shortly with a tall glass. The ice clinked noisily as she sat it down in front of him. He ordered a burger, medium-rare, and fries.

“So, almost mooing but not quite,” Celia joked. He chuckled as she took his menu. “Only guys seem to order their meat rare. Why is that?”

He shrugged. “It just tastes better that way, I s’pose. You don’t know guys who like their food bloody?” He was staring at her again. Something about his tone indicated he wasn’t talking about burgers. That was unsettling.

Without answering, she turned slowly for the kitchen. She glanced back at him on the way. His green eyes were still on her—well, her butt.

Celia put his order in then waited inside the kitchen until it was ready. The cooks were dancing to a hip-hop song playing on the radio. They were all Brazilian who barely spoke English but they knew all the words and dances to the Soulja Boy song.

Two of the other servers—young college students—were talking animatedly while chomping on warm focaccia bread. They were still going over the story of the man found in the alley. Celia cringed. She had been horrified last night when Carson had spread the news of police activity. The steely detectives made Mickey cut the music, then sectioned off the crowd to begin interviewing. The staff started to clean during this process. The club patrons were released and the detectives asked the staff questions as a whole, though no one had any answers.

Last night, after dropping off Trixie, Celia had asked Victor what happened with the fighters.

"Those bouncers took them out back. They continued to fight. One of them almost killed Bryce. The two humans were killed."

She gasped. "Two? But they said there was only one body!"

"We took one of them with us, but he died."

Uneasy images wafted through her jumbled brain. Obviously, if these men were attacking Victor and his friend, they would need to defend themselves. Except these were the second and third deaths in so many days . . . presumably at Victor's hand. She was shaking by the time she had parallel-parked on her street.

Upstairs, she didn't bring the subject up again. She knew to expect chatter at work; it was definitely a newsworthy story. And with Carson drumming up intrigue the previous night with his stupid and wild-fetched stories, there would be talk for weeks.

"They said he had a piece of wood in his chest," the first boy replied. He rubbed his own chest. "Shit, man, that's gotta hurt."

"Of course it hurts, dumbass."

The first one lowered his voice. "You don't think security did that, do you? They'd have reason to, since he was one of the guys Bobby was telling us about."

"No! It had to be those guys they were fighting."

"I never heard of gangs using sticks as weapons."

"They're not a gang, you idiot."

"Alright, can we talk about something else?" Maria chimed in with a visible shudder. Her Colombian accent overwhelmed her words at time. “I hate thinking about that. My husband almost made me not come in today,” she told Celia.

“Order’s up,” one of the chefs called, sliding a plate onto the service window counter. “Twenty-three.”

Celia checked that her outfit was still neat before heading out again with the plate. “Here you go,” she said politely, placing the food in front of her patron. She reached for his empty cup and was surprised by him gently taking hold of her wrist. His hand was big and warm. She looked at him, wondering why she wasn’t snatching her hand away.

“You got a boyfriend, Celia?” he asked outright. There was something harsh just below the surface of his eyes that made her a bit nervous about where this question was coming from.

“I do,” she said firmly, attempting to appear unperturbed. “And he wouldn’t be happy that some stranger’s trying to hold my hand.”

He didn’t release his hold. “I’m Jay.”

“Hello, Jay. Can I have my arm back?”

She held his gaze so he wouldn’t think he was intimidating her. Unfortunately, those damn shivers were back. His eyes were just so piercing.

He finally let go of her wrist. She took his cup to the dispenser behind the bar and refilled it. She planned to just place the cup down and retreat to the kitchen, but he stopped her with more strange questions.

“You ever wonder why your boyfriend’s never around during the day?”

“What?” she said, sounding more outraged than surprised like a normal person would. How would he know that? She’d never seen this guy before that she could recall . . .

“Why he’s so pale? Or so strong? Or—”

“Look,” she said tersely, putting a hand up to stop him. “You don't know me or Victor or what you're talking about."

"I think I do." He looked at her meaningfully. "What do *you* know about him?"

She fixed her mouth to tell him off. At the last second, she decided that wasn't a good idea. She came to the quick conclusion that he had sat in her section on purpose.

She backed away, and then hurried to the kitchen.

When Celia peeked out fifteen minutes later, Jay was gone. She went to clear his food. He'd taken a huge bite of the burger. The pink of the meat was clearly visible, the juices drenching the bun. He left a twenty on a ten-dollar tab and a napkin with a phone number scribbled on it.

She should've thrown it away. Instead, she slipped the napkin in her back pocket.

Celia's shift ended at four. Bobby was doing paperwork in the office when she entered. She went to the lockers in the corner to retrieve her purse as Carson strolled in.

"Celia," Carson replied. "Why don't you stay and have a drink with me?"

Celia chuckled humorlessly. "Wow, the balls on you," she said as she pushed the locker closed. She clocked out, waved to Bobby, who was staring at Carson, then bounced out the office. Bobby would definitely ream him out for that. He didn't allow fraternization.

Celia put her sunglasses on as soon as she stepped out onto the sidewalk. She sighed happily as the hot sun beat down on her face and shoulders. The heat absorbed into her pores and she closed her eyes.

"Hello."

She nearly jumped out of her skin as the voice jarred her from her mini-trance. She looked around to find the culprit and groaned when she discovered Jay leaning against the wall.

God, is he following me?

She stomped past him on her way to the parking lot. His gait was longer than hers. He easily fell into step beside her. When they made it to the parking lot, she spun on him and reached into her bag.

"I have mace," she warned. Her fingers grasped the travel-sized bottle of musk body spray. He didn't have to know it wasn't true until the last second when she would run for her life.

He put his hands up in surrender. "Easy."

When he raised his arms, his shirt lifted slightly. The sun glinted off the gold badge clipped to his waist. She looked at it, then back to his face. "You're a cop?" she demanded.

"You know," he said casually, "that's a really derogatory term—"

"Are you? What's this about?"

"I'm investigating a murder." Well, it *was* true. His target was still on the loose.

She stiffened, looking all kinds of guilty as her eyes widened and her jaw dropped slightly. Her voice was a whisper. "A murder?"

"Yeah."

"The one last night?"

He raised a brow. "You know of others?"

"No!" she said quickly. He didn't look convinced. "You think Victor had something to do with it?" She was becoming scared and she couldn't keep it from her face.

He just shrugged, contented with letting her incriminate him. Not that he was going to arrest him and take him to trial. Though, the fact that she blanched showed there might be some relevance in scoping out her long-toothed BF.

Abruptly, a brick wall shot up across her face as she got control of herself. "Well, you're wrong!" she exclaimed.

She turned and rushed to her car. He was still where she left him as she sped by. Checking the rear-view mirror often, she made sure he wasn't following her. She went straight home and ran inside, turning all the locks just in case. In the living room, she went to the window to peek out.

Everything was still. The block was deserted: a few lights shone in windows across the street; a yellow Chrysler squeezed into a spot. She moved away to the sofa while chewing on her thumbnail. Thank goodness for acrylics.

Was he really looking into the death of the blonde guy? Why would he think Victor was involved? He hadn't been around when the fight broke out. Could he know about Trixie's date?

Celia sat there for an hour before she groaned miserably. She went to the kitchen. She had some time before Victor came and she needed to keep herself occupied. She pulled down ingredients to make cookies and set to work.

Just as she was placing little drops of batter on a cookie sheet, the buzzer sounded, making her start. She glanced at the intercom. Her heart pounded. Images of Jay standing on her stoop, reinforcements crowding the sidewalk like in a gangster movie, flashed in her mind.

The buzzer sounded again in three short bursts. She let out a sigh of relief.

She used her pinkie to let Trixie in. She then stepped out into the corridor, watching as her dark head bounced up the stairs.

"What're you doing here?" Celia asked. She looked over her jeans and red tank top with a puzzled frown. "Don't you have to work tonight?"

"Nope," she said merrily. She reached out and ran a finger along Celia's cheek, then brought it to her mouth. "Ooo, chocolate chip."

They went inside the apartment. Trixie stood next to the counter, watching Celia arrange the balls on the sheet. "What's the occasion?"

"Nothing, I just wanted cookies," Celia said, avoiding her eyes.

"Liar. You only bake for barbeques and when you're upset."

Damn, Celia thought. She placed the cookie sheet in the oven. She then went to the sink to wash her hands, taking her sweet time. Trixie was no fool. She folded her arms at the chest, patiently waiting.

Celia tossed the towel she used to dry her hands on the counter and faced her friend. "This cop was hounding me today. I think he wants Victor."

That took Trixie by surprise. Her arms slipped to her side and tears welled in her ice-blue eyes. She'd been crying about Donny for the last two nights. He was a cool guy and, hey, she could've gotten a discount at Best Buy where he was a manager if things went well. Okay, that was mean.

The police had spoken to her on Sunday and brought her in to meet with a sketch artist. She had purposely screwed up the image so it wouldn't look like Victor. Even now, she didn't know why she had done that.

"Was it Officer Keegan?" she asked in a small voice. "He's the one who questioned me about Donny."

Celia shook her head. "His name was Jay and he wasn't wearing a uniform so he must've been a detective."

"Maybe it was about something else," she said cautiously.

Celia took a deep breath wrought with concern. Her shoulders slumped as she looked to the floor. "That's not very comforting."

She shuffled to the living room and sat on the sofa. Trixie followed. There was only the sofa and a tall director's chair in the corner to sit in Celia's small living room. Trixie pulled herself up onto the high chair. It was brown with pink psychedelic flowers emblazoned on the seat.

Celia flipped on the television as a distraction. "Why don't we go out?" Trixie suggested after a moment. "Let's get plastered."

Normally, she would decline because of Victor. Except after the past couple of hours of fretting, she didn't know if she wanted to see him. Bonus: she didn't have to work the next day. She jumped up, determined.

"And let's stay out all night," Celia said. "We can get a hotel room."

"Yay!"

Trixie hopped down, clapping her hands together. She helped Celia choose an outfit: denim mini-skirt and fluttery flowered top. Celia slid her feet into her sandals, freshened her makeup and pulled her hair into a ponytail. Trixie borrowed a gold tank top with sequins on the shoulders to be a little dressier. She also borrowed a pair of gold flats.

After removing the cookies from the oven, they headed out with their arms linked. Working at Cage's had its benefits. Celia and Trixie knew the bouncers of most of the clubs downtown and in Faneuil Hall. They were able to hop from club to club and bar to bar. It was Tuesday night, but there was still a good turnout in most of the places. Two of the clubs were hosting parties—one for a birthday of a local celebrity, the other a going-away celebration—and the girls slipped in with ease.

They knew the bartenders as well, plus Trixie flirted constantly so they didn't have to worry about drinks.

By one forty-five, as Trixie wished, they were both wasted. Outside, the air was still warm, though not as sticky as earlier. Celia stumbled against Trixie, who laughed like it was the funniest thing in the world.

"I . . . I love you, Trix."

Celia had a silly grin on her face as she rubbed Trixie's arms. Yeah, she was one of *those* drunks.

"I love you, too, Seal. I love Seal!" she shouted at the top of her lungs.

Two guys passing by smirked at them. They were wearing matching rugby shirts—one green, the other red—and shorts. Yeah, that didn't scream "losers" at all.

"I love seals, too," Red Shirt said.

"You're awesome!" Trixie cried and threw her arms around his neck for a sloppy hug.

"Where you ladies headed?" Green Shirt asked. Celia and Trixie looked at each other before bursting out in laughter.

"Sorry, hon," Celia said. "We're married."

"To each other," Trixie replied. She grabbed Celia's cheeks then kissed her with a loud smack. Just like any hetero guy presented with the opportunity to witness females making out right in front of them, their little faces lit up. Trixie wrapped her arm around Celia's shoulders, wiggled her fingers at the guys, and pulled her down the sidewalk, pursued closely by the guys' calls for them to stay. Good thing they had arranged for the hotel room before clubbin'.

"Where wuz it 'gain?" Celia slurred. Her eyes were half-open and her arms felt numb.

Trixie was genuinely confused. "Where was what?"

"The hotel, stupid," Celia chuckled.

"Hey! I'm not stupid, stupid."

"Don't call me stupid!"

"Don't call *me* stupid!"

They stared at each other in shock at the name-calling. Then they laughed again and staggered on. They turned down a tight, deserted street that smelled like garbage. The brick buildings were all closed and dark. Some abandoned flyers rustled in the wind, dancing off the curb and into the ditch up ahead. Trixie, through her haze of inebriation, didn't realize they were coming to the alley where she'd stumbled upon Victor munching on her date.

A glass bottle hit the concrete somewhere and rolled across the bumpy surface. Celia stopped short from the noise. Trixie stumbled since she still had her arm around her.

Celia looked around with wide, frightened eyes. "What was that?" she said in a stage whisper.

Trixie's expression matched hers once she sensed her fear. "I don't know," she said in the same whisper.

Celia looked around slowly. She wasn't even sure of what she was searching for. When her eyes went to Trixie again, Trixie's face crumbled into a snicker. She put a hand to her mouth then pointed to Celia.

"You should see your face!"

Celia started to laugh, too. "Boogity boogity boo," she said, wriggling her fingers in front of her like she was a witch.

They had only taken two steps to wherever the hell they thought they were headed when a dark figure stepped from the alley a few feet ahead of them. They didn't see him at first—he had to clear his throat to get their attention.

At the sight of the man, their smiles faded simultaneously. He was average built and so pale he was nearly gleaming in the light of the streetlamps. You could say he almost . . . sparkled. His golden hair came to his ears in soft curls. A pair of blue-rimmed, square-framed glasses sat on the bridge of his nose. He grinned at them, his eyes as dark as the night. His gaze sent a chill through Celia. Her brain was too addled to comprehend the danger quick enough.

He studied them for a long moment, as if waiting to see if they would run now. The two just stood there, frozen in confusion and distant fear. Seeing that they needed further motivation, the man's grin melted into a snarl. Celia saw the flash of his fangs as they extended menacingly from his extra pink gums. He hunched forward, arching his back; a predator that just found two stupid pieces of fresh meat.

He charged.

The girls turned to run. He was behind them before they'd even faced the opposite direction. He shoved Trixie. She went flying into the street. Her head hit the ground and she lay there, unmoving.

Celia was still in the process of turning when he grabbed her shoulder and pinned her against the wall. His blonde curls swung into his face as he hissed at her. Her heart pounded, making him grin again, excited. His problem was that he liked to play with his food.

His fingers caressed her cheek. Cold, thin fingers. She noticed how long his nails were, like a guitarist. She wondered if he played. Maybe the Spanish guitar? Then she questioned if she really *was* dense. Here she was, picturing this vampire crooning to a crowd in a dimly lit lounge when he was trying to kill her.

He put his face in the crook of her neck. She winced, anticipating his bite. All she felt were his chilly lips, then the tip of his tongue against her skin. She cringed.

Time seemed to stop as horrible images of being molested in a dank alley flooded her mind.

No! Celia told herself.

It was fruitless, but she struggled against his hold, even kicked him in the shins. His chuckle warmed her neck.

His voice rattled in her ear. "Mm, I like you."

She yanked on his hair. "Let go of me!" she screamed as loud as she could. He chuckled again.

He moved closer to cease her kicking. His mouth was at her neck again when suddenly he rammed into her, as if by force. He didn't bite, like she thought he was trying to do. Instead, the vampire released her, hissing and clutching the back of his neck. White smoke rose from his skin. He shifted. Celia saw Jay standing behind him, a silver bat in his right hand.

The vampire growled something fierce.

"You," he said.

Jay shrugged nonchalantly. "Me."

He swung the bat with both hands, grunting from the exertion of popping him one. The vampire went down. His glasses landed on the sidewalk beside him. There was a red mark on his cheek and jaw where the bat had come into contact. Jay swung again and again.

The third time the bat came down, the vampire caught it. He didn't even care that it was making his hand sizzle. He pulled it from Jay's grasp and tossed it aside. He then jumped at Jay, who caught him at the collar and fell backward. Once his back hit the pavement, he put a foot in the vampire's stomach and launched him overhead.

Jay's legs kicked out. The force of the movement propelled him forward from the pavement. His boots hit the ground and he spun around. He pulled a stake from his side and pounced on the vampire. The vamp had already regained his steam and punched Jay off of him.

Jay rolled from the impact until he landed in the gutter. The vampire appeared at his side with lightning speed. He wrenched his arm and pulled him to his feet. Jay grunted in pain. The vamp threw him against the opposite wall.

Jay's head jerked back and forward, hurting his neck. The vampire again was in front of him, striking him in the stomach with an uppercut before Jay realized he was there. He clocked him in the face. Jay landed on his hands and knees on the ground with a groan.

The vampire hunched over him, fangs bared, ready to bite, when there was a crack. The vampire hadn't heard Celia run up behind him since he had been preoccupied. She didn't have as much strength as Jay but she brought the bat down on the exposed skin of his neck where Jay's mark was still visible.

The silver helped. The sound of sizzling followed the vampire hissing. He reached out and grabbed her ankle. She gasped because that was all she could muster. His grasp was like a vise. She thought fleetingly that he was going to snap her ankle in two.

Jay turned slightly underneath him. The stake he still held in his hand poked into the vampire's chest. The vampire reached for it, knocking Celia on her ass as he let go of her. The bat dropped to the pavement with a hard thud. They wrestled for the grip on the weapon. The sharp tip pierced through the vamp's shirt, through his skin. Blood dripped down the side of the stake onto Jay's torso. The vamp put a hand around Jay's neck. His hold on his throat cut off oxygen to his brain. Jay resisted the blackness threatening the edges of his vision. He used all his might to ram the wooden stake in farther.

The vampire screamed and went crispy. His ash trickled onto Jay's stomach and legs.

"Argh!" he exclaimed, jumping up. He tossed away the recently vacated jeans and shirt and brushed the ash off. It would still leave that nasty smell on his clothes. He'd have to get rid of them.

He glanced at Celia. She stared up at him in astonishment. A red ring had already appeared around her ankle where the vampire had held her. He stuck out his left hand—his right shoulder was aching from being thrown around like a rag doll. He pulled her to her feet.

She dusted her hands off on her skirt, her eyes still on Jay. He flashed a sexy smile and she felt that good sort of tingling.

"So," he said, drawing out his Southern accent. "Enjoyin' your night out, ma'am?" He even tipped an imaginary cowboy hat.

"Don't call me 'ma'am,'" she muttered irritably. All the excitement had cleared her brain. Well, for the most part. Her arms still felt numb and she was having a hard time standing still.

She glared at him. "Were you following me?" she snapped.

"No."

It wasn't a complete lie. He'd been scoping out a bar called Ned Devine's, looking for vamps. That's when he saw the two dancing together, surrounded by a group of guys watching them avidly. He wasn't having much luck on his own so he thought he'd see if her vampy boyfriend would come to her.

Celia didn't believe him. She was going to argue when she suddenly remembered Trixie. She looked around frantically. Trixie was still lying in the street where she had been tossed. Celia ran over to her, panicked. She stooped beside her and gently rolled her onto her back.

Trixie groaned. "What happened?"

She adjusted her tank top. It had moved to the side, revealing her marigold bra. She rubbed her forehead where a round bump sat. There was a small, pink scrape on her cheek.

While Celia examined Trixie, Jay gathered his bat and stake and stuffed them in a well-used leather satchel the color of sandalwood. He must have set it aside when he realized this was his vamp. He flung the strap across his chest now. The bottom of the bat stuck out the side, pressing against his back. He then crossed over to them and slid his hand under Trixie's arm, bringing her to her feet. She held his arm to steady herself.

"You okay?" he asked.

She was feeling light-headed. "I think so." Trixie looked up at him and her face softened. "Oh," she said.

She stumbled dizzily and, for once, it wasn't an act to touch a guy to increase her tip. He draped her arm across his shoulder and held her up. "Come on," he said gruffly.

They walked back toward Faneuil Hall. It was nearly three in the morning. That didn't deter the people still milling about, looking in on dark store fronts or making out under trees. A short queue stood to the side of the Sausage King's cart stationed on a corner, outside the Black Rose bar. His competition was parked across the street, next to the 7-11. The delicious aroma of onions and green peppers clung to the night.

"Our hotel's on, um, Union Street," Celia said after a moment of hard thinking.

"Hotel?" he asked with a frown.

"That's right," she snipped. She actually wanted to call the night a bust and crawl into her comfy bed. She didn't because she was afraid Victor would be there, looking for her. She didn't want Jay to see him.

"Whatever," he mumbled, unruffled. It took them fifteen minutes to find the small hotel because Celia couldn't remember which way to go. She tried to ditch Jay in the lobby to no avail. He insisted on making sure they were settled upstairs.

Their room was on the top floor. Celia, annoyed, jabbed at the four in the elevator. Soft jazz playing over the speakers was the only sound in the tiny box. Jay stood on one end with Trixie draped over him, her head tipping forward every once in a while. Celia, on the other side of Trixie, stared at the numbers above the door as they lit with each floor. Her arms were crossed tightly. She could feel Jay's eyes on her but she kept her gaze forward. The elevator eventually dinged and they stepped out.

Inside the room, Jay deposited his cargo onto the double bed. Celia took the gold shoes off then sat beside her. Trixie had been falling asleep on the trip over and now that she was on the bed, her eyes closed, her mouth fell open. Celia bit her bottom lip, anxious that her friend might be suffering from a concussion.

"She'll be fine," Jay replied at her expression. "Just a little bump on the head."

Celia concealed the wave of relief before turning to Jay. "Okay, I think we're good."

He rolled his neck a few times, trying to loosen the tight muscles from the whiplash. He then put his hands in his pockets and leaned against the wall—lucky wall! He didn't appear to have any intentions of leaving.

"What kind of cop are you?" Celia asked. She slid her own sandals off and rested her ankle on her knee to rub her foot. Jay strolled over. He sat down on the other side of Trixie's legs. Gently, he took Celia's foot and massaged her sole. She didn't even have a chance to protest. His strong fingers expertly worked the kinks. She let out a contented sigh. She then shifted on the bed so that her leg was more comfortable, which meant it was draped across Trixie's prone legs. He caught a glimpse of her orange panties as she moved.

"So, what kind of cop are you?" she repeated, only without all the damn hostility. His fingers were like magic.

"Did I say I was a cop?" he asked quizzically. She narrowed her eyes. "I was investigating a murder and I just killed the suspect."

She decided to play dumb. It seemed like the best option. "What *was* that back there?"

He eyed her, trying to figure out what was her game. She kept her expression neutral; she even threw in a little fear since he was watching her reaction. Who said acting was hard?

"There are a lot of things that go bump in the night. That was a vampire. You know, *I vant to suck your blood*," he said in a Dracula accent that didn't quite translate with his Texan one. She had to fight to stifle her giggle.

Jay placed her foot on the bed. The ring around her ankle was now a deep shade of red. He reached down to take the other that had been dangling over the side. Trixie mumbled something inaudible about the extra weight on her legs. Celia propped a pillow against the headboard behind her for more comfort.

"Silver and garlic hurts them," he went on. "A stake to the heart kills them, as you saw. And, of course, the sun."

Those were all things she knew. She shook her head, mystified. "Wow, I don't know what to say. It would be easy to just write you off as fucking nuts except I saw . . . with my own eyes . . ." She trailed off and stared at his hands on her foot. She was glad she'd refreshed her toenail polish over the weekend—a relaxing shade of turquoise as the bottle proclaimed.

"Better?" he asked, motioning to her feet. She nodded. He kissed the top of her foot then placed it on the bed.

She watched as he stood, adjusted his bag, and headed toward the door. "Where are you going?" she asked, then winced. She'd sounded too eager. And he heard it.

He smiled a little, the cocky bastard, and faced the room.

"I've got another three or four hours of huntin' time left. Maybe I'll see you for lunch tomorrow."

"I'm not working tomorrow."

"Even better. You can sit with me."

She shook her head. "I am not going to Cage's on my day off."

"Well, let's go to The Pit," he suggested. That was the greasy spoon diner where he'd first seen the hunters.

"Ick," she said, scrunching her nose. "I heard that place gives you the runs."

"Have you had it?" He sounded offended.

"Did you not hear what I just said?"

He rolled his eyes. "Just meet me there at one."

"That's kinda late for lunch—"

"Look," he interrupted, annoyance seeping into his voice. "Just fuckin' be there."

He turned and left the room before she could protest further.

Six

CELIA FELT GUILTY as she searched her closet for an outfit. She and Trixie didn't leave the hotel until nine that morning, which was on purpose to make sure the sun was good and settled in the sky.

The ground was still wet from the early morning rain shower. They shared a cab home that smelled so strongly of patchouli that they had to roll the windows down, prompting an irritated look from the driver. He had had the AC on. When she went inside, Celia ate some fruit, cleaned the kitchen and bathroom and hopped in the shower.

She stood in her room with a light purple towel wrapped around her body, her brown skin still damp from the shower. It was going to be hot today, according to the news reports. What else was new? From the closet, she took out a yellow sundress with spaghetti straps and pockets at the waist. She had to wear a strapless bra because the top of the dress was no match for her bad boys.

After dressing and tightening her ponytail, she headed out. She took a cab since parking would be impossible in the South Station area of downtown. The station was where buses and trains out of town loaded. There were always cabs and cars clustered out front of its tall, tinted glass walls, picking up tourists and relatives.

Jay wasn't at The Pit when she arrived a little after one, so Celia took a seat in a booth by the window. The diner was small on the inside. There were about ten booths along the walls and a counter with stools in the center. The color scheme was navy blue and white, with artsy-fartsy pictures of dishes of food on the wall that really didn't go with the atmosphere.

A waitress sauntered over, popping gum. She looked to be eighteen or nineteen with curly blonde hair, short brown shorts and a pink top under her stained white apron. She placed a menu in front of her.

"Would you like something to drink?" she asked politely. That surprised Celia. She'd been expecting attitude. The girl smiled warmly.

"Yes, a Sprite, please," Celia said.

"Sure thing."

As she walked away, Jay came inside. He glanced around until he found her, then headed over. He was limping slightly and sat with a sigh. Heavy bags hung under his sleepy eyes and he was wearing the same clothes from last night. Also, he smelled like bologna and rotten eggs.

Celia put a finger under her nose as she recoiled. He nodded in agreement. "Sorry. Got thrown in a dumpster and didn't have time to change."

"It's one o'clock in the afternoon. Did you fall asleep in that dumpster?"

The waitress returned with Celia's soda. "Coffee," he said at her. Celia was going to add the "please" since Jay appeared to have misplaced his manners this morning, but the girl didn't seem to mind his tone. She brought him a steaming cup right away.

"Thanks." He downed the drink, burning his tongue. "Fuckin' shit," he muttered. He glanced up at Celia through his lashes. "Oh, sorry."

"Did you find other . . ." she lowered her voice, "vampires?"

"One other," he said. "Motherfucker fought hard but I got 'im." His smile shone through the weariness and she could see he was proud.

"Hmm," she said. She glanced down at the menu, trying to seem indifferent though her heart was racing. Good thing he didn't have the super hearing of his quarry. "What, uh, what did he look like?"

"Average height, light hair, kind of geeky."

She nodded slowly. That didn't sound like Victor at all. She stopped tugging at the hem of her dress. Jay raised his cup to the waitress, indicating a refill. She brought the carafe and took their orders.

Jay drank the second cup more slowly, able to savor it this time. Celia surveyed him a moment. She could see the fresh cuts and bruises on his face, neck, and hands, along with a few old ones. They really did make him look manly . . .

He glanced up, probably feeling her stare, and their eyes met. She could get lost in that sea of emerald green. She found herself not wanting to look away. It was as if he were trying to enthrall her but he wasn't a vamp since, you know, he was out in the daytime.

It took some effort to avert her eyes. She looked at the napkin between her fingers. "How did you get started doing this?" That seemed like a safe direction.

He took a sip of the coffee. When he spoke next, his voice was steady, yet strained.

"I was sixteen when a bloodsucker attacked my house. He was a newly turned son-of-a-bitch so he didn't know what the hell he was doing. He did manage to kill my two sisters. He was working on my dad, who had been trying to stab him with a broken chair leg while he was attacking my mom. I picked up the leg and jabbed it in his back. I only made him angrier.

"Then I remembered about the stake to the heart, which, up until then, I had thought was all bullshit. I found the sweet spot and he fuckin' burned. But during the fight, the bloodsucker had bled onto my mother. What the hell did I know? I thought she was going to be alright.

"She slept through the night and the next day, then the next night she started shaking and convulsing and crying out in pain. That lasted for hours and it was the worst sound anyone could hear."

He paused to bring the coffee mug to his mouth.

"Then she was quiet," he continued. "The doctors didn't know what was happening. It just appeared she was in a coma. The next night, she rose and killed my father. He was sleeping beside her."

He stopped. His face had taken on hard lines as he remembered that time. He gulped down more coffee. Celia reached across the table and placed her hand on his. She didn't even think about it, the gesture was instinctual. He accepted the comfort.

"It took me two months to track her down," Jay went on, his voice low and purposefully even. He stared her in the eye. She couldn't help a twinge of fear at his intensity. "After that, I made it my business to stake as many of those sons-of-bitches I could get my fuckin' hands on."

Celia retracted her hand as Victor crossed her mind. The waitress came with their food. Jay didn't waste any time chowing down on the steak burrito. Celia ate her Cobb salad slowly, turning his story over a few times in her head. Her heart ached with his pain and loss. She couldn't even start to imagine hunting and killing a loved one. That took a lot of courage and determination and she knew her emotions would get in the way.

Ten minutes later, Jay was leaning back in his seat, stuffed and satisfied. His knees brushed hers as he relaxed in the chair.

"I'm surprised you didn't lick the plate," Celia commented. He chuckled, then thumped his chest with his fist to ease out a belch, which was disgusting. Luckily, she couldn't smell it over his more pungent stenches.

"Where are you from?" she asked.

"Dallas. Is waitressing your full-time job?"

"I'm a bartender mostly. I actually prefer being behind the bar. Time goes by quicker and I don't have to interact as much." She shrugged as if to say, *go figure*. "Where are you staying?"

"This guy's basement," he said vaguely.

"That sounds sketchy as hell," she said seriously.

"I guess it is."

Celia looked down at her salad as a thought began to take shape. "So, you probably only eat food from places like this."

"The food here's good," he protested, affronted. "Your problem is you're prejudiced."

She scowled at him. "I don't think so."

"Yes, you are. You didn't wanna come here because of something you heard. You didn't even order food. Look at that shit. You can get a fuckin' salad at home—"

Celia rolled her eyes. "See," she cut across him, "I was *going* to invite you over for real food. But if you're going to be a jerk, forget it."

He was quiet. A smile tugged at his lips. "You wanna cook for me?"

There was coyness to his tone that snapped her back to reality. What the fuck was she thinking? She couldn't invite him over. What about Victor? This was a tricky path she was headed down; she needed to get out and *quickly*.

"No, because I just remembered I don't allow assholes in my house." She munched on a piece of lettuce to avoid speaking.

He chuckled, and took the soft breadstick from her plate. It was gone in thirty seconds. Her lips pursed in annoyance. She was going to eat that.

Jay stretched against the faux leather and draped his arms over the back of the seat. The sun was coming in now, lighting their table. She glanced outside. A cab nearly rear-ended a Benz that had stopped short for two teenagers haphazardly crossing the street. The girls barely glanced back.

Celia wanted to change the subject. "How many years have you been doing this?" she asked.

"Eleven. I guess I found my career path early. How long have you worked in the lounge?" he bounced back.

"Three years. I used to be a temp in this law firm but it was *so* boring." She pointed an imaginary gun to her head and pulled the trigger. "I did that for like a year after jumping around with retail jobs. Not as exciting as staking motherfuckers but, hey," she replied with a casual shrug, "I make a living."

Uh-oh. He was really starting to like her. You could tell from the look in his eye, the small relaxed smile making him look younger. He glanced at his watch and saw that it was a little after two. He called the waitress over to order dessert.

"You want anything?" he asked Celia. She declined.

The waitress brought him a slice of apple pie with a dollop of whipped cream. He did take his time with the pie (there's a joke in there somewhere).

"You got any kids, Jay?"

He snorted. "None that I know of."

"Do you just . . . move around like this? You don't have any other family?"

He paused for the briefest moment where she saw his jaw clench. “Nope,” he said lightly, but she could tell he was troubled.

“Does that mean you want to?”

“Do you always ask so many questions?”

“I’m just curious, is all.” She looked down at her plate. “I don’t know if I want kids. I . . . just want to be with somebody who can take my shit and not complain.”

He stared at her a moment but didn’t answer her question. He was probably wondering where the hell that had come from; she was wondering the same thing. The talk of family brought that argument with Victor to mind. He wanted something he could never have. Getting married, having kids . . . they were both options Celia could make . . . but did she want that?

Jay had those options as well. He would grow old—if he didn’t become a statistic with his line of work. What did he want?

She’d never let herself think these thoughts before with Victor. It was easier to ignore them, to live in wonderful denial. And to add more frosting on that particularly bitter cake, the latest murders weighed heavily on her mind.

Jay’s voice broke through her debating. “What’re you gonna cook for me?” he asked around a mouthful of cinnamony apple. She tried not to wince. She hadn’t been successful in making him forget her unwise invitation.

“I thought I told you, you weren’t invited,” she said snippily.

“Personally,” he carried on as if she hadn’t spoken. “I like steak and potatoes. But I’ll take whatever froufrou thing you’ll make.”

She frowned. “Froufrou? You think I’m *froufrou*?” She was a little hurt by that. She didn’t think she had given off signs that she was stuck-up in the brief time that they’d known each other.

He could see that she was upset by the way her forehead crinkled. “Calm down. I was joking,” he said. “I just meant that obviously you weren’t gonna make greasy burgers and fries cuz I can get that right here."

She eyed him suspiciously but that did make her feel better. "Lasagna," she said after a pause.

He nodded approvingly. "I like lasagna. When are we doing this?"

"Tomorrow," she said, giving in. That way, she could avoid Victor. He didn't always stop by when she was getting ready for work. She assumed he was coming by tonight. She'd tell him she was hanging with Trixie or something.

Ugh, that wasn't good. She felt bad that she was considering lying to Victor. He wouldn't want her making dinner for some guy. Some *hunter* guy. Except she wanted to see more of Jay.

Bad, she told herself over and over. *Bad, bad,* fucking *bad.*

She should have told him that it was all a mistake. Reminded him that, you know, she had a *boyfriend.* They may have their arguments but they were a couple and she always thought she respected that. So, why did her mouth remain clamped closed?

Jay finished his pie. A smear of whipped cream sat lazily on his top lip. He didn't seem to notice. Oh, how she wanted to lick it off.

"You got a little . . ." She inclined her head toward his mouth. He slowly licked his lips, all the while gazing at her significantly. As corny as it was, her knees went weak. Good thing she was sitting.

"Let's get outta here," he announced. He lifted his hand to signal the waitress. She came by with their check and cleared the table. Jay took the bill as Celia was reaching for it. He pulled out a battered leather wallet and paid.

Outside was still hot but it was a nice hot, minus the mugginess with which August usually subjected Boston. The rain earlier had helped clear the air. They walked down the street at a leisurely pace. The food seemed to have eased his aching body; he was only limping slightly, like how guys do.

It was so comfortable, their pace, that if she had taken his hand, she was sure he wouldn't object.

She immediately chided herself for even thinking such a thing.

They had been walking around for a while, talking about little things, and ended up in a quiet section where Chinatown met Downtown. They came across a tiny park tucked away on a tiny street. Celia entered first. The playground was meager, with a silver slide reflecting the sun, peeling monkey bars, and two swings. One of the swings had been swung and swung until it was wrapped around the top bar. Celia sat on the one functioning swing and pushed off. Jay stood to the side.

A cloud passed across the sky, shading the park and bringing a slight respite from the sun. Jay watched her kick off, swinging high into the sky. The wind she was creating whipped her ponytail across her face. She had sat on her dress so it wouldn't fly up over her head and reveal her black boy short underwear.

Playing on the swing reminded her of when she was younger. She always loved things that made her stomach fly into her throat, things that frightened her. Like swings and roller coasters and that yo-yo ride at Six Flags.

"Is this what you do on your days off?" Jay asked, amused.

"No, but I should," she said, sounding breathless.

He let her do a few more swings before insisting it was his turn. She sighed, slowed down, then hopped off. Jay caught the swing. Her eyes locked on his stake that was holstered at his side under his shirt. He had to adjust it so he could sit.

"Are you expecting dangers in the daytime?" she asked with a raised brow.

"No. But I never know where I'll be when the sun sets."

He ignored her staring and pushed off lightly. He kept his feet on the ground, not at all getting into it like she had.

While gazing at her, he started to hum a song. Celia didn't

recognize it at first. It sounded like a rock song, which wasn't really her forte.

"*Smoooooke, on the water*," he sang suddenly. His voice was really quite pleasant. "*Fire in the sky. Smoooke on the water.*"

"Dun dun da. Dun dun dun da dun. Dun dun da, dun dun," Celia added, singing the beat while flexing her fingers on an air guitar. Jay was impressed.

"*When it all was ooov-ah. We had to find another plaaaace. But swiss timeeee was running out. It seemed we would lose the race.*"

"*Smoooooke on the water*," they sang in unison. "*A fire in the sky.*"

"Well," he said through his smile. "I didn't think you'd know that."

She shrugged indifferently. "Guitar Hero."

That, he did not find amusing. In fact, he stopped swinging so abruptly, his feet dragged in the sand, creating little ditches. She chuckled at the horrified expression on his face.

"Come on," she said. "Let's do a spider."

"A what?"

She walked up to him, gathering her dress in her hand. His expression was still puzzled but he looked intrigued as well, now that she was so close. It took some balancing but she was able to straddle his lap on the seat, with her legs on either side of him. It was one of those hard bar seats, not the kind that curved to accommodate your hips, allowing more room.

Celia kicked her legs to make the swing go. It didn't work until Jay moved his legs. Something hard pressed into her knee. She felt around to see what it was.

Just as her fingers closed around the barrel of the gun, Jay's hand grabbed her wrist.

Her eyes widened in surprise. "Is that a *gun*?"

"Yeah."

Her mouth hung open. She was about to ask a really stupid question but she already knew why he was carrying a gun. She'd never been this close to one before. Her uncle had a few hunting rifles his father had handed down to him. Those were always stored away in the basement, the shells locked up in a cabinet in the living room.

Jay gave her a crooked grin to relax her.

Besides the garbage smell, it was exciting being that close to him. Hearing his breath escaping his nose; seeing the gold traces in his light brown hair; looking into those green eyes up close and feeling the muscles of his chest and thighs against her.

This is bad, she chastised. *So fucking bad.*

Yet, so good.

"You have family here?" Jay asked. His voice was low and soft.

"Just my aunt and uncle." She waited for the normal lump to form in her throat at the mention of her family but it was a no-show. She hadn't felt the need to compose herself or go off on her own in a while now. She was okay talking about her lack of family, but it had taken her a long time to get to this point.

"My mom died when I was younger. Breast cancer."

For whatever reason, Jay's eyes drifted to her breasts. Well, they *were* in his face, especially with her posting up and down in his lap. He was stealthy though, and his gaze went back to hers before she had a chance to really notice.

"I'm an only child and I don't know my father. My aunt doesn't talk about anyone else, if there are any."

"But you have your friends," he commented.

"And boyfriend," she added with a warning tone that did not befit what she was doing at the moment.

"Where is that boyfriend?" Jay asked lightly. Her hands were above his on the chains. He used his left thumb to make little circles on her right hand.

"Working," she said. She looked at his mouth as she spoke, hoping he couldn't tell she was lying. His lips were fuller than Victor's. They had a light tint of pink with just the right amount of moisture. She realized she was inching forward and started slightly. She hoped he hadn't noticed.

"Where does he work?"

"Starbucks," was the first thing to pop in her head.

"Starbucks?" he repeated dubiously.

"Yeah," she said bitingly, her eyes returning to his. "They treat him right *and* he gets benefits."

Jay's hearty laugh vibrated through her thighs and crotch. "You are something else," he said.

She frowned. "What's that supposed to mean?"

He shook his head in silent mirth. "Nothing."

They were quiet a moment, the only sounds from nearby birds and the creak of the swing. Jay was still caressing her hand and peering up at her.

"You're very beautiful, Celia."

She felt her cheeks flame. "Thank you."

He touched a lock of her hair, twirled it around his finger and pulled until it was straight. He released and the strands bounced back. There was a small smile playing at his lips. He looked like a child discovering a new invention that gave him unexpected pleasure. Could she have actually elicited such a reaction?

His gaze came to hers. "Would you hit me if I kissed you right now?"

Her head jerked back in surprise. "Yes."

Jay laughed. "I don't believe you."

"Don't test me."

He leaned his head to the side; the pointy ends of his hair caressed her arm. "Then it would be like I stole it. I think I like that."

Celia leaned back in his lap like she actually wanted to put distance between. Like she wasn't smiling on the inside while imagining his lips on hers. "Don't even think about it."

He turned away with an airy shrug. "You can't tell me what to think."

He was quiet for a while, staring off in the distance as if in a trance. Every once in a while, he'd chuckle to himself or shake his head amusedly. She scowled and slapped his shoulder.

"Stop it!"

Jay laughed. He grabbed her hand to stop her from pelting him. She tried to yank her arm free and almost fell backward in mid-swing. His warm hand clutched her back in time and pulled her into him. They were chest-to-chest, panting into each other's faces.

The swing continued its pendulum motion as they stared into the other's eyes. Celia chewed her bottom lip. That same electric current she experienced from Victor's magic cursed through her from his palm on her back. She found irresistible urges to run her hands through his hair, over his chest, into his jeans threatening to overtake her.

Suddenly, she felt something on her thigh. It took her a second to realize what the hard, thick object was. The bedroom eyes he was giving her were a major tip-off as well. Celia nearly toppled over scrambling from his lap.

"You're disgusting!" she shouted at him. "You—I—ooooo!" She couldn't even form sentences she was so aghast.

He shrugged insouciantly. "What you expect when you're molesting me in a swing?"

"Ugh," she groaned and smoothed down her dress.

It was almost four when they left the park. They continued to amble. She showed him the duck boats in the Public Gardens and Frog Pond. A family of ducks made their way to the small, makeshift pond in the Boston Commons. They very much resembled the bronze duck family near the entrance of the Public Gardens. Very recently, one of the ducklings was stolen by a heartless idiot. Luckily, it was returned shortly afterward.

The family dropped into the pond. A tiny tot crouched on the edge, leaning over the water, trying to touch a duckling. The little bird scuttled closer to its mother.

By the time they made it back to South Station and the diner, the sun was setting, tinting the sky pink and lilac. Celia's feet were aching. Flats were meant to be cute, not to be used to traverse the entire metro Boston area. She needed to get home and shower. She smelled like Jay, so like garbage that had baked in the sun. She figured she could fool Victor's sharp nose with her new cocoa butter shower scrub.

"Well," Celia said as they came to a stop in front of the diner. "I should be getting home."

"Boyfriend?" he asked with a raised brow. He seemed both amused and challenging.

"Maybe." She looked to the street for a cab. A yellow one turned sharply around a corner and headed to her like she were a beacon. Celia raised her hand anyways and the cab pulled up.

When Jay leaned forward, his breath tickled her shoulder. She took a step back, her heart pumping faster. He only smiled and opened the door for her. "I'll see you tomorrow then?"

She cleared her throat to regain her composure then told him her address. "You're gonna remember that?" she asked.

He tapped a finger to his temple, indicating he'd remember. She didn't have to know he'd been staking out her place for a few days. She smiled a little, and then sat in the seat. She glanced back at him through the rear window as the cab creaked down the street. Jay waved.

* * *

Victor knew something was amiss the minute he showed up at eight. The burning candles filled the apartment with curls of raspberries and currant. Under that, he could smell her shower scrub and what must've been her dinner of chicken and veggies.

Celia was in the living room, watching TV. He was his usual soundless self so she jumped when he walked into the edges of her vision.

"You really need to start wearing a bell," Celia cried, breathless. He sat next to her and kissed her lips. When he tried to make it more meaningful, he could tell she was holding back. There was another smell on her skin but he couldn't quite distinguish it through the other scents bombarding his nose. Unfortunately, he was above straight-out sniffing her neck.

"Where were you yesterday?" he asked in a thin voice. He was fighting to control his temper. Celia hadn't called or sent a message, like she usually did when she wasn't going to be around. His immediate thought was that she was avoiding him after that hunter was found.

"Trixie and I went out."

Her cheeks were pinking just slightly. She was feeling nervous. "Went where?" Victor pressed, studying her.

"A few clubs in Faneuil Hall."

He could tell something was wrong, something off about her. "Did you two have fun?" It was a simple question but his tone was rigid.

"Mm, hmm," she said with a nod. She faced the television again, hoping he'd let it drop.

He paused. She had been freaked about the dead hunters. He feared she was afraid of him. He had had no choice with the hunter. Did he really have to explain that?

"I just wanted to stop by and see you. I have to go to Ramsey's."

Victor nuzzled her neck with his nose. She shivered, but because his face was cold, like he'd been outside in a blizzard. His hand inched over her stomach, up to her breast. His thumb rubbed across her nipple in tiny circles. At the same time, he nibbled her ear how she liked but she still wasn't responding.

He turned her face to his and pushed his tongue through her lips. His frustration was mounting. She was hiding something from him and now she wouldn't even kiss him back properly. A tingly feeling started behind his eyes, signifying that he was close to ensnaring her with his magic. Except he knew she'd hate him and he'd hate himself. Plus, Celia seemed to have some unnatural power to get herself out of his grip. He'd never seen a human with the ability to withstand a vampire's preternatural mind-control. He'd have to work overtime to keep it up and that would take away from any pleasure.

"Victor, I'm not really in the mood," she murmured, a statement you would think was unnecessary.

He tensed, then leaned away. "What the hell's the matter with you?" he demanded, his expression wounded.

She scowled at his tone. "I don't feel like having sex with you. Why's that so fucking wrong?"

He shook his head. "Why are you behaving so strangely?"

She stared at him. Even in the dim room, she noticed how dark his eyes were, how pale his skin was. She'd have to tread lightly if she didn't want a sofa-shaped hole in her living room wall.

"Look," she said after a pause. "Rain check, okay?"

"Whatever," he grumbled as he stood up. "I'll see you tomorrow."

"After work," she said feebly. "I'm going to visit my aunt tomorrow."

Her voice was even and her heartbeat regular. Even so, it didn't seem like truth to him. In response, he wasn't breathing and his eyes were harsh as he struggled to keep his fangs in check. Beyond that, he was trembling. He was hungry and getting angry wasn't helping one bit.

He didn't say anything, just disappeared. Teleporting always took him off kilter for a few seconds. When he fed, it made the trip easier. So when he appeared in Ramsey's front hall, he stumbled. He caught himself on a side table against the wall and held his head in his hand.

"Victor? Is that you?"

He didn't really have to ask; he knew his scent. Ramsey appeared around the corner. Victor straightened up, still dizzy, and inclined his head to him. Ramsey gave an abrupt nod then walked back the way he came, Victor trailing behind. The first thing he noticed was the smell of blood.

Bryce and three other vampires sat in the living room. Annie, a model-thin vamp with a curtain of blonde hair that flowed past her hips, was holding a red-stained towel to her shoulder. She also had large cuts across her arms and rips in her jeans. Dried blood painted her forehead, cheeks, and hair. She growled softly from the pain.

Bryce stood by the window, staring out into the dark night. Elizabeth, who was curvier than Annie with thick, dark brown hair that stopped at her shoulders and milk chocolate skin, and Josiah, a small Dominican guy with a clean-shaven head and tattoos on his neck, were on either side of Annie. Elizabeth held her hand comfortingly in her lap. Annie's blood was sliding down her arm, staining Elizabeth's sheer brown one-shoulder blouse with its light purple and gold design.

They were all tense and preoccupied and, therefore, weren't keeping up their human facades. In fact, Bryce looked like a marble statue erected in front of the window to ward off vandals. He needed to stand still though, to focus on other things besides the tantalizing allure of blood. His bloodlust trigger was extremely sensitive.

Victor took in all of this in a few milliseconds. He looked to Ramsey for explanation. "Annie was just attacked," he said, stating the obvious. Victor would never say anything so flippant, though. "They knew where she slept."

That brought Victor up short. Vampires guarded their hidey-holes with their lives—or else; hence the need for their magic. He looked to Annie. She was pissed the fuck off. The cuts on her arms were already healing, looking more like ugly red bumps. She pulled the towel from her shoulder. Bryce groaned from his post. You could see her collarbone through the gaping hole. Splinters were visible from whatever crude object her attackers had used as a stake.

"Let me," Elizabeth said. She ran from the room and was back with tweezers and some other medical objects. She carefully removed five splinters and placed them on the coffee table.

"It was a vampire," Annie griped while Elizabeth worked. "A damn vampire tried to kill me."

Ramsey's hands clenched at his sides, as they did the first time she'd told the story.

"How did they know where you slept?" Elizabeth asked, awed. She had placed gauze on the hole and was now using a tan colored wrap to hold it in place.

"I don't know," Annie said so softly that human ears wouldn't have even heard her. She was still astonished by a vampire working with hunters. Josiah rose up to stand next to Ramsey, his way of seeking guidance.

"How many were there?" Victor asked.

"Three, including him."

"Did you know the vampire?"

She shook her head. "Out-of-towner," Bryce muttered. "I didn't recognize his scent." He was upset that he hadn't been there. He was older than Annie, by a couple decades. His age meant he didn't need to sleep as long. Everyone in the nest knew that and could understand his anguish. Vampires literally died during the day. Newer vamps needed longer to rouse from that sleep, from their deadened state. Over time, they could rise as soon as the sun set below the horizon.

"Bryce," Annie whispered. He was next to her in a flash. He rubbed the base of her neck soothingly, and then pressed his lips to her temple. It was a way to comfort himself as much as her. His eyes focused on the room instead of her, to keep his control. Any other person bleeding like that and Bryce wouldn't have been allowed in the room.

"They came just as I was waking," Annie continued.

Vampires were dazed when waking, as they tried to regain their bearings, to maneuver their extremities. They felt light, like a feather, for as little as five minutes and as long as a half hour. Their vision was fuzzy, their hearing hollow. Humans would definitely have an advantage finding a vampire at that moment. Of course, most would jump at the chance of killing them *before* they woke. The ones out for blood and no fight, that is.

"I knocked one of the humans around but that fucking vampire was harder. He almost got me in the chest but I moved just in time."

"I came back to meet Annie and heard the heartbeats so I rushed in," Bryce chimed. "But they got away."

"Only because I was hurt," Annie replied, her fist tightening on the sofa. "If I hadn't let them overpower me, we could've gotten them."

"Don't be so hard on yourself," Ramsey said. "You fought them off."

"What do we do?" Elizabeth asked.

"We find those pricks and snap their necks," Annie growled. Josiah took Bryce's place at the window.

"They're not going to find the house," he replied. He kept watch anyways.

"The hunters wouldn't," Victor said. "If they have vampires working with them, that's another story."

"Annie, Bryce. I want you to stay here," Ramsey said. They looked at him questioningly. "I can't lose any more." His voice was as smooth and resolute as the rest of him. Being leader of the nest, they had to follow his commands.

They both nodded courteously, even though staying in the house would seriously cramp their style.

"She needs to feed," Bryce commented. Feeding would help with healing.

"Cindy and Mallory are upstairs," Ramsey said, speaking of two of their groupies.

Annie shook her head with a scrunch of her nose. She didn't like Cindy, with her blonde blonde hair, fake breasts, and Botoxed face. Not to mention, she had quite a lot of attitude for someone who tasted like plastic. She was almost chewy even. How can blood be *chewy*?

"I think we'll go out for a bit," Bryce said diplomatically. They stopped off in one of the spare bedrooms on the first floor to allow Annie to change before heading out.

Ramsey was still holding his ground, silently fuming over the attack of his territory. "I haven't dealt with hunters in fifty years," he said. "They drove me out of Macon. They won't drive me away from here."

He looked at Elizabeth, then Josiah with determined eyes. They each nodded their agreement. His eyes landed on Victor.

"I'll help in any way I can," he said immediately.

Ramsey squeezed his shoulder affectionately. "Josiah and I are going to patrol. I've already sent Milo and Clarice into the city."

"I'll come with you," Victor volunteered.

Ramsey smiled at the request, but it didn't reach his eyes. He was too upset to fully show his appreciation. Josiah left the window to bring the sexy, candy apple-red Infiniti sedan around. Ramsey got in next to him, Victor in the back, and Josiah sped off.

Seven

CELIA SPRINKLED THE last layer of cheese over the lasagna before covering the pan with foil and placing it in the oven. She set the timer to twenty minutes, then started the salad. She was already showered and her hair done. Straight, her auburn hair stopped between her shoulder blades.

She moved around the kitchen in her silky kimono robe, humming a Duffy song. The robe was black with pink flowers. It had slits on either side that went to mid-thigh, revealing a silver lining. She had every intention of being fully dressed long before Jay arrived but the buzzer rang before she'd even finished slicing the tomatoes for the salad.

She went to the intercom next to the door and pressed the Talk button. "Yes?"

"It's Jay."

She gawked at the intercom for a second before pressing the Release button. Why was he so damn early? It was only five-thirty. Granted . . . they hadn't set a time . . . but still! She wasn't expecting him until six. Wasn't that more of a reasonable dinner time?

She opened the door and a minute later, he appeared at the top of the stairs. This coquettish look came over his handsome face at the sight of her robe.

"Get your eyes back in your head," Celia replied. She double-checked to make sure it was cinched. "You're early."

He followed her inside. She had pulled down two wine glasses earlier and placed them on the kitchen counter. She went to the fridge, and then rustled in a drawer until she found a corkscrew.

"Do you have beer?" he asked, eying the bottle of pinot grigio. She looked down at the wine in her hands. "I don't really like the stuff," he explained.

She rolled her eyes, then pointed to the fridge. "Knock yourself out," she grumbled before turning back to the tomatoes. Jay pulled a Corona from the bottom shelf and used the bottle opener magnet on the freezer door.

He stood close to Celia as she worked. He swiped a tomato slice before she placed the pile on the lettuce. His aftershave was musky, she noticed. It was really nice actually. To pass the time, he wrote his name on her shoulder with his finger.

"What's it like in Dallas?"

"Hot."

She looked at him. "That's it?"

"Yup." He grinned.

"Let's hope the city of Dallas never asks *you* to be a spokesperson."

Celia cut up half a cucumber and added the slices to the salad, then moved away from his touch.

"I'm going to get dressed," she said.

"I like what you're wearing now."

He trailed behind her. She faltered because it appeared he

was going to enter her bedroom with her. Her heart fluttered into overdrive as she tried to figure out what she would do if he came into her room. The debate was moot as at the last second he veered off and sat on the sofa.

She closed the door behind her. A pair of blue plaid shorts and a white top lay across the foot of her bed.

After dressing, she checked herself in the full-length mirror. As if of their own accord, her eyes drifted to a picture of her and Victor. It was tucked in the upper right corner of the mirror that hung on her closet door. Victor's arms held onto her. Celia's arms were outstretched beyond the picture because she had been holding the camera. It was taken in Celia's living room after Victor had made her dinner for her birthday. He used to love to cook, and still remembered a lot of his old recipes. Since he had traveled so much, there had been all kinds of spices and herbs that made her tongue dance in delight.

A flood of guilt washed over her as she stared at the picture. It was so strong she rushed out the room with the purpose of forcing Jay to leave. She'd drag him by the heels if the need arose.

He glanced up from a book of hers he was perusing. She opened her mouth, trying to avoid giving her brain time to confuse her. Just as some words started to form, the timer went off in the kitchen.

He stared at her and it was too late. She couldn't do it. Her mouth opened and closed a few times but the timer was persistent. She stomped into the kitchen to shut it off with a groan. She slid an oven mitt on her hand and took the pan from the oven. She then leaned over the stove, attempting to steady her breathing.

She was rifling through her conflicting emotions, trying to figure out why she wanted Jay's company so badly. He was different and mysterious. And Victor was complicated. She could never have a future with him. Could you imagine her walking down the street, a seventy-year-old woman with a twenty-seven-year-old on her arm? Oh, the stares and whispers. That is, if they hadn't bored each other to tears in all that time together.

So, was that even a future for them? Did she love Victor? Every once in a while the thought would creep up. Usually when they were lounging together, talking about nothing or watching television or walking along the beach at night. She'd wonder if that contented feeling in the pit of her stomach was love.

"Are we gonna eat that or should I join you in staring at it?"

She looked up to Jay's quizzical expression. She sighed as the power of his eyes took over.

She didn't have a table proper. They used the coffee table to hold their plates and drinks. She played Alicia Keys from her iPod dock on the bookshelf. Jay was on his second beer and Celia sipped her wine.

"Supposed to be a full moon tonight," Jay announced. Celia looked to the window. The gauzy curtains were closed but she could see that the sun was in the beginning stages of setting. The rays were bright orange as they fell onto the sill.

"I guess the werewolves will be happy," Celia commented with a snort.

"There's no such thing as werewolves." His tone was serious. She frowned at him.

"How do you know? Up until last year, I didn't think vampires were real either." She shook her head and took a drink of wine. When she set the glass down and picked up her fork for more lasagna, she noticed that Jay was still staring at her with the strangest expression.

"What?" she asked before taking a bite.

He looked like he was considering something. It was a little unnerving how intense and measuring his gaze could be. A crawly feeling circled the base of her neck, like she was guilty or something.

He shook his head finally, indicating nothing was the matter, and picked up his beer for a long swig. They were quiet for a moment.

"How long have you been with your boyfriend? Victor, was it?" He was playing coy because he definitely remembered his name.

She shrugged. "About nine months."

"How did you meet?"

She stared at him, nonplussed. "Why?"

"Just making conversation. Is it some kinda state secret?" His tone was casual but his gaze was alert.

She eyed him a moment longer, her guard going right up. "Trixie and I were at this bar. I used to smoke then and I couldn't find my lighter. Victor had matches. We talked a little and he asked me out."

He smiled because he was about to be a jerk. "That's sweet," he said cheerfully. "I mean, at a bar. That's the best place to meet that special someone. Did he at least buy you a drink? Some fried cheese, perhaps?"

She glared at him. He chuckled. "Don't get mad. My most meaningful relationships start in bars."

"You're being an ass."

He shrugged. "I do that."

In an effort to steer the conversation, Celia asked, "What about you? Is there some girl out there who can stand your company long enough to call herself your girlfriend?"

"Nah," he replied, swigging the beer again. "I move around too much, remember? Out at all hours of the night, always bruised or bloody." He shook his head. "I'm not what they call 'boyfriend material.'"

"Hmm," she said. She was quiet, unaware of the holes she was spearing in the remainder of her pasta with her fork. "So, you probably have *friends* in every city, huh?" The way she said "friends," it was obvious she didn't mean Scrabble buddies.

Her eyes were on her plate so she didn't see his amused grin. "Is there a problem with that?"

Sudden anger swelled in her chest, making her cheeks warm. She jerked her head to him. If they could change color, her eyes would've been as black as Victor's got when he was incensed.

"Yeah, if you think I'm gonna be your Boston booty call."

He frowned, tilting his head to the side quizzically. "What makes you think I don't already have friends in Boston?"

She pursed her lips furiously, then slammed her fork on her plate. She shot up so quickly that the napkin on her lap dropped to the floor.

"Get out."

He laughed at her reaction. "Celia."

"Out!"

She grasped his arm and tugged. Wow, those muscles were nice. She was surprised she'd made him budge. Being around Victor so much made a gal feel puny. Her pulling made him lean to the side but she couldn't quite get him to his feet.

"I'm serious," she said, sliding in her slippers from the effort.

"Celia," he said, standing. He was still holding his beer bottle and he put his napkin on the table. "I was joking—"

"I don't care," she said determinedly. "I want you to leave."

She was pushing him now, toward the door. It took all her strength and she grunted a little as she threw her weight into his back. He was still protesting when they made it to the door. She opened it and shoved him over the threshold.

Jay turned, stunned. "Celia, come on. Why are you making a big fuckin' deal? Don't you have a boyfriend—?"

Celia slammed the door in his face and turned all the locks. She then stomped to her room. She yanked off her clothes and pulled on black jeans and a t-shirt with thin, horizontal black and blue stripes. The jeans were a little tight. She had to jump up and down to get them over her hips. That activity meant she had to adjust her panties, which only served to make her more livid as she shoved her hand into the back of her jeans. She brushed on a little makeup more out of habit because she always wore makeup to work.

She was still fuming as she hurried out of the apartment at seven-thirty, silently daring Jay to still be around. She swore she would kick him if she saw him. Right in the nuts.

At this rate, she was going to be early for work. She didn't care. She just needed to move. After stalking down the concrete stairs of the building, Celia stomped the two blocks to her car. Inside, she slammed the door shut. She gave an indignant huff and sped out of the spot.

She was normally a patient driver, especially by Boston standards. Tonight, she weaved in between cars, tailgated behind slow drivers, and laid on the horn whenever fuckers didn't take their foot off the gas at the same second the light switched to green. Basically, she was behaving like your typical Boston driver.

She found a parking spot in the lot quickly. Rick was at the door. He looked at her questioningly as she approached.

"You okay, Celia?"

"No," she said coldly.

"Man troubles?"

She narrowed her eyes to slits, warning him not to start. He lifted his hands in surrender, his back against the open door. She dumped her purse in Bobby's office and sat on his leather couch. It was comfy and formed to her shape and she felt her tense body relax after fifteen minutes.

Bobby strolled in with Carson at eight forty-five. He frowned at Celia as he headed to his desk.

"I didn't know you were here," he said. "There's salad and chicken in the kitchen."

"Thanks," she muttered. She rested her head on the back of

the sofa. Her mind was still on Jay. Did he really have "friends?" Of course he did, she thought. He was sexy and cute and had this . . . *air* about him that made you seek his company. Who wouldn't want him?

Me, you dumb bitch, she scolded herself.

Her eyes drifted to the bulletin board next to the cube-shaped lockers, seeking a distraction. Posted prominently over the call for auditions and roommates, a homemade flyer displayed five male faces.

The back of her neck got all prickly when she recognized two of them; the blonde and red head from that night in the kitchen. "Drug dealers" was just their guise for scoping out vampires amongst the breeding ground of horny, drunk humans.

Celia stared into the brown eyes glaring from the blonde one's mug shot. He was dead, found in a most undignified way. She wondered what the cops thought. A man turned up, a stake through the heart, drained of blood. It was pretty damn scary.

"Bobby, are those cops still around?" Carson asked, as if somehow reading her mind.

"No," Bobby answered tightly.

"Damn, I wanted to get some details. I've seen that guy here before, you know. About a month ago. Rick threw him out. You think that was some kind of turf war? Like, maybe, they got upset that those other guys were trying to sell here? Wouldn't that be something?"

Leave it to Carson to be excited about a scandal.

"I don't want to hear any talk like that," Bobby snapped. "Drugs are not allowed here in any form."

"What if I have a headache?"

Bobby wisely ignored that. Carson could go on for days with only the smallest ammunition. "Just go about your day as normal."

She heard papers rustling on the desk.

"Don't think you'll get paid for being early," Carson said suddenly, a laugh in his voice. She knew he was talking to her but Celia kept her eyes on the poster.

The papers stopped abruptly. "Do you ever shut your goddamn mouth?" Bobby asked.

Carson snickered even though Bobby sounded irate. After a pause, in which Carson was eyeing Celia, he asked rather eagerly, "What's wrong, Celia?" She had a feeling he was going to say something stupid so she didn't respond. "They run out of shoes in Macy's?"

That pulled her attention back and she hurt her neck as she sat up straight. "You take lessons to be an insensitive shithead or does it just come natural?"

She jumped up from the seat and stormed out to the main area before he could say he took lessons at the Y, which he would have. Trixie and the two other dancers were stretching in the middle of the dance floor, much to the excitement of four guys eating boneless hot wings in a nearby booth.

Trixie smiled when she saw Celia. Her hand froze in mid-wave when she quickly noticed her sour mood. She rushed over to the bar where Celia was slamming things and throwing towels around.

Trixie leaned on the bar. "Uh, Seal?" She laced her fingers together and watched her hasty movements. "You're gonna break something."

"Oh, who cares?" Celia cried, throwing her hands in the air. "What does it all fucking matter? Men will always be shits and we just have to suck it up and deal, right?"

Trixie's eyebrows hiked up her forehead. "What happened? Did Victor do something?"

Celia groaned at the mention of his name. Jay's last words finally registered. She did have a boyfriend. What the hell was wrong with her?

Suddenly, all the fight went out of her and she wanted to sink beneath the floor. "No," she whined. "Victor didn't do anything. I'm such an ass!"

"Seal, you're scaring me. What's going on?"

"Oh, I'll tell you later," Celia said with a wave of her hand. She was deflated now. "I can't go into it because I think I might break down."

Trixie's look was skeptical since it appeared she was already starting that aforementioned breakdown. She reached over and squeezed her arm, then went back to stretching.

Celia felt so low. Here she was, getting angry with some jerk when her boyfriend hadn't done anything to warrant such transgressions. Who cares how many fuck buddies Jay had? It was none of her damn business.

Suddenly, she wanted nothing more than to see Victor, to feel his arms around her, his lips on hers. She'd rejected him the last time she saw him. She could only imagine what he had thought of her. She pulled out her cell phone but he didn't answer.

"Hey, baby, it's me," she said softly. "I just wanted to see if you were coming by Cage's tonight. I'll buy you a drink," she added with a light laugh. She then bit her lip, trying to think of something more to say. When nothing came to her, she hung up.

"I'm such an ass," she muttered again.

* * *

Victor and Josiah picked their way through the empty streets of Downtown Crossing. The only signs of life were the cat-sized rats rummaging through the dumpsters, and the one or two homeless sleeping in the tight corners of stores shut up for the night.

This was their second night on the lookout for the hunters. They passed the Macy's and rounded the corner at a 7-11 store. There were a few people at the counter, paying for their late-night munchies.

As they neared a garage coming up on their right, a sound made Victor's ears perk. He listened for footsteps or heartbeats but none followed. No, the sound he had heard was from someone taking a drag of a cigarette. They blew the smoke out, then there was utter silence. Not even subsequent breaths.

He looked to Josiah, who nodded, acknowledging he'd heard the same thing. Victor used silent hand gestures to tell Josiah to wait on that side of the garage opening. He jumped in the air, high enough so his feet wouldn't be seen, and landed on the other side.

Victor hugged the wall until he came to the corner. The gray garage was bare. The arms of the gates were down on both sides and the attendant's box was dark. Even so, he could smell the cigarette.

Victor looked at Josiah to do more military hand signals when he froze. The vampire was almost a blur, even to Victor's eyes, as he ran up behind Josiah. He had a crew cut and was wearing all black, that he could see. The most essential part was the wooden stake in his hand, raised menacingly in the air.

"Josiah!" Victor called. He turned just in time for the stake to sink into his shoulder instead of the middle of his back where it surely would've found his heart, easy. Josiah hissed and sputtered and dropped to his knees.

Victor rammed into the vampire. The vampire stumbled, lost his balance, and rolled ass over tit on the pavement. Josiah was still on the ground, clutching his shoulder in immense pain. He should've recovered already. Or at the very least had removed the stake from his shoulder. Victor didn't understand and stooped down to help.

He caught a whiff of that cigarette a millisecond before a fist slammed down on his upper back, right on the scapula. There was an audible crack. The second vampire, this one with the same crew cut as the first but much broader shoulders and legs, kicked Victor and he flew to his side.

The vampire jumped and, anticipating where he was going to land, Victor rolled out of the way. The vampire was quick and stomped his chest before he could fully get away. More cracks, this time from ribs.

The first one had recovered in the two minutes all of this was happening and joined in on the assault of Victor's chest and sides. He was already too weak to teleport from not feeding the past couple of days. All he could do was cover his face with his arms.

Getting the shit kicked out of you by vampires as a human meant death for sure. As a vampire himself, Victor had more of a chance. However, these two were fast and strong and he was having a hard time regrouping under the constant barrage.

The precise moment came when both attackers swung their feet back at the same time. Victor rolled to his left and barreled into the first vampire, snapping the ankle of the leg on which he was balancing.

Victor pushed off the ground so that he was on his feet in a crouch. He snarled nastily and exposed his fangs. The first vampire scrambled up and bounced a little on his good foot. The second one's nose flared like a bull. He ran his tongue over his own fangs, hungry for more.

Now that he had a moment, Victor saw that they both had similar features—the same eyes and brow bone and the same shaped head. They were related was his best guess. And both sets of eyes that were glaring so sinisterly were crimson red. Like, freaky red. Even the pupils were red.

He'd never seen that before. They were both swaying slightly, like leaves in a soft wind. Yeah, there was something more than a little off about these two.

For the first time, Victor noticed that Josiah had fallen silent.

"What do you want?" he demanded, his voice barely more than a growl.

The second one responded in a language Victor did not know. It sounded Russian or the like.

"If you're hunting here, you've already taken a misstep. You have to speak with Ramsey first. This is his territory."

Victor never lessened his defensive stance even though he was aching all over. His ribs were a mess and something was punctured because it felt like his belly was filling up with each passing second. He could smell his own blood; it was streaming down both sides of his face, pooling at his collarbone. One or both of them had gotten in a couple kicks to his head.

The two vampires were conversing. Victor's eyes darted between them. They were arguing it appeared. The first one with the hurt ankle pointed down the street, like he wanted to leave. The second one shook his head vigorously.

It was *so* frustrating not knowing what someone was saying, whether it was trying to get the hell out of dodge or seeing who would get to kick his head around first after ripping it from his shoulders.

Victor waited. When the second one took a step toward him, his snarl was like an animal's. The first one said something, his tone pleading. Maybe Victor had done more damage than he had thought. Not that he cared since he was the one bleeding internally.

Ugh, blood. It was making him dizzy. He wanted it, needed it. He fought the hunger, trying to focus on the matter at hand.

The first one must've worn him down. The second huffed, then jerked his head to the side. They ran at that lightning vampire speed, even the limpy one.

Victor didn't move for twenty long seconds. His muscles were too tense. When he could no longer hold himself up, he sank to one knee, his fangs retracting. He panted and clutched his side.

There was a groan. He looked over at Josiah, who lay face down with the stake still in his shoulder. He wasn't breathing but, duh. Victor pulled himself up and staggered over. He wasn't able to teleport him, not in this state. Ramsey and Milo had the car. Victor patted his pockets but his phone was missing. He must've left it in Milton.

Squealing brakes and motor oil caught his attention. A car was traveling down Tremont Street, about a mile away. Victor concentrated. Based on the labored breathing and the sportscast on the radio, he figured the person to be a man. Victor closed his eyes.

A picture formed in his head of a middle-aged man behind the wheel of a Ford Taurus. He had a serious beer gut and receding hairline. A collection of multi-colored air fresheners shaped like trees was clustered around his rear-view mirror, which had to be creating an unnecessary blind spot. Empty soda bottles and crumpled fast food bags littered the back seat and floor. Why this man was driving downtown at four in the morning, Victor did not know or care.

He dug deeper, through the internal musings of the latest Sox game. A name floated to the surface.

Fred.

His call was like a sweet breeze on a humid night. Fred's eyes glazed as he let it wash over him. Whoever this voice belonged to claimed him and he couldn't resist—didn't *want* to resist.

Come here.

Victor looked down at Josiah again. He grasped the stake and tugged. There was a gross sucking sound, like a suction cup. Victor was put off by that. Normally, the wound would have already started closing, making it hard to extract the stake.

The blue Taurus turned the corner. When he pulled up, Fred jumped out and rushed to Victor's side. He was so enthralled, he looked like he wanted to reach out and run his hand through his hair or something. It was *really* nice hair.

"Help me with him," Victor said. They heaved Josiah into the backseat and Victor got in after him. He directed Fred to Ramsey's, hoping he was there or at the very least, Elizabeth, who was the resident MD.

The seat was too comfortable. Victor's eyes drooped dangerously. His stomach was tight and his chest hurt, but a soothing wave of unconsciousness was washing over him. If he just drifted away, only for a minute, he would feel better. Vampires didn't sleep in the same fashion as humans. They were able to sink into themselves at will, appearing to be in a coma-like trance.

When he felt the car slowing, he opened his eyes dazedly. They were on the expressway, passing the Fields Corner exit.

Fred was glancing around, confused. His hands clutched the steering wheel, going toward a destination he did not know. Under Victor's spell, he could hear his thoughts. Fred was wondering why he was in Dorchester when he had originally been on his way to Somerville, which was north of Boston, not south like they were heading.

Irma, his wife, was already mad at him for getting back so late and now this. He wouldn't get home until the sun was coming up. Oh, God, what if she started crying? He hated when she cried. It always made him feel like the scum of the earth. No, the scum of the scum of the earth—

Victor tightened his grip on Fred's mind. Fred immediately relaxed, his brain going (pleasantly) blank. Victor forced himself to stay awake though the pain in his body was fighting hard to overcome him. Fred pulled off the expressway and ten minutes later stopped in the circle in front of the white mansion.

Fred kept the car running. He got out, helping to carry Josiah up the stairs to the door. It was unlocked. They went to the first room they came across, which was one of the spare bedrooms next to the sitting room. The bed was neat with a yellow bedspread. It was ruined the second Josiah was placed on it.

"Elizabeth!"

That was a testament to how weary Victor was because he didn't have to yell. She had heard the car when it turned down the street half a mile away. She hung up with her friend, who was on sojourn in the Amazon. He'd need to get to his resting place soon at any rate since it was nearly six-thirty there. She rushed downstairs.

"What happened?" she asked, her brown eyes taking in everything. She stopped at Fred, who stood by the door, staring vacantly at Victor.

"Uh, Victor . . ."

Victor looked up as she trailed off, his brows furrowed deeply.

"Go home," he ordered Fred.

Fred spun on his heel and ambled outside. A moment later, the front door opened then closed. Victor would release his hold when he was certain Fred was out of Milton.

Elizabeth didn't like the looks of Victor. She flitted to the bathroom for towels and rubbing alcohol and bandages. She handed a blue towel to him. He mopped his face weakly. She couldn't tell his internal problems yet so she turned to the more pressing matter of Josiah, who was unconscious. She touched his face for a moment.

"He's alive," she reported. "Barely."

She looked him over.

"Where's he hurt?"

Victor clutched Josiah's side and rolled him onto his stomach. The hole was still there, red and messy.

"Oh!" Elizabeth gasped, covering her nose with her hand. A putrid smell emanated from the wound now, kind of like rotting lettuce.

"I've smelled this before," Victor said gravely. "When Andy was killed."

"Dead Man's Blood," Elizabeth choked out. "It gets like this when it mixes with vampire blood." The odor was like a vise on their noses, even though both had stopped breathing. It was too much. Victor's head spun.

"Go to the storage room in the basement," Elizabeth said as she examined Josiah's wound. "I need ginger root, chamomile, and Epsom salts. Oh, and dandelion to flush the poison—Victor!"

He had collapsed, hitting his head on the bed as he fell to the floor. Elizabeth hurried to him and touched his chest. "Oh, no," she muttered as she registered the broken bones and severed spleen.

She ran to the phone in the living room to call Ramsey. He didn't answer. She called Bryce.

"Yeah?"

"I need you," she said urgently before hanging up in his ear.

She went to the cool, concrete basement. The lower level was mostly empty. An old leather sofa sat against a wall, as well as about a dozen sealed brown boxes. There was a door at the base of the stairs that was closed and locked with three gold deadbolts. She didn't hear his usual pacing. Cillian must've been resting.

The storage room was at the far end, concealed by a black door and a waterfall of red beads. They clinked together as she pushed them aside.

Elizabeth took a white plastic basket from one of the shelves and loaded it up with ingredients and tools. Back in the room, she used a pestle and mortar to crush peculiar herbs that smelled like mint and rust. She poured them into a glass with vinegar and stirred with a wooden tongue depressor.

Josiah's eyes were still closed, adding to the corpse-like effect. His skin was gray under his black tattoos, his lips white as paper. Elizabeth slipped her left arm under his head and lifted. She then tilted the concoction to his mouth. It was an awkward angle. She had to use her left hand to open his mouth to ensure that more of the potion went inside instead of out. She did manage to trickle some on her arm and the bed. The thick mixture tingled at the touch. She quickly wiped it off with the pillowcase.

When the glass was empty, she laid him against the pillow. The front door opened then Bryce and Annie were in the room. Bryce's chest heaved as he panted with his worry. Annie's jaw was clenched, as were her fists. Her skin was as pale and smooth as it usually was; no signs of her earlier trauma remained.

"What's that smell?" Annie asked, removing her baseball hat.

"Dead Man's Blood," Bryce answered. "What happened?"

"I don't know," Elizabeth said, her voice steady though she was anxious. That came from years of practicing emergency medicine, staying calm in the presence of confusion. "Victor's unconscious. Help me take him to that other room."

Bryce scooped Victor into his arms and carried him across the hall. Elizabeth touched his chest again. "The bones are only just starting to heal," she said after a moment. "Ten ribs—four of them broken—and his scapula. Annie, I need that basket in Josiah's room."

She brought it to her. Among the tools, Elizabeth had put in a scalpel, surgical needles and thread. Annie's eyes widened when she saw her extract them.

"He's not healing properly," Elizabeth explained at their tense silence. "I'll have to cut him open and fix his spleen. You should leave," she said to Bryce without malice or judgment. It was only a statement.

Annie rubbed his arm gently. "Go check on Josiah." Bryce paused a moment. He looked from Victor's prone body to Annie's soft yet stern expression. He consented with a brisk nod. Annie closed the door behind him.

Elizabeth ran her hands along Victor's abdomen, searching out the problem. She stopped on his left side, ripping his shirt open to see his skin. Dark red and purple bruises covered his stomach. He looked like an odd Dalmatian. Elizabeth crossed to the desk, picked up the scalpel, and dug a lighter from her jeans. She ran the blade through the flame.

"Why isn't he healing?" Annie asked. She was staring at the spot Elizabeth had cleared. The contusion there was especially ugly.

"I don't know," she admitted. "Maybe he hasn't fed tonight."

She went to the left side of the bed. "Hold him, Annie," she instructed. "In case he moves."

Annie laid her arms along his shoulder and stomach on the opposite side. Elizabeth leaned forward then sliced, leaving a trail of blood that slid to the hunter green sheet beneath him. Victor flinched. Annie held on tighter. Elizabeth parted the skin and muscle, using makeshift retractors made of steel to hold the incision open. They normally didn't last long if Elizabeth had to use them, since vampire bodies heal so quickly, breaking the instrument.

She set to work examining his spleen. With the pooling blood, she could barely see. She began to pack gauze inside the incision. She tossed them to the floor as they became saturated. Waiting until she found the wound first, she sterilized the needle. Blood poured out of the wound but she could still see what she was doing.

Just as she repositioned herself at his side to start mending, a loud crash on the other side of the wall made her stop.

Elizabeth and Annie exchanged glances—Elizabeth's apprehensive, Annie's saying, *fuck*. A short silence followed. The seconds seemed to tick by. They didn't fool themselves into thinking the trouble was over.

Suddenly, the bedroom door flew open, hitting the wall with a whack. Annie had forgotten to lock it.

Bryce growled hungrily, fangs out, his face furiously distorted. When blood—human or otherwise—was in the air, he was no longer himself.

"Annie!" Elizabeth shouted. Annie spun around and lunged at Bryce just as he was building the strength to pounce. He snapped at her. She raised her forearm to shield her face. A fierce tug-of-war ensued. Annie's strength was amazing considering how lithe she was.

Elizabeth worked quickly, sewing the hole in the spleen. There was still blood in the incision and no more gauze and Bryce was growing frantic in his bloodlust. His growls were strangled by desperate whimpers.

Thinking hurriedly, Elizabeth lowered her mouth to the opening she had created and sucked the excess blood. She didn't like the taste of vampire blood. If Bryce had had at it in this state, though, Victor would have been ripped in half.

Annie managed to shove Bryce out the door, receiving more than a few bites and cuts for her troubles. With Bryce out of the room, Elizabeth could slow to human speed with sewing Victor's side.

When she finished, she placed her hand over the suture. The spleen was the same. The skin under her hand was still puckered and red from her sewing.

"What's going on with you?" she whispered.

After cleaning up and covering him with a blanket, she checked on Josiah. He was still unconscious; however, the color was rising to his skin. She rolled him gently to scope out the wound. It was smaller now, the smell abating.

Elizabeth took a towel and doused the corner with rubbing alcohol. She dabbed the hole. There was a hiss from the pillow that sent waves of relief throughout her. She checked for splinters before covering the hole with large bandages.

She returned him to his back and laid the sheet across him. She noticed the thrashing upstairs as she closed his door. Annie obviously found another way to direct Bryce's aggression. Too bad their bedroom was on the *first* floor.

Elizabeth went to the living room. A square armchair was embedded in the wall above the sofa. It teetered uneasily. Only two of the short legs were in the wall. She reached up and pulled it out, then returned it to its spot next to one of the windows.

She then sat to wait for Ramsey. All the adrenaline from earlier died away as soon as she sank into the comfy sofa. She was exhausted now. She closed her eyes and drifted away into a comatose state.

Eight

CELIA CARRIED A tray of white chocolate, macadamia nut cookies she'd baked that morning. The sun was blazing. Luckily, plenty of trees lined the street for shade. A cool breeze kicked up every once in a while to cool things down.

Twenty-five or so people were gathered in the middle of the block. Children chased each other, using a wooden fence as base. Three tables were set out under the shade of trees, laden with potato salads, pasta salads, regular salads and a variety of sodas and juices.

The street was blocked off for the party by blue police blockades. They were already blasting the oldies. Her aunt and uncle lived in Lower Mills, a somewhat lofty section of Dorchester. It was located on the border of Milton and Quincy.

The house was small and cozy, a few blocks from a T stop and a cemetery. At least it was quiet, her uncle always said. Celia thought the close proximity to the graveyard was creepy. When her mom died, she had been fifteen. She lived with her relatives until she was twenty. In high school, she had to pass the cemetery to get to the train. She tried hard not to look as she walked.

Celia spotted her uncle flipping steaks on the grill. He was stationed close to the barricade at the end of the street. Max was in his late forties. His mostly gray hair was cropped close. His silver aviator sunglasses sat on the bridge of his nose. He was wearing khaki shorts and an orange Hawaiian shirt. Her aunt's choice, no doubt. He was more of a solid-colored shirt and slacks kind of guy. No frills, nothing too showy.

She dropped the tray of cookies off at the desserts table, threw on a false smile, then snuck up behind her uncle to give him a hug. She came to his shoulder blades and rested her head on his back for a second. He smelled of smoke and sunscreen.

He rubbed her arm. "Hey there, Celia." He peeked around at her. Her uncle wasn't much for smiles but she knew he was happy to see her.

"Steak?"

"Maybe later."

There was a sudden whoop of laughter. Celia looked around. Her aunt Meg was laughing it up with three of her friends at a plastic picnic table. Celia strolled over, trying hard to seem excited though her mind was on Victor. She hadn't seen him since Wednesday. It was Saturday now.

She slid in the seat next to her aunt. Her face scrunched into a grimace when the skin of her thighs touched the hot plastic.

"Celia, you made it," Meg replied, giving her a half hug. Her aunt had the same curly hair as Celia, only hers was dyed honey blonde and parted into two braids. She was wearing a red- and black-checkered dress over black capri leggings.

She glanced over her niece's shoulder. "No Victor?"

Celia's lips pursed. All she could do was shake her head in response.

"If Meg hadn't insisted that she's seen this Victor with her own two eyes, I'd say he didn't exist."

Celia fought hard to keep her mouth shut. Meg's friend Peggy laughed lightly, as if she were actually joking. Her black hair was shaped in a short bob. She wore a Celtics' jersey and denim shorts. Her lips formed a thin line as she observed Celia.

"Peggy," Meg chided slightly. She smiled at Celia, trying to lighten her words.

"I'm just saying it would be nice to meet this young man. Of course, we never see Celia anymore either." She took a drink of her wine, her dark brown eyes boring into her. "You still work in that bar?"

"It's a restaurant, too," Celia replied tightly.

"They're always enrolling at Bunker Hill, dear. RCC, too. That's closer, right?"

Celia gritted her teeth. Meg swooped in and changed the subject but Celia knew her aunt agreed with Peggy. She would love for her to take classes at one of the community colleges and get a degree.

The three friends continued their gabbing while Celia sat beside them, miserably chomping on cookies and pie and brownies. Ugh, she was going to be sick later.

After growing tired of her aunt and her gossipy friends, Celia wandered off, her mind in a daze. Her aunt and uncle's house was two stories and pale yellow. There was a large porch, fenced-in yard, and plenty of windows for natural light.

On the side of her old house, three trellises arched above the path, supporting vines from heavy grapes and rosebushes that snaked through diamond-shaped openings. She glanced up at the sun peeking through the vines.

She went inside the house through the back door. The kitchen was cool. It was one of those houses with glorious and inexplicable internal air conditioning. All her aunt had to do was open a few select windows and maybe the back door and the house would stay at a comfortable degree for most of the day.

Celia ambled through the hallway on the first floor, being pulled forward by a mysterious force. She stopped in the hallway. Hanging on the walls were framed pictures of Celia; of her aunt and uncle and their two sons, who both lived out of state; of Celia's mother. She liked to take a few minutes with the photographed memories whenever she came by, especially of her mom.

In one of the black-and-white photos, her mom was laughing and squinting from the sun. The dogwood trees in the background were in full bloom. You couldn't see her but a three-year old Celia sat in her lap, getting peanut butter all over her face and dress.

It was odd, and possibly a figment of her imagination, but to Celia, there was a twinkle in her mother's eyes that couldn't be explained away as a reflection.

Celia had to fold her arms around herself to contain the nostalgia that flooded her at the moment. She loved her aunt and uncle, appreciated their hospitality, but she missed her mother. She had seemed to be encased by this cloud of comfort; whenever you were in her presence, any physical ailments lessened. Bad headache? Just stand next to Daphne and you'd forget all about it.

There were no other family members in the photos. Celia didn't wonder the reason for that very often. In fact, she hadn't thought about it until Jay asked on the swing. The world had only encompassed her, Daphne, and Meg (of course Max and her two cousins were included). After Daphne died, Celia had hidden inside of herself for almost two years. It had been hard enough watching her mother deteriorate over the course of eight months. She needed that much time to mend the hole her mother had left behind.

Celia never complained about her modest family tree; they

were all she needed.

"Every day you look more and more like her," her aunt said gently. Meg had been standing in the threshold of the kitchen, watching her. "Daphne would be amazed." Celia smiled softly and followed Meg into the kitchen.

"Aunt Meg? Do I have a grandmother?"

Meg laughed out loud. "What kind of question is that? Of *course* you have a grandmother."

"Where is she?"

Meg's eyes went to the wall somewhere beside Celia. "She lives in Groton."

Celia frowned. "Groton? Where the hell is that?"

Meg looked at her sharply. "Language!"

Celia rolled her eyes. "Is that in Massachusetts?"

"Yes," she said, a bit tightly. She turned toward the kitchen. Celia hurried after her.

"Do you talk to her?"

"Yes—well, sometimes. Usually on holidays. Well, on Christmas. Where is this coming from?" She sounded flustered now, and she wasn't looking at her.

Celia put a hand on her hip as she watched her aunt open cabinets, stare inside as if she'd forgotten what she was looking for, and shut them. Why was she so ruffled? If anyone should be upset it should be Celia. How come Meg never talked about her grandmother?

"I'm thinking of repainting the shed," Meg finally said as she crossed to the pantry. She pulled out a bag of paper plates from the floor. "It's chipping on the door. I was thinking a nice, bright yellow, to match the house. The white's too plain."

She'd never seen her aunt like this. Instead of pressing the issue like she wanted to, Celia said, "I like that."

"How did that date go?" she asked suddenly. "Trixie's?"

Celia glanced sideways. "It didn't work out."

She gave her a pitying look. "Aw, that's too bad. She needs to find dates outside of that place."

Celia groaned. "Auntie, please, not again—"

"I can't be concerned with your safety?" she cried. "You're dealing with drunks and fools and dead bodies. Are you trying to give me a heart attack?"

"Auntie," she moaned, shaking her head. She so didn't want to have this conversation again. Her aunt had been calling her, leaving messages almost every night since that hunter was found. Celia had mostly been ignoring her but that was a little hard to do when she was in the same room as her fretful aunt. She could just *kick* Peggy for reminding her.

"The police are investigating. Everything's the same as before. This was just some random act that just *happened* to occur behind Cage's. That's all."

Her aunt didn't look convinced. To Celia's immense delight, she didn't argue more.

Meg headed back out and Celia followed. She was downing her third cup of Kool-Aid by the drink table when she felt her uncle's hand on her shoulder. "Everything okay?"

She nearly coughed on the drink because he surprised her. "Mm, yeah," she said, wiping her mouth with the back of her hand. She looked up into her own reflection in his glasses and sighed. "I'm a little worried about Victor. I haven't heard from him in a couple days."

"Sounds like he's just being a guy. He'll come around."

She shrugged, not comforted at all. Victor wasn't a regular guy. And he didn't disappear for days on end, not even when they had first started dating, when that type of behavior could be excused as "playing the game."

She cocked her head to the side. "Where's Groton?"

"Western Mass," he answered simply. "That's where Nancy lives."

Celia's brows raised slightly, her heart suddenly pumping in her chest. Was that her grandmother's name?

Max squeezed her shoulder. "Don't worry about Victor. Just make sure you give him a piece of your mind as soon as you see him."

Right. Victor. The breaking news that was the discovery of newfound relatives slipped away.

She chewed her bottom lip as she watched her uncle wander back over to the grill, where he was more at ease. Standing by the table, holding her cup, she felt . . . alone. Everyone around her was having fun, laughing and eating. It was like she was in a different world; her own bubble of wretchedness.

How could people be smiling, the sun shining, butterflies fluttering when she was worried out of her mind?

Ten o'clock the next night, Celia was still a wreck. She called Victor for the fifth time but voicemail picked up straightaway. She called Trixie.

"I think something's happened to Victor."

"Why do you say that?"

Celia sighed. "I haven't seen him in four days. I'm afraid . . ." She shook her head, trying to erase the thought. It was just too stressful to tuck away. "What if Jay did something?"

"He wouldn't do anything." She didn't sound too confident.

"How do you know? He would just be doing his job."

"I thought you said he didn't know about Victor."

Celia shook her head. She had been pacing, crossing the room in ten strides each way. "Nah, I think he knows," she muttered.

"Well, maybe Victor knows about Jay," Trixie tried. "And he's staying away to protect you."

"To protect me?" she cried, bewildered. "I saw him lift a

fucking car with one hand once when my earring rolled under it. I don't think some stupid asswipe from Texas with a stupid name and a stupid, sexy smile would scare him."

Wait, that wasn't right. Celia squeezed her eyes shut in guilt. She had been able to avoid Jay as a customer since it was the weekend and she was behind the bar. She'd seen him on Friday, making sure she was "busy" when he headed her way. When she had looked up a minute later, he disappeared in the crowd. She frowned, confused and a little hurt.

"I don't know, Seal," Trixie said.

Celia took a deep breath. It didn't help. She hung up with Trixie and sank to the floor in the middle of the room. The television was playing softly in the corner, the floor lamp at the dimmest setting.

She closed her eyes and pictured Victor's lovely face. Those gray eyes were as light as burgeoning storm clouds, only, you know, the good kind. Like when the ground had been parched for days and a nice ol' rain would hit the spot.

She breathed deep through her nose. *Victor*, she thought. *Victor? Where are you?*

She sat completely still until she was dizzy, then blew out the breath she'd been holding. She waited to feel his cool fingers on her face or for his unique scent to fill her nose. She could never describe his smell. It was like leather and the ocean, as weird as that sounded.

No touch or scent came. She became highly aware that she was utterly alone in the apartment. She opened her eyes, feeling numb. Had she screwed everything up in so short of time and without even as much as a kiss or moan shared with another person? Was that how karma worked?

Celia pulled herself up, shut off the television and lights, and climbed into bed for another sleepless night.

* * *

Victor drifted in and out of consciousness. He didn't know what day it was or the time. All he knew was pain. Pain from his mending body and pain from his hunger. That cursed through him like electric shocks. In his fingers, his legs, his belly. He was grateful for the unconscious, the blackness allowing him a respite.

This time when he surfaced from the dark undertow, it was for a different reason.

Where are you?

The words were so faint that he almost missed them. Celia's voice was thick with concern. She was calling him, something she'd only done once before. Victor had told her about the process and she figured she'd test it out.

Victor left her alone in the apartment, having given her instructions to wait five minutes. She didn't have to speak aloud but there was nothing wrong with that. Victor went to get her pad thai at her favorite restaurant in Jamaica Plain. He was just pushing the door open to go inside Wonder Spice Café when he heard her voice.

Victor? Is this thing on? Um, can you hear me?

To his surprise, it had worked. By all logical standpoints, they wouldn't have had that psychic connection because they had never shared blood. He knew where she was but the call was always accompanied by a psychic GPS location in his head. That's how vamps were able to track their charges. Victor rushed to her house with the takeout and stared at her, amazed.

"What?" she had asked. She sounded distracted because she was tearing into the brown paper bag.

"I heard you."

She looked up and smiled. "Cool." Then she went back to her food.

She had lost interest and distracted Victor with the next night's dinner plans with her aunt and uncle. He had meant to inquire of Ramsey and Elizabeth about this strange phenomenon. The thought completely left his mind when she climbed on top of him later and traced his lips with the tip of her tongue. The lingering scent of peanuts greeted his nose.

Celia filled his mind now. He couldn't move from the bed. The electric jolts kept his muscles locked. He wanted so badly to go to her. He would've run if he could. She must've been frantic to resort to calling him. How long had he been out of it like this?

He groaned in frustration. A hand grazed his forehead, then his cheek and for a second he thought he had teleported and he was there with Celia. He even smelled her.

"Victor? Is something wrong?"

The relief and happiness that had just begun to swell and match the agonizing throbbing vanished. It was Elizabeth, checking her patient. He didn't bother opening his eyes, hoping she'd go away. He wanted to be alone in this misery.

* * *

The club let out a little late. People didn't mill outside until around two-thirty. The club was small and almost hidden on the little street downtown. No one lingered. There had been a launch for some new foundation that helped youth at risk or something of that nature. All that mattered to Jay was the vampire mixing in with the crowd.

Said vampire: Newborn Trent.

His shoulder-length brown hair was tucked behind his ears. He had a thin face and acne marks across his jaw that would stay with him for eternity, wearing nice pants and a fashionable polo.

Trent's white glow was distinct since he was a newbie. Jay had first seen him at a table near the bar. He had been discreetly leaning to the side, sniffing a girl's hair.

Fuckin' loser, were the exact words to cross his mind.

The partygoers rounded corners, seeking out their cars or cabs. Trent was talking to a different girl a little ways from the entrance. She had short hair the color of an oil slick and one of those Monroe lip piercings—a silver ball sitting above her top lip like a mole. Jay was a few feet away but not close enough to hear what they were saying. He wasn't too confident with Trent's macking skills.

He felt in his back pocket for the badge. He had only taken one step when two guys approached Trent from behind. Trent jumped when one of them put their hand on his shoulder. Jay immediately recognized them as those hunters from The Pit.

The red-haired hunter smiled unctuously at Trent. He was tall and pale and you could see the budding muscles of his arms and shoulders. The other was short and barreled-chest with hairy arms. He looked to be in his late twenties. They were hounding Trent, who put his hands up as if saying he didn't want trouble.

The girl took an uneasy step backward. The red head's grip tightened on Trent's shoulder and to Jay's astonishment, the vampire crumpled. The other hunter grabbed him before he sank to the ground. They carried him off, ignoring the few bystanders' stunned glances. Jay trailed behind.

The farther they traveled down the street, the quieter the night became. It was a Monday after all, and most people were home, asleep. The hunters approached a plain, black van, which, come on. How typical. It was parked in front of a vacant building. An orange parking ticket rustled in the wind from its spot under the wiper.

"Crap!" the short hunter exclaimed when he caught sight of the ticket. "Snipe's gonna kill us."

"You, Harold." The red head's voice was a grunt under the weight of the vampire. "Snipe's gonna kill *you*."

"You're with me, aren't ya?"

"Dude, just get the door open."

"Need a hand?"

They were such *amateurs*! How did they not know Jay was

following them? He'd startled them so badly that Harold's hold on the newbie slipped and he drooped to the ground. The red head was only holding his upper arm now.

They both spun around at Jay's voice. Harold fumbled with pulling a gun from his waistband. He cocked it and pointed the barrel at Jay's head. Jay raised his hands to show he wasn't a threat. He even smiled.

"I just gotta know one thing," Jay drawled. "How the hell did y'all manage to incapacitate a vamp?"

That brought both men up short. They looked at each other with eyes so wide they could've popped out and bounced off the other's forehead.

"How did you—who are you?" the red head stammered. He was glaring suspiciously at Jay now.

Jay kept it cool. "Like you, I'm ridding the streets of scum."

"Let's just get outta here, Colin," Harold said hastily. Jay didn't like how his hand was shaking so much.

The vampire's glow began to pulse ever so slightly. Jay's eyes shifted from the gun to their catch. Yup, the newbie was stirring. You didn't want to be around a newborn vampire when he was disoriented. He'd take out his own kind if they were close enough. Colin was still holding his arm.

"Uh, guys," Jay tried to warn.

"Shut up!" Harold shouted at him, jabbing the gun in the air. "I don't know who you are, mister, but you better be on your way. Come *on*, Colin. Let's just take this trash and get out of here."

"Well, if you'd help me, I could get him in the freaking van—ahhhh!"

His sentence was abruptly cut off as Trent came back to life, so to speak. He jerked his arm away so quickly that Colin didn't even have a chance to release him. Colin's arm twisted. A popping sound followed. He fell against the van.

"Crap!" Harold shouted. The vampire advanced on Colin.

Harold fired the gun three times into the vampire's back. He wailed and reached behind him as if he were trying to touch the wounds. White smoke floated around his back. Silver bullets, Jay assessed.

Jay pulled out his holstered stake. Harold hit Trent on the back of his head with the butt of the gun. The vampire swung and Harold caught his fist in the face. He fell hard to the ground, his jaw bouncing off the sidewalk.

Trent turned back to Colin, who had been fumbling with the van's sliding door, trying to find refuge inside. Like the vamp couldn't tear it off its track with his fucking pinkie. When you're panicked, you didn't think about those things.

Trent's lips pulled back over his teeth, revealing his sharp baby fangs. He reached out for a handful of Colin's red hair and jerked his head at an angle. Colin yelped, as the skin around his eyes grew taut. Just as he thought this was it, the vampire froze, his fingers still tangled in his hair. Jay grunted as he pushed harder on the stake he'd rammed between his scapulas.

Trent's head turned slowly, like a freaky ventriloquist's doll. His hazel eyes were both shocked and scared. He didn't know what was happening to him. He had just gotten used to being strong and fast and now his skin was charring, his body burning hot.

The white glow radiating from his skin vanished. He crumbled between them.

The stake hit the sidewalk with a loud clatter. The only sounds now were Colin's whimpering and Jay's haggard breathing at the effort to get the stake though his vampire skin.

Jay bent over to retrieve the weapon, then surveyed the other two. Harold sat up on the concrete. His fingers grazed the nasty, red scrape running the length of the side of his face. He winced like it was stinging really bad. Colin was holding his right shoulder, his face twisted in pain.

"Here," Jay said, placing a hand on his arm.

"What—"

"Try to relax."

Colin, of course, tensed. Jay held his injured arm at his side with his elbow bent at a ninety-degree angle. He slowly moved his arm to his stomach and back the other way. Colin turned his head from Jay, biting his lip to muffle his scream. It took three turns for the shoulder to pop back into the joint. Colin groaned as he fell against the van. It was more of a dull ache now instead of piercing jolts.

"Dude, that hurts."

"Better get some ice on that," Jay advised. "You'll probably wanna lay off any strenuous hand movements." He held his fingers in an "O" while jerking his wrist back and forth a few times to demonstrate. "Unless you're a lefty, of course," he added with a chuckle. Colin wasn't hurting enough to keep from chuckling along with him.

Harold came up to the van, keys in hand. "Snipe's gonna be mad," he griped. He shuffled his foot in the ash.

"Snipe sounds like a dick," Jay commented. Harold looked scandalized. Jay ignored him and started back toward the club. He wanted a shower and his pillow.

"Wait!"

Jay paused. He turned slowly on the ball of his heels and faced them. Harold was still upset. Colin looked thoughtful through his pain. "Why don't you come with us?" he said, grimacing. Jay cocked an eyebrow. "I think Snipe would like to meet you."

He considered it for a moment. With a shrug, he said, "What the hell."

They climbed in the van. The last row had been removed. A few dirty blankets and black trash bags were strewn across the floor in its space. Jay made himself comfortable on the hard second row, the leather seat stained and torn. Harold pulled off.

Harold was listening to classical music from the radio. After a minute, Jay leaned forward through the opening between the two front seats and turned the dial.

"Hey!" Harold shouted. Jay found a station playing Iron Butterfly then settled back in his seat, satisfied. Harold shot Colin an irritated look.

"So," Jay said. "How did y'all take him down?"

"This concoction of Special K and Dead Man's Blood," Colin answered. "I kept the syringe in my sleeve." He couldn't lift his arm to show him since it was concealed in his right sleeve. "The blood poisons them and the Special K works as a tranq."

"Interesting," Jay said with an impressed nod.

"And we use silver bullets to slow them down."

"How did you know that he was a vampire?" Harold asked in a strange voice. He was fidgeting a lot, like he was fiending for caffeine. His head darted from side to side as if he were expecting someone to jump in front of the van at any moment.

"How did you?" Jay countered in order to avoid answering. Really, how *do* you explain seeing something glow?

"We've seen him a few times," Colin said. "He's newly turned. This was the first time we ever saw him alone."

"That's why Snipe's gonna kill us," Harold piped. "We were just supposed to knock him out so we could put a tracker on him. Then we could find the nest and get rid of those bloodsuckers for good." He shuddered. "I hate having them here, wandering the streets like a bunch of animals."

Colin turned as best as he could to look Jay in the face. "Where are you from?"

"Dallas."

"See a lot of vampires over there?"

"Sure."

"Do you work alone?"

"Yup. I mean, I come across the occasional hunter but I mostly stick to myself."

Colin nodded. His eyes were full of reverence. Jay glanced out the window. They were in South Boston, although he didn't know that. They had been riding for twenty-five minutes when Harold pulled into the driveway of a nondescript home. The yard was neat but littered with bouncy balls and baby dolls. A silver chain-linked fence surrounded the house, which was a large, white rectangle, with no porch, just stairs that led to the door.

The front door opened right into the carpeted living room. The olive-skinned guy was sitting in his Barcalounger. He was staring intently at a news report on the television. Jay heard the reporter say there were no updates on the downtown murder. It still appeared to be a random and senseless act.

Snipe looked up when the door moved.

When he saw Harold and Colin, he was on his feet instantly. He had a slight but noticeable limp from his stiff left leg. His eyes quickly assessed them for damage but they seemed fine, meaning no dangling limbs or sucking chest wounds. He halted when Jay entered.

"This isn't the bloodsucker," he said simply. His voice was smooth, deep. He could definitely lull someone to sleep with that soulful tenor.

"He killed him," Harold said, quick to place the blame. He even pointed.

Snipe frowned at Jay, like he was debating something in his head. "I've seen you before," Snipe finally said. "Are you hunting here?"

"Nope," Jay replied. "Just tracked a fangy son-of-a-bitch here. That's all taken care of now."

"Sweet," Colin said, thinking it was under his breath. Harold frowned at Colin in displeasure.

"I'm Snipe," he said, extending his hand to him.

"Jay," he replied, shaking it.

Snipe motioned to the sofa. Colin disappeared into the kitchen and Harold went off to clean his face.

Jay let out a sigh as he sat. Harold returned shortly with his cheek shellacked with enough Neosporin to cover his entire head. Jay looked down to hide his grin.

Snipe was unfazed by Harold's silliness. "We've been dealing with these bloodsuckers for a couple of years now."

"I've seen them around," Jay confirmed. "Staked two myself last week. One was in a club downtown."

Harold stiffened. "It wasn't Cage's, was it?"

"Yeah."

Harold quickly looked to Snipe. Snipe's expression had grown cold but it wasn't directed at Jay. "We lost two men at that club," he said grimly.

"They left Booth in a dumpster, drained," Colin chimed in. He strolled out of the kitchen holding an ice pack to his right shoulder. "We can't find Teddy but we're sure he's dead."

Jay shook his head. "Shit. I was the one who found the kid in the dumpster."

Everyone stared at him. Colin and Harold exchanged stunned glances.

"You called the police?" Snipe asked.

"Yeah. I didn't know where to find y'all and I couldn't let him sit there like that."

Snipe grounded his teeth, obviously not happy with the outcome. What could he do? Someone was bound to find Booth and call it in.

"They ran the story on the news last week," Colin added. "The police don't know what to think."

"They said something about gang activity," Harold replied.

"I'm sorry for your loss," Jay said sincerely.

"Thank you," said Snipe.

The hunters were quiet for a moment. Jay's eyes roamed around the room. It looked so homey. Toys were piled in one corner and pictures of Snipe with two little girls hung on the wall. Among the array of photos was an elegant silver frame housing Snipe's wedding picture. His wife was very pretty in her white sheath dress and flowing chestnut curls. It looked like they were standing on the steps of a Catholic church, based on the Gothic arches above the doors behind them.

There were also old-school soccer and swimming trophies on a bookshelf and the entertainment center was overflowing with kiddy movies. Jay looked at the agitated man in his brown leather chair and wondered if his family knew about his late night excursions.

"How do you do this?" Jay asked. "How are you a hunter and still manage to take care of a family?"

Snipe shrugged. "It's usually fine 'cause I work second shift as a dispatcher. But lately, I haven't been getting much sleep. We've had to pick up the slack since we're short-handed at the moment."

There was a scary vein throbbing on his temple. He seemed to be containing the urge to throw something, if only just barely.

"Well, I got time," Jay offered. "I can help if you'd like."

Harold and Colin looked at each other. They turned to Snipe. Colin was eager. He liked how Jay worked. Harold, as usual it seemed, was nervous.

"I'll have to speak with Harold and Colin but I thank you for your generous offer." He looked at the clock on the entertainment center. It was a quarter past four. "Where are you staying, friend?"

"In Quincy. My car's back at the club. Hopefully."

"You're more than welcomed to stay here. I'll get you some bedding," he said before Jay could decline. The old floors creaked under his feet when he went into the hall. He returned shortly with a pillow and light blanket.

"You can have the room," Harold said to Colin, who nodded and shuffled off. Jay was given the sofa, which left Harold with a fold-up bed that Jay hadn't noticed before now. It had a ratty mattress and squealed loudly at the slightest movement. He just hoped Harold didn't move around a lot in his sleep.

With the lights out and Harold already snoring, Jay closed his eyes. He tried to sleep. Unfortunately, his mind was on Celia. The last three nights, he'd waited in his car outside her apartment. He saw her leaving for work each morning but there was no sign of the boyfriend. Celia seemed to be fraying at the edges as a result. He went to Cage's on Friday with all intentions of talking to her. At the last moment though, he had reconsidered.

He was thinking about her cute little smile and the way her brown eyes lit up when she laughed. How her nose reddened just slightly when she was angry. He remembered their "spider" and how warm she felt in his lap. How close she had been, how she smelled of strawberries. He should've stolen that kiss. She probably tasted like strawberries.

His eyelids had slowly drifted closed at the memory of the swing. Now, they sprang open. He looked down. He could've waved and his willy probably would've waved back. He threw his head back with a groan.

Okay, he thought. *Bloody stubs. Pus-filled pimples. Aunt Sophie's neck rolls.*

It wasn't working. As Jay visualized the back of his great-aunt's bulbous neck, he remembered the silver necklace she always wore. It held a heart-shaped pendent that reminded him of Celia's necklace and he was back to where he had started: hard dick in a stranger's home.

"I need to get laid," he said under his breath because that was always a viable option to him.

As if he had heard and agreed, Harold grunted in his sleep.

* * *

The next morning, Jay was roused by the smell of bacon. His eyes opened and he blinked a few times, trying to remember where he was. It wasn't a dumpster, he established.

"He's awake," a tiny voice whispered.

Jay turned his head. Two round faces peered down at him. One of the little girls from the pictures gave him a toothy smile. The other stared at him as if examining some strange life force taking up space in her living room. They both had dark hair like their father. Their eyes were green instead of black.

"Hi!" said the taller one, who must've been about six. The other looked four. "I'm Morgan. This is my sister, Jessa. What's your name?"

Oh Lord, she was *way* too perky for it being so early. Well, it was ten, but that was pretty damn early for a hunter.

"Girls, leave the man alone," came a female voice from somewhere.

There was no way he'd get to sleep longer. Jay sat up on the couch. Harold's bed was back in its spot in the corner of the room. Stuffed toys littered the floor in front of the sofa. There was a woman in the kitchen, her back to him, scrambling eggs in a pan.

Morgan flipped on the television to cartoons, turning the volume up to deafening levels. The mother stalked out of the kitchen, her ponytail switching behind her authoritatively. She picked up the remote from the floor and lowered the volume.

"Aw, Mom!" Morgan cried.

"Hush." "Mom" turned to Jay with a smile. Her face was round, her nose pointed at the end. She had a triangle of beauty marks on her left temple, just above her thin eyebrow.

"I'm sorry about that rude awakening. The boys stepped out for a moment but they should be back any minute. Breakfast is just about ready if you're hungry."

He was starving. He followed behind her into the kitchen. A wooden table had been pulled away from the wall. There were five settings consisting of glass plates the color of cobalt and matching silverware. Jay sat on the side with a single setting. She placed a tall glass of OJ in front of him. He seemed to radiate sunshine from inside out at the sight. She chuckled.

"I'm Lauren, by the way." She watched him throw back the glass. "Snipe says you came by late."

"Yes, ma'am," he replied after swallowing. Then he frowned. "That his real name?"

She chuckled again. "Stanley Snipes."

"Ah."

He took another long gulp of juice. "Snipe always have late night visitors?"

"No."

"I guess he trusts me."

With a grin, she nodded to the knife block on the counter behind her. "I have the best aim."

Jay took that sweet little threat in as she went back to the stove. Lauren was putting the final touches on breakfast when Snipe and his fellow hunters came in the house.

Morgan screamed "Daddy!" from the other room. It was a minute or two before the three men entered the kitchen.

Snipe wrapped an arm around his wife and softly kissed her cheek. It was the first time he didn't seem wound-up, and as soon as he released her, the grim expression returned.

Colin and Harold took their places across from him at the table. Colin was wearing a makeshift sling crafted from what appeared to be a black t-shirt. Harold's scrape was still shiny.

"Was that sling okay?" Lauren asked over her shoulder. She

sounded concerned, yet professional.

Colin glanced down at his arm. "Yeah, it hasn't moved much. The painkillers helped, too."

"I'll see if I can get a real sling from the hospital."

"My cheek's kinda burning, Lauren," Harold replied, holding his hand over the scrape. She reached over and slapped his hand away. Harold turned beet-red from the contact.

"Stop touching it. God, you're worse than the kids!"

Snipe took his seat at the head of the table. "Where'd y'all go?" Jay asked.

The atmosphere in the room shifted perceptibly. Jay frowned. "We, uh, got a report earlier," Colin said somberly. "This cop friend knows what we do. A woman from Beverly was found with punctures on her neck. She was left behind the Stop 'n' Shop in the South Bay Plaza."

"She was exsanguinated," Snipe added.

Jay lowered his head as grief and anger for the unknown woman settled over him. He was wise enough not to feel guilty about her death. Not to think that maybe he could have protected her, that he could have somehow prevented this. He'd been working long enough to know that sometimes you couldn't save people, even ones close to you.

To cut the tension, Lauren served eggs, bacon, and home fries. She took two plates out to the plastic kiddy table she had arranged in the living room. It was close enough for her to keep an eye on Morgan and Jessa, yet far enough away for the adults to speak candidly.

When she returned to the table, the others lowered their heads and closed their eyes. Jay looked around, surprised. Lauren said a short prayer giving thanks for the nourishment and safety of loved ones. They sat in silence for a few minutes as they began to eat.

"So, Jay," Lauren said. "Are you traveling alone?"

"Yes, ma'am. I had some business to take care of," he said vaguely. He still wasn't completely sure how much she knew.

Snipe looked down the table at his wife. "He tracked a vampire up here," he informed her, effectively clearing that up.

"He's going to help us for a little while, until he gets sick of us, I guess," Colin piped with a chuckle.

Jay looked to Snipe. He nodded. "We'd like to take you up on your offer."

"Okay."

After breakfast, Snipe dropped Jay off at his residence so he could shower and rest. They made plans to pick him up at five to do a little shopping and reconnaissance.

Jay's place was pretty much what you'd expect of a basement. Unfinished cement walls and floors. A slight moldy smell that you hoped didn't cling to everything. There was a futon, a small fridge, and an ancient television set on the left side of the room. An efficiency bathroom with a toilet, sink, and shower stall was tucked in the back corner.

The other half of the basement was sectioned off by a pale blue sheet suspended from a clothesline at the ceiling. A bunch of boxes and containers, plus the washer and dryer were behind it. Jay had access to the appliances, as well as the kitchen, though he didn't go upstairs. He had his own private entrance around the back of the house.

Jay showered and changed. Instead of taking a nap like he should have, he headed back out. There was a fifty-fifty chance she was working the day shift. He felt confident.

It had gotten a lot muggier in the hour Jay had been inside. The air was so thick it made it hard to breathe. He tugged at the collar of his gray t-shirt, creating a slight breeze that didn't help one bit. The AC was beautiful inside Cage's and he let out a little sigh.

"Hello."

Trixie stood just beyond the door. She wore light gray slacks and a lavender blouse. Her black hair was pulled up into a loose bun. The little scrape was barely visible and the bump had gone down. Little tendrils framed her face and her makeup was very understated today. It all made her look soft and pretty compared to her va-va-voom, vixeny persona at night.

"Hey," he said giving her a smile that could melt an iceberg. "Is Celia on today?"

"Yup. But maybe I should seat you somewhere else." Her tone was teasing and, at the same time, cautionary. It made him wonder what Celia had been saying about him.

"Do *you* have a free table?" he asked huskily, leaning closer. He was fucking with her, and she knew it.

"I'm not a server," she replied simply.

They stared at each other for a moment; Trixie testing how determined he was going to be, Jay waiting her out.

"Is your seating criteria always this demanding?" he asked.

"Just when my friend's involved."

He looked over her shoulder into the lounge. It was nearly full, business people and such having meetings or late lunches.

"Well, don't worry. I'm just getting a salad."

She gave a snort of laughter. "Something tells me you aren't a salad kind of guy."

She turned and he followed her to a round table near the bar. Trixie disappeared into the kitchen. A minute later, Celia came rushing out.

Her expression was harried, to say the least. Her apron was crooked, her bun frizzy. As she came closer, he could see she wasn't wearing makeup, not that it detracted from her beauty or anything, just an observation.

She was a couple feet away when she finally looked up and halted. He couldn't quite decipher her expression now. Some mixture of surprise, anger, and relief.

He smiled.

Celia looked like she wanted to turn right back around. Instead, she sighed and trudged to the table. Her voice rang with false cheeriness. "Trixie didn't say *you* were here."

"Hey, what can I say?" He shrugged insouciantly. "I'm like an itch. You can't get rid of me."

"More like a rash, you mean."

She tried to hold on to her irritation. Looking at his handsome face and his crooked grin, a reluctant smile broke through. She pulled out her pad and pen.

"What can I get you?"

"Another home-cooked meal, for starters. With your froufrou wine and music, the whole nine."

She rolled her eyes and decided not to respond to that. "How about I get you a Coke while you look over the menu?"

She left before he could say anything. Jay chuckled to himself, amused that she was trying to show attitude when it was obvious she couldn't stay mad at him. A minute later, she placed a glass down. She then put a hand on her hip, giving him a no-nonsense look. Jay decided to drag it out to annoy her.

"Ummmmm, let's see." He looked over the first page of the menu, letting his eyes scan each and every word. "Salmon?" he muttered to himself. "No. Maybe a turkey sandwich? Ummm."

She glared at him, irritated, and snatched the menu. "I'll surprise you," she said, then added a terse, "Jackass."

He watched her as she moved around her different tables. Her attitude had lifted considerably. She was even smiling.

She served Jay chicken parm and spaghetti. It was one of her favorite dishes at the lounge, simple and delicious.

He picked up his fork. "Join me."

"I'm working," she replied matter-of-factly. "You know, what *normal* people do to make money." She paused a moment, thinking. Her tone shifted. "How *do* you get money?"

He shrugged while chewing the chicken. "Random jobs here and there. Sometimes I work cases for the police. It's not Starbucks, but I don't mind." She gave him a weird look until she remembered that she had told him that's where Victor worked. She fixed her face.

"Doesn't sound like it's enough to cover everything."

He shrugged again. "That's when the credit cards come in." She frowned, not understanding. He didn't say more because he figured she was smart and would get it later.

"Are you working tomorrow?" he asked.

"No."

"Good. Then I'll stop by."

She scowled, outraged. "You can't just invite yourself over my house!"

"Why not?"

"I might have errands to run."

"Cool. I like errands."

She huffed. "If you come to my house, I won't answer!" And with that she stomped off to the kitchen. Jay finished up and left some money on the table before leaving. It was two and he needed to get that nap before it was time to meet Snipe.

Nine

THAT NIGHT, CELIA sat in her living room, bored and anxious and still worrying about Victor. This was not like him at all, disappearing for a long stretch of time. She had tried "calling" again at eight, nine, and nine-thirty, to no avail.

At ten-thirty, she changed the channel once again. Then she groaned. She would've gone to Trixie's but she was working a double. The lounge closed at eleven-thirty during the week. She wouldn't get home until close to one. Celia could very well drop dead from boredom by that time.

A thought came to her, creeping its way down her neck, through her spine to her legs. It compelled her to stand and go to her room. It made her search through her work pants, pulling out the pockets. She found five dollars and a flyer for an art show that had just occurred. Patrons were always handing her flyers about different events they hoped she would pass along.

She rifled through her dresser, discovering she was getting low on panties. She'd have to do laundry soon. She finally opened her jewelry box and there it was: the napkin with the phone number. She carried it to the phone with shaky hands, like she was afraid it would disintegrate. She picked up the phone and dialed. He wasn't answering quickly enough. Maybe this wasn't such a good idea. She was just about to hang up when Jay answered.

"Yeah, who's this?" he said gruffly. He was ready for a fight.

"Nice phone manner," she grumbled.

His voice lightened. "Celia. What can I do for you?"

"Um, I just needed someone to talk to." She sounded so lame; she even cringed into the sofa.

His chuckle was soft and gentle. "I see."

"What are you doing?"

There was a pause. "Working."

She didn't like the sound of that. "Oh?" she managed to croak out.

"Haven't had much luck so far," he replied lightly. "I guess I'm pretty damn bored myself."

"Yeah, I'm just sitting here, watching TV," she said.

"Mmm. What're you wearing?"

She rolled her eyes. "Scratchy flannel pants and a wool turtleneck sweater."

"Liar," he said with a smile in his voice.

Celia smiled herself, then bit her bottom lip. She wanted so badly to ask him if he'd seen Victor. Unfortunately, that would entail actually telling him about Victor. She hated this. Her worry and anxiety had somehow manifested itself into a cold piece of steel that had settled in the pit of her stomach, which was quite uncomfortable, to say the least.

"What do you do when you're . . . working?" she asked carefully.

"They like to hang out in the clubs," he told her. "You know, find a fine honey and take her home."

"Basically what everyone else does. How do you know the difference?"

"I just do."

"That's not cryptic at all." He laughed again. "What if the vampire had no intention of causing harm? That they just needed to feed?"

"A vampire's a vampire," he said forcefully. All signs of laughter and smiles evaporated. "When they're *feeding*, as you call it, they lose whatever human aspects they had and turn into the monster. If they can't or aren't willing to control the monster, that piece of cattle they're sucking on is dead."

From his tone she could tell he was getting angry, so she should've shut the hell up. She was thinking of Victor and how she didn't want Jay to kill him if he came across him.

"But how do you know they're all the same? What if they don't kill?"

"They all kill at some point. They shouldn't be here in the first place. Their blood is toxic. A human is drained until the very last moment, and then they give their blood and it makes the human undead. Nothing should come back from the dead. It's unnatural."

His voice was scary and she was glad she wasn't face-to-face with him.

"Put some clothes on," he said suddenly. "I'll be there soon."

He hung up before she could fully understand. She gaped at the receiver before putting the phone down. She pulled herself up as a new set of anxious butterflies irritated her stomach.

Jay rang her buzzer thirty minutes later. She went downstairs. It was kind of cool out because that's the way Boston weather goes. Jay wore his leather jacket. Celia was happy she'd worn a shirt with sleeves.

Jay's car was double-parked. He opened the door for her as she approached. The gesture would have been nice, were it not for the harsh shadow darkening his features that made it seem like she was headed for the electric chair. She gulped.

He shut the door behind her then climbed in on his side and drove off. The silence was deafening. She glanced up at him a few times. His grip on the steering wheel was eerily close to Victor's when he was angry.

"Where are we going?" she asked in a small voice. He didn't answer.

Ten minutes later, he found a spot in front of Boston City Hospital. She was very confused as she trailed behind him to a side door that read "No Public Admittance."

They entered a long, beige hallway. The few offices in this part of the hospital had their doors shut for the night. At the end of the hall, they turned left and went down a flight of stairs. The temperature dropped considerably. Celia shivered.

They came to a set of swinging doors. Jay pulled something from his pocket as they went inside.

A desk was placed in the corner of the small lobby, with a computer and lamp. The man sitting behind it was young, about twenty-five. He'd made the area his own, with posters of various rock bands on the walls next to the desk and *Family Guy* figurines clustered around the computer.

The man wore a white lab coat over a black Ramones t-shirt. His nametag read "Phillips." His dark hair was slicked back and gleaming with too much gel. His glasses slid down the bridge of his nose a few times as he pored over some kind of crossword puzzle.

Phillips glanced up when the doors opened. He nodded to Jay amiably, obviously familiar with him. His eyes settled on Celia and he frowned.

"Who's your friend, detective?"

"This is a colleague of mine," Jay said firmly, clipping to his belt the badge he had taken out of his pocket. He walked up to the desk and flipped a page in a binder sitting on the corner. Celia stuck close to his side. He scribbled something under the Visitor Sign-In but it was illegible.

"We'll be quick," Jay said. The guy saluted him in a cheesy way. Jay and Celia walked through another set of swinging doors to the left of the desk. Celia didn't want to go farther into the morgue but she was too freaked out to stay near the door. She stayed at his elbow.

Four silver tables were lined up at the far end of the big, laboratory-looking room. Masses of different sizes lay under white sheets. Jay walked purposefully to the head of the second table.

"Come here," he grunted.

Celia had stopped at the end of the table. Now, she swallowed hard. She was trembling, from the cold and from fear at what he was going to do. She wrapped her arms around herself to control it. What was he going to show her?

His eyes narrowed warningly. She didn't know what he would do if she didn't move. She forced her legs to go.

Jay pulled the white sheet back from the body. It was a woman. She was so white and still that Celia's stomach churned. The woman was probably Celia's age, though being dead made her look older. The two puncture wounds on the neck didn't escape her notice.

"What happened?" Celia whispered.

"A vampire got carried away. He didn't even cover the fuckin' wounds," he added with disgust. "She was found last night. Those two fools," he said, pointing to the tables to the left of this one. "They were found Friday night, after a Red Sox game."

He turned around to face the other table. "And this one was found today."

He pulled the sheet back gently. A teenaged boy, pockmarked and bony, lay there. He was probably very awkward,

Celia pondered, being tall and skinny. He hadn't had a chance to learn how to manage his lengthy limbs, to bulk up.

His blonde hair hung limply around his face. Celia was amazed at how pale he was. How could he have only been found that day? There were the same wounds on his neck, as well as scrapes and cuts on his neck and face and shoulders. They would've probably been red and bruised if, you know, he had blood in him.

He was so young. Couldn't whoever had done this have picked someone bigger, stronger? Granted, humans weren't always up to par with the strength and speed of a vampire, but come on. He was just a fucking kid.

Celia put a hand to her mouth, feeling sick and repulsed and sad all at once. Jay watched her like a hawk.

"Do you understand now why I have to do what I do?" he asked sternly. He pointed to the teenager. "This kid was gonna start high school next month. That woman was a vet and both of those two men had wives and kids."

"This is horrible," she muttered, shaking her head in disbelief.

"You're damn right it's horrible!" he bellowed. She tore her eyes away from the poor boy's face.

She asked, quite reasonably, "Why are you yelling at me?"

"Because you're being stupid," he said flat out. Her jaw dropped. "Because you're standing by while all this shit goes on."

She slowly closed her mouth as the confirmation that he knew what Victor was sunk in. Her hand went to the gold heart. Her mouth had gone dry. She didn't know what to say anyways. She lowered her eyes to the floor, making her look guilty.

Jay took a deep breath to calm himself. His voice was soft but his tone steely. "Do you know where he sleeps?"

A lump was forming in her throat and she choked as she spoke. "Victor is a good guy. He'd never—"

"He's not a *guy* anymore. Let me do my damn job, Celia. Let me protect the people of this city. Let me protect *you*."

Her eyes flashed angrily. "I don't need you to protect me. People die every day, you know! Guns, car accidents, bar fights, suicide. It doesn't matter, people are gonna fucking die! Victor didn't do any of this. And I won't let you kill him," she added resolutely.

"You're fuckin' crazy."

"And you're an asshole. Is that why you came to my job? Is that why you asked me to lunch?"

"You love him?"

The question was so abrupt and curt that she didn't know how to answer. "What's that have to do with anything?" she finally demanded.

"It has to do with alotta things. But if I can't make you see the seriousness of all this, then there's no fuckin' point in me wasting my breath anymore."

"You're being a real dick. You can stand there and try to be all high and mighty and as fucking moralistic as you want but this is really about wanting something you can't have."

He glared at her. "And what's that?" he challenged.

"Me!"

She spun on her heel and stormed out the room. Jay fixed the sheets across the bodies then left the way she'd gone, only, he was taking his time. When he made it outside, Celia was nowhere to be found. That's because she had continued down the street, rifling in her pockets for bus fare.

It took her an hour and a half to get home, what with the transfers and waiting. Her anger had subsided by the time she got on the second bus. She just sat on the hard blue seat, staring dejectedly out the window, assessing her feelings for Jay. Much to her chagrin, there were feelings.

Yeah, he was mad and there was the chance that he was just

using her to get to Victor. She didn't think that was completely true. She saw the way he looked at her; you could hear it in his voice, too. That excited her. Made her feel desired. And like shit.

Victor deserved better than her, she told herself. No wonder he wasn't around. Maybe he had sensed her pulling away. Maybe he was letting her go. The thought made her nuts. She didn't want this. She wanted Victor. Would he ever forgive her?

She shuffled her feet as she walked down the street to her building.

"Celia."

She frowned at the Southern accent because it wasn't Jay's. She glanced over her shoulder from the bottom step. Ramsey was leaning against a silver Infiniti G convertible with the top down, looking not at all like himself. That lazy smile and carefree air she had always associated with him were nowhere to be found. Tonight, he had about as much enthusiasm as a mourner at a funeral.

She turned slowly, a terrible sense of foreboding making her tense. She figured something had to be bad if the vampire leader was at her doorstep.

"Ramsey, right?" she asked cautiously.

He nodded. He then pushed off the car and strode to her. She saw his feet moving but he was so graceful, it was like he was floating. He stopped in front of her. She was put off by how incredibly massive he was up close. It was a little intimidating, actually. How powerful his arms and chest looked, the chest that was not rising and falling. She wanted to take a step back but was afraid of his reaction.

"I need your help," he said. "Victor's taken ill. Come with me, please."

Her heart began to pound as she tried to imagine what could possibly make a vampire sick. Ramsey stiffened a little at the rise in her pulse. His face was already flushed so it seemed he had fed before coming to get her. Her scent tonight must've been very appealing.

"What happened to him?" she asked, trying hard not to think about the shift in his posture, like he wanted to pounce.

When he spoke, there was no indication of any change. "He was attacked. Will you come with me?"

"Of course."

She moved around him to get in the car. He put a hand up.

"I have to do this," he said as she looked into his eyes. She could feel that familiar tug, as if his sea green eyes were magnets.

She managed to take a breath and pulled her eyes away. She shook her head. "You don't have to." She sounded just the slightest bit out of breath. "I'm not going to tell anyone about the house."

Ramsey cocked his head to the side, examining her. His expression was quizzical, like he hadn't expected her to stop him.

"And if you get angry and wanna be vindictive, will you still be able to say that?"

Her eyes narrowed to angry slits. "You really think I'm trifling like that?" she demanded. "There may be other girls out there who would spill her boyfriend's secrets at the slightest indiscretion but I have better things to do with my time—"

Growing tired of this, Ramsey silenced her by placing a hand on her shoulder. His thumb grazed the skin on her collarbone. His allure worked best with skin contact. She didn't resist as her eyes automatically sought his.

She was being pulled in again. His eyes melted into the greenest ocean that surrounded her with its radiance. The water was so warm and luxurious. She floated on her back, the brilliant sun shining down on her. A contented sigh rose in her throat.

Ramsey was there. He held out his hand to her. *Why not?* she thought. She placed her hand in his. Suddenly, they were back on the sidewalk in front of her apartment building.

She looked up at him with a silly grin. The spell had taken effect. She wrapped her arms around his waist and rubbed her cheek against his chiseled chest.

"Alright, alright," he said, patting her back. "Let's get in the car, brown eyes."

"Okay, whatever you want, my dear," she said dreamily.

Ramsey opened the door for her and she sat inside. He had to reach around her to buckle her in because she wasn't making moves to do the task herself. She rubbed his arm with her hand as he did.

He drove as fast as Victor however Celia didn't fret. She enjoyed the wind in her hair. She felt she could trust Ramsey. After all, he was tall and strong and handsome.

Ramsey drove up the driveway that led around back of the white house. The brick path ended at a three-car garage. The garage door cranked closed as they got out of the convertible. Celia rushed around to Ramsey's side to snake her arm around his waist. She couldn't stand not being next to him, even for a few seconds.

The side door opened into an expansive kitchen, with all sorts of state-of-the-art equipment and fixings.

"Silly, Ramsey," Celia said, still in that dreamy voice. "What do you need a kitchen for?"

"It came with the house," he said lightly. She laughed like it was the funniest thing the funniest person in the world could come up with.

They went to Victor's bedroom. The only source of light was from a lamp on the dresser. The windows were sealed and covered with paintings of snow-capped mountains. Victor lay on the bed, under a gray jersey sheet.

He was still very pale, with dark circles around his closed eyes. They fluttered open when the door opened. He tried to smile when he caught a faint whiff of her scent. It never fully formed once he saw Celia wrapped around Ramsey, enthralled.

Ramsey, seeing Victor was troubled, placed his hand on Celia's shoulder again and released his hold on her. She stared at him blankly for a moment. Her eyes deglazed and she slowly came back to reality. She looked around the room, befuddled.

She remembered how enamored she had been with Ramsey. Those feelings were gone now and she felt kind of silly about her actions, even though she hadn't had any control. This room was a mystery to her. She hadn't paid attention on the way because her focus had been on Ramsey and his luscious arms.

There was a soft intake of breath. Celia looked to the noise.

"Victor!"

She threw herself across him on the bed, hugging him tight. She was so relieved that he was alive. It hadn't been her fault that he wasn't around. Tears spilled from her eyes onto his face as she laid rapid kisses on his cheeks and nose and forehead.

"Hey, Celia." His voice was just a whisper.

She leaned back to get a better look at him. His skin was ice cold and the muscles of his jaw were strained as he fought to conceal his pain.

"Am I hurting you?" She tried to shift so that she was sitting beside him but he grabbed her waist. Even in his weakened state, he was able to keep her still.

"No," he breathed. "You're perfect."

Her eyes watered again. "What happened to you?"

"It's nothing," he said dismissively, closing his eyes. "Some guys downtown."

"Guys? Like hunters?"

"Vamps," Ramsey said from the door. "What do you know about hunters?"

"Nothing," she said quickly. "I don't understand. Why would they attack you?"

"I don't know," Victor whispered. "I don't think they really knew."

She was all kinds of confused. "Huh?"

"We're still working it out," Ramsey said. "In the meantime, he's refusing to feed." Celia looked at Ramsey. "He needs it to heal properly."

Celia turned back to Victor. "Why aren't you eating?"

He was quiet for a long time and if she didn't know better, she could've suspected he'd fallen asleep.

"Victor," she said sharply.

He took a deep breath then opened his eyes. They were pitch-black. "I had made a promise to myself a long time ago that I would not take any more lives while feeding or bring anyone to this kind of life."

He paused significantly.

She raised her eyebrows. "Is this about Trixie's date?" He didn't answer. She glanced back to Ramsey. "That was a week ago. It could affect him this badly?"

"Yes," was all he said.

She chewed her bottom lip, worried. She examined Victor again and hated what she saw. She closed her eyes, debating. After a minute, she sat up determinedly.

"Take my blood." She even pushed her hair aside so he could see her throat.

He looked stricken under all that pain. That didn't stop his canines from sharpening slightly.

"No," he said.

"But you need it to get better. You're punishing yourself too harshly, baby. It was an accident."

"It doesn't matter," he said, shaking his head weakly. "I'm old enough to know self-control."

Tears stung her eyes yet again. Her bottom lip trembled. "It's all my fault!" she wailed. "If I wasn't being a bitch, you'd never have stormed off."

He put his hand over her mouth, cutting her off. His eyes were harsh now. "Don't be stupid. *You* didn't make me do what I did."

"But—"

He tightened his hand, which hurt her a little.

"Shhh," he said gently. He waited a moment before lowering his hand.

She stared at him as she fought back the anguished and guilty tears. "You have to feed," she said softly. "What about me, huh? What do you think's gonna happen to me if you waste away? What do you think I've been going through? I've been out of my mind with worry. I couldn't think of anything else."

"I see," he said jokingly as he ran his hand over her unkempt ponytail. She sucked her teeth and swatted his shoulder. He smiled. It was small but it was genuine.

"Please, Victor," she pleaded, growing serious again.

Her words had touched him. He sighed, giving up. "Fine." She was about to smile happily. He cut her off once again. "But not from you."

She was surprised. "Why not?"

"Because when I first told you what I was, I asked and you said you weren't comfortable with it. And remember what I told you?"

She shrugged dejectedly. With a put-upon sigh, she said, "That you would never do anything to make me uncomfortable."

"So, it's settled."

He turned his head to Ramsey, who had his eyes closed. A second later, a vampire named Milo walked through the door. Milo was short and petite, wearing black skinny jeans and a fitted white tee under a black vest. His straight hair was nearly white it was so blonde. It was brushed back in a mini-pompadour.

"Milo," (pronounced mee-low) "bring Victor some company, please."

Celia didn't like how he said that and was about to open her mouth to complain when Victor squeezed her waist. She looked at him. He gave her a half smile that told her to relax. At least he hadn't said bring Victor a nice, juicy piece of meat.

She didn't know how long it would take for Milo to return. She moved on the bed to sit beside him, her back against the headboard. Victor shifted, too. She gave him a hand in sitting up so that they were shoulder-to-shoulder.

He kissed her cheek. It was like he'd placed an ice cube on her skin. She leaned against his shoulder, quickly slipping back into that serene piece of mind she usually experienced when in his presence. Something, she realized, she hadn't felt in the last couple of days.

"How are you doing, Seal?" he asked. His voice was still so soft. At least he was moving some.

"I'm not the one on bed rest."

He shrugged a little, lifting her head in the process. "I'm okay. How was work?"

Her face lit up. "Oh, there was this girl this weekend wearing this really cute bubble dress—"

"Bubble dress?" he asked with a frown. *Obviously*, he was not up on the latest female fashion trends.

"Yeah, you know, those dresses that kind of scrunch up at the bottom. Well, it was this really nice shade of blue and her shoes were cute, too, and . . ."

She went on like this for ten minutes. Victor just smiled to himself as he listened to her. He could listen to her prattle on about anything. He just loved hearing her voice, and the fact that she could tell him anything.

"So, I found out I have a grandmother in some place called Groton."

"That's near Shirley and Dunstable," he informed her.

She stared at him as if he were speaking Arabic. He chuckled, and held his side tighter. “It’s a little over an hour away.”

“Why would I have a grandmother living in the boonies?”

He only shrugged.

“And why would that be such a secret?”

“What did Meg have to say?”

“Not much at all,” she pouted. “She changed the subject.”

He took her hand in his. She was talking about different shoes when Victor suddenly went all rigid.

“But the strap dug into my ankle, which was so damn annoying! I really liked the turquoise color. Trixie wears them whenever she can, that heifer.”

A low hiss escaped Victor’s lips, causing her to stop. She frowned up at him, confused. She was about to ask what his deal was when she heard a voice in the hallway.

“Lovely. Simply lovely.” Cillian drifted to the doorway, wearing a snappy charcoal suit, with a cobalt blue dress shirt underneath. The tie was the same shade of blue as the shirt, with small burgundy and gray diamonds. His dark hair was neat and swept away from his face.

He only had eyes for Celia—deep, penetrating eyes that instantly scared the shit out of her.

He lifted his hand gracefully, stirring the air, and inhaled deeply as if he were wafting something to his nose. “Like the sweetest wine,” he said in that wispy voice. “So . . . strong. So distinctive. It reminds me of Greece. I had a lady there who smelled like her. I enjoyed her very much, I must say. Yes . . .” he replied, drawing out the “s.”

While he was speaking, Victor crawled over Celia. She wanted to tell him he shouldn’t be moving but Cillian was freaking her out. She tried to take hold of his arm. He got out of her grip easy, peasy.

Cillian continued on. He didn’t seem to notice Victor. “Her blood was so . . . warm. I made it last as long as I could but, ah,” he paused to shake his head regretfully, "these affairs don't always work out the way you want."

He looked at Celia again with a blank expression. The film over his eyes seemed to be moving; a creamy fluid cascading down over his blue irises. She had no idea what he was thinking. All she knew was that something about him screamed *danger*. Strangely, she could not look away from him. She didn't feel that tug. Nope, just paralyzing fear.

Victor took more steps toward Cillian, and he finally acknowledged his presence. He smiled at Victor, showing his fangs.

"Is she a treat for me?" he asked pleasantly.

"You stay away from her," Victor growled with more intensity than Celia had thought possible.

Cillian's smile faltered. He was confused. He took in Victor's stance and the fact that his fangs were down. His eyes slid to Celia. He surveyed her, and then looked back to Victor.

"But she's special," Cillian protested. "Can you not smell it? That sweet—"

"Out, Cillian."

Suddenly, Cillian's face twisted into a scowl. His hands became taut at his sides, the muscles tightening, ready for a fight.

Celia's breath caught in her throat. She didn't want Victor to fight but she didn't know what to do to stop this. She sat on the bed, feeling completely scared and completely useless.

Just when it appeared that Cillian was going to take what he wanted, something changed. Cillian's expression went blank again. He stared at Victor with unseeing eyes, focused inwardly. They waited. Celia was confused as hell but Victor understood what was happening.

After a moment, Cillian heaved a disappointed sigh. "Very well," he said. "I never have treats anymore—she was a gift I never expected . . . No, it's unjust. I will leave you one of these days, Ramsey, for the way you treat me . . . She smells like her. Why is that? Is she one of them? Umami, they are called. Blood like sugar they say.

"Stop right there." He pressed two fingers to his forehead. "Always in my head, damn Ramsey. Always in my head." He continued to mutter to himself as he exited the room.

Celia stared after Cillian. "Who was that?" she whispered as softly as she could.

Victor closed the door before returning to the bed. He limped a little now that the adrenaline wasn't so high.

"Cillian. Ramsey's project," he added with a note of discord, knowing full well Ramsey would hear him.

"What does that mean?"

Victor shook his head. "He's the only one Cillian listens to."

"What was he talking about? 'Blood like sugar?' Was he talking about me? I couldn't really follow."

Victor clutched his side. "I don't know what he was rambling about. He's not well. He confuses things. Time, places, people."

Celia didn't completely buy that nor did she appreciate Victor's dismissive tone. She didn't know Cillian but the way he spoke about the woman in Greece, the passion in his voice made her think there was something to what he said, even if his recall wasn't always accurate to the others. What did he call the woman? She couldn't remember.

"What's with his eyes?" she whispered.

"A witch put—"

"A *witch*?"

"Yes. She cast a spell to blind him but it didn't work correctly. She only succeeded in making him colorblind. If it weren't for Ramsey, he probably wouldn't be alive. He's very old and sometimes needs . . . help. To make sure he stays manageable."

He ended with that. The finality in his voice told her to drop it for now.

She had just started to relax again when Victor glanced toward the door. She tensed up, expecting Cillian to sidle through again. Try as she might, though, she couldn't hear a thing. The house was very still around them.

She looked back to Victor. He stared unblinkingly at the door. His hands were gripping the sheet at his waist. She could see the strain on his knuckles. He wasn't growling, though, so it couldn't have been Cillian. It finally dawned on her: his food must've been near.

Celia had to fight to keep her mouth clamped. She knew Victor needed this and she didn't want to upset him more. After all, she was forcing him to do something he'd been vehemently avoiding.

The front door opened. She heard that. "My friend's in here," Milo said playfully. "You girls are going to love him."

Girls? Celia thought. *As in . . .* girls*?*

The door opened and Milo stepped in with his arms around the waists of two women. One was full-figured with chocolate hair, caramel skin, and a mole above her top lip. The other was tall and athletic-looking. The muscles in her arms and legs were toned, but not intense, body builder status. She had blonde hair with fringe bangs that nearly covered her eyes. She kept sweeping them out of her face, which Celia found irritating. Why wouldn't she just cut them a little shorter?

They both smiled at Victor, completely ignoring Celia. Though they looked pleasant enough, there was no flicker in their eyes, no emotion. They appeared to be life-like mannequins, waiting to find out their next move.

"Victor," Milo said. "This is Tonya—" (curvy) "—and Elise." (blondie) He looked at Celia like he wanted to say something but didn't quite know how to phrase it. Maybe something along the lines of, you gonna sit there or you want some, too? Celia was too busy glaring at the two women to notice anyways, focusing her resentment and impotence in this situation on them.

Victor placed a hand on hers. She turned to him. "Why don't you wait in the living room, Seal? The coast is clear," he added at her unwilling expression.

She quickly decided that she didn't want to see this. So she might be eaten by a numb vampire. That couldn't be as bad as watching her boyfriend feed, right?

She gave him a quick peck on the cheek, swung her legs off the bed and left, peeking around cautiously as she went. The living room was right next door to his bedroom, just across the hall. It looked more like a swanky lounge, if anything.

There were plush sofas and square ottomans, all of them white, which seemed impractical. What if something spilled on them? Blood being the number one concern in a vampire home. A medium-sized bar occupied the far right corner, fully stocked. The paintings on the walls were beautiful and abstract. All that was missing were sparkling white lights and a view of the beach.

She frowned when she saw the holes from that armchair, still in the wall next to the door.

As she contemplated what that was all about, noises from the other room wafted to her. She didn't want to listen as soon as she recognized them but her body wasn't obeying her. Her muscles had gone all tense and she was holding her breath.

There were moans. A female at first. It must've been when she was bitten. That was more like a gasp. A male's soft moaning came next. Her frown deepened. Was that . . . *Victor*? She listened closer for bed creaks or small utterances that indicated sex. None followed.

He sounded like he was really enjoying himself, although, not in the getting-his-rocks-off type of way. That would've meant he was a guy. No. This was more intimate and . . . sweet, even. She couldn't believe it. She hardly ever heard Victor make noises, whether they were kissing or making love. And here was some stranger, making him sound like that.

Her anger built slowly. She wanted so badly to storm in that room and yell and scream and kick. She was frozen to her spot as she listened to her more rational self. He needed this. Those girls didn't know the situation, which was another issue in itself. She couldn't screw everything up.

Celia groaned miserably and sank into one of the sofas. Her resentment abated but oh, goody, was replaced with gloom. As she listened, she wondered if maybe it were her. Maybe *she* was the reason he never made noises . . . Maybe she didn't pleasure him enough . . . Or he didn't feel he could open himself up to her when they were intimate? So she could see and feel the real him?

She covered her ears with her hands and closed her eyes, imagining she was somewhere far far away.

* * *

The curvy girl, Tonya, sat on the bed first. Victor so didn't want to do this. Except he ached all over, and not just from the pain of his slowly mending bones. His mouth watered as she neared him. The only thing keeping him from pouncing on her like a rabid dog was sheer determination. He was afraid he was too enervated now to control himself once he started.

Their pulses were strong, calling out to him. His hands tightened around the sheet. A third heart beat in the house—Celia's in the other room. He took a deep breath, thinking of her.

"Don't be scared," Milo said gleefully. "Get over there."

Tonya edged closer. "What would you like to do? Milo said you're hurt. I give a wonderful massage," she added, her face almost lighting up with her pride.

He really despised these games sometimes. It was incredibly tiring. Plus, Milo's "catches" were always so vapid under his control. They needed direction for every movement, every word, every emotion. He seemed to prefer it that way.

Victor sighed as those thoughts slipped out of his head and his hunger grew to lethal levels. He leaned into her, not even giving into the pretenses. His gums tingled as even his fangs seemed to tremble in anticipation. He unintentionally nuzzled her neck as he moved into a better position. He felt her shiver. So, there *were* some emotions in that empty head of hers.

Out of pure habit, he kissed the spot right below her jaw.

"Mm," she purred, awakening just a little. "That's nice."

He hesitated. Her reaction had been way too sexual for his liking. Her pulse pounded loudly in his ears and the scent of her humanness was overwhelming, filling his head. He needed her blood. Now that he was this close, he wasn't going to back down.

Victor opened his mouth and bit her. She gasped, then fell quiet. He could feel the effects almost immediately. Her warmth spread through him slowly, luxuriously. He took his time, letting the blood pool in his mouth before swallowing in gulps. His eyes were closed as Victor, the man, drifted away, along with the aching. No one else was in this space. All around him was heat, like he was sitting on the sun.

Suddenly, there was a tugging. No, it was more like shoving. The strange interruption triggered something and Victor became aware of his own hands, then his arms, then his shoulders. Someone was gripping his shoulder and pushing him roughly.

Victor frowned as he slowly came back to the room.

"Victor!"

His eyes sprang open. He pulled away from Tonya's neck. He panted hard, as he looked around the room. Tonya stared at him with those dead eyes. Three red marks circled her upper arm from where he had had her in his grip. Blood dripped down her bicep. His talon-like nails had stabbed her flesh.

Milo had been leaning over the bed. He released Victor now and stepped back. He hadn't wanted to pull Victor off of her. He could've ripped her skin or attacked. Milo's expression was mild though. He wouldn't have cared if Victor had killed her but he knew Victor—and Ramsey—would.

Milo took Tonya's hand and helped her stand. "Is he going to be okay?" she asked Milo like Victor couldn't hear her.

Milo nodded. He rubbed her shoulders soothingly. "Yes, yes, don't you worry." He kissed her lips, then made a trail to her neck. He used his tongue to clean her wounds.

He looked at Victor, who was still breathless. He wanted more but was scared. His body was healing; he could feel it already. He had been deprived for too long. One feeding wouldn't be adequate.

Milo took Elise's elbow and brought her to the bed. She was enthralled. Any sane person would've run screaming with their arms flapping in the air at what they had just witnessed. There would be no shame in that, either.

Instead, Elise took up Tonya's spot next to Victor.

"Easy this time, tiger," Milo chided cheerfully.

Her heart beat just as loudly as Tonya's had. The rhythm pulled him in. He was able to stay in the room this time, instead of floating up there somewhere with the sun. He moved away after a minute and cleaned her wound. Tonya's was already pink.

"Alright, ladies," Milo announced when Elise stood. "Let's go see what we have for music."

He took their hands and led them out the room. Victor breathed deeply, mentally examining himself. The blood cursed through him, filling him up *everywhere*. He felt immensely better. And incredibly horny.

He pushed the sheet aside, climbed out of bed, did a good stretch then followed the melody of the lone heartbeat into the living room.

Celia was sitting on a sofa, crouched forward with her hands over her head. Guilt hit him like a truck at the sight. He thought she was still upset from seeing him emaciated and in pain. He sat beside her. When she didn't move, he placed his hand on her knee.

He took hold of her wrists and gently pried her hands from her face. She looked up into his light gray eyes with sad brown ones. He hated to see her upset. It made the space where his heart sat ache.

Victor rested his forehead on hers, fighting to keep from throwing her down on the sofa and ravaging her.

"You're warm," she whispered.

She smelled good. Like strawberries and cherry blossoms. Even her breath, so warm and full of life. The predator in him wanted to seek it out, find the core and take it. Although most of him just wanted to sex her up.

His hand closed around the cushion he was sitting on. White bits of cotton tumbled to the floor.

"Are you okay now?" she asked, completely and infuriatingly unaware of his turmoil.

"Yeah, baby," he whispered back.

"Good."

She rubbed his knee. Now, why did she go and do that? Victor's jaw clenched as his arousal piqued even more. He took her wrist as gingerly as he could. Judging by her wince, it hadn't been gentle enough. He brought her hand to his mouth and kissed her palm. His tongue ran along her wrist, the heat from her skin enticing him.

He looked up at her, his lust in his eyes. She seemed to understand. She didn't protest when he pressed his lips to hers. She did cringe from the taste of blood on his tongue. He moved on to laying kisses on her neck and collarbone. His hand slipped inside her jeans, into her warmest space.

Before he could lose himself in the moment he was creating, he paused. A vaguely familiar scent was on the back of her shirt and, now that he noticed it, mingled with her hair, too. He'd been too focused on Celia and her body to notice anything out of place.

He recognized the leather seats of Ramsey's car right away. There was also the sterilized smell from the morgue. He would ask about that later. What made him pause was that other scent.

"What's wrong?" Celia asked, puzzled. She had just been sitting there, letting him do what he wanted without much response. She was still preoccupied.

Victor sniffed her shoulder, trying to recall why it was so familiar. It hit him in an instant. That night when she had the candles burning. And had also refused him. This time the scent was more concentrated. He could tell it was a man.

He tilted away to stare at her harshly. She frowned.

"What?"

"Where were you tonight?"

Her frown deepened. "At home. Why?"

"You had company?"

Her expression shifted to surprise. She looked away. Victor shot up and was across the room in a flash. He picked up an ottoman and hurled it across the room. Celia shrieked because it happened so fast. She looked to where the loud *thwack* had come from. Victor appeared in front of her. She gasped back a second shriek.

"Victor—"

He cut her off by grabbing her shoulders and pulling her up from the sofa. "Who is he?" he demanded. His eyes were no longer gray.

"What're you talking about?"

"Don't, Celia!" he cut across her. "Don't do that. Be a fucking adult." She flinched when his fingers tightened.

"You're hurting me!" she cried.

He released her instantly and stepped back. There were tears in her eyes. He was still angry as all hell but he knew he needed to calm down a bit so he didn't hurt her or the house. He paced a minute, then stopped abruptly and faced her.

"Are you seeing someone else?" He sounded more hurt than he had intended. How else to explain this foreign scent?

"No!"

"You smell like someone else."

She shrugged, not quite meeting his eye. "It's probably someone from work. Carson's always touching me."

"No," he said, shaking his head. "I know... him." He didn't want to say he knew his scent. That just sounded weird.

He surveyed her. Her cheeks were pink, her heart still racing. Instead of his anger flaring up once more, he was more saddened by this. She was lying to him and it was not a good feeling.

His eyebrows pulled together gloomily. He folded his arms at the chest. "Fine," he said softly. "I'll go see if Ramsey can give you a ride home. You probably need to get up early."

He turned to leave. He walked at human shuffling speed, disappointment and sadness weighing his shoulders down.

"Victor."

He halted at the door. She sighed behind him.

"Come back."

He turned slowly. Celia returned to her spot on the sofa. He hadn't been playing games; he was truly going to let her go. If she felt she had to lie, obviously she didn't trust him anymore. It was shitty but he wasn't going to force her. They argued whenever the future was inadvertently brought up. At least then she didn't lie.

He took a couple of steps until he stood a few feet away from her.

She stared down at her fingers in her lap. "There's this guy," she began. "He's a hunter. He came to Boston looking for a vampire and he killed him."

She paused.

"Yeah?"

She groaned. "I think he has his sights on you," she added

reluctantly.

"He's been pestering you?"

She shook her head. "No, not really."

Just then, a slender woman appeared at the door. She had dark brown hair in a chignon at the base of her neck. Her skin was so pale. She wore a leather pencil skirt and a red and black chiffon top. A pair of gold sunglasses sat on her nose. She smiled at Victor. Her fangs were out.

"So this is your human, Victor," she purred. She spoke with a pure South Boston accent, dropping the "r"s like they were the plague. "You never bring her around. Don't want to make me jealous, huh?" She began to unbutton her blouse.

Victor darted a harsh stare at her. "Get out of here, Clarice." She was always trying her best to get under his skin. She'd been infatuated ever since she laid eyes on him when he arrived in Boston.

The vampire shrugged. "You're always such a freakin' stick in the mud. Fine. I'll go join Milo then." She turned from the doorway as she slipped her shirt off her shoulders. She wasn't wearing a bra. Both nipples were pierced by barbells with silver balls on either side.

Celia's jaw dropped to her lap. Her head jerked to Victor, her face outraged. He took her hand and brought her to her feet. Before she could shove him away, he wrapped his arm around her waist and held her close.

"Hold your breath," he instructed. She nodded, though she was confused. He waited until he felt her chest contract with her breath. He teleported. Relief flooded him at the feel of the icy currents running beneath his skin, indicating the power involved.

They materialized together in Celia's living room. She immediately began coughing and gasping, like she was imitating an asthma attack. Victor rushed to the kitchen for a glass of water. Celia had dropped to her knees without his support as her body reconditioned itself to being whole again.

"Here," he said, kneeling beside her. She took the glass with shaky hands. The water sloshed over the sides. He helped her bring it to her mouth. She took a sip, and choked.

Victor rubbed her back and her hair until her gasping slowed. When she was calm enough, she peered up into his gray eyes indignantly. "Don't . . . ever . . . do that . . . again," she panted.

He smiled and kissed her forehead. He didn't want to move her just yet. He sat in front of her with his legs on either side of her body. Her palms were flat on the floor and her legs tucked under her. She looked like she was bracing for impact.

"Who the hell was that, *Victor*?" Celia asked after a moment. She was still trying to get her bearings but her words dripped with venom.

He rubbed his temple. "Clarice. She's one of Ramsey's."

"And does she always feel the need to undress in front of strangers?"

"She doesn't normally do that. She . . . likes me," he said, sounding embarrassed. He kind of shrugged and avoided her eyes. Celia's lips jerked, as if she felt an urge to giggle. "She was trying to get a rise out of you."

Celia shook her head. "Mission accomplished."

Victor squeezed her shoulder. "Who is this hunter bothering you?"

"Jay. His name is Jay. And he hasn't been bothering me. But he's searching for vampires." She looked at him. "Why did we leave?"

"I didn't want anyone to hear us," he said. "There is already a group of hunters attacking us. I don't know what Ramsey is planning. He doesn't like bloodshed, but he will protect the ones he loves."

"What's so secretive about that?"

"You don't question the motives of the . . . let's call him the dominant."

She frowned. "I thought you weren't in his group. Not officially, anyways."

"I'm not. But I still want to show respect."

"Why aren't you in his group? I mean, they bring you people to drink from. They walk around half-naked with piercings that make it look like they have six nipples . . ."

Victor grinned. "Stop it, Seal. Clarice means nothing to me." He shrugged. "I prefer the solitude."

She took a drink of her water. "What's Ramsey doing about these other hunters?"

He sighed. "I'm afraid Ramsey doesn't have a plan. He's very upset. He's lost two already and then Josiah was hurt badly."

"And you," she added.

"I just have the distinct feeling he's hoping this will all blow over. As if maybe the hunters will move on."

Celia touched his chest. He took her hand in his. So small and frail. It was amazing to him how easily he could crush it. He cradled it like the fragile vase she was and kissed each finger.

"Please be careful out there," Celia whispered.

"I'm always careful," he said playfully.

She looked gloomy again. He rubbed her cheek. "Do . . ." she started but trailed off. He tilted his head quizzically. She chewed her bottom lip like she did when she was contemplating something. After a second, she closed her eyes and spat it out.

"Do I do it for you?" Her words were a jumble as she rushed them out.

He wasn't quite sure of the vernacular. "What?"

"Am I . . . enough for you?"

Now he was really confused. "What the hell are you talking about? What kind of question is that? I told you Clarice was just being—"

"I'm not talking about her anymore." She shrugged timidly, her gaze on his chin. "I heard you with that girl. You sounded like it was . . . pleasurable."

He thought back to the bedroom. He didn't remember making any noise. All he could recall was the warmth, the same warmth still pulsing through him at the moment.

She saw his confusion. "Surely you heard yourself," she said crabbily. "It was loud enough."

He shook his head slowly. "I wasn't myself at that moment. I apologize profusely, Seal. Why would you think you weren't doing it for me?" he asked, using her phrase.

She got all bashful, tucking her chin to her chest and not meeting his eyes. "I don't know. You're kinda quiet when we're together. I thought that was just the way you are but then you were with them and . . ." She trailed off again and bit her bottom lip. That was always so sexy to him; she didn't even realize.

He smiled warmly. "Celia, please. I wasn't having sex with those women. You're beating yourself up for nothing."

"Don't say that!" she cried, snapping her face to his. "It's not 'nothing.'"

"Okay." He lifted his hands. "I'm sorry. Wrong choice of words." He took a moment to organize what he wanted to say in order to make it just right. "You're the only one for me. You're the only one I think about, dream about, care about. I only curse the heavens for not allowing me to meet you sooner. I'm so happy you're in my life. I wouldn't trade it for anything."

For some reason, that made her look guilty. She leaned forward to kiss him. A gentle kiss that quickly grew more real. She took his face in her hands as she became persistent.

Victor effortlessly lifted her so that she straddled his lap. She gasped lightly from the quick movement. It didn't distract her from his lips. He wanted to show her just how much she meant to him. It took all night, with breaks for ice cream in between. The good stuff, too, since she just bought a pint of dulce de leche Haagen Dazs.

They made it to her bed for the last round. The ice cream sat melting on her nightstand. The covers were a swirly purple mass under their writhing bodies. Her legs were bent, his arms behind her knees. Victor kissed then nipped each of her calves. He purposely eased in and out in a slow rhythm, even when she kneaded his back to make him go faster. He put her legs down to be as close to her heart as possible.

Victor took hold of her hands and squeezed a little too roughly. He stared into her eyes, his own penetrating her deeper than his body.

"Do you feel me?"

His question was a firm whisper, his breath in her face. His fangs weren't even extended; this was from him, not his other nature.

Her eyes were already drooping, signaling she was close to her end. She only managed to nod. He could see that she understood. That she felt the same way. He kissed her intensely to seal it. He finally increased his speed. It felt like he was trying to reach her stomach.

"Yes," she managed to sigh, before her eyes rolled into the back of her head.

The sun was just beginning its slow climb into the sky now. Celia was moaning softly in her sleep, her hair strewn across her pillow. He loved to watch her sleep. All the little noises and facial expressions. Vampires had to practice those nuances in order to blend in: blinking, breathing, making their faces soft and inviting.

Victor traced the outline of her cheek with his finger. He picked up the gold pendent, then ran his thumb over it. He longed to stay in bed with her, to spend the day with her. To see what the sun did to her hair and skin. He knew she tanned because her skin was bronzier now than when they had met that cold night in November.

He needed to leave so she wouldn't wake up to a pile of ash staining her sheets. Damn.

He kissed her lightly on the forehead before he disappeared.

Ten

THE NEXT NIGHT, Victor found out about all he had missed while on bed rest. Elizabeth, Annie, Bryce, Ramsey, and the Italian, Arturo, were in Ramsey's living room, arguing.

"You were supposed to be watching him," Bryce was saying. He pointed a finger at Arturo. "Trent's death's on *your* hands."

"I'm sick of defending myself," Arturo exclaimed. "*Trent* left *me!* He was with *una ragazza* the last time I saw him. Who am I to deny him when girls surround him?"

Bryce shook his head. "You know you have to keep your eye on him. He's new. What if he had killed someone?"

Arturo shrugged, as if saying *not my problem.* Bryce stood menacingly but Annie had his wrist. Arturo looked at him with disgust.

"You are one to talk about watching someone. You can barely control yourself, *amico.*"

Bryce stormed at Arturo, who stood to meet him. They bumped chests. Bryce took hold of Arturo's shirt. Ramsey quickly stepped in, grabbing Bryce into a half nelson. Bryce tried to shrug him off but Ramsey's grip was deceptively strong, especially compared to Bryce's massive self. Annie looked on with an expressionless face. She was used to this, and was probably thankful Ramsey was there to act as barrier.

Victor stood to help Ramsey. Bryce calmed enough for Ramsey to let go. He released Arturo's shirt, then moved his head from side to side, cracking some bones. He gave Arturo one last, long stare before leaving the room.

The air was still laced with tension as everyone settled back into their seats. "What do we do about these hunters?" Elizabeth asked gently. She wore a black jumpsuit tonight with a slit that stopped above her navel. Silver Grecian sandals were on her feet. "They're using Dead Man's Blood. Who knows what else they have up their sleeves." No pun intended.

"Besides having vampires in their employ?" Annie added, adjusting her cap.

Ramsey looked to Victor. "Josiah doesn't remember much of that night."

"There were two of them," Victor reported. "They spoke a language I didn't understand. And they seemed unsteady once they were standing still. Ramsey, they had red eyes."

Ramsey frowned. "Elizabeth?"

She shook her head. "I'll have to do some research. I don't know what that means."

"Maybe Cillian knows," Annie suggested. Elizabeth looked at her sideways. She was not comfortable in the least with the idea of having a conversation with Cillian.

"I'll ask him later," Ramsey stepped in. He looked back to Annie. "That sound like the vamp that attacked you?"

She shook her head slowly as she contemplated. Annie had a heart-shaped face with a full, round mouth, like Kerry Washington. Her small eyes were the color of toffee, and her eyebrows seemed non-existent because of the blonde color. You could always find her in jeans and the latest pair of sneakers.

She blew out a breath. “I’m not sure. Could be. I think I would’ve remembered the eyes, though.”

If she were just rising for the night, she would’ve been disoriented. She may not have noticed or even seen the red eyes.

Ramsey turned to Victor. “Do you think there were more?”

“I don’t think so. But I don’t know for certain.”

Victor watched Ramsey. His brow was furrowed and his jaw set. Victor debated the most diplomatic way of asking his next question. “Ramsey,” he began slowly. “What are you thinking?”

Everyone looked at Ramsey. “That I want this to stop,” he said after a moment. “I’m going to find their leader. I’ll talk to him. Make him see we’re not a threat.”

That was not what Victor thought he was going to say. And judging by the eerie silence in the room neither had anyone else.

“Talk?” Arturo asked dubiously. He shook his head and spat rapid Italian. Ramsey glared steadily at him.

“And that’s your opinion,” he told him. “I’ll at least try for peace first.”

Arturo looked like he wanted to say more but he refrained. That didn’t erase the hostile grimace though.

Elizabeth tossed him a scornful glare for his disrespect. “Milo and Clarice are out tonight,” she reminded Ramsey. “Maybe they’ve seen one of them.”

Ramsey closed his eyes. Arturo stood and left the room, avoiding Elizabeth’s harsh look. Two minutes passed before Ramsey opened his eyes again.

“The hunters haven’t been out tonight. It’s still early.” It was only nine-thirty. “I told them to let me know immediately. Annie, will you and Bryce patrol as well? It’s Restaurant Week. A lot of humans will be in the North End.”

Restaurant Week was a bi-annual event in Boston where

people could try different eats for a prix fixe. Many foodies went out during the week, doing their own versions of restaurant hopping. It just sounded funny to hear such a normal, human event roll off his tongue. Then again, Ramsey had been in Boston for a while now. He knew what attracted humans, and surely that would attract the hunters.

"Sure," Annie said, then flitted out the room.

Elizabeth hesitated a moment, before clearing her throat. "Perhaps," she began, "Celia could be of service?"

Victor did not like that, as evidenced by his growl. "I don't think so."

"She knows one of the hunters, right?" Wow, there really was no privacy in that house. "She can help."

Victor shook his head, resolute. "I won't put her in this."

"Victor," Ramsey said. "If we can't find these people on our own, they'll keep coming after us. Coming after you. I'm sure those vamps wouldn't have attacked unprovoked."

"What makes you so sure? They could be rogues." Victor knew it was unlikely; he was trying to keep Celia away. Rogues were more dangerous than newborns. They broke away from their kind after losing their humanity to old age. They were careless, killing without any concern for discretion. Cillian was a rare example of a rogue who had been reigned in. Most rogues needed to be put down.

"From what you said, they were probably drugged." Ramsey shook his head. "No, they weren't rogues. I think they were instructed."

Victor leaned forward so that he was squarely facing Ramsey. "I can't. If anything were to happen to her . . . I don't know what I would do."

Ramsey could see his pain. He placed a hand on his shoulder and squeezed. "We'll find another way." His tone was too distant to be comforting.

Elizabeth stood then. "I'll be back later," she told Ramsey. She leaned down to kiss his temple then left out the front door, no doubt to start her research.

Ramsey bowed his head, thinking. Victor left the house as well. He was determined not to include Celia. He didn't know what Ramsey thought talking to the hunters would accomplish. He figured he would find them on his own. Anything to keep Celia as far away as possible.

* * *

It was nearly ten when Jay pulled up in front of Snipe's house. He had had to disentangle himself from Kathy, who had been trying to convince him to go a third round. She was a cocktail waitress at Gypsy Bar, located a few blocks over from Cage's. He had been more than willing to go that extra mile with her if he wasn't meant to meet the hunters. They were going to patrol tonight. Jay was ready with his stake strapped to his waist and his gun in the holster on his hip. The strap of his satchel was across his chest.

The air was still hot, even for such a late hour. He dressed for the weather with jeans (natch) and a loose tee to conceal his stake. If anything, it appeared he had a rolled-up newspaper in his back pocket. The shirt still managed to show off his muscles nicely, not that he did it on purpose. Sexiness just happened that way.

He walked up the stairs and raised his hand to knock. Before he made contact, the front door swung open.

"Wow, you must have that ESPN I've heard about," Jay joked.

Snipe looked extremely harassed when he opened the door. Surprise was added when he saw Jay.

Jay cocked an eyebrow. "Everything okay?"

"Jay," he sighed. "I forgot you were coming by tonight."

"Should we reschedule?"

"No, no. That's not necessary. Colin!" he shouted over his shoulder. Jay rubbed his ear. "Let's go!"

Snipe stepped out and headed down the stairs in an even stride, which was intriguing considering that limp of his. Jay glanced into the house. The living room was empty. Colin rushed out of the kitchen with a sandwich half in his mouth. His arm was still in a sling and he was stuffing his wallet in his pocket.

"Mey, May. Mow's mit moing?"

Jay was surprised he understood that muffled language. "Everything's still attached. What's going on?"

Colin closed the door and took the sandwich from his mouth. "Harold's MIA." There was a loud honk from the street. "Dude!" Colin called, annoyed. "Come on, before Snipe has a coronary."

They climbed into Snipe's light blue mini-van. Snipe weaved through the streets to the Savin Hill part of Dorchester. Harold's house was at the end of a dead-end road. It was dark green with a wrap-around porch and an overgrown yard to the left.

The black van was parked in front of the house. Snipe found a spot across the street and they all got out. Their weight made the wooden stairs creak and groan. The porch was cluttered with weathered lounge chairs and potted plants strangled by the humidity. The light was out and all was still in the house.

"You sure he's here?" Jay asked skeptically.

In response, Snipe pounded on the door. Colin rolled his eyes to Jay. Snipe pounded again. A light came on behind the curtained window on the door. The locks turned and the door opened.

Harold was breathless. His chest heaved heavily. Red scrapes littered his forehead in addition to the one on his cheek. Two small wounds punctured the left side of his neck. His eyes darted anxiously from each of their faces.

"Harold," Snipe bellowed. "Where the hell have you been?"

He pushed his way inside before Harold could answer and

looked around.

"I've been . . . busy," he responded lamely.

Everything seemed to be in order, as best as Jay could tell. He could see into the living room, where two lamps were on. Nothing was overturned or out of place. In fact, the home was quite neat.

Snipe was still looking around. Colin took a step closer to Harold. He surveyed the wound on his neck.

"What the hell, man?" Colin exclaimed, reaching out to touch it. "You got bit?"

Harold clamped a hand over his neck, taking a step back. Snipe looked furious. "What's going on here?" he demanded.

Harold's face turned fire engine red. "I . . . We—um, I—"

"Goddammit, Harold, spit it out!" Snipe thundered.

He gulped and his eyes lowered to the floor in shame. "You know how Booth had captured those two bloodsuckers? The ones from Europe?" He swallowed again. "Well, he didn't quite . . . kill them."

The hallway was silent for a moment. Everyone gaped at Harold. Snipe finally opened his mouth to say something when a giant crash shook the floor beneath their feet.

"What the fuck?" Jay cried.

Harold's eyes went all wide. He ran for a door under the staircase. The others followed. An old set of stairs led down to the finished basement. There was a makeshift laboratory in one corner, comprised of a metal table clustered with test tubes and chemistry looking things, a computer and two stools.

In the back corner, three cages stood. They didn't allow much room for occupants to move around. The foreign vampires occupied two of them. They turned their freaky red eyes on the newcomers. The bigger one was fidgeting back and forth, with his head ducked so as not to touch the top of the cage. He growled softly, hungry and sore. His bare feet were smoking. Silver bars.

"Shoot," Harold said. "He knocked his cage over."

Sure enough, the concrete part that was supposed to be the bottom of the cage was now one of the walls, leaving the bars horizontal. The vampire lunged at them. He jumped back quickly with a loud hiss when he touched the bars. White smoke rose from his palms.

"What is this?" Colin asked, astonished.

"It was Booth's idea," Harold said quickly. "He thought we could use them to get rid of the other bloodsuckers and then we'd kill them. But Booth was the only one who could understand them and they've been going wild these last couple of nights. I don't know how to feed them."

"How did you *used* to feed them?" Colin cried. None of them wanted to think that they had brought humans down here as chow.

"Booth stole some bags of blood from a blood bank. I only have two bags left but they won't take it."

"How'd you get them to work for you?" Jay asked, unable to hide his disdain.

"Booth heard them talking one night about making sure they bring someone home for their maker. We followed them. They both drank off this guy who was tweaking bad and you know how drugs are. You can't tell how it'll affect vampires.

"The small one, Eugene, passed out but Balthazar went on and on about the Ukraine or Poland or somewhere. Booth was the one talking. All I know was that they were laughing like old pals.

"Booth got Balthazar to show him where they were staying since they were passing through to Canada. We came back the next day and kidnapped their maker while she was still sleeping."

Jay looked around. There was nowhere else to hold someone in the basement. "Where is she?"

"Booth put her away."

"You don't know where she is?" he asked incredulously.

"Um . . . not really. I just know it's secluded and dark." He glanced to the vampires. "I haven't been able to talk to them or tell them what to do. After taking the maker, Booth ordered them to help or he'd kill her in front of them. He'd been creating this drug to keep them in line and it worked for, like, two weeks. We tested them out in Rhode Island. They killed four vampires.

"I let Booth's friends use them. They said they almost killed a blonde vamp. The other night was the last time I let them out. Eugene came back injured. I had to shoot Balthazar to get him in the house." He looked at the floor. "I think they've built up an intolerance."

Jay was perceptively furious. His hand moved to the stake at his side. "This ain't right," he grumbled.

"What am I supposed to do?" Harold cried. He sounded frantic now. "I'm all alone and they can't understand me."

"You shouldn't've aligned yourself with goddamn vamps," he barked.

"You aren't alone, you jerk!" Colin said at the same time.

"Harold," was all Snipe could say.

Jay pulled out the stake and stalked to the overturned cage. Balthazar glared at him with unwavering eyes. He may not have understood his words but he understood his intentions. Maybe he welcomed the sweet release of death after all he'd been through.

"No!"

Harold rushed forward, planting himself in front of Jay. "You can't! It was working, I'm telling you. I just gotta fix the drug and—"

He'd been too close to the cage. Without concerning himself with the consequences, Balthazar stuck his huge arms through the bars and grabbed Harold by the collar. Harold choked as he pulled him back. He tripped into the cage. The vamp sank his teeth in the meat of his shoulder, just below the other wound.

Jay produced his gun and shot the vamp. The silver bullet grazed the left temple. Harold screamed but he was uninjured. The vamp cried out and moved away just enough for Jay to shoot him in the face. He got him in the cheek, which caved in on impact. Blood and saliva leaked out of his face. The vampire stumbled backward, startled.

The pain in his face and feet and arms registered all at once. He went crazy. He threw himself into all sides of the cage. Each time was met with a sizzling sound and more white smoke. Silver couldn't kill vampires but it was supposed to render them weak. This treatment just seemed to make him more enraged.

Snipe picked up a stake from the metal table. Balthazar was blind in his rage, and, possibly, due to a bullet to the face? As he neared one side of the cage, Snipe reached in to grab his upper arm. He jerked Balthazar forward and rammed the stake into his heart. The other vampire, Eugene, had been watching all of this. He cried out now, and ran to the edge of his cage.

Balthazar swatted his hand off him. Snipe grunted when his armpit caught on a bar. Balthazar staggered until he was backed up against the bars, burning himself on the silver. It didn't last long. Small flames actually erupted from his hands and feet and quickly engulfed him. The poison they'd been giving him must've triggered the fire. He screamed terribly; the sound hurt their ears. The smell of burning flesh and hot garbage was overwhelming. They all ran for the stairs, followed by white smoke that hugged the ceiling.

On the main floor, they coughed and coughed as their lungs fought for clean air. Colin closed the basement door. The odor still managed to seep through the cracks. Harold threw open some nearby windows in the living room. Jay spotted a pile of towels on a side table in the hall and snatched them up. He stuffed two along the bottom of the door.

"Not it," he said as he straightened up.

"Not it for what?" Colin asked. He was rubbing his nose as if that would clear it.

"Not the poor fool who'll haveta go down there and make sure Harold still has a fuckin' basement."

"Oh. Me neither!"

"I—I'm sorry, Snipe."

Jay and Colin followed the voice into the living room. Snipe stood in the middle of the room with his arms crossed stiffly. Harold was cowering by a window, staring at Snipe's feet. The blood from the new wound on his shoulder seeped through his striped shirt.

"You could've been seriously injured," Snipe reprimanded. "You and Booth were reckless with this..." He thought of a word. "Project. You should've told me what you were doing."

"That's what I told Booth."

"You're an adult, Harold. Do I have to remind you of that?"

Harold blushed again. His shoulders hunched forward, like he was trying to protect his ears.

"It's too late now for shoulda, coulda, wouldas." He sighed. "Go ahead downstairs and check on the basement. And take care of that other vampire."

Harold jerked his head up suddenly. "But it was working!" he cried. "Snipe, we just need to perfect—"

"No," Snipe said. "We don't use vampires as weapons."

"But they're strong and disposable and—"

"Harold." His tone was final.

Harold nodded somberly then shuffled out the room. The door to the basement opened. There was a loud gasp as he sucked in fresh air, then the door closed. Colin plopped down on the floral sofa and propped his feet up on the wicker coffee table.

Jay looked around at the room. All of the decorations screamed "older female." From white doilies lounging on the back of the sofa to rosy-smelling potpourri in ceramic bowls on the end tables.

"This is Harold's place?" he asked dubiously.

"His mother's out of town," Colin said. "Her sister's sick."

"I guess this is party central," he quipped dryly.

"That's what I said!" A slow smile spread across his face. He was in complete awe. "You know, you were really good down there, man. I don't think I've ever thought that fast."

Jay shrugged modestly. "Comes with experience."

He'd told them his story and had listened to theirs. Colin had been the newest recruit. Senior year of high school, he'd stumbled across a vampire feeding on a teenaged girl under the bleachers in the football field. At first he thought they were just making out, and was going to carry on his merry way. On second glance, however, he saw that something was off about the couple. The guy was sucking hard on her neck. Her head was slumped to the side; her eyes stared off, unfocused.

Colin had picked up a stray football and threw it. The pointed end hit the back of the vampire's head. That normally would've meant certain death. Especially when the vamp hurled a loud growl his way. Lucky for Colin, Snipe and his crew were around to intervene before the vampire could attack.

That was a year and a half ago. Snipe had been impressed by Colin's quick thinking and brought him in, like he'd done with the others. He had been a hunter for the majority of his life. He got his limp from protecting Teddy, his first recruit.

Teddy was being attacked by two vamps when Snipe met him. He was thrown into a guardrail, breaking the femur and tibia of his left leg. It took too long for him to get to a doctor. His tibia never fully mended. While recuperating in the hospital, he figured it was about time to bring on more hands. A little prodding from Lauren helped.

Snipe had been protecting Boston for fifteen years. Somehow, Ramsey's nest had grown under his nose. They didn't keep track of which vampires were local and which were passing through. Procedure was stake-to-the-heart, then breakfast at Snipe's. Jay had pointed that out to Snipe, who'd considered it thoroughly.

"I guess we can mark those two as 'visitors,'" Colin replied with a chuckle. He was referring to the bulletin board in Snipe's living room. They usually wheeled it out before patrolling. It was where they tacked up descriptions and pictures of the vampires they'd come across. Colin took much pleasure in marking red "X"s across the dead ones.

Thanks to Jay, they'd identified three vampires that they figured to be locals: Milo, Arturo, and Trent. A thick "X" marred Trent's face on the board. Jay still didn't explain his ability, no matter how many times they asked how exactly he knew. The origins of this . . . ability were unknown to him. The vampire that attacked his family was the first he'd ever seen and he had glowed as bright as a light bulb.

Harold came back upstairs in a cloud of coughs and odor. "They're gone," he wheezed. He made a path to the window and stuck his head out. "My mom's gonna kill me if the house smells like this when she comes back."

"Would that mean a spanking?" Jay asked. Harold gave him an irritated look. "You guys still up for some patrolling? Didn't you wanna go to that restaurant thing?"

Snipe looked at his watch. It was eleven. "I guess we should. Let's go now."

"Harold," Jay said, putting his hand up when he tried to pass him. "You better change first."

* * *

Victor strolled down the narrow streets of the North End. This was Italian central, home of quality restaurants and the best damn pastries ever. Too bad Victor couldn't partake. The closest he could get to experience a cannoli was by feeding on someone who had just eaten one. He'd be able to taste the sweetness.

Many of the people out tonight were already drunk on food and wine. You could tell in the way they laughed or walked. Victor was getting hungry himself. He'd been out for an hour now with no sign of anyone who could be a hunter.

It was getting late, by human standards that is. The time was almost midnight when Victor turned down a street and stopped at a little library. Lit up by soft white lights, stands of children's artwork were on display in the window. Construction paper filled with colorful handprints. He smiled a little as he imagined the tiny hands wielding paintbrushes.

Someone laughed. Victor had heard their footsteps before they turned the corner. He glanced up the street to see Milo with his arm draped over a girl's shoulders. She stumbled a little, like she was tipsy.

"Careful, now," Victor heard Milo tease. "We don't want you hurting yourself."

"Well," she purred, smiling up at him. "That's what you're here for, right?"

He leaned down to give her a kiss. When he pulled back, he was still staring into her face.

"Victor," he replied. They were only a few feet from him now. The girl looked at Victor. Milo kissed her cheek. He stayed close, inhaling her scent like he was checking for freshness or something.

He smiled at Victor. "What're you doing down here?"

"Nothing in particular," he said. "Aren't you supposed to be on patrol?"

He shrugged casually. "Eh, just taking a break. Shana, here, lives right up there." He nodded over Victor's shoulder to one of the brick buildings.

The girl grinned when they stopped in front of Victor. "I have a roommate," she added with a suggestive lick of her lips.

Victor's eyes were on Milo though. "Ramsey gave you a job," he said tightly.

"Oh, calm down. The hunters will keep."

He kissed the girl again and she giggled. Obviously, she wasn't under his spell because she was a little too... lively. They started to go around Victor when both vamps heard the heavy footsteps turn down the street. Their heads jerked around.

Jay and Colin were together.

"Speak of the devil," Milo replied, loud enough that the hunters heard. "And I was just going to have dinner."

Jay's fists clenched. "Sorry, fellas. Your heartburn's gonna come a little early tonight."

Milo chuckled. Even when the hunters pulled out their stakes, he appeared amused, his arm dangling lazily on Shana. Shana, for her part, looked nervous. Victor planted his feet, ready for an attack. The wind shifted. He received a good whiff of Jay. His eyes widened for a second in recognition, then narrowed in anger.

Fuck the rules, he thought. He rushed at Jay in that lightning speed and knocked him to the ground. Jay's head hit the pavement. His stake skidded away.

Victor punched him twice in the face before Colin realized what was happening. He shoved Victor with his good shoulder. Victor pushed him away, and he stumbled into a parked car.

With the momentary distraction Colin gave, Jay elbowed Victor in the face. When his head jerked back, Jay pushed him and rolled from under him. They were both on their feet in an instant. They sized each other up, waiting to see what the other would do.

Just when it looked like they were going to run at each other, a police siren whooped at the top of the street.

The cruiser slowed and parked. Two officers stepped out. "What's going on, gentlemen?" the older cop asked. His hand was on his holstered gun.

"Just a little misunderstanding," Jay offered, dusting off his pants.

"Let's move it along then."

The officers waited. Jay glared at Victor with as much animosity as he was showing him. Something about that look clued Victor in that Jay knew who he was, Celia-wise. There was more than indignation in his eyes. She'd told him she had a boyfriend. That gave him satisfaction, though you wouldn't be able to tell from looking at him.

Jay stooped down in the guise of fixing his shoe in order to retrieve his stake. He kept it at his side so the officers couldn't see. Jay and Colin walked back the way they came. Victor glanced over his shoulder but Milo and the girl were strolling into a building.

That just left him. The older cop raised an eyebrow. His expression clearly read *we're waiting*. Victor went the way Milo had and crossed the street to head up a different one. He doubled back to find the hunters. The street was deserted.

Eleven

JAY AMBLED BACK to Snipe's living room from the bathroom. It was a little after six the next night. He and Snipe were waiting for Harold and Colin to show up so they could plan out their patrol tonight.

Snipe was sitting in his chair with both Morgan and Jessa in his lap. He stroked their hair as they watched the ending of *SpongeBob*. Jay was trying hard not to throw himself out a closed window. It wasn't his house, he kept telling himself. They had to watch whatever the kids wanted.

At six forty-five, Lauren came through the front door, clad in peach scrubs. Her face was flushed from the heat. It didn't detract from the happiness that lit her up at the sight of her family.

"Hey, guys," she said, walking over to give Snipe and the girls kisses.

"Where's mine?" Jay joked, even though Snipe didn't like that. She ruffled his hair as she passed to the hallway. Ten minutes later, she scooped up Morgan and Jessa.

"Aww, Mommy!" Morgan complained. She hopped down from the seat.

Lauren ignored her oldest. She took their hands in hers. "Did you guys eat?"

"Daddy made mac and cheese," Morgan reported.

"Sounds yummy. I hope you saved me some."

"Nope. It's all in my belly!"

"In your belly?" Lauren exclaimed in mock horror. "Oh no!" She reached down to tickle Morgan before switching off to Jessa. The girls' laughter filled the house. Jay found himself once again wishing for a settled life. He'd even sit through cartoons, he told himself.

Lauren chased the girls out of the room. The water ran in the tub a few moments later. A half hour after that, they bounced back in the room in their nighties to give Snipe goodnight hugs and kisses. Morgan even did the same to Jay. She smelled of lavender.

She giggled and rubbed her cheek when she stepped back. "Your face is scratchy."

He smirked. "Some girls like that."

"Yuck!"

Lauren ushered them off to bed. At seven forty-five, Harold and Colin came through the front door. They looked exhausted. They both plopped down, Colin heaving a satisfied sigh.

"Where've y'all been?" Jay asked.

"We *finally* found that vamp Booth had stashed away," Colin answered. "Dude, she was totally wasted away. It was kinda gross, actually. We've been riding around all day and I'm friggin' tired." He glanced to Snipe, gave him a pleading smile. "Think I can get a quick nap in?"

"Your idea of a nap is two hours," Harold complained.

"So? You rather me falling asleep in the van?"

Harold rolled his eyes. "That's fine, Colin," Snipe said. "I figure we do the regular rounds tonight and that doesn't have to start until ten."

"Cool," Colin said. He pushed himself out of the loveseat and shuffled off to the spare bedroom. Lauren returned, wearing plaid boxer shorts and a white tank top. Harold looked at her, and then immediately averted his eyes. His cheeks flamed under all the scrapes. He was constantly shielding his eyes whenever they were in the same room together, Jay noticed.

Jay, on the other hand, was always one to take in a fine form. Lauren crossed the room to turn on the oscillating fan in the corner. She stood in front of it for a moment, letting the air cool her skin. Wisps of lavender floated on the breeze.

Harold hazarded a glance. Sneaking peeks at Lauren was the only time he didn't look like a neurotic dingbat. Jay saw him watching her, with all the longing in the world, and elbowed him in the ribs. Harold jerked his head to him questioningly. Jay shook his head in admonishment. Harold gave a soft sigh and looked at his lap.

"My sister wants us to visit Saturday," Lauren replied. "There's a carnival in Nahant she wants to take the girls to."

"That's fine," Snipe said. "I need to fix the back windows in the van first. That's a thirty-minute drive to Revere and you know how Jessa gets when it's too hot."

Lauren nodded in agreement. "Poor thing and her heat rashes. She's going to love Nahant. The beach air will do her wonders. I'm glad she's old enough to make the drive."

She walked over to Snipe and sat on his thigh. She draped an arm over his shoulder and caressed his chest.

"How was your day?" Snipe murmured.

She placed her forehead on his temple. "Long," she replied with a sigh. Snipe had his hand under her shirt, massaging her back. She ran her fingers through his hair, which was loose over his shoulders tonight.

"I have something to show you," Lauren said in a husky, let's-get-out-of-here voice.

She took his hand and led him out the room.

"Well," Jay said, getting up. "I guess we have some free time. Wanna get a beer?" He surprised himself because he wouldn't normally hang with Harold alone.

Harold shook his head. "No, thanks." His voice was a little strained.

Jay shrugged. His funeral. He wanted to say something along the lines of Harold being pathetic if he was trying to catch sounds from their bedroom. Instead, he took out his keys and left the house.

* * *

Thursday night, DJ Mickey was spinning. Celia was in a good mood. She bopped and swayed to the music while fielding drink orders. She didn't even care when that one guy copped an attitude with her for not coming to him soon enough. Or when Carson pretended to trip so he could touch her ass. Or when the airhead girl knocked her drinks across the bar the second Celia placed them down. Oh well, she was wearing old sneakers anyways.

Trixie was finishing up her break at twelve-fifty when Celia bounced into the kitchen. She smiled up from her salad. "Seal, this really cute guy asked for my number. And he wasn't even that out of it either."

"Oh yeah?" Celia called as she went to the walk-in for a bottle of water. "He liked your dance moves?"

"I guess so," she said. "I mean, I get hit on all the time by drunken idiots." Celia laughed in agreement. "I'm not looking for anything serious right now, but I could use a little fun."

"Well, do you, girl."

Trixie frowned a little, though she was still smiling. "You're in a good mood."

Celia rolled her eyes playfully. "Why does everyone keep saying that? Like I'm always moody or something."

Trixie shrugged. "It's just nice to see."

"Well, thank you, friend of friends."

She was in a great mood since Victor spent the entire evening with her again the previous night. They had gone out for dinner in Cambridge to keep out of sight of the hunters, though Celia didn't know this. Dessert was at Finale in the Park Plaza Hotel. They played Monopoly later, even though Celia thought the game was boring and too long and didn't know why she even had it in her possession. Since Victor had won, he got her as a prize.

The rest of the night went by smoothly. Rick and Meat had some troubles with a group of guys who didn't want to leave. Bobby threatened to call the police if they didn't get the hell out and they finally did. Bobby had one of the bartenders call them a cab.

Celia and Trixie snagged their paychecks before skipping off to Celia's car. They arrived at Celia's house at two forty-five. To her amazement, she actually found a spot in front of her door.

"Would ya look at that!" she cried from the sidewalk. She stepped back to admire the wonderful spot that had been waiting for her to drive up. "It kinda makes me not want to move it."

Trixie laughed and they went upstairs. Celia opened a bottle of chardonnay that had been chilling in her fridge and laid out some cheese and crackers. They watched an old *Grey's Anatomy* episode—Trixie's choice since Celia had never seen the show. They were talking over it about trivial things, all the while laughing and drinking.

At three forty-five, they danced around the room to a new mix on Celia's iPod. They could play music since Celia's neighbors weren't assholes. They kept it at a respectable level because of the hour.

By four-thirty, Trixie was passed out on the sofa. Her arm lay across her stomach. Her toes grazed the shag carpet, right next to the hole Victor had dug that night. Celia was about to stagger into her room to collapse in bed when her buzzer sounded.

She turned her head in the direction of the door. It took a minute and a second buzz for her brain to tell her legs to move. At the door, she pressed the Talk button and breathed into the intercom.

"Oh," she said when she realized she needed to actually *speak*. "Who is it?" she asked sweetly.

A male's voice answered. "Celia?"

"Hey, that's my name, too!"

He chuckled. "It's Ramsey."

She frowned. "Celia Ramsey? I don't know a Celia Ramsey."

"No, no, brown eyes. This is Ramsey, Victor's friend. Do you remember me?"

She did. "Ramsey! Yay!"

She pressed the Release button, then opened her door to wait. She rocked back and forth on her heels with a huge smile. Ramsey glided up the stairs, looking more like he was riding an escalator. She waved and stepped inside the apartment.

He waited at the threshold. "Ah, Celia," he said lightly, his eyes twinkling. "You have to invite me in."

She covered her mouth and giggled into her hand. "Sorry. Coooooome iiiiiiinnnnnnnn," she crooned, and swept her hand out in a grand gesture.

Through the fogginess in her brain she remembered the first time Victor had come to her place. It was after their fourth date: dinner at the Hong Kong restaurant in Harvard Square. She really liked him. She enjoyed making him laugh. And he smelled good. Like the ocean. They kissed on her stoop. She then shielded her eyes a bit and asked if he wanted to come inside.

"I'd love to," he'd said huskily.

She opened the door and they went to her floor. She stepped inside her apartment but he didn't follow. She frowned back at him.

"Is something wrong?" she asked, and she was amazed that she had been able to keep the sting from her voice.

Victor had given her a crooked grin and leaned on the doorjamb, his hands in his pockets. "May I come in?"

She put a hand on her hip with an incredulous sigh. "I thought I said that already."

"Say it again."

She rolled her eyes but she was smiling. "Come in, fine sir, if you please."

They'd made love for the first time on the floor just inside her door.

Ramsey looked around, surveying her and the room. His eyes lingered on Trixie a moment.

"Hmm," he said, and a smile touched his face. "Did I miss the party?"

The alcohol was making her stare at him with that silly smile. Normally, she wouldn't look him in the eye too long, something Victor had taught her. It made it too easy for vampires to use their magic, though he'd done that already, huh?

She was taking in his sandy hair and how outdoorsy it made him look, especially with the stubble. He had nice lips, as well. Small, but not too small where you'd be kissing the skin under his nose.

Ramsey grew serious again. "I need your help, brown eyes."

She put her hand to her heart in surprise and gratitude. "Really?"

His gaze went to Trixie again, as if making sure she was actually asleep. When he seemed satisfied, he turned back to Celia. "Your friend, the hunter. I need to meet with him."

She gasped, horrified. “Oh, no no no, you mustn’t.” She lowered her voice to a loud whisper. “He would kill you.”

Ramsey nodded, amusement shining in his eyes. “I ’preciate your concern. I just wanna talk to them. Would you be able to set up a meeting for me?”

She shrugged. She already forgot why she’d been upset. “Sure. You can go for ice cream.”

Ramsey chuckled. “I see why Victor enjoys your company so.” He went to her coffee table and picked up a little spiral notebook. He scribbled his phone number on a clean sheet.

“Have a good night.”

Celia walked him out, then trudged off to bed.

The next morning, Celia woke around eleven. She groaned from the pounding in her head. She didn’t want to move but she knew she needed to. Eventually, she tossed the sheet aside and stumbled into the bathroom. She swallowed two aspirins and ducked her head under the faucet to drink.

When she straightened, the reflection of someone in the mirror standing just behind her made her shriek. She clutched her chest. Her heart beat against her hand.

“Dammit, Trixie!” she cried. “You scared the shit out of me.”

“It’s a good thing you’re already in the bathroom,” she muttered as she stepped inside. Her hair and clothes were tousled, her eyes squinting. She took the bottle of aspirin from her hand and shook out two pills. She copied Celia’s drinking from the faucet then pushed her out the bathroom so she could use the toilet.

Celia went to the kitchen to find something for breakfast. She was frying eggs and bacon when Trixie called out from the living room, “Who’s Ramsey?”

“What?” Celia called back. She hadn’t heard what she said

over the grease popping in the pan.

Trixie entered the kitchen. "I said who is Ramsey?"

Celia glanced over her shoulder with a confused expression. "Why do you ask that?"

She held up the little notebook. Celia's frown deepened. She fought through the haze of last night in an effort to recall where that had come from. Disjointed images popped in her head of Ramsey coming up the stairs, of him standing in her living room. But she couldn't remember what he had asked her.

Trixie cleared her throat to get Celia's attention back. "I think he stopped by last night," Celia said. "He's a friend of Victor's."

Trixie's face stiffened. "A friend *like* Victor?"

"Don't worry; he didn't sniff you or anything." She went back to the pan. "I don't think," she added under her breath.

They ate swiftly, stopped off at Trixie's place so she could change then headed out to the mall. Celia bought a pair of gold hoop earrings from Claire's. They both bought gauzy scarves in H&M—Celia's orange, Trixie's purple. Trixie poked her head into the Verizon store to say hello to a guy named Lee while Celia smelled fragrances in Victoria's Secret.

At three, she dropped Trixie off then drove to her aunt and uncle's house for a quick visit. Her uncle was there. He had been under the weather and was working from home, which mainly entailed ordering supplies for his flower shop.

After heating up chicken noodle soup for him, Celia went to the grocery store to pick up a few items before heading home. The sky was turning purple as she drove to her apartment. She had just showered and was pulling out her Kabuki brush to start her makeup when a soft, tinkling sound made her step out of her bedroom.

Victor held her tiny gold bell between his fingers. Her aunt had given her the souvenir after a trip to Philly. Victor wiggled his eyebrows at the bell. Celia laughed then rushed over to give him a long, deep kiss.

He groaned when she pulled away. “What’re you doing to me?” he complained halfheartedly. She was only wearing her kimono robe and she knew it wasn’t leaving much to the imagination at the moment since she was still a bit damp. She glanced at the time on the cable box.

“If you don’t mess up my hair, I’ve got twenty minutes,” she said with a sly smirk. He lifted her like she weighed nothing. She wrapped her legs around his waist. He was already planting kisses on her neck as he carried her to the bed.

As she commanded, Victor did not touch her hair. She straddled his middle, her robe still cinched with one boob peeking out. Victor gripped her waist. He directed her movements, moving her hips in wide then tiny circles. She went with his flow. He arched his hips upward, rubbing against her, making her shudder.

Her breath escaped in little gasps. Victor’s breathing was even but she heard his soft moans. She quivered all over. She came before he did; she felt like she was floating high above the bed. When she slowly drifted back to him, she let her head fall to his chest. He chuckled a little, his chest vibrating against her cheek.

“Okay,” she said in a gasp of air. “I need to get dressed.”

He borrowed her slang. “Wow, it’s like that?”

She rolled off him, careful with her hair. She had blow-dried it and given herself loose curls that she prayed would last through the night. Victor laid on his side with a lazy grin, watching her pull on bright pink underwear, black shorts and a black cami under a sheer, black top. He was always amazed at how much black she owned.

“Ramsey stopped by last night,” she said, somewhat distractedly as she stared down at her shoes.

"Why?" Victor's voice was suddenly tight.

"Trixie and I got shitfaced so I have no idea. I was hoping you knew." She cocked her head to the side for a second as a thoughtful look crossed her face. "Unless he was planning a surprise party for you, in which case, I just fucked it all up."

She looked at him regretfully. "I'm sorry . . ." The words died on her lips. Victor was standing now, so enraged, he was trembling. Tiny prickles of fear rippled down her back.

"Victor?"

"He came to you?" he asked. Disbelief and anger strangled his words.

"Nothing happened," she said a little too defensively. He didn't notice. He shook his head a couple times. Then without so much as a goodbye, he vanished.

Celia blinked a few times. She didn't have much time to contemplate it all because she was going to be late. She slid her feet into black sneakers, grabbed her purse and hurried out the house, wishing, not for the first time, that she could teleport like Victor.

* * *

Any pleasure from being with Celia had evaporated like a puff of smoke at the mention of Ramsey. Victor could not believe he went behind his back. And while he had been out patrolling with Milo and Bryce for him.

Victor appeared in Ramsey's hallway, startling a woman passing through in a bikini. Seeing his fierce gaze, she hurried into the living room. Quickly, he became aware of the music, voices and heartbeats coming from the room. There were about fifteen of them, overlapping and pulsing in unison. That stalled him.

Victor walked to the doorway. Female and male humans were clustered around the room. They were drinking and talking, all clad in swimwear. The woman from the hall looked to her friend then pointed surreptitiously to Victor.

There were no vampires in the room. Victor continued on, checking in the kitchen and other rooms as he passed. He went upstairs and knocked on Ramsey's door but there was no answer.

From the bottom of the stairs, Milo's voice rang out. "The pool's nice and warm. Let's take this party outside."

Whoops of enthusiasm followed his announcement. The people tagged along like a herd of cattle to the sliding door in the kitchen that led out back. Victor trailed silently behind.

Josiah and Bryce were in swim trunks on the edge of the pool. The entirety of Josiah's chest was etched with different drawings, mostly depictions of old-school Asian monks doing karate. They had bald heads like Josiah and long, thin mustaches. There was a story within the drawings, of the progression of the monks as they learned the complexities and the art of karate. The colors blended and mixed with the black. It was all very intricate, like a painting that stretched up to his jaw.

Bryce's chest was just . . . muscular. Yum.

Bryce stared hungrily at the people as they neared the pool. Annie and Clarice lounged on chaises in cute string bikinis with ruffles on the bottoms. Clarice wore round, Chanel shades as if the sun was out. Her dark hair was as long as Annie's only she had hers pulled back into a bun. She was examining her blood-red nail polish until she noticed Victor. Well, she smelled him and, boy, how she loved his smell.

Clarice was on her feet and floating to him before he had taken two steps out of the kitchen.

"Victor," she purred. She removed her shades, revealing almond-brown eyes. "Where's your human? She was cute."

He didn't want to tangle with her. "Where's Ramsey?"

"Out. Why do you think we're having this little get-together?" She waved her hand over her shoulder, indicating the revelers. Splashes and laughter filled the air as people jumped into the pool.

"Do you know where he is?"

She shook her head and stared up at him through her lashes. "Why don't you stay for a drink?"

She touched his cheek. The pull of her persuasion—the magic that even worked on vampires—worked toward his brain. He started to relent. Of course he wanted to stay and take part in the . . . festivities.

"You haven't fed yet," she said. She was right, he hadn't. His hunger magnified, since she mentioned it. His gums throbbed as his fangs lengthened.

Some part of him that hadn't weakened yet from her touch made him remove her hand before the power took control of his brain. The motion broke the spell. He'd learned years ago, when he first arrived to the area, how to discern when she was using her magic. Of course, she'd trapped him a few times before he wised up, but never since.

"No, that's okay. I'll figure something out later."

"Victor, don't be a buzzkill. Come on, relax a little with us."

He really had no desire to relax with them. He knew what these little parties became after the vampires mixed in. He wasn't in the mood.

"I need to find Ramsey."

She pouted. He ignored her and vanished. Ramsey frequented a club on Washington Street, downtown, called Felt. It wasn't too far from Cage's; it shared a block with the Boston Opera House and a Hyatt. Ramsey liked to watch the people play pool. Sometimes he'd even join in. He took great pleasure in out-hustling the hustlers.

Victor appeared in an alley one street over. He was wearing black slacks and a hunter-green dress shirt that Celia had wrinkled. It didn't look bad enough to be turned away. The green normally made his gray eyes stand out, however, they were black at the moment.

He paid the cover and went to the lounge on the fourth floor. It was only nine-thirty. Most of the patrons occupied the lower floors, playing billiards and drinking at the bar. Two humans sat at the bar, talking with the bartender. A Sara Bareilles song played softly from the speakers in the ceiling. He found Ramsey tucked into a booth in the far corner.

Victor slid in across from him. He didn't even need to say anything; his heated glare was enough. Ramsey nodded in concession.

"I'm sorry. But we were getting nowhere with the canvassing. I don't want anyone else to die."

Victor shook his head stoutly. "You had no right."

Ramsey raised his hand. "I'm doing what I can to protect us." His tone wasn't really apologetic any more.

Victor stared at him as he attempted to see things from his point of view. Ramsey was trying to stop this before it steamrolled into a battle for territory. These hunters had tricks up their sleeves and wouldn't go away easy. Besides, Ramsey liked his life. He was able to have a home and a family here. He enjoyed mingling with the humans. They kept him grounded, helped him retain his humanness. He didn't want to upset the balance he'd finally gained.

Victor sighed, relenting. "I'll talk to Celia about setting something up. For future reference," he added with a smirk. "Don't expect her to remember anything if she's been drinking."

Ramsey smiled. "Good to know."

Twelve

IT WAS ONE pm on Sunday and Jay was thinking of Celia. He didn't feel bad for taking her to the morgue, just for the way they had ended things. He didn't think she would want to see him so he was completely surprised when she called.

"Jay? It's Celia." Her tone was businesslike.

"Oh," was all he said. He kept his tone bland to disguise the thrill that went through him at the sound of her voice. "What can I do for you?"

"I was, uh, wondering if you could meet my boyfriend."

He couldn't believe his ears. In fact, he stared slack-jawed at the ceiling. He was laying on the futon in his boxers, sweating it out in the basement.

"Jay? You still there?"

He chuckled in amazement. He decided not to mention that if he hadn't been interrupted in the North End, there wouldn't *be* a boyfriend for him to meet.

"Why do you want me to meet your boyfriend?"

"They want to talk with you. You and the other hunters."

He didn't like this professional tone at all. It made it sound like they didn't really know each other. Like she hadn't climbed into his lap on the swing that sunny day.

"Can I set something up?" she asked.

"Sure. How about Starbucks in an hour?"

He heard her sigh through the line. "There's a little park on Adams Street in Dorchester. Across from the Cedar Grove cemetery. Ten o'clock okay with you?"

"What do they want?"

"I don't know for sure."

"What do you know not for sure?" he pressed.

She groaned. "They just wanna talk to you guys, okay?"

His gaze narrowed. "So, we're just supposed to walk into a possible ambush with our fuckin' dicks in our hands?"

"God, you can be so infuriating!" she cried. "They want to *talk*. You know, to hopefully squash all this fighting. Are you gonna go or not?"

He sat quietly for a moment, just to drag it out. He could nearly see her aggravation, as if she were standing there in front of him.

"I guess so."

"Jay," she said, her voice suddenly softening. "Promise me something. Promise me you won't hurt Victor."

"Is there any particular reason why you're asking me that? You expectin' a fight?"

"With you, who knows?" She paused, waiting. "Well?"

His jaw clenched. He could barely get the words out. "I don't think I can make that promise."

"Please?" Her voice was tiny in his ear, pleading, breaking through his resolution. He hated that he was relenting. He couldn't even fight it.

He'd been silent for a full minute. "Jay?"

"Fine," he sighed.

That lifted her spirits slightly. "And you think you can find the park?"

"I'm sure the others will know where it is," he grumbled, completely irritated now. "Unless *you* wanna take me."

There was a pause. "I'm not going," she said. He picked up on the note of frustration in her words.

"Well, I'm not going if you're not," he said immediately.

"What?"

"Like I said before, I'm not walking into a goddamn ambush."

She huffed. "Victor doesn't want me to go. He didn't even want me to be the one making this phone call but I said I had to."

"And for that same reason, you need to be at that park at ten," he said brusquely. She was quiet again. "You tell your boyfriend he can forget about it unless you're there."

"Why are making this more difficult—?"

His answer was the click of the phone.

***

It took some convincing and a little bit of yelling but Victor finally relented to letting Celia go to the meeting. She had still been in her work clothes. Now she rushed to her bedroom to change. She could hear Victor on his phone in the living room, though he spoke too low for her to make out any words.

"What to wear to a meeting between vampires and hunters?" she muttered under her breath while riffling through her dresser.

"Baggy jeans and an equally baggy sweater," Victor answered from the other room.

Celia threw an irritated glare at the door for his eavesdropping. She pulled on a pair of jeans and a pink t-shirt. She was tying her hair into a ponytail as she walked out into the living room. Victor gave her a once-over.

He looked so on edge. She stepped up to him and gave him a

kiss. It was a small gesture but she hoped it helped soothe him. He held her to his body with his strong arms. A warm smile touched his face. She couldn't help but respond in kind.

The smile disappeared. "I'm sorry for this," he replied after a pause.

She shook her head, ready to protest that she was okay with helping them settle things with the hunters. That this was a good thing. That he didn't need to apologize.

The words never formed. A fierce iciness radiated from his body. It crashed into her like a sub-zero tidal wave and she lost her breath. She knew this feeling. She just didn't have time to brace herself as everything but Victor's remorseful face shifted and changed around them.

Suddenly, they were outside. The tidal wave relapsed, replaced with sticky heat from the summer night. Celia could only gasp as air suddenly filled her lungs. Her knees went weak but Victor held her up. Her head was spinning. She closed her eyes.

"Breathe," he coaxed, which only made her angry. Like she needed to be told to fucking breathe.

She pushed against him. At first he wouldn't let go, afraid that she might fall. When he did, she staggered a few feet away, toward the small, well-worn baseball diamond. Getting angry only made her head spin more. She bent over, panting in deep breaths. Her mouth was dry. She carried herself over to the water fountain. Normally, she would never drink from a public fountain in the middle of a park. Tonight, she sucked down the water as quickly as she could.

She didn't hear the other vampires approach. Everything was quiet, save for her slurping, and then suddenly someone was speaking.

"What's up with her?" She recognized Milo's voice.

"She just needs a moment," Victor said, his voice going all

rigid again. "Are they here yet?"

"No." That was Ramsey.

When Celia felt herself again, she straightened up. She had dribbled water down the front of her shirt. She used her hand to wipe at it ineffectively.

When she turned, she saw five vampires standing in a semicircle where she had left Victor. Puffy white clouds were scattered across the night sky. The silver moon shone through, lighting the park around them. The guys had their arms crossed at the chest. All of them looked serious and fully alert. Celia took a last deep breath and trudged over.

All of their eyes were on her, which was incredibly unnerving. Her every movement was processed under those intense glares.

She gulped and stood at Victor's side. He put an arm around her, pulling her closer. After a second, he glanced down at her with a puzzled frown. She must've been trembling.

"Celia," he said, then motioned around the circle. "This is Bryce, Annie, and Elizabeth."

Her eyes roamed across them quickly. Bryce unfolded his arms and cracked his neck with his introduction. She remembered him from the fight at Cage's. Annie's long blonde hair glistened in the moon. She wasn't wearing a baseball cap tonight but her white sneakers were spotless. Elizabeth waved amiably. Celia's eyes were drawn to her pale pink maxi dress that was cinched at the waist with a matching belt. It was very pretty, very seventies' chic like her other ensembles.

"You know Ramsey and Milo."

"Someone's coming," Milo said. Their eyes went to the street.

Celia stared in the same direction though she could not distinguish one car from the many others traveling down the main road of Gallivan Boulevard, about half a mile away. As she stared off, she realized something. This park was only three blocks away from her old house. She had chosen it because it was quiet and a bit secluded—the nearby houses didn't have a good view of the park. Now that she realized her family was so close, she started to worry. How could she have been so careless?

A few cars rode down Adams Street. The only one to slow and pull over was a black van. It parked at the curb. The occupants hopped out. Jay had been in the passenger's seat. Celia stiffened at the sight of them. They looked almost as intimidating as the vampires with that professional air about them. She wondered if they were packing. Then she rolled her eyes because *of course* they'd have weapons. She remembered Jay's mini-arsenal that day in the park.

Victor's hand tightened on her shoulder. The four hunters approached the group. The vampires kept their positions in the semi-circle. Only Ramsey and Milo stepped forward to greet them. Well, Milo was acting more as bodyguard. His body was crouched slightly, ready to pounce. How that was possible in those skinny jeans was a bit of a mystery.

The hunters stopped a good distance away, leaving plenty of space between but they could still talk without yelling.

"Hello," Ramsey said immediately.

Snipe nodded. Celia's eyes drifted to Jay. He wore baggy brown cargo pants and a khaki shirt. His hair was getting longer, she noticed. He must not have had a chance for a cut. His expression was harsh under the stubble. How could he look so attractive when he appeared so extremely angry?

He examined the vampires as Ramsey and Snipe made introductions. He caught Celia staring at him and she thought she saw his jaw tighten more. She looked away.

"This is Jay," was all Snipe offered up about him. He didn't waste any time. "Now, what's the cause for this meeting?"

Ramsey took a breath. "I was hoping to speak with y'all before there's any more bloodshed. We've all lost these past few weeks. I wanted you to see we aren't a threat."

There was a snort from the hunters. Bryce growled in response. It was so guttural that even though he wasn't standing directly beside her, Celia could feel it penetrate to her bones. Annie placed a hand on his arm warningly.

The only hunter who seemed fazed was Harold. His hand jerked to his side, making Celia nervous. Was he reaching for a gun or stake? Was it there now or was the gesture only instinctual?

Celia was certain that if she had noticed the movement, the vampires had also. Nevertheless, no one acknowledged it and Harold had already removed his hand from his hip.

"We've had five bodies show up, drained of blood," Jay piped crossly. "How do you explain that?"

This was news to Ramsey. You could tell because his back stiffened. He kept his eyes on the hunters.

His voice was flat when he responded with, "Everyone makes mistakes."

"Yeah, but how many people *die* because of a mistake?" Jay spat at him.

"Plenty," Celia said before she realized what she was doing. She didn't appreciate Jay's attitude. "Stop being all high-and-mighty."

Oh, if looks could kill. Celia would've toppled over from the one Jay turned on her. Victor didn't like the look either. From the sound of his growl, she wondered if his fangs were out.

"Celia," Jay said in a cool voice, ignoring the others. "Nice to see which side you're on."

"There doesn't have to be sides—"

Abruptly, Victor pulled her back. He stood between them now, picking up Jay's furious stare. Celia had to peek around him.

"Are you asking for a truce?" Snipe said, not shielding his

disdain.

"Of sorts, yes," Ramsey replied.

"We don't hunt you . . . and you keep drinking from innocent people? Where's the balance in that?"

Ramsey sighed. "We don't have to . . . use the people in the city," he said in an offhanded way.

Harold shook his head in disagreement. Jay looked at Snipe, his disgust as plain as day. Some of the vampires shifted at this prospect.

"We don't kill people, whether you believe that or not. And we don't turn anyone. Those were my rules from the very start." He was directing that to his own as well, judging by the sharpness of his tone.

Harold was getting all fidgety again. Celia frowned at him, then to where he was staring. Bryce pulled away from Annie and had been slowly inching forward. It appeared she hadn't wanted to cause a scene by gripping his arm. She was watching him like a hawk.

Harold's hand went to his side again. This time she saw the gun holstered at his hip.

Everything happened so fast.

Bryce's shoulders hunched forward. Annie ran to his side but he had already taken off in a run at Harold. A gunshot rang out and Celia screamed. Annie dropped to the ground, mid-stride. Her body convulsed violently.

Bryce stopped his stampede when he heard her grunts. "Annie!" he shouted and rushed to her side. Celia looked to the hunters. It had been Colin who'd fired. He still held his gun in the air.

Milo jumped at Colin, his teeth snapping. Ramsey lunged at him, too, only to control Milo. Colin cried out from surprise and his injured shoulder. Milo had him by the neck, with his teeth bared and ready. He had moved too quickly for the other hunters to get to him. Ramsey was closer. He snaked his arm around Milo's chest. He pulled him away just as he was leaning in to bite. Victor was at his side in a flash, tugging Milo's arms. The both of them wrestled him off as Snipe and Jay ran over.

Celia's eyes were wide in terror. She had been gripping Victor's shirt. When he left so suddenly, she stumbled forward. She looked over to Annie. Her convulsions were slowing. Elizabeth was doing . . . something. Celia thought she was taking her vitals from the way she was touching her neck and wrists. She hadn't known it was possible to take a vampire's vitals.

Snipe snatched the gun from Colin. "Put that away," he snapped at Harold, who was standing stock still with his gun pointed at Bryce.

Bryce rose to his feet. "What did you do to her?" he demanded.

Victor released Milo, who was still thrashing against them, trying to have at Colin. He vanished and appeared in front of Bryce, with his hands on his chest. Bryce pushed his hands away but Victor put them back.

"She'll be fine," Colin grumbled, almost too low for Celia to hear. "It was just one shot."

Victor was straining under the effort to keep Bryce back. "Bryce, man, calm down."

He jerked his hands away for the tenth time. "Get the fuck outta my way, Victor," Bryce growled.

"Bryce—"

Swiftly, he shoved Victor to the side and he went flying. Celia gasped. She instinctually took a step toward them but her fear got the better of her. She froze, her hands covering her mouth. Victor rolled on the ground then sprang to his feet.

Bryce barreled toward Harold. Harold fired. Bryce kept going. Harold had to shoot three times before Bryce's steps faltered. He panted and clutched his stomach where the last bullet had hit.

Bryce looked down, then grasped something. He held it up. In the illumination the moon provided, Celia saw that it was actually a dart with a small red flag or something on the end. Bryce sank to his knees and fell onto his side.

An eerie silence cloaked the park. Everyone stared at Bryce, the huge football player, dropped by a couple of darts. The vamps turned their stony gazes on the hunters. Jay and Snipe stood up, Jay with his chest thrust out. Colin stood behind them, cradling his sore shoulder with a grimace on his young face.

Snipe raised the gun he had taken from Colin. He then nudged Colin, who was closest, and indicated the van. They moved cautiously. Jay had his stake out. Harold stumbled as he rushed to his group, his tranq gun still pointed at the vamps.

No one said a word as the hunters picked their way to the park opening. The vamps must've been holding off because of Ramsey. They'd need his go-ahead.

Snipe kept his gun trained on the vampires as they climbed into the van. The engine revved and the tires squealed. Snipe whipped the van into a U-turn. Celia got one last glimpse of Jay's contemptuous face.

Elizabeth, furious, ran by Celia in a flash of pink and brown. The wind she stirred up made Celia's ponytail sweep into her face.

"Elizabeth!" Ramsey called.

She jumped over the stonewall that stood about four feet tall, enclosing the park. She stopped in front of the van, her face pale in the headlights. Snipe slammed on the brakes. Elizabeth jerked her arm back and punched the grill. A loud metallic crunch permeated the air from the hood rippling. White smoke rose from underneath it. Luckily, Snipe had stopped with enough distance to prevent a ton of damage.

Elizabeth glowered at the humans in the van, making sure

they got the message, before she slowly extracted her arm. Blood dripped from her elbow to her fist. She walked to the sidewalk with her shoulders squared, her pink dress fluttering around her ankles. The van started off again. Something was clicking under the hood now. Elizabeth kept her controlled pace until she came back to the park, where she went to Bryce.

"What the hell was that?" Milo exploded. "Why didn't you *do* anything?" He was yelling at Ramsey, who had been staring at his fallen vamps. Ramsey threw him a harsh glare. Milo shut the hell up.

"There's no time for this," Victor said. He placed a hand on Elizabeth, then pointed to Annie. She nodded, understanding his silent command. She scooped Annie up in her arms then took off in a run across the street. She easily vaulted over the rusted fence of the cemetery and disappeared into the darkness.

Victor pulled Bryce into his chest as best he could. He looked at Ramsey. "Get her outta here." He gave Celia a last look before vanishing with Bryce. Just as they melted into thin air, sirens began to build in the distance.

Ramsey crossed to Celia and held out his hand. She was too shaken to move. She stared at his hand like it was some foreign object. Ramsey walked up to her slowly, so as not to spook her. His strong hand took her left bicep and gracefully whipped her onto his back. She didn't even have time to understand what was happening until it happened.

She wrapped her legs tightly around his waist and her arms around his neck to ensure she wouldn't slide off. He nodded to Milo and then they were off. He was moving fast but his legs pumped smoothly, like a marathon runner. The night air slapped her face. Her eyes watered. She squeezed them shut and buried her face in his back. She didn't know how he could navigate at this speed but then she stopped concerning herself with that and instead on keeping her heart from bursting her eardrums.

After two minutes, she became aware of Ramsey slowing down. She peeked out the corner of her eye but couldn't tell where they were. The houses and streets were still a blur.

He finally came to a stop. She clung to him like a cat. He walked up steps. She caught a glimpse of the white pillars and the ornate black door before they went inside.

"Celia."

That was Victor's smooth voice. Her muscles instantly relaxed. She felt his hands on her arms, gently coaxing them free. She thought she was going to fall backward to the floor but Victor caught her. He carried her in his arms to the living room, where he sat on one of the sofas, cradling her like a baby.

He stroked her hair as he waited for her to get it together. After a moment, Celia shifted. He placed her on the sofa beside him. They were alone in the room, which was comforting. She didn't want people thinking that was a normal thing they do, like she always needed to be cradled. Although it was the second time it happened in a month . . .

Celia rubbed her face, exhausted. "That didn't go so well, huh?" she muttered through her fingers.

Victor didn't say anything, just rubbed her back. It felt nice. His hand took her away for the moment. She didn't have to recall Annie's body jerking in quick spasms. Or Bryce being shot point-blank.

Tiny moans escaped her. Victor nudged her after a minute. She groaned because he stopped. She lifted her head, ready to question him, when she realized that Ramsey and Milo had entered the room. They might as well be ninjas they were so quiet. Ramsey looked murderous. Milo was smirking a little. He had obviously enjoyed the little noises she had been making.

Milo sat in the loveseat that was positioned next to the sofa. He crossed his legs, his right ankle resting on his left knee. Draping his arms across the back of the sofa, he openly leered at

Celia.

She felt like a piece of meat under his stare. It must've been all the excitement from earlier, she figured. He was probably looking to release that and she was the only live thing around at the moment.

That was no excuse, mind you. She scowled at him.

The bad news: she had looked him in the eye too long. He was drawing her in. His pull was different, though. There were no niceties or warm, tingly feelings. By contrast, it was as if an invisible rope had just encased her body like a snake—an itchy, constricting snake. It tugged her forward. She didn't want to go. Usually that was enough to get her out. This time it didn't work. She was confused and scared and her mental struggling was making her dizzy. Her thighs tightened as her body tried to stand. Her heart rate jacked up a notch when she felt herself lifting up from the cushion.

Victor's hand cupped her knee subconsciously; he probably noticed her anxiety. It was enough to break the spell. The rope was gone. Or perhaps Milo released her. She blinked at him, not quite certain it was over. He tilted his head, fascinated, like he'd just received a positive reaction to a scientific experiment.

She looked away quickly, relieved she hadn't done anything inappropriate. That's just what they needed, another fight.

She didn't like Milo, she decided. And she couldn't believe he just tried enthralling her right in front of Victor.

Victor, for his part, hadn't noticed because he was watching Ramsey. "Elizabeth said Bryce and Annie will be okay," he said consolingly.

Ramsey shook his head. It looked like an entire conversation was roiling through him but he wouldn't let it come out.

"She doesn't know what drug was in that dart they shot Annie with but she's stable. She'll probably be out of it for a little while," Victor continued. He must have just been talking to help

Ramsey calm down since Elizabeth had more than likely already updated him. Or maybe he was saying it for Celia's benefit.

"And there was Dead Man's Blood along with a tranquilizer in the darts used on Bryce."

"Do you think they actually had any intention of making a pact?" Celia asked. She turned her head so that she couldn't see Milo.

"I don't know," Victor answered since Ramsey still seemed too tight to form words. He looked at her. He must've seen the disappointment in her face. He cupped her cheek and rubbed his thumb under her eye.

"What are you guys going to do?" she whispered.

"Take their heads off," Milo growled. She didn't dare look at him. She could hear the hunger in his voice. That did not sit well with her. He could be an asshole, but she didn't want Jay to get hurt or worse.

She figured that maybe she could talk to him. Maybe she could convince the hunters to back off. She looked from Victor to Ramsey.

"Are you really going after them?" she asked anxiously.

Again, Victor answered, though not with what she wanted to hear. "Celia, it's getting late."

She shook her head fiercely at the brush off. "No, Victor. I want to know."

"We don't know anything just yet," Victor said gently. "It's probably best if you go home. You're already more involved than I ever wanted."

She glared at him as a realization sank in. "You think I might tell them," she accused. "You think I'm gonna call them and tell them what you're planning!"

She bolted up from her seat. Anger and disbelief sent shockwaves through her. Victor sighed. "I already told you I don't want you any more involved."

"That's bullshit!"

"Hey, I say use the little lady," Milo replied in a lazy tone. "She can tell us where to find those grimy fuckers. They can't just get away with what they did."

"Bryce started it!"

"They were able to walk away. Let her help, Victor. She wants to be of service."

She darted him a hostile look. "Why don't I show them where to find *you*? That would rid the world of a huge nuisance."

The room was suddenly very still. Even Milo looked at her more seriously. She glanced at Ramsey, who was surveying her, then Victor. After a moment, he and Ramsey exchanged a look she didn't understand.

Victor stood in front of Celia and held her shoulders with both hands. There was sadness, reluctance to his expression. She looked into his eyes. Suddenly, she was melting. Like her bones had vanished and she was just ooze in his hands.

The blackness of his eyes expanded and surrounded her, closing off all sound in its wake. Victor was gone, too, and now she was scared. Time stretched on. The bleak blackness held her in its grip for an eternity. It made her nauseous and claustrophobic. She couldn't move. She didn't know where to go.

Then it just . . . lifted. She blinked a few times as her eyes focused on her surroundings. She was in her bedroom, that she knew. The cushiony fiber bed under her sheet, her light comforter around her waist, they were all familiar.

The lamp on her nightstand casted a yellow glow on the room. She frowned because she thought she had been with Victor. The image of him standing in front of her was hazy at best. Was it a dream? Did she miss the meeting at the park?

Her eyes darted to the alarm clock. It was nearly midnight. She gasped, then snatched up her cell phone. She called Victor but there was no answer.

"Victor, what happened? I think I fell asleep. Did you all meet tonight? Please call me."

She closed the phone and held it in her hand for a moment. This was like the next day after drinking with Trixie. She could feel that things had happened; she just couldn't quite remember what.

The thing was, she knew she hadn't been drinking tonight. She'd gone to work at Cage's. Her shift had ended at five, a little later than usual because she had to cover for Maria, who had had trouble getting a babysitter in time for the start of her shift. She came home, made dinner. She could even smell the fresh cotton candle she had burned to combat the fried chicken odor that usually clung to everything.

After that was a blank. Kind of like a hole. That made her nervous. And the more she thought about it, the more alarmed she became. She wondered if she'd been drugged somehow. Had someone broken into her home?

She flung the covers off and rushed to the main apartment. The moon pooled onto the floor through the thin curtains on her windows. The AC swished on the softest setting. The cool air made her shiver. Or was it dread?

The room was empty. She flicked on a light and went to the door. All of the locks were where they were supposed to be.

She checked the windows. The living room was closed tight. There were none in the kitchen. She moved on to the bathroom. As she pushed the door open, a warm breeze skirted her ankles. Her heart immediately accelerated. She stared at the curtain fluttering gently in the night wind.

She ran over and shut the window. Alarmed, she turned on lights, checking for any signs of a stranger in her home. She went through every single inch of her place. She lived on the second floor of her building and the fire escape was outside the other window in her living room, the one without the AC. Short of

Spiderman, no one would be able to sneak into her apartment windows. Unfortunately, that bit of logic didn't penetrate her panic.

She came back to her room and dialed Trixie's cell phone. She was greeted with a lot of commotion on her end, loud talking and metal clanging. Someone shouted for more Bud Lights to the bar.

"Trixie," Celia breathed before she could even answer. "I think someone broke into my house."

"What?" she said, alarmed. "Why do you say that?"

"My bathroom window was open and I can't remember what happened to me after I got home. I think someone drugged me."

"Do you feel sluggish or tired?"

She thought for a second. "No, not really."

"Do you have a headache or a bump on your head? Like if you were hit with something?"

She ran a hand over her head. Normal. "No," she whispered.

"Um, I don't think it was a roofie," she said contemplatively. "I don't know, Seal. Do you want to call the police?"

She bit her bottom lip. "I don't know. What if I'm wrong? What if I just fell asleep?"

"Possibly. Do you have any bruises or pain?"

She did another mental examination. No, no pain anywhere, not even down there. She sighed. "I must've fallen asleep. But why wouldn't Victor wake me? We were supposed to go somewhere tonight."

"Well, you are so incredibly cute when you're asleep," Trixie teased, trying to lighten the mood.

It worked for the most part because the tension in Celia's back and shoulders receded. "Yeah, I'm sure drool is *such* a turn-on."

Trixie stayed on the phone with her for another minute before she had to get back to the front door. The restaurant was closing in a few, meaning the delicate process of shooing people from the premises needed to commence.

Celia sat on the edge of her bed. She wanted to call Victor again but figured he was with the other vampires. She didn't want to disturb him. She climbed back into bed, leaving the light on.

Thirteen

THE NEXT MORNING, Jay stood by, watching Snipe tinker under the hood of the black van. He and Jay had already banged out the sides and hood, making it somewhat straight. The hood was able to close, which was about all they could ask for. At least they wouldn't have to drive in fear of it flapping back against the windshield.

Currently, Snipe was putting a hurting on a bolt in an effort to loosen it. The wrench slipped, making a clanging noise. His knuckle hit on something sharp.

"Shit," he grumbled, the first time Jay had ever heard him swear. He pulled his hand from under the hood. A nasty cut sliced the hills of his knuckle. It was only red at first, then blood bubbled to the surface, as if his body had needed a second to get over the shock of the injury. Jay tossed him a rag from the bench he was leaning against. Snipe blotted it on the cut before wrapping it around his knuckles.

He was already pissed. The cut seemed to really set him off.

He even kicked a stool over in his aggravation. Jay watched the metal stool fly into the side of the van—leaving a small dent to add to the collection—then clatter loudly to the cement ground.

The garage was quiet. A sedan passed on the street. The brakes squealed when it slowed at the corner.

"Jay," he said after a moment. He was looking at his rag. "There's no way in hell I'm going to agree to any kind of truce." Jay waited to see where he was going. He still wasn't looking at him. "You think you can get your girlfriend to find out where they sleep?"

The mention of Celia sent an unexpected jolt through him, a combination of anger, resentment, and desire.

"She ain't my girlfriend," he grumbled.

Snipe faced him. "She can find out where they stay."

Jay shook his head slowly. He didn't want to involve her, no matter how much he wanted to stick it to the vamps. "She probably doesn't know anything."

"You can at least try."

Jay was growing uncomfortable under his dark gaze. He wanted to get out of that garage. "I'll see what I can do," he said vaguely. "I'm gonna go see what Colin's up to."

Jay slipped through the door that led to the kitchen of Snipe's house. Lauren was making sandwiches at the counter. She smiled when Jay entered. He crossed through and into the living room. Colin was sitting on the couch with Jessa. A cartoon pig was counting toys on the screen.

Jay made a face at the show as he plopped down in Snipe's chair. Jessa's full attention went to him. He could feel the heat of her little green eyes without even turning to her. She always stared at him with open curiosity, and he was beginning to get used to it. Today, however, it was annoying.

He glanced at her sideways. A silent staring contest ensued. Unfortunately, Jessa was winning. His eyes burned. Colin must've felt the crackling tension because he pulled his attention from the television to look down at Jessa at his elbow, then to Jay.

Jay finally gave in. He groaned in defeat and rubbed his eyes. Jessa turned back to the television with not even a trace of triumph in her expression. Jay didn't get it. What a conundrum that little girl was.

"Come and eat, guys," Lauren called from the kitchen. She didn't allow meals in front of the television. They all rose and went to the table. Colin helped Jessa into her booster seat with his one good arm. Lauren placed paper plates holding turkey sandwiches and chips in front of each of them.

"Thanks, Lauren," Jay replied before taking a huge bite and losing all ability to speak.

"Thanks," Colin said. Lauren sat beside Jessa to help her eat.

Lauren brought a chip to her mouth. "How did last night go?"

Jay and Colin exchanged the same questioning looks. If Snipe hadn't told her, should they? Jay took another bite to stall for time. Colin saw this and did the same eagerly.

Lauren opened her mouth to say something, maybe to complain judging from the troubled expression on her face. Before she had a chance, Snipe traipsed in through the side door, grease smeared across his forehead. He sat heavily in his chair at the end of the table. He chomped his sandwich with dirty hands and glared at Jay, who stared pointedly at his own sandwich.

Colin and Lauren both picked up on the strain flowing between the men. Colin cleared his throat.

"I got us a job," he announced. "The sister of that Beverly woman, the one found last week behind the grocery store, doesn't believe the police report. She wants us to find her killer."

"Fat chance on that one," Jay quipped.

Colin shrugged. "Dude, it's money and I can't keep asking my moms. 'Til I can find a part-time job, it'll do."

"Ever thought about working in a comic book store?"

"I used to work at Game Stop but they closed," he said in all seriousness. "I was thinking about applying to this pub near here. Snipe knows the owner."

Snipe didn't seem to notice the acknowledgement. He chewed his sandwich like it had insulted his mother. Jay quickly finished his food then stood. He dumped his plate in the trash and pulled out his car keys.

"I'll see ya," he called out to no one in particular and left before anyone could stop him. It was late afternoon. The humidity was no joke as he walked down the stairs to his car. He didn't complain because he was used to it. Dallas could get pretty stifling when it wanted to. At least he didn't have to carry his weapons during the day, and he usually didn't. They were currently stashed under his seat in his satchel.

He climbed into his Mustang. The windows had been left down but it was still uncomfortable. He immediately drove off to get a wind going. When he glanced at the time, he saw it was nearly six. Celia was probably done with work now. He wondered if she would go straight home or run errands.

Someone beeped behind him. "Yeah, yeah, hold your fuckin' horses." He pressed a little harder on the accelerator. His feet and hands had the reign and in no time he found himself turning down Celia's block. Her black Honda was parked at the beginning of the street.

Outside her place, he paused in front of the buzzers. He licked his lips slowly as he contemplated.

"Ah, hell."

He reached out and pressed the little button next to her name. A few seconds passed before her voice came over the speaker.

"Yes?"

"It's Jay." He winced, bracing for the worst. Instead of a barrage of insults, the door buzzed. She was letting him inside.

He pushed the door open. "Okay," he said uncertainly. She was waiting for him at her door in denim Bermuda shorts and a purple Hello Kitty top. Her sizable breasts made that cat's already sizable head seem even larger. He noticed that she didn't seem upset, like, at all. He surveyed her with a frown as he approached.

"Celia?"

She tilted her head to the side, obviously puzzled by his caution. "What?"

He followed her inside. The air smelled sweet, like buttercream. He trailed behind her into the kitchen. A yellow cake sat on a plate on the counter. It was only partially covered with frosting. A pink bowl sat next to it with a plastic spatula leaning against the side. He glanced around in search of the cake mix box and frosting canisters but found none.

"You made this?" he asked in disbelief. "From scratch?"

She scoffed. "Yes, is that so hard to believe?"

Ignoring her indignation, he ran a finger along the edge of the frosting bowl and brought it to his mouth. It was really good, just sweet enough but still light. She slapped his hand when he reached for another taste.

"What's the occasion?" he asked.

She shrugged, looking bashful all of a sudden. "I just felt like it," she said in a soft voice. He watched her put the final touches on the cake. She then placed the plate in a plastic cake holder and closed the top.

"You're not gonna eat it?" he asked, bemused.

"No, making it was enough."

He just nodded. She was quiet as she set the cake holder on top of her fridge. Suddenly, she turned on him. She had a hand on her hip and a determined expression on her pretty face.

"Please tell me you all met last night even though I wasn't

there. I must've fallen asleep..." she added with a shake of her head, still not quite believing that. "Victor didn't wake me and I didn't see him last night. So, did you all meet or not?"

Jay stared at her with his mouth agape. "You're shitting me, right?" he finally said.

Her brows pulled together. There was something in her eyes that told him that she was completely serious.

"Yeah, we met last night," he said. "And you were there. What, you fall on your head or something?"

She looked shocked. She rubbed her cheek absently as she stared off somewhere. "But . . . why don't I remember?" Her voice was faint again.

It didn't take long for Jay to understand. His back went rigid as his fury sparked and flamed. "Those fuckin' bloodsucker sons-of-bitches," he growled. "They erased your memory."

She shook her head, her eyes as wide as saucers. "No . . . That can't be right. Victor wouldn't . . ." She trailed off. The fear in her eyes made his stomach ache. She looked so betrayed. And now her eyes glistened in the light from above.

Celia bit her bottom lip in an attempt to suppress the tears. She shook her head again, deep in a silent debate. He wanted to put his arms around her and pull her close. To feel her body next to his and smell her hair and—

He stopped himself because that particular train of thought was not going to lead anywhere good—or appropriate, rather. She was gaining control of herself now anyways. She turned back to the counter and pulled down two plates from the cabinet. Then she took the cake holder from where she had stashed it on the fridge. She cut two giant slices of cake. She thrust a plate at Jay, then stalked out to the living room. There, she plopped down on the sofa and snatched up the television remote.

She turned to some sitcom and brooded as she used her fingers to eat the warm cake. Jay went to the director's chair in the corner and stayed quiet. Ten long minutes passed before Celia slammed the plate down on the table.

"Why would he do that?" she cried. She turned her angry, confused eyes on Jay. "He said he would never do anything like that to me. Do you know I actually thought someone had attacked me? I thought that someone had broken into my apartment, knocked me out and did things to me that I couldn't remember."

Jay's hands gripped the plate like he might break it. "How do you know he's never done this before?"

She shook her head resolutely. That was a thought she was not going to entertain. "No, I would remember feeling like this. This is new. What happened last night?"

He gave her a quick rundown. "And after she fucked up the van, we left," he finished.

She still looked confused. "So something must've happened after that," she muttered, more to herself. She took another bite of cake as she visibly contemplated. Bits of frosting clung to her thumb. It was no use.

This was his chance, Jay thought. She was angry and confused and questioning her boyfriend. He'd have to be careful.

"Celia," he said. She looked at him. "Have you ever been to Victor's place?"

"No, only Ramsey's."

"Ramsey's the leader, right?" She nodded slowly, but with a suspicious frown. He could see she hadn't been as distracted as he had thought. So he said, fuck it.

"Would you remember how to get there?"

She jumped up like she had just been shocked. "Un-uh, no way," she exclaimed.

Jay stood as well, placing his empty plate (because he was never one to turn down dessert) on the seat. He closed the distance between them and held her shoulders. He was trying hard to make her see how important this all was.

"Let me do my job," he said earnestly.

"Your fucking job means killing Victor. I don't think so. Even if I did remember, I would *never* take you."

He released her and took a step back because his anger was rising to dangerous levels. "So, you'd just stand by and let them keep killing? I'm sure he didn't erase your memory of those people lying in the morgue. Remember them? The woman, the boy. You think they knew what was fuckin' coming?

"How long do you think it takes to drain a person?" he asked, changing tracks a little. She was shaking her head vigorously, as if that would make him stop. "Five minutes," he answered. "Maybe seven if the bloodsucking bastard's having a little fun. May not sound long but there's the pain from the bite," he went on, ticking off his fingers, "and the numbness from losing blood and the fear of dying that makes your heart pump harder, speeding up the time."

Her voice was shaky. "Why are you doing this?"

"Because I wanna protect you," he said without hesitation.

"I don't need protecting."

He snorted. "Yeah, that's real fuckin' convincing coming from the person who can't remember leaving the damn house last night."

Her eyes flashed furiously. "I want you to leave," she said.

He rolled his eyes. "Oh, great. It's a pattern."

"What?"

He looked at her harshly. "Anything gets tough, you push it away. Anything that threatens your little bubble, you lash out 'cause that's the only way you know how to handle it."

"Hey, screw you. And get the fuck *out*!"

Jay threw his hands up and marched to the door. He gave her one last reproachful glare over his shoulder. "When you're through with the lies, come find me."

She shook her head in astonishment. "You've known me for,

like, five seconds. You have no right trying to tell me how to live my fucking life."

He grumbled something inaudible and left the apartment, slamming the door shut behind him.

* * *

Celia was still fuming, even more so since the sun had gone down. Victor didn't come around until ten. He appeared so suddenly and right in front of her pacing path that she shrieked.

"Sorry, baby." He moved to hug her. She maneuvered out of his grasp.

"Don't 'sorry, baby' me," she snapped. He jerked his head back, baffled. "How could you?" she demanded. All of the fury that had been building made her hands ball into tight fists. She lunged at him. She knew it didn't have much physical impact but she pounded on his chest anyway.

"Celia," he said, trying to catch her hands so she wouldn't hurt herself. "Celia, what the hell?"

"You bastard! You *fucking* bastard! How could you erase my memory? You promised!"

He froze, then stopped resisting her wailing on him. He stood there, looking miserable, as she beat on him. After a moment, she backed off. She panted from the exertion and the throbbing in her hands. She shook them out as she paced the room.

"I didn't want to," he said softly. "I broke my promise, I know. But I couldn't let Ramsey do it. I knew I could control the . . . outcome better."

His voice tugged at her. A part of her started to relent. She could hear the pain, but she couldn't face him. She just kept up her furious pacing.

"We had to protect the nest."

That made her stop. She looked at him in utter confusion. "What? You thought I was going to give up the nest?"

"You got angry with Milo. We couldn't risk—" He broke off.

She tried so hard to recall the night, to remember why she would get angry at Milo. It was all gone. Frustrated tears prickled her eyes yet again. She rushed at him, punching his chest and slapping his face. He took it.

She didn't realize she was sobbing until Victor's arms closed around her. He pulled her tightly into him. "I'm so sorry," he whispered into her hair. "I'm sorry."

He did sound genuinely apologetic. She couldn't give in. The betrayal she was experiencing had caused a knot in her stomach that just would not let up. It was so easy to do things and apologize later. Who knew what would happen in the future? What if something else came up and he felt the need to erase her memory? What if he erased this moment so that they could go back to the way things were? How fair would that be? And *had* he ever done this before?

She rubbed her face against his shirt as those questions and others swarmed her head, which was starting to ache from dehydration. His scent filled her runny nose. It was tantalizing but still did nothing to comfort her. She didn't like this at all.

Celia sighed then pulled away from him. She used the back of her hand to wipe her face. She knew it was swollen and red because that always happened when she had a crying jag. She sniffled a few times to make sure what she was about to say was crystal clear.

"I want you to leave," she said evenly. There was a sharp intake of air. Her eyes were being pulled to him like a magnet. She didn't resist. He looked shocked and sad and irate.

"Celia—"

"No," she said, though it was more strained than she wanted. She was being sucked into his gray eyes. Her strange ability to break away actually worked this time. She jerked her head to the side. She closed her eyes and took a few deep breaths, making sure she was still herself. For a brief moment, she considered rescinding his invitation into her home but quickly dismissed the thought.

She had kept her eyes closed and her head averted so she didn't see him leave. She felt it, though. It was strange, like a vital part of her had just up and disappeared. She finally faced the space Victor had occupied. It was vacant and empty.

Another round of sobs threatened to overtake her. She rushed to the shelter of her covers.

Fourteen

THE NEXT DAY, Celia called out of her day shift. Bobby yelled at her a little but she basically told him to fuck off, especially if he was thinking about firing her for missing a shift when she hadn't called out in five months.

Bobby sighed. "Fine," he said. "I'll call Lynn. You think you can bless us with your appearance tomorrow?"

She had figured she'd go in the next day but she didn't like his attitude. He must've been having troubles at work because he had never spoken to her like this before.

"No, I think I need the week," she said, just to be spiteful. He groaned and she rolled her eyes. "I'll let you know Thursday," she added. Everyone else shouldn't have to fear being in the weeds because of her personal shit.

She hung up and pulled the covers over her head again. She drifted in and out of sleep all day. Her cell phone rang at eight pm. She figured Trixie was calling to see what was up. She made no moves to answer it. It rang three more times before the voicemail alert pinged.

Celia rolled over, turning her back to her phone on the nightstand. However, she only stayed there for another ten minutes. Her bladder was full and her stomach growling. She took care of the bathroom first, then brought the cake holder to the sofa.

She began watching an episode of *Reaper* that had been taking up space on her DVR for months. Regrettably, they were dealing with an escaped soul who sucked the life from humans through a bite in the neck. She switched to her *Fringe* episodes post-with. There were no supernatural creatures on that show. Just freaky science experiments. She figured she could deal with that.

Around nine-fifteen, her phone rang. For whatever reason, instead of ignoring it, she pressed Pause on her remote and went to her room to retrieve it. Jay's name flashed across the display. She sighed.

"Hello," she answered in a bored voice.

"Hey," he said softly. She was instantly suspicious.

"What do you want?"

He paused. "I'm sorry, Celia."

"Not the first time I've heard that recently."

He chuckled, which would've normally set her off. Conversely, a calming wave flowed over her at the sound. She didn't let him know that, though.

"So, what do you want?" she repeated brusquely.

"Just that," he said. "We seem to part in unfriendly ways lately and I don't like it. So . . . yeah. I'm sorry."

It wasn't as lame as it sounded. She actually found comfort in the sentiment. He wasn't just throwing words out there. Plus, Jay didn't seem the type to apologize often. He hadn't broken any promises. He was just a *really* determined asshole at times.

She chewed her bottom lip then sank to the bed. "I yelled at

Victor," she told him. "For what he did."

"Uh-huh."

"I had made him promise not to use that hoodoo mojo shit on me and he said he never would. I mean, I know sometimes he slips up with his magic, or whatever they call it. But, he promised."

"Hey, sometimes situations change and you can't always keep your promises. No matter how much you want to."

She rolled her eyes to the ceiling. "Great, you're siding with him."

"Not really. *I'd* never do that to you. Of course, if I became a bloodsucker, I'd run chest-out into the first pointy thing I could find."

She sighed. "You know, not everyone has a choice in the matter," she said wearily, already tired of this repeated argument.

"That's why I'd *choose* a way out."

"Whatever," she grumbled. "Not everyone has brass balls like you."

"That's too bad. So, what're you doing tonight?" he asked, like they had just been discussing the weather.

"Gorging myself on cake. I'm hoping to eat my way into a sugar coma."

"Now, we can't have that. Get dressed. I'll be there in ten."

She was about to protest because she was in no mood to leave her cavern but he hung up too fast. She tossed the phone aside and pulled herself up. She was sure it was still stifling out there seeing as how the city was in the grips of a full-on heat wave. She dressed in white linen pants that bunched at the ankle and a brown tank top layered over a white one.

She was closing the clasp on her gold gladiator sandal when the buzzer sounded. She grabbed her wristlet and went outside. Jay gave her an appreciative glance as she climbed in beside him, exciting an unbidden rush of warmth. She tried to keep herself in check, determined to be morose and gloomy. Something about Jay and that lazy smile he was directing her way—not to mention his extra fly car—made it difficult to hold onto that resolution.

"Where are we going?" she asked, keeping her voice as neutral as possible.

"You'll see." He pulled off. She rolled her eyes.

"It better not be The Pit again."

He laughed. "Shut it, okay? Just sit back and relax."

She gave him an incredulous look. "You know where you're going now, is that it?"

"Didn't I say shut up?"

He drove down Washington to Columbia Road, then continued on past Franklin Park Zoo and the golf course until he came to a rotary. He took the second exit and joined the light traffic on the Jamaicaway, a winding road also known as the "Green Belt" that flowed past Jamaica Pond towards Brighton and Kenmore Square.

He parked in the Landmark Center garage near Fenway Park. They walked to Longhorn Steakhouse, which was located next to the movie theater. *Figures,* she thought when she saw the steakhouse sign. She didn't voice the sentiment. She had nothing against steakhouses; it just seemed to be such a *Jay* choice.

There was a ten-minute wait before they were seated in a booth near the door. They had stood off to the side, not quite looking at the other. People passed them by, chatting and laughing. At one point, a couple crossed in front of them, going toward the door. The woman rolled her ankle on her heel and she stumbled into her date. The guy was very concerned that she had hurt herself. Celia and Jay each hid their smirks. Their eyes met once the couple left and they both laughed. A nervous tickle started in her stomach.

In the booth, Celia scanned the menu, fully aware of Jay's knees pressing against hers. She could barely concentrate.

Their waitress was medium height with firm boobs that wanted so badly to break free from their cottony prison. That was exactly where Jay's eyes went when she approached. Jealousy flicked at Celia. She kept her eyes down as she manhandled the menu in her grasp.

They ordered and, to his credit, Jay tried not to make his ogling of her walking away too noticeable. Unfortunately, Celia *did* notice.

In retaliation, she curled her toes in her sandal so that she wouldn't hurt herself then kicked him in the shin. He looked at her, stunned.

"What the hell was that for?"

Ignoring him, Celia unrolled her napkin, neatly placed the silverware on the table and laid the red cloth across her lap. Comprehension and amusement made him grin as he watched her little act.

The waitress brought Jay's beer and Celia's Cosmo, along with their appetizers. This time Jay didn't look, though he would have just to annoy her. Celia dug into her chopped salad.

"You want any of these?" Jay offered of his chili-cheese fries. She looked down at the conglomeration of fries and chili and peppers and could almost feel it coating her stomach already. She shook her head.

He shrugged and went to work. God, he ate like a pig. He dug in with his fingers, licking up chili and sour cream that didn't go into his mouth the first time. She scrunched her nose in disgust.

Then she thought about how strange it was for her to be sitting there, with Jay. A hunter. Who was gunning for her boyfriend.

She found herself glancing around the restaurant. Of the other booths she could see, all the people were eating and drinking merrily, without a care in the world. Certainly none of them were dealing with the problems she was having at the moment.

She took a long gulp of her drink to combat the sudden ache of sadness as she thought of Victor. The vodka warmed her insides, starting the process of dulling the pain.

The waitress came back to clear the plates and bring their meals. Celia cut into her salmon, though she was no longer hungry.

"How long are you in Boston?" she asked.

"Dunno," he said through the steak he was chewing.

"Must be nice. Drifting."

He shrugged. "There're some benefits, like not paying taxes, but I'd like to settle down some day. Get a normal job. A normal life."

"Then who'd fight the boogey man?"

"Some other dumb motherfucker." He swallowed the food. "I'd take a break if I could. Is your place hiring?" He actually sounded serious.

"Sure. We can always use extra hands cleaning the toilets." She gave him a teasing grin.

"Har, har," he chuckled sarcastically. "So, is this it for you?" he asked suddenly. "Bartending. Dating a vampire."

He had meant no harm but the words stung. "It wasn't like I chose Victor because he was a vampire. I found out about that later. By then I already liked him too much to walk away. And what's so wrong with working in a bar?" she snapped defensively. "It's a job that pays the bills. I'm not walking the streets or stripping or cheating people out of their money."

"Whoa!" he said, leaning back in the seat as if she had taken a swing at him, which she kind of wanted to do. "I just meant—"

"I know what you meant," she cut across him, suddenly extremely angry with him. "So, I'm not a schoolteacher or a doctor, so what? Does that make me less of a person? I happen to *like* where I work, okay? I'm not looking to be there when I'm forty but it's what I need now."

"Celia," he said gently.

"Shut up," she grumbled, taking another gulp of her drink. He gaped at her a moment before his face softened. He chuckled.

She glared at him. "Don't laugh at me, asshole."

He waved his hands in front of him in surrender. "Sorry!" He took a drink of his beer. "So, I take it this is something you've thought about before?"

Her brows furrowed as her words came flooding back to her. She hated having to defend her job to people. She felt no shame in what she did, for not going on to college, for having a daily routine. Why was it that she felt people always judged her? Her aunt's friends, even her aunt.

Jay reached across and cupped her hand with his. She had her little hand balled into a fist so tight it was trembling. The heat from his touch soothed her and she found she could breathe steadily again.

The waitress approached them to see if they needed anything. Celia used her free hand to down the last of her drink and ordered another. Jay surveyed her, trying to gauge what she was thinking.

She finally sighed, releasing the anger. "Sorry." She brought her hand to her mouth and pretended to pull something out of it. "Here's your head back."

He smiled. The gesture made his eyes twinkle. "You are something else, Celia."

There was no mistaking the yearning in his eyes. His hand tightened on hers and instead of fighting it, like she knew she should, she adjusted so that their fingers were entwined.

They stared into each other's eyes. A full conversation seemed to pass between them. A discussion that swept away the obstacles and awkwardness people testing out their chemistry had to battle.

The waitress interrupted the moment by setting Celia's drink in front of her. She gave Celia a tight smile, then left quickly. She must've liked Jay's attention but now he was holding Celia's hand. She actually felt triumphant, as childish as that sounded.

They finished eating in relative quiet while playing with each other's fingers. When leaving, Jay held the door for her. She stepped outside into the sweltering heat. Sweat beaded on her forehead. She used the back of her arm to wipe it away.

Jay's hand was on her back first, then he pulled her to the side. She still had her arm on her forehead when he leaned down. The kiss was deep, hungry, like he was searching for the meaning of life through her lips. She melted into it instantly. His mouth suckled her top lip; she had his bottom. She tasted the warmth of his breath, felt the pressure of his tongue. He opened her mouth insistently and caressed her tongue with his. An electric jolt shot down her spine to the meeting of her thighs when he stroked the top of her mouth. His hands gripped her lower back, pulling her hips into his. She cupped his face. His stubble tickled, making her moan even more.

It was Jay who ended the kiss. They huddled together, foreheads pasted from sweat, each panting like they'd just been running. His hands squeezed her waist. Her head was swimming now, even more so than the two Cosmos had accomplished.

Without a word, Jay took her hand and led her in a purposeful stride down the sidewalk. They passed the Quiznos, the Cold Stone, the Best Buy. She was practically jogging to keep up with his dogged pace. Her sandals slapped against the pavement. They were headed toward the entrance of the building. She could take a guess as to where he was going.

To his car.

To go back to her place.

If they made it out of the garage.

She was debating on what she *should* do. Of course, what she *wanted* to do was shove him up against the window of the store and have her way. Was that so wrong? Look at him, all serious and intense. He was hot.

She tried pushing Victor's remorseful face out of her mind. She didn't want to think about him or what he had done. It made her feel like her insides were being yanked from her with a rusty nail. She could use the distraction Jay could more than adequately provide. His stolen kiss proved that.

As they neared the entrance, Jay began to slow. Celia looked up at him in confusion, especially when his hand squeezed hers. He was glaring straight ahead, a thick vein pulsing in his temple.

She looked to see what had captured his attention. Leaning against the window next to the front door, like this was some kind of high school hangout, was Milo and Clarice. Celia remembered Milo as the "take-out delivery guy" at Ramsey's. Of course Clarice's pierced tits flashed in her mind at the sight of the vamp. Celia looked over the tight black pants that hugged her long, long legs and her pale skin peeking from under her leather vest. Her hair was held back and out of her face with sparkly clips.

Suddenly, the wind shifted. Milo raised his head. A serene smile crossed his face, like he'd just smelled something delicious.

He looked to his left. His smile widened, having received confirmation. Without hesitation, he pushed off the window and began strolling toward where they had halted. Celia saw Clarice pull out a cell phone, a devious smirk on her face. Neither she nor Jay could hear what she was saying.

Milo stopped a few feet in front of them. His gaze slid from Jay to Celia, making the little hairs on the back of her neck stand on end. She inadvertently stepped closer to Jay because she was having one of those bad feelings.

* * *

Victor was at Ramsey's, wishing alcohol had any effect on

him. He was throwing back glasses of Jack just for the motions. The only way for a vampire to really get a buzz was by drinking the blood of a person who was completely trashed. One or two glasses of wine wouldn't necessarily do the trick.

Victor glanced at the old, wooden clock on the mantelpiece. It was a little after eleven. He considered going to one of the sports bars near Fenway Park. There was a Red Sox game at Toronto that would've just ended. If they had won, the Sox nuts would be celebrating.

He was just conjuring the parking garage on Lansdowne Street where he could appear when his cell phone rang.

It was Clarice. "Yeah?" he answered, annoyed.

"Hello, Victor," she said swiftly. "You better get over here. There's something you should definitely see."

He didn't like the unctuous tone or the mystery. "I don't have time for your games," he spat.

"Just get over here. Brookline Ave, at the Best Buy next to the movies."

She hung up. He rolled his eyes and, instead of getting himself drunk off his ass, he appeared in a dark corner next to the Bed Bath and Beyond, on the other side of Landmark Center from the Best Buy.

A woman gasped when he stepped out into the light. She was a little shorter than Victor, with curly blond hair and freckles. She'd been rushing to the Green Line train stop when he startled her. Her pulse pounded loudly in his ears and the tingly feeling indicating he was about to entrap kicked in.

Her steps slowed. She stared at him with sudden rapt interest. He didn't reel it back so she approached him. He welcomed her like a lover, wrapping an arm around her waist and caressing her warm neck. They stepped back into the shadows. She moaned when he penetrated her and he let her warmth fill him.

He stopped himself after a minute. She sighed with pleasure when he licked the wound. He sent her on her way. She wouldn't remember the experience once his hold wore off, which would probably happen while she was riding the train underground.

Victor stalked around the building to the Best Buy. He didn't see Clarice or anything of interest.

"Great," he muttered to himself.

She'd wasted enough of his time. Instead of teleporting, he decided to walk up Brookline Avenue toward Lansdowne Street and the sports bars. He made it two blocks when his nose stopped him. Spilled blood tinged the night air. Now that he was alert, he could hear the punches, the curses. The accelerated pulses.

He walked cautiously down the quiet street. A few parked cars lined either side; the meters blinked red since the hours of operation were up. The end of the street flared slightly to allow more parking spaces. It was empty of vehicles tonight.

Instead, there were four bodies in the open area, two of them human. He knew all of their scents, which stunned and propelled him forward. Milo had Jay on his back, punching him in the gut. Clarice was with Celia. Celia leaned against her, her face blank. She was using her magic, Victor quickly ascertained, which explained why Celia wasn't fighting back.

Clarice sniffed the air, then closed her eyes. "You came," she said. Both she and Celia turned just as he rushed at them. He shoved Clarice. She held on tight to Celia. They both stumbled backwards to the ground.

"Victor!" Clarice exclaimed in surprise. She shoved Celia off of her—effectively removing her magic—and jumped up. She stood squarely in front of him, fury distorting her face. She wasn't necessarily pretty. In fact, she had a sharp chin and small eyes. That didn't matter, at least to humans. Her vampireness made her exceptional.

Her voice caught Milo's attention. He, too, jumped up to face

Victor. His ultra-blonde 'do was spiky tonight and not a hair was out of place. Jay rolled onto his side, groaning. Celia shook her head a few times to clear it. When she saw Jay distressed, she appeared to want to run to his aid. She stopped herself from moving. Victor's fists tightened.

"What do you two think you're doing?" Victor demanded, turning back to the problem at hand.

"Just having a little fun," Clarice replied. She had already regained her composure and that smug smile of hers. She turned her focus on Jay. "You know what would be wicked fun? If we turn him." She jumped in the air and landed softly next to his head. She pressed a stilettoed foot on his chest. "How about that, little hunter boy? You wanna be what you chase?"

Milo laughed, loud and grating. "I like that."

He started back over. Celia ran at him, shouting, "No!" The force from the hit didn't have the intended purpose and she ended up on her ass again. It didn't even faze Milo. He continued on toward his prize.

The two vamps were out for blood. And they wanted Celia to see it. Since Clarice had called him, they must've had plans to hurt Celia as well, and wanted an audience. Victor rushed over. Clarice had grabbed Jay's collar, pulling him up from the ground. His feet dangled in the air. He grasped her wrists as he fruitlessly fought against her hold.

Clarice brought his face close to hers. Her tongue licked the blood from his lips. She purred then kissed him roughly. He grunted as he tried to pull away but she had him in a death grip. Milo had been holding Victor back. When she was finished, she handed Jay off to Milo. She was the fastest in the nest so she was able to jump in front of Victor before he could get Jay away. Jay's shouts of protest were muffled as Milo took his turn kissing him.

"Stop it!" Celia cried.

Out of sheer panic, she ran over to the group. "Stay back!"

Victor ordered but Celia hurried forward anyways. She grabbed and twisted Milo's hair, yanking his head back. It was the first thing to come to mind.

Milo laughed heartily, his fangs glinting in the streetlights. "Foreplay. I love it."

In swift movements that only the vampires could keep up with, Milo dropped Jay, grabbed Celia's wrist, twisted her arm behind her, then sank his teeth in her throat.

Everything seemed to freeze at that moment.

Celia's eyes widened in surprise for a second before the pain registered.

Clarice's face brightened in glee.

Electric volts cursed through Victor's body, holding him in place. It was the only way he could explain why it took him two whole seconds to respond.

In a rage, he used both hands to toss Clarice out of his way. She soared through the air then crashed into a parked car ten feet away. The alarm sounded. Clarice's head lolled to the side. She was embedded in the trunk, the metal bent and distorted around her body. One of her red heels dropped to the ground.

Milo pulled back. Celia's blood dripped from his lips. His gaze was both triumphant and arrogant.

Victor's growl nearly matched Bryce's as he ran at Milo and grabbed him by the throat. Milo released Celia, who sank to the ground, clutching her neck. He punched Victor in the stomach but it didn't have much effect. Victor was too far-gone in his fury.

With a grunt, Victor yanked on Milo's arm. A sick snapping sound filled the air. Milo howled in pain. He tried punching Victor in the face with the other hand but he knocked it away. Victor put a hand across Milo's mouth, the other on the back of his head, then broke his neck. The vampire dropped to the ground with a thud.

"Behind you!"

That was Jay, who was still on the ground, hunched to the side. Victor spun around as Clarice rushed toward him unevenly in her one heel, the trunk's hood in her hands (whoever's car that belonged to was going to be *pissed*). She swung the dented piece of metal at Victor's head. It made a grinding noise as it connected, spinning Victor around so that he was facing Jay and Celia.

A line of tears streamed from Celia's eyes as she gazed up into his. She looked so small in her shock. Her fingers grazed her neck where he had bitten her, as if she weren't completely sure that it had happened.

Victor was resolute. He'd deal with Clarice later; he had to get Celia away. He crouched down quickly as Clarice was winding up for another hit. He took Celia's hand, then reached across and grabbed Jay's knee, the closest thing he could touch.

It took a lot of effort to transport himself and the two humans. The ice-cold currents shooting through him intensified into sharp shards in his veins. A jolt of pain sliced through his spine to his head. He steadfastly kept the visual of where he wanted to go in his mind's eye until it became real around him.

Both Celia and Jay gasped for air. Victor crumpled to Celia's living room floor, holding his head. That random woman's blood hadn't been even *close* to sufficient for such a trip. Most of that had been used up during the fight.

From his vantage point on the floor, Victor saw Celia's feet as she rushed to the bathroom. She'd recovered quicker this time, probably getting used to this form of transportation. Jay was coughing then groaning from the pain of coughing.

Now that he had a moment, as he waited for the ache in his head and back to subside, he wondered why Celia was with Jay. Had they run into each other? Were they together when Milo and Clarice came upon them?

He wanted to know. He sat up slowly. Even that cautious

movement made his head spin. He rolled onto his back and closed his eyes. The water that had been running in the bathroom sink stopped. Celia's feet returned to the living room and continued on to the kitchen.

The fridge opened. Ice cubes clinked as she dropped them into a Zip-loc bag. "I don't know where you wanna put these," she said to Jay. He just sort of grunted.

Something damp touched his cheek. A washcloth cleaning the blood that no longer had a source since the cut had healed. The cloth was then placed on Victor's forehead like a compress. He sighed in relief as the coolness began to soothe his head. He could smell Celia hovering next him, her strawberry shampoo and the tantalizing blood still bubbling at her neck.

He'd never smelled her blood before; she'd never even so much as had an accident in his presence. It was sweet as it filled his nose, like vanilla. His mouth watered, his fangs lengthened, his nails sharpened. Cillian's words suddenly returned to him. He'd been able to smell her distinctive blood.

"Victor," she said gently. Her hand touched his chest. "Are you okay?"

All he could do was shake his head. His arms were trembling from the effort to keep himself still, to ignore her blood that was calling out to him like a Siren's spell. He wanted to stop breathing but he just couldn't force himself to do it. He *wanted* to smell her.

"Celia," Jay said gruffly. "Move away from him."

"What?" she asked, baffled.

"Now." From his tone, Victor could tell Jay understood his turmoil. Celia's hand was gone and the scent drifted away. After that, Victor's muscles were able to relax. His fangs and nails retracted. There was still a dull ache in his back and he was a little dizzy but he sat up and opened his eyes.

Celia stood in the threshold of the kitchen, two tan bandages on the right side of her neck. She was no longer wearing the tank top. It had been stained with her blood. Instead, she wore an old AIDS Walk t-shirt. She was biting her nail anxiously as she stared at Victor. She stiffened when he moved. Her leg twitched, like she wanted to go to him, but she held still, remembering Jay's warning.

Victor took a deep breath. The vanilla-y scent was still there; it was best that Celia stayed put so he could be sure to contain the animal. He looked around to Jay, who had pulled himself up on the sofa. His head rested on the back. His breathing was even, like he was sleeping.

"Are you okay?" Celia asked, drawing his attention back to her. Her forehead was crinkled with worry.

"I'll live," he muttered. A derisive snort rose from the sofa so, obviously, Jay was not asleep.

Celia looked like she would burst into tears at any moment. "What happened tonight?" he asked calmly.

Her voice was shaky. "Those two just came at us. We ran and they just sort of skipped behind us but then that bitch, Clarice, caught up and forced us down that street. She grabbed me and, I don't know. I couldn't move or fight or anything. Milo got the best of Jay and then you showed up."

There were more pressing questions he wanted to ask. He kept them to himself. He didn't like the state of their relationship but he couldn't pressure her either. The room spun a little as he got to his feet. She must've seen he was disoriented because she rushed to his side.

"What's wrong, Victor?" she asked, her voice thick with concern.

"Nothing, that just . . . took a lot out of me."

"I'll say."

He glanced over to the sofa when Jay spoke. He squinted at Victor, as if he was shining a flashlight in his face.

Victor scowled, his anger flaring up again. "I just saved your ass and you're giving me shit?"

"Look," Jay snapped. "I'm in pain and you're blinding me, so, sorry if I don't seem my usual appreciative self."

That was a strange thing to say. Not the, oh, so very funny statement of Jay's self-awareness. The other part. Victor looked to Celia for an explanation. She was just as puzzled.

"He's blinding you?" Celia asked.

He paused, then groaned when he realized he had misspoken. "Fuck."

"What is it?" she pressed.

He rolled his hand as if it were no big deal. "Vampires have this . . . glow," he said grudgingly. "That's how I recognize them."

"A . . . glow?" Celia stared at him. Hey, at least she didn't laugh.

"Yeah," he replied bitingly. "And this one's glowing like crazy. You must be hungry," he lobbed at Victor as he glared at him in the eyes.

Jay groaned again as he stood. He held his arm around his stomach with the ice pack on his ribs. Celia crossed over to the sofa. "Maybe you should go to the hospital," she suggested. She reached out to touch his side. Victor's eyes narrowed.

"And pay for it how, exactly?" She cocked an eyebrow at his attitude.

"You know," Victor said because Jay was annoying him. "A little vampire blood would do you wonders."

"No, thank you."

Jay shuffled past Celia toward the front door. "I'll see ya," he called over his shoulder as he left.

Celia frowned after him, and then looked at Victor. "Is that true?" she asked.

"Yup."

"Oh. I think I read that in a book or something."

An awkward silence fell over the room. She avoided his eyes.

She scratched at the bandages on her neck.

"Come here," he said.

She obeyed. She stood in front of him with her arms at her side. He looked at her a moment, sensing the growing distance between them. He'd really fucked up.

Victor reached out and gently pulled off the bandages. His fingers on her skin made her heart flutter. He was careful and controlled as he leaned down into the crook of her neck. His tongue slid over the red, swollen bumps.

She sighed in pleasure. Her breath warmed his cheek. Was that just a normal reaction to vampire tongue on your skin?

Standing that close to her, he wanted to kiss her, to make love to her right there. You'd think they'd been apart for months. That's how badly he yearned for her.

The other problem was that he also wanted to bite her. The little remnants of her blood he tasted were so sweet, alluring. However, that would more than likely be a mood-killer for her, especially after tonight.

"Blood like sugar" was right. He didn't know how to explain it. How just those little drops filled him with enough warmth to last all night, he was sure. There must've been a connection to her knack of getting out of a vampire's control. What else could she do? And could he manage another taste before the wound healed completely?

He eyed the two punctures. The skin was slowly sealing, the redness lightening in front of his eyes. With great effort, he stepped back.

"There," he said in a soft voice. He could still smell her blood, but he was certain it was only a phantom scent, lingering in his subconscious. Teasing him.

"Thanks," she whispered. They stared at each other again. This was all wrong. They were like strangers. No, worse. They were like lovers who suddenly couldn't be in the vicinity of the other because of the huge elephant in the room—said elephant being vampire mind-fuckery.

Okay, so that wasn't really an analogy. In either case, this was awkward, uncomfortable. Miserable.

"I better go," he muttered reluctantly.

She bit her bottom lip as she trailed behind him to the door. In the threshold, he stopped and turned so quickly that Celia walked into him. He held her in his arms before she could back away, feeling her warmth soak through to his bones. He kissed her forehead, released her, then left down the stairs, something he hadn't done in a long, long time, back when he was pretending to be human.

* * *

Jay waited in his car for no particular reason. He figured Victor would use his regular mode of transportation or, worse: stay the night. So he was pretty surprised to glimpse him coming down the stairs not even five minutes after he'd dropped his sore body into his Mustang.

On the last step, Victor pulled out his cell phone. He spoke for half a minute then sat on the step. Jay watched him with interest, wondering just what Celia saw in him. Was there any of that "hoodoo mojo shit" involved?

Victor was staring glumly at the ground, drained of his usual vigor. He was still extremely handsome. With his dark eyes downcast and him absentmindedly playing with his nails, he looked like a man defeated. Jay could feel for him... but he wouldn't dwell on that too long. It would suit him just fine if the vampire disappeared into the night, leaving Celia unattached. As far as he was concerned, Celia would be better off as well.

Ten minutes later, the red Infiniti stopped in front of Celia's building. More accurately, it screeched to a halt from sixty mph to zero. The loud bass rattled the car, and the music screamed louder when Victor opened the passenger door.

"Shit, Bryce, turn that down," he complained as he climbed inside.

The red car sped off down the street then zipped around the corner. "Dammit," Jay muttered as he rushed after them.

Bryce was being careless. He weaved in and out of cars, running yellow lights. Even with all that, he didn't notice the black Mustang tailing him.

They drove through Mattapan, a smaller section of Dorchester, on to Milton. It was a quiet, but extremely bumpy road, thanks to the horrendous job of filling potholes. Bryce turned left off the main road. Jay slowed though Bryce raced on.

As Jay neared the end, he saw the cul-de-sac. The white mansion was very dark, with only a few lights on the first floor illuminated. He pulled over two houses before the circle and turned the engine off.

Bryce had already parked in the driveway. He, Victor, and a third vampire (Josiah) got out of the car. Bryce was laughing and talking animatedly. Those tranquilizers must not have had lingering effects.

He said something and clapped Victor on the back. Victor looked too preoccupied to respond. The light above the porch came on suddenly. Jay noticed for the first time the two females walking up the stairs. Their pace faltered as they stared, amazed, at the three vamps.

They grasped each other's arms in nervous excitement. The white light above them was soft, making their blond hair glitter. They were both wearing some skanky outfits—short dresses with holes and strips of fabric in strategic places. Bryce nudged Josiah conspiratorially and they both went up the staircase to let the ladies into the house.

Victor took the stairs much slower. Halfway up, he turned his head. The movement was so swift that Jay wouldn't have had time to duck even if he had thought to. Victor stared in his direction. Jay held completely still. Though he'd love another go at the vamp, he knew that now wasn't the time.

After a long moment where Jay didn't even breathe, Victor finished his ascent up the stairs and closed the door behind him. Jay turned the key, threw the car into drive and sped away.

* * *

"I can't believe you're showing your face here!"

Clarice yelled at Victor as soon as he entered the living room. Josiah ushered the two girls out of the room. They didn't seem to notice the outburst anyways; they were so busy gazing at Josiah like he had an orange aura or something. Bryce stayed put with an intrigued grin.

"Victor," said Ramsey. He was sitting on one of the sofas with his legs crossed, next to Elizabeth.

Victor spoke directly to Ramsey. "They attacked Celia."

"She was with that *hunter*." She spat the word out like it was rotten. "They're attacking us, and since she hangs with them then—" she added a nonchalant shrug "—*she's* attacking us."

He wheeled on her. "That's not true."

"You are the company you keep." She gave him a haughty smirk.

"Oh, shut up! You were just angry and saw an opportunity to take her out of the equation. Well, forget it, Clarice. No matter what you do, I won't want you."

The words were like a slap. Her face paled in shock. She looked around at the eyes of the others, mortified. Her magic swelled and pulsed throughout the room, touching everyone. Eyes averted as her embarrassment and anger hit them as if it were they who had been affected. Only Victor stood his ground, immune.

Clarice spun and ran from the room in a flash, her hair flowing behind her. It took a moment for her presence to dissipate and the room to be released.

Victor faced Ramsey again. In the heat of the argument, he forgot that he wanted them to scan the grounds. He had a strange feeling that someone was out there, watching them. Bryce had been driving like a maniac, which was saying something since Victor usually drove like the speed limit was sixty-five everywhere. He had been calling way too much attention. But that had slipped from his mind with Clarice's outburst.

Ramsey pinched his sinuses, obviously annoyed. Victor didn't like to see him like this. He wasn't going to apologize for what he did, though. Besides, Milo would be back to his slimy self in no time, if not with a sore neck to slow him down for a few weeks. Sunlight and foreign objects to the heart were what killed vampires.

"It's bad enough we got hunters after us, now we have to watch each other?"

"Tell that to Milo," Victor replied coldly.

"I don't want to argue." His tone brokered no arguments. He glanced to Elizabeth. His voice automatically softened. "What've you found?"

She shook her head grimly. "Nothing. I even went to Maine, Vermont, and New Hampshire. No one has seen red eyes like how Victor and Josiah described. I called Manny. He said he would check with the vamps in his area but he hadn't seen anything personally.

"I brought the darts to Thomas but all he could discern for certain was the Dead Man's Blood and mercury in the one that hit Annie. He says there are more elements, foreign elements he can't explain."

Thomas was a scientist at Harvard University, who helped Elizabeth out from time to time. His services were payment for her saving his sister. Plus, he was more than a little frightened by the vampire, not that she'd been anything but courteous. His sister had been hiking in Maine when she came across a grizzly. Elizabeth had been running with the Monte Carlos and pulled the sister to safety.

Unfortunately for Elizabeth, the woman had seen her fangy side while she was fighting off the bear. Even more unfortunate, and unbeknownst to Elizabeth, the woman had snapped a few pictures with her phone. She had promised not to tell a soul, which apparently hadn't included her brother, Thomas.

Thomas, a skeptic, had his sister arrange a visit. He showed Elizabeth the pictures. Instead of using her magic to make them both believe they were chickens, she decided to take advantage of Thomas's credentials. They had met behind his lab. Not the smartest idea.

At the mention of Annie's name, Bryce cursed. Annie was awake but still on bed rest as a precaution. The two girls were for her.

"So, what's next?" Victor asked, no longer fretting about stepping on his toes. "Obviously those goddamn hunters don't want any kind of truce."

Ramsey was quiet for a long time as he debated. He looked at Bryce, then Elizabeth. She smiled a little in encouragement.

He sighed. When he spoke, it was grudgingly, but with authority.

"If you see a hunter," he said. "Take him out."

Fifteen

TRIXIE HAD WEDNESDAY night off. She came over with a bottle of wine she snagged from work. Celia did not ask how she swung that. Instead, she quickly grabbed two glasses.

"Are you coming back to work any time soon?" Trixie asked once they settled in on the sofa. They had ten minutes before the show they wanted to watch started. Celia wanted her to get her questions out soon so she wouldn't have to yell at her to shut up. It was some summer reality show about people doing things. To Celia, they all tended to blend with each other after a while.

"Probably tomorrow. Bobby was being a dick."

"When's he not?" she asked with a snort.

Along with the wine, they were eating butter pecan ice cream. Celia had already explained to Trixie what had happened over the last couple of days. Trixie shook her head again in amazement.

"Is your life always this dramatic?" she asked.

Celia rolled her eyes. "Believe me, I do not like drama."

"Well, what are you going to do? About Victor."

She was quiet for a moment, pondering the question, like she'd been doing ever since she made Victor leave that night.

She sighed. "I don't know. But I miss him."

Trixie licked her spoon. "What about Jay?"

She groaned. "I don't know. But I miss him."

Trixie patted her knee with a chuckle. "God, I wish I had your problems."

"Trying to choose between the guy you might love and the guy who wants him dead?" Celia asked dubiously.

Trixie looked at her seriously. "Do you love him?"

Celia sighed again. "How should I know?"

Trixie frowned because, yeah, that didn't make much sense.

"I *can't* love him," she grumbled, her frustration rising. This wasn't a new feeling. "He's a fucking vampire. I don't want to become like him—not like he'd do it anyways—and he'll live forever if Jay doesn't have his way. How could we have a life together? I wouldn't want him to see me wasting away from old age. It would be different if we were both going to be dealing with brittle bones and bad backs and gray hair. But we aren't. Just me.

"So, how can I love him?"

She shook her head despondently. Her eyes dropped to her melting ice cream. She felt . . . vulnerable, miserable. She spooned some ice cream into her mouth, letting the cold dessert sit there until it melted, freezing her teeth in the process.

"It was just about spending time together," she went on, even though the seconds were ticking down until the start of their show. Her voice was low and depressed, her shoulders slumped. "I try not to think about the future. Just the here and now. It's the only way to make it with him."

Trixie smiled in support. She bumped her shoulder lightly with hers.

"Okay," was all she said.

* * *

"Did you get the stuff?" Snipe asked as soon as Colin and Harold entered the garage. He was still dressed in his work uniform—khaki pants and a navy polo—having just gotten home ten minutes ago.

"Yup," Colin said cheerily. He dropped a black duffle bag on the workbench. Snipe quickly opened it. He pulled out seven clear beer bottles that clinked together in their own melody, their labels mostly peeled off. There were also rags and planks of wood in the goody bag.

Snipe handed Harold the wood. "Get to work," he said brusquely. Harold bundled them in his arms and went to a smaller table in the far corner. He set the wood down in a neat pile. He picked one up, weighed it in his hand for a moment, and placed it in some kind of carpenter's clamp. Next, he pulled out a chisel and began whittling the wood.

Jay wandered over to watch. He was still favoring his right side and it hurt a little when he breathed.

He hadn't made a new stake in a while and was intrigued by Harold's technique. Harold worked the chisel along the wood in almost a caress, shaving it down to a point on the end. This contrasted greatly with his normal neurotic self. Jay raised an eyebrow, but decided to hold in his snarky remark about him playing with his wood like it was a virgin.

He went back to Snipe and Colin. They were pouring gasoline into the beer bottles. The strong smell filled the confined space, prompting them to work swiftly. Next, rags were stuffed inside. They were careful to leave pieces hanging over the side. Colin set the bottles in a crate, cushioning them with the extra rags so they wouldn't move.

The reason why they hadn't gone back to the white mansion the night Jay had followed the vampires was because Colin wanted Harold to make more of his tranquilizing concoctions.

That meant Harold had to find Dead Man's Blood, which was harder to obtain than the Special K, believe it or not. Jay had to use his contact, Phillips, from the morgue (without his knowledge, obvs).

Into the van went the crate of Molotov cocktails, stakes dipped in Dead Man's Blood, and the tranquilizers, already loaded in guns with silencers. It was five am. The sun was set to rise at five forty-nine according to the local news' website. Most vamps would already be in their sleeping places unless they enjoyed risks.

Jay wanted to be there when the vampires realized something was wrong. He wanted to see their faces as they stirred, conscious of the presence nearby. Lying in wait to snuff them out. The predators becoming the prey.

It was all so exciting to him. Adventure was his drug of choice.

Colin had disappeared into the house ten minutes ago. Snipe glanced at his watch agitatedly. He had already directed Lauren and the kids to stay at her sister's place in Revere, just in case. He must've been nervous about them.

"Colin!" Snipe shouted.

"Coming, coming!"

He bounded out the door carrying a paper plate of four sandwiches. He smiled sheepishly at Snipe when he caught his glare. "For the road," he explained. Snipe was not amused. Colin scrambled into the back next to Harold.

Because his stomach growled, plus he loved to eat, Jay reached back and took a sandwich. Roast beef on whole wheat. He had even taken the time to add lettuce, Dijon mustard, and tomatoes.

Snipe reversed out of the garage and started down the street. The sky was lightening, shifting from midnight blue to a softer cobalt. The streetlights were on and it was still pretty dark but

Jay felt they were pushing their luck.

Jay pulled a sheet of paper from his satchel at his feet. It was a printout of a map of Milton, near Mattapan Square. They had been using it to track where the vampires had driven. None of the winding side streets in the area had cul-de-sacs according to the map, which puzzled Jay. He pointed out Central Avenue as the bumpy main road they had been traveling on. So, that's where Snipe headed.

It was only about a fifteen-minute drive from Southie to Milton, especially with the light, early morning traffic. Snipe turned onto Central Avenue and slowed so that Jay could survey the streets.

About halfway down, he recognized the dark purple Victorian house with the turtle-shaped mailbox on the corner. The odd decoration had stuck in his mind when he passed the other night.

He nodded to the street. "That one."

Snipe drove up the quiet street to the very end. The white mansion looked cold this morning, like it somehow knew its fate. It sat far from the street, guarded and faceless. Jay actually got a shiver. Snipe stopped before the circle. An odd silence filled the van.

Jay turned to unlatch his seatbelt when he saw the deep frown on Snipe's face. "What's wrong?" he asked.

Snipe slowly turned to him. "Where's the house?"

Now Jay frowned. He looked out the windshield, up at the mansion. "Uh, right there," he said, pointing.

He looked at Colin and Harold in the back, whose confused expressions matched Snipe's. "What the hell's the matter with you guys?" Jay asked, getting annoyed.

"Jay," Colin said. "There's no house here."

Indeed, the vampire mojo worked on them. All they saw was an overgrown field at the end of the street. The weeds were waist high. The thick grove of trees hung low, making the area dense and foreboding, like the sun never penetrated it.

Jay sighed, realizing why he was the only one to see the house. "Look," he said. "You're gonna have to believe me on this one. There's a white house there. The bloodsuckers are using magic to conceal it."

"Then how come you can see it?" Harold asked, his nerves making his voice shake.

"Because, for whatever reason, vampire magic doesn't work on me. Well, for the most part anyways." He looked at them harshly. "Are we gonna do this or not?"

"But we can't see the house!" Harold complained.

In response, Jay turned and got out of the van. Snipe and Colin followed. Harold didn't emerge until they'd unloaded the weapons from the back. They strapped on the tranq guns and stakes and Harold held the crate. He trudged along with them into the "field." The mirage was complete with mosquitoes that nipped at his bare arms and neck.

"Gah!" Harold cried, slapping his leg and fumbling with the crate. The bottles clinked together. "This is stupid."

"Shh!" Snipe said severely. Harold's mouth clamped shut. He swatted at a mosquito buzzing in his ear.

After a few yards, Jay held up a hand for them to stop. They were standing in the middle of the road, though they didn't know that. Snipe glanced around at the neighboring houses to make sure they didn't have an audience.

Jay moved forward ahead of them. He mounted the stone staircase to the porch. The others stared in wonder, their jaws slacked—even Snipe's. He must not have fully believed Jay. To their eyes, he seemingly rose into mid-air.

Jay didn't notice their reactions. He was busy inspecting the house. There wasn't much to see. The light was off, the porch bare. Heavy curtains covered the windows on the main level.

There were no movements or sounds, no signs of life inside.

He checked the door but of course it was locked. He waved the others forward. Colin and Harold exchanged astonished glances. Snipe walked to where Jay first started ascending into the air. He raised his foot gingerly, then lowered it. The hard step met his foot though he could not see it.

The three of them joined Jay on the porch. They didn't move around much. It was freaky standing eight feet above the ground. As they were cautiously coming toward him, Jay had pulled out his little B&E kit. He had already opened the first lock, above the handle. Now he was fiddling with the deadbolt. He wasn't all that surprised about the security. Even though they knew humans couldn't see their house, they were still on high alert when it came to their resting place.

Jay had only come across one other resting place. This woman in Corpus Christi had been hiding her vampire pimp in her basement. She had been displaying some of the classic signs of addiction: bite marks on her forearms; dazed, withdrawn expression; pale skin; lethargy. Jay followed his gut and trailed her to the rundown house not far from the Corpus Christi International Airport.

There, he burst in, scaring the shit out of the junkie whore. She had been eating a bowl of Fruit Loops on her sofa, which she spilled on the carpet. Jay had his gun drawn.

"Where is he?" he demanded.

"Where's who?" she cried between choking coughs.

"The vampire who's been sucking off of you."

Her eyes narrowed. She threw the bowl at him, then made the mistake of dashing to the basement. Jay wiped the milk from his eyes and chased after her.

"Laurent!" she screamed. "Help me!"

Of course, it was three o' clock in the afternoon and Laurent was dead in a locked room. She rushed to the door. Lifting her hand, she felt around on the edge of the doorframe until she produced a gold key. She immediately dropped it.

Jay stalked over and knocked her to the ground. He retrieved the key. As he slid it in the door, something heavy cracked him up side the head. With a grunt, he fell against the door. He could feel his blood sliding down the back of his neck.

"Fuck."

"Get outta here!" she shouted. She slid between him and the door, still wielding the cast iron pan she had used to hit him.

He was trying hard to maintain his temper. "Look," he barked. "Step the fuck aside or there's gonna be trouble for you, too."

"You leave my Laurent alone, you cocksucker!"

From a distance, the woman had looked to be in her late twenties. Up close, she looked a good fifty-five.

Tired of her and her rotten breath, he snatched the pan from her grasp and knocked her on the side of the head. She fell to the floor and stayed there. He stooped down to quickly take her pulse. She was still breathing. He went in the locked room and staked the vamp. He called for an ambulance anonymously before heading to his no-tell motel to sleep.

The memory of that day flashed in the back of his mind briefly. He turned the pick. The lock clicked. The others heard it as well. Jay slid the door open. He entered with his tranq gun raised. The others followed.

The spell wore off as soon as they crossed the threshold. They could all see the expansive hallway with its expensive paintings on the walls, though only barely. Up ahead was the staircase to the second floor. It was so dark you'd think it was midnight, not dawn.

Snipe silently motioned for Harold to come with him upstairs while Jay and Colin scoped out the first floor. Harold left the crate by the front door.

Jay and Colin stepped into the living room. A single shaft of light filtered in from a window where the curtains hadn't been completely drawn. The room was still.

"We need night vision goggles," Colin whispered. Jay put a rigid finger to his mouth, wordlessly telling him to shut the fuck up.

Colin made a *whoopsie* face as his cheeks reddened. They came to the first bedroom, next to the living room. It was open but empty. The windows were sealed, leaving the room pitch black. But Jay didn't see a glow, so no vamps.

The next door didn't budge. Jay set to work picking the lock. Colin wandered a little farther down the hall and peeked into the kitchen. By now, their eyes had adjusted. Even still, all he saw were shapes and shadows.

A strange noise wafted through the darkness. Colin frowned, clutching his gun tighter. He reached out with his left elbow, since his right arm was still in the sling. He used his knobby elbow to feel along the wall, while keeping his gun trained on the center of the kitchen as best he could. His elbow found what he'd been looking for and he flipped the switch.

That sound he'd heard: Josiah growling. The sudden light blinded the vamp. He put an arm up to shield his eyes. His pupils had been like pinpricks, they were so small.

Is that what happened to their eyes when they went to sleep?

Colin shot him twice in the chest. Josiah pitched forward, landing on his belly.

Jay rushed in. His quick eyes took in the scene. Colin smiled at him proudly. Jay patted his back lightly, so as not to disturb his shoulder. They approached Josiah. Colin nudged him with his foot. As was probably expected, Josiah grabbed his ankle. It wasn't normal vampire speed because the drugs were taking effect, plus he was weak from the sun rising. Colin was going to yelp but he held it just in time, only emitting a gasp.

Jay was about to pull the trigger on his gun when Josiah's hand dropped feebly to the floor. He groaned, then fell silent. Jay wondered why Josiah was still up since usually the older ones got up right when the sun went down and could stay up until the sun rose. But Josiah's white glow was almost as perceptible as a newbie's.

Whatever, Jay didn't care. He left when Colin went to work staking him. The death smell escaped into the hallway a few moments later. Jay buried his nose in the crook of his elbow as he tinkered with the lock.

He wasn't having much luck. He cursed in his head. He was going to start all over but stopped.

The lock had clicked open.

He jumped back, gun at the ready as the door swung wide. The vampire was fast, his glow faint as he bobbed and weaved out of the path of darts Jay fired at him.

It was Bryce. He ducked as a dart sailed over his shoulder. He was close enough to whack Jay in the ear, of all places. It stung like hell.

"Fuck!" Jay grunted as he fell to one knee. Annie flitted from the room as well. She was too quick. She kicked him hard in the balls before he knew to protect himself. Stars actually burst in front of his eyes. The breath caught in his chest and a wave of nausea clenched his stomach.

He squeezed his eyes shut, waiting for his body to behave, and to make sure he didn't embarrass himself.

Annie zipped away. Colin's scream came from the kitchen but Jay couldn't move, paralyzed by the radiating *agony*. There were heavy boots on the stairs: Snipe and Harold, each shooting their tranqs. Someone grunted from a hit.

"Get the bottles!" Snipe ordered and Harold ran for the front door. Snipe stopped at Jay but he waved him on. His crotch and his ear throbbed equally but Colin needed backup. It wasn't until he felt Harold's hand under his armpit, tugging him up insistently, could he find the strength to stand. Snipe and Colin held the four vampires at bay.

With his free hand, Harold threw one, then two already-lit bottles up the stairs. They crashed, and orange flames engulfed the landing.

The four hunters scuttled to the door. Unfortunately, Colin made the unwise decision to turn his back on the vamps.

Annie jumped and landed on top of him like a graceful cheetah, bringing him to the floor. She swiped her sharp nails along his back and he cried out.

Snipe ran at her, stake drawn. She hissed at him but flitted backwards, just missing the arc of his swing.

Harold tossed another bottle, creating a line of fire between the vamps and the hunters. The blaze licked the hunters' faces. They lurched and staggered backward onto the porch. The dry, morning air rushed inside, fueling the flames. The sky was even lighter now, though the sun wasn't visible.

They didn't stop until they were at the van, stumbling down the invisible stairs and all. You could smell wood burning but there was no evident fire. It would be a conundrum for the neighbors.

As Snipe sped off, Jay spied through the side-view mirror bright blurs escaping to the woods around the house. He couldn't count how many. *Burn bitches*, he thought bitterly, which was kind of rude.

He slumped into his seat, closing his eyes for a moment. It wasn't until the van jerked to a stop when Jay realized he had passed out. His eyes sprang open and he looked around, disoriented enough to forget his pain. As Colin's distressed moans hit his ears, his own throbbing returned.

Harold and Snipe carried Colin inside. It was a bit awkward maneuvering Colin's long legs and arms without aggravating his back and shoulder. They crossed through the living room to the hallway, past the girls' room and the bathroom. The spare bedroom was at the end of the hall, on the right. Jay snatched back the green covers on the queen-sized bed before Snipe and Harold deposited Colin. Jay saw the scratches, the blood and sweat on them; they matched his own battle wounds.

Snipe wiped his eyes to get a better look at Colin's back. "Get me the first-aid kit," he told Harold, who hurried off to the bathroom.

He used the scissors Harold handed him to cut Colin's shirt. Four deep gashes sliced his shoulder blades. It looked like the work of a scalpel, that's how clean and precise the cuts were. Snipe let out a slow breath to steady himself.

"He's going to need stitches," he said wearily. He touched a spot above the wound. Colin flinched and snuffled. "I don't see any muscle damage; the cuts aren't as deep as they look."

Snipe had gained almost as much emergency medical training as Lauren over the years. It came with the job. It was too complicated trying to explain various, bizarre wounds to doctors without fear of law enforcement intervening, especially with his hunters' ages. Booth, Teddy, and Harold were all in their twenties, but they had been teenagers or just out of their teenage years when he had first recruited each of them. Harold specifically had been the most accident-prone of the group. He was the first one Snipe had to learn to stitch up. He still had the lopsided scar on his left calf where a stake had impaled him during a fight in Provincetown.

Jay shuffled to the kitchen for two makeshift ice bags, then leaned heavily against the wall of the bedroom, out of the way. Colin was whimpering. Snipe was on one knee beside the bed, bent over his back, carefully stitching his wounds.

Jay sighed to himself. Colin was too young to be dealing with this shit. And at that moment, Jay felt he was too *old* to be dealing with this shit.

"Where's the gauze?" Snipe asked after a half an hour. Harold opened a few packs, then handed him white athletic tape to hold them in place. With that and the shoulder, Colin was going to be out of commission for a while.

Snipe grunted as he struggled out of his kneeling position. Harold gave him a hand, helping him to his feet. Snipe limped, more than usually, to the kitchen and brought back three beers and a glass of water for Colin. He had his face buried in a pillow, clutching his sore shoulder, his wounded back still exposed. Snipe set the water on the bedside table along with a bottle of Percocet.

The others went to the living room. Jay settled into the loveseat with his ice packs.

"Where're you hurt?" Snipe asked Harold.

"I already bandaged the cuts. Not too bad."

"Any bites?"

"Just one."

He lifted his shirt and removed the gauze he had taped to the right side of his belly. The vamp had meant business, since you could see the imprint of his regular teeth along with the two puncture wounds. Harold had cleaned the dried blood away, leaving behind a ring of red and yellow, like some kind of grotesque Christmas wreath. He replaced the gauze because it was still leaking.

Snipe sighed because the wound looked bad. "Lauren'll be back in the morning. Wash it out and keep pressure on it until then."

Harold nodded and disappeared into the bathroom. Snipe looked to Jay wearily, as if expecting the worst. Jay shifted the ice in his lap. He gave him a humorless smile.

"Don't worry 'bout the boys," he said, motioning to his 'nads. "They'll be alright."

Snipe sank into his recliner with a groan. No one said anything. The fridge grumbled from the other room. Water swooshed through pipes overhead and the air conditioner, on a low setting, rattled in the window.

There wasn't much else for them to do at the moment but rest. Jay figured they'd swing by the house a little later to check the damage. He didn't think they'd taken out the nest though, and that weighed on him. He hadn't seen Ramsey there either, and he highly doubted that he had slept through all the commotion (the other vamps there had been Bryce, Annie, Elizabeth, and Arturo).

Those vampires still had a short time to find a dark place to hide. He hoped some of them fried in the morning sun. Of course, this definitely meant a full-on attack would come. Snipe was always careful when going to any of their houses, choosing to take circuitous routes just in case, but Jay wondered if they should move their headquarters.

He sighed, deciding to think about that later. For now, sleep fell over him like a thick blanket and he was knocked out.

Sixteen

VICTOR STOOD BESIDE Ramsey, staring up at the house. The fire had eaten away at the living room and top floor, and consumed most of the roof. A mid-morning shower had squelched the flames, leaving a dilapidated . . . structure in its wake. The white of what was left of the house seemed to stand out even more in contrast with the blackened sections.

Ramsey trembled in rage. Victor could practically feel it rolling off of him. He took a step away to give him space. Elizabeth and Bryce emerged on the porch, each carrying water-stained paintings. They'd been taking inventory of the inner damage. Ramsey hadn't been able to bring himself to go inside yet. He felt like his home: exposed and violated.

The injured vamps were looking like themselves. There were only a few marks and Annie's hair was just about the same length again. Once the sun went down, Bryce and Annie, both covered in burns that had bubbled and blistered, had found solace in the basement of a neighbor's house two streets over. The humans—

four people in their late twenties sharing the house—hadn't heard anything. Two of them were home when the sun set at eight. They had just finished cleaning up after dinner when the sound of something heavy hitting the floor beneath their feet carried them downstairs to the basement.

They were considering how the storage crates had fallen when Bryce stepped out of the shadows of a corner, panting in pain. One of the nastier blisters took up residence on the left side of his head. The hair had burned away in the sun. The plum-sized blister on his scalp trembled then ruptured as he neared the frightened humans. Yellow pus and light pink blood squirted onto his shoulder.

The female human's scream filled the room. She spun around for the safety of the stairs but Annie was there behind her. The fire had licked her face. Her skin was red and shiny, like plastic. The ends of her hair were singed, leaving it uneven. It was sticking to the sores on her shoulders.

The woman backed up, bumping into her housemate. In a flash, Annie was on her neck. Bryce grabbed the man's throat and craned his head to the side. He sank his fangs into his neck. They only took enough to make the humans pass out. Annie had to tug on Bryce's ear, her reminder to him when to stop. Bryce looked up at her with reluctant eyes. She stared back adamantly. Lucky for them, the other housemates came in and they were able to feast some more. Their skin was bright pink like newborn babies when they emerged from the house.

Bryce's control was surprising, especially since he was hurt.

Elizabeth had lost her heels when she scaled a house to hide out in an attic. She wasn't able to find nourishment in the inhabitants because the single mother had three small children. Standing over the crib of the youngest and sucking her teeth at her bad luck, she caught the scent of charcoal and grilled meats. A group of six was in the next yard, drinking and laughing merrily. The man behind the round kettle grill went to the side of the house to take the stairs inside. Elizabeth grabbed him on the bottom step, pulling him into the bushes separating the houses with a hand over his mouth to silence him. They were interrupted by a black-and-white cat. Elizabeth and he locked eyes. He hissed, all his fur standing straight up, and raced off. She hadn't experienced as much trauma as the rest; that one man's blood did the trick.

Arturo wasn't as mindful as the others. He had been awoken by the sound of someone cursing.

"What the fuck is this shit?"

The owner of the shed he had hidden inside had just discovered the broken lock. The metal clasp clanged against the wooden door. Arturo kicked it open. The door hit the man in the nose. He stumbled backward. Arturo snatched him by the collar before he fell backward and yanked him inside the dark, cool shelter.

He didn't stop, even when the man ceased his struggling, even when his heart raced faster to compensate for the loss of blood. Not until his heart stopped and there was no more to take. Arturo grunted, and let him drop to the floor. His head hit a rake on the way down. The wooden handle banged against the wall. Arturo stepped over the body then closed the shed. He hung the useless lock on the door for effect and made his way to Ramsey's.

Annie and Arturo were currently making piles of rubbish in the front yard. The magic that hid the mansion was still in effect and the vampires had their own hoodoo up so the humans that were moving about in their houses—eating dinner or watching television, or having some damn good sex judging by the sounds from next door—were oblivious to their cleanup work.

"Leave it!" Ramsey suddenly barked. He had gotten a look at the waterfall painting Bryce was carrying down the stairs (it used to hang in his bedroom). All of the vampires looked up at him in surprise. "Just leave it all!"

"Ramsey," Elizabeth said, her tone soft and unchallenging. "There may be some things that can be saved—"

"No. Leave it all." His voice was gravelly. He began shaking his head slowly, like a thought was creeping into his mind that he was fighting. "This is too much. It's time to stop being idle."

Arturo and Bryce equally lit up. "Does this mean we can add some new meat?" Bryce asked, a hungry glint in his eyes.

Ramsey hesitated, Victor noticed, as if considering this notion. He shook his head, though. "No."

Bryce gave a huff and folded his massive arms at the chest in annoyance.

"Milo and Clarice are supposed to be on lookout," Annie replied.

"I don't think they'll be out tonight," Victor commented. "They're probably lying low, recuperating."

"And I don't like only having Milo and Clarice on patrol," Ramsey added.

"They'd create a bloodbath in the middle of downtown just to draw them out," Elizabeth said, a hint of disgust in her voice. She looked at Ramsey. "We could call in the other nests."

"Bryce, Annie, Arturo, go do some looking," Ramsey dispatched. They each nodded then dashed down the street. Bryce and Arturo were especially eager now that Ramsey gave them permission to take out the hunters.

Ramsey looked up at Elizabeth, who was still on the porch. "I don't want a war, love." Elizabeth nodded slowly. She didn't seem to be in complete agreement with his decision. Victor didn't understand either. If Ramsey had other vamps at his disposal, vamps he allowed to live in his territory, why not use them in his time of need? What was the point of being the leader?

"Victor, would you help Elizabeth find whatever's salvageable?"

"Okay."

He left Ramsey on the curb in his silent lamenting. The basement of the house was undamaged. As soon as they descended the stairs, they knew Cillian was in his room. He was walking in circles, singing a song in a rich baritone. The words sounded Welsh.

Victor and Elizabeth exchanged glances. They went on to the storage closet, hoping he'd ignore them. They found empty boxes to fill with her miscellaneous medical supplies.

Victor was placing a scale into a plastic storage container. "Where will you go?" he asked her.

She shrugged as she closed a box with tape. "Probably to Ramsey's house in Brookline."

Victor paused, puzzled. "He has a house in Brookline?"

She chuckled. "There are humans living in it." Her face grew cold for a moment. She obviously didn't like that particular living arrangement.

Victor decided not to pry. Besides, it wasn't his place. He and Elizabeth were friendly, but not the tell-each-other-everything kind of friends.

They went through the rest of the house in relative silence. In the shell of the living room, Victor saw that Ramsey was no longer out front.

"How do you think they found the house?" Elizabeth asked Victor's back since he was staring out onto the front yard.

Victor shrugged, completely forgetting about the other night when he thought they were being watched.

At ten-fifteen, while bringing up the boxes from the basement, Elizabeth went very still for a moment. Her eyes stared blankly at the floor. Victor recognized this so he wasn't too concerned. He just stood by, waiting for her to come out of the trance.

"Ramsey said the house is ready," she told him. She glanced

to the closed door of Cillian's room. "He said to leave him. He'll collect him later."

The fire hadn't made it to the garage. They piled as many of the boxes they could into the Infiniti and Ramsey's convertible. The rest were stored along the back wall. Elizabeth drove the convertible, with Victor right behind.

The house in Brookline wasn't as concealed. It sat at the end of the street (another dead-end road) and there were a couple of yards between each house. It was a nice house, painted a light blue you couldn't see at night, with two floors and a flower garden out front.

The lights were on for the benefit of the neighbors. Elizabeth parked in the driveway, Victor at the curb. They carried the twenty boxes into the house. In the living room, they stopped, looking around at everything. The house was well lived-in. It still smelled of them, a woman and three kids. Their scents traced a path of them packing and leaving the front door together.

There was a banging noise that Elizabeth and Victor followed into a spare bedroom off the kitchen. Ramsey was hammering drywall over the windows.

"I've already done the upstairs rooms," he informed them without turning around.

Elizabeth went to his side to hold the drywall while he hammered. She watched him work, concern on her pretty brown face.

He drove the last nail through the panel. "I'm fine," Ramsey said softly. Elizabeth faced him, waiting. He finally sighed then pinched his sinuses. She reached out and rubbed his back, trying to comfort him.

Suddenly, it was very much like Victor was intruding on a private moment. He left the room to explore the rest of the house. The woman who lived there must've been married very recently. A man occupied some of the photos and he detected a male scent in the master bedroom. It was the only room where the scent was most discernible.

This would be the perfect house for him and Celia, he mused. His sharp eyes sliced through the darkness of the master bedroom. There was a queen-sized bed with framed photos of the family littering the two circular end tables. He imagined him and Celia, lounging there in each other's arms. Talking about nothing; hearing her soft laugh. It was dangerous territory, he knew this. But he couldn't help pining for a future with her. A future he could never have because Celia didn't want to be a vampire. And he didn't want her to be one. This life was too hard. There was so much to sacrifice. Her loved ones. Her job. Daylight. Her personality could change drastically. He wouldn't wish it on his enemies.

His enemies.

The thought made his spine hunch, like a cat. He wanted this over. To be rid of those filthy humans who were making their lives a living hell. He was angry he had saved Jay's life. It had only been because he knew Celia would never forgive him. Now he wished he had left him to Clarice. For her to turn him, force him to go through the painful process of coming over. Not everyone could survive the turn but he was sure Jay would do fine. What would he do if, without his permission, he became this powerful creature who lived for an eternity off of human blood?

It was an interesting prospect that actually gave him a thrill of excitement. No matter how Ramsey's plan went down, Victor was concocting his own at that very moment. It relaxed his hands. They had been balled into tight fists as he stared down at the faces of that family, their happy smiles frozen in time.

He knew what he was going to do.

* * *

Bobby hadn't said anything to Celia when she came in on Thursday; in fact he pretty much avoided her. On Friday, when he handed out paychecks at the end of the night, he barely spared her a glance. Celia rolled her eyes. She'd fix it later. Last thing she needed was tension at work. Well, besides the whole Carson thing, which she had gotten good at ignoring.

Speaking of which, Carson strolled up behind her. She hadn't been paying attention since she was opening the envelope containing her check. He put his mouth really close to her ear and whispered, "Boo!"

She jumped at the sudden voice. She spun on him. He chuckled at her furious glare. "You're such an ass."

He shrugged. "Sorry, I couldn't help it. You're just too easy." She gave him the finger then hurried off. The anger wore off quickly during her march to her car. Her misery returned along with sweat from the blaring sun above.

She thought of Victor every second. It was Sunday evening when she finally made her decision. She slammed her fork on the table in resolution. Trixie frowned at her. Celia was actually giddy as she jumped up and raced to her room. She snatched up her cell phone and dialed Victor's number. The call went straight to voicemail since it was only seven and the sky was just beginning to darken.

"Victor," she breathed after the beep. "Can we talk?" She paused, trying to form the right words. "I . . . miss you. And I want to see if we can work this out. Please, come by tonight. I'll be up."

She couldn't think of anything more to say so she closed the phone. A fresh wave of anxiety made her stomach hurt. She returned to the living room. Trixie's eyes were on her the whole time. She had muted the television and had heard her message, the nosy thing.

When Celia sank back into the sofa, Trixie squeezed her shoulder. Celia gave her a small smile that didn't reach her eyes, then picked up her wine glass for some liquid courage.

The sun set at seven-fifty. Victor arrived at eight twenty-five.

"Celia." His smooth voice seemed to fill the room. Trixie shrieked. Celia jerked her head to him then slowly stood without realizing it. Victor glanced at Trixie. "I didn't know you had company."

"It's okay," Trixie said quickly. "I was just leaving."

She grabbed her wristlet, kissed Celia's cheek, and hurried out the door. They were both quiet. Celia swallowed a few times, trying to find her voice. She was happy he was there though she still wanted to go over the ground rules.

They both opened their mouths to speak. The buzzer went off. They stared at each other, then grinned simultaneously.

"Of course," Celia said of the interruption. She trudged to the door and pressed Talk. "Yes?"

"It's Jay."

Her finger dropped from the button. "Oh." She bit her bottom lip nervously and glanced over her shoulder to see what she should do. She was looking at an empty room.

"Victor?"

Abandoning the intercom, she peeked in her bedroom. He wasn't there. Her ears perked when she returned to the living room. She rushed to the window and pulled back the curtains.

Victor and Jay were fist fighting, right there in front of her stoop. She gasped, then ran out the apartment. She pushed open the front door of the building just in time to see Jay knee Victor in the stomach. Victor responded with an elbow to his face.

Celia was going to do something incredibly stupid. She propelled forward, hoping that if she stepped in, the boys would stop. Victor, seeing this and realizing her impending stupidity, grabbed Jay into a bear hug. They both vanished right before her eyes.

"No!" she screamed, stumbling to a halt. Her shout startled a woman coming out of the opposite building.

They were gone and she had no idea to where.

* * *

Victor and Jay appeared in the basement of the Brookline house. Teleporting knocked the air out of them both and they fell to the ground. Clutching his head, Jay reached for his gun in the waistband of his pants. Victor kicked out as he pointed it at him, knocking the gun from his hand.

Victor was able to recover quicker. He was on his feet in a second, with his arm around Jay's neck the next. He squeezed hard against his jugular. Jay blacked out before he could retaliate.

Victor dragged him to a nearby chair. He held him up with one hand while using duct tape to bind him to the seat. Ten minutes later, he came to. He glared at Victor in odium.

"Where're the other hunters?" Victor asked in a calm voice, a façade hiding his own abhorrence.

Jay's face softened as he smiled. "Is that all you wanted?" he asked in a carefree way. "Well, hell, you didn't have to kidnap me. All you had to do was ask." Victor's gaze narrowed. "They're up my ass. Wanna look?"

Victor neared him to punch him twice in the face. Jay's lip split and he spat blood onto the floor. The smell set off tingles in Victor's arms. He punched him a few more times, in the face and stomach. Jay took them with grunts and grimaces. The more blood he spilled, the more Victor lost himself to his other nature.

After a few glorious minutes of this, that human side finally took reign and he stepped away. Jay slumped forward, his chest heaving against his constraints, making it hard for him to catch his breath. His face was bloodied and bruises were already turning his cheek and nose red and purple. The collar of his shirt was ripped from when Victor grabbed it.

"You're wasting your time," Jay said between pants. "I'm not gonna tell you a damn thing."

"But I'm having fun in the meantime."

Jay smiled, a scary smile with the blood and saliva coating his teeth and dripping from his lips. "Huh. I didn't think you knew *how* to have fun."

Victor's eyes were savage. "You don't know me."

Jay shrugged as much as he could. "You're right. But like I said, I ain't telling you shit."

Victor knew he was right. He had no leverage.

Cue the dramatic chords.

Victor heard the car pull into the driveway, immediately recognizing the roar of the engine. He frowned as he listened to the car doors open. Two vampires and one out-of-control heartbeat.

The front door opened. Victor froze, anger rising in him for a different reason now. The feet moved above their heads. The cellar door opened and he received visual confirmation of what he had smelled.

Milo came down the stairs first, followed by Clarice. Clarice had one arm around Celia's neck, the other twisted Celia's arm behind her back. She didn't bother with her art of persuasion because she wanted her to be panicked.

Celia stumbled on the stairs. Clarice yanked her back to her chest before she could fall.

"Well, well," Milo crooned, rolling his neck a few times. "Did we miss the party?"

His eyes were on Jay, his fangs already bared. Clarice giggled. "I forgot how nice he smelled," she purred. She rubbed her nose along Celia's jaw, making her whimper. "Almost as good as you, my dear."

Victor took a step toward her but Clarice showed her fangs meaningfully. "Un, un, un," she said. He halted. "I've heard about her. I could use a sugar rush." Her free hand inched up Celia's stomach and cupped her breast. She laughed when Celia struggled to knock her hand away.

Celia was looking at him, her brown eyes glazed with unshed tears. Her despair was too much. Victor calculated that he could reach her before Clarice could do too much harm.

Just as he moved his leg to run at her, something hard crashed against the back of his head.

He hadn't registered the look of alarm on Celia's face when Milo appeared behind him.

The last thing he saw was the ground rushing to his face.

* * *

Celia fought hard to keep from screaming out. It would do Jay no good. It was a tough task containing her agony. She struggled weakly against the duct tape binding her arms and legs to the chair. The parts of the tape she managed to loosen with her wiggling left a sticky residue on her skin. Blood and sweat slithered into her eyes, and she blinked to clear them.

Clarice was enjoying this entirely too much. She licked the blood from the blade she'd been using to cut Celia's arm. She came closer now and stooped next to Celia.

Jay growled and strained at his binding.

"Leave her alone," he barked.

Clarice dragged her tongue slowly over the last cut she'd made with the knife, this one along her bicep. The others were already starting to heal, thanks to their saliva.

"Mmmm," she moaned. "I could do this all night. It's like . . ." She squinted as she debated. "Vanilla bean ice cream. Yeah, that's it. I just want to eat you up." She giggled. "Why are you so friggin' sweet?"

She smiled up at Celia. Celia's look was murderous. "Fuck off."

Clarice threw her head back and laughed. Celia could see Victor over her head, tossed in the corner like a discarded towel by the other vampires. Milo had hit him with a lead pipe, and proceeded to hit him a few more times just to be sure. Celia had screamed at him to stop. He blew her a kiss.

Celia took a deep breath as the pain eased. "Don't tell them anything," she told Jay.

Milo sighed. He'd been perched on an overturned milk crate for the past five minutes, opting to sit out on the latest round of Torture the Human. She tried to suck it up for the cuts and bites though they hurt like hell. No matter how much she braced for them, she couldn't properly prepare herself for the sting.

It was to the point now where she actually felt *grateful* when they healed them. And she knew they knew. She wasn't that good at hiding her relief. Yeah, they knew what they were doing.

Milo stood and stretched his lean body. He ran a hand through his white-blonde hair. He strode over to Celia, straightening his vest.

"Enough of this bullshit."

Clarice stood back, eager to see what he was going to do.

Milo lifted her chair and brought her to Jay. He set her down so that their knees were just about to touch. His fingers grazed the sides of her neck, massaging the muscles and tendons beneath.

Very gently, he tilted her head to the left, exposing the flesh of her throat. They had left that area untouched. He leaned down slowly—his lusty, cocky eyes on Jay—and showed his fangs. Celia winced. He bit down. Jay groaned and sputtered furiously.

Celia's heart raced. She still wasn't used to the pain. This was a weird feeling; like Milo was tugging, pulling strings from her arms, shoulders, and chest through her neck. She'd been holding her breath when she was waiting for the bite. She released it now, which had an adverse effect. It made her relax. When she stopped fighting, the tugging relaxed as well. Now the strings were rhythmic, soothing. Her eyes drooped then closed on their own accord. She didn't want him to stop. She almost said so, but was too lost in this newfound bliss to form any coherent words.

"Stop it, you sick son-of-a-bitch!" Jay yelled. His voice sounded distant to her ears, like he was calling from the end of a tunnel.

Milo pulled away after a minute. His mouth was dry, as if he hadn't wanted to waste a single drop. When he laughed, his face became even more flushed. Jay's eyes darted from her neck back to the vampire.

Milo rolled up the sleeve of his right arm. He took the knife from Clarice and made a vertical slice along his inner arm. Deep red blood dripped from the cut onto the basement floor beside her chair.

Jay stiffened when he saw the blood. He knew what he was threatening. Celia's head felt like a spinning top. She would certainly be swaying if she hadn't been secured to the seat.

Milo stroked her head as he brought his arm closer to her face.

"You better not," Jay said, his voice low. "You better fuckin' not."

Milo just smirked. He was so close. Celia was starting to feel loopy. She just wanted to lie down and go to sleep. Milo's fingers in her hair felt incredibly nice, adding to the effect. His arm hovered in front of her and she wondered through the haze in her head what he wanted her to do.

"Fuck!" Jay shouted. "Alright, alright! I'll tell you where they are."

Milo glanced at him. His smirk widened into a grin. "Yeah?"

He heaved a sigh. "They've been using this place in Boston, near a train station. South something."

"South Station?" Clarice asked.

"Yeah," he said reluctantly. "It's a letter—A Street, I think. A gray building. Number three forty-five. Now, leave her alone, dammit."

Milo considered him a moment while tonguing his fangs. Then, without warning, he shoved his bleeding arm to Celia's mouth. Too slow on the uptake and groggy from the blood lost, she didn't move away. She gasped as his blood passed her lips and over her tongue.

"No!" Jay bellowed. "Celia!"

She tried to turn her head away since Jay seemed so adamant but Milo held his arm tight on her mouth. She didn't know what to expect vampire blood to taste like. This . . . was like nectar, like a warm glass of milk on a freezing cold day, like double chocolate chunk ice cream. She could go on forever about how blissful she felt. He was inside of her, penetrating her every corner. Celia found herself drawing him in, his blood warming her cheeks and throat.

"That's right," Milo whispered. His face was soft in ecstasy. His hand tightened in her hair. He pressed his nose to her temple. His tongue flicked out through his fangs, running along her skin.

"I'm gonna kill you," Jay growled. "You hear me, you piece of shit? I'm gonna fuckin' kill you!"

Milo rolled his eyes. He pulled away like his mood was just killed. Her lips made a sucking sound when he removed his arm. She hadn't expected him to take the goods away so suddenly. Droplets of blood snuggled at the creases of Celia's mouth. The blood worked through her system, awakening things she hadn't known were asleep. Little sunbursts appeared in front of her eyes and she stared at them in wonder.

Milo rolled down his sleeve. The cut was already mending itself. He pinched Jay's cheek affectionately. They were off, with Jay glaring after them.

Celia gazed at his face, amazed at the premature lines forming around his eyes. She'd never noticed them before but her eyes were sharper now. She could see the individual hairs of his stubble, the folds and creases of cuts, the varying shades of bruises as well.

Jay's green eyes shifted to her. There were flecks of gold near his pupils that she'd never seen before either.

"You okay?"

His voice was gentle, concerned. She wanted to tell him yes except she was distracted by a car driving down the street, and a dog's collar clinking as he was walked by his owner, and the leaves blowing in the wind. She hadn't been able to hear anything but her and Jay's haggard breathing before.

Victor groaned from his corner. They both looked. He sat up, rubbing the back of his head as he surveyed the room.

"'Bout time," Jay grumbled. "We gotta get outta here. Those two are gonna be mighty upset when they get to that abandoned warehouse."

Victor immediately became alert. He stood and yanked Celia's tape. He touched her cheek, saw the blood on her mouth. A low growl rumbled in his chest. He used his thumb to wipe it away.

She gazed up at him, mesmerized. He was truly beautiful, she thought. There were no lines, no flaws in his skin, unlike hers and Jay's. She ran her hand up his arm, to his shoulder, until she was cupping his cheek. It was so smooth under her fingers.

"Celia," he said softly, warningly. But she wanted to kiss him. She didn't understand why he didn't want her to.

She pulled his face toward her and actually made him move. He had to put his hands on her shoulders to stop her.

"It's okay," he said. "It'll wear off in an hour or so."

He took her hand and led her to the stairs. "Hey!" Jay called. "You wanna give me a fuckin' hand?"

Victor ignored him, opting to continue toward the stairs. Celia, however, stopped. He was annoyed but remained silent.

Celia pulled her hand from Victor's and went back to Jay.

She tugged on the tape around his wrists, astounded at how easily it ripped. Unfortunately, she also got some of his hair.

"Careful," he snapped.

"Sorry."

She removed the rest of the tape, a little gentler this time, and the three of them rushed upstairs. As they neared the front door, Celia halted. Suddenly, she was looking at something completely different. She'd just seen the door right there in front of her but now she was staring at an empty, dark warehouse. It was almost like she was there, it was so real. She could feel the humidity, smell the must from the closed off place. The vision moved from side to side, showing her the empty space. Her blood boiled in rage.

No, not *her* blood. Milo's.

"They found the warehouse."

Jay came to a stop beside her. "What? Already?"

She nodded. Milo's vicious scream resounded in her head. She clapped her hands on her ears but she could still hear his cry. The vision turned abruptly and she knew he was running.

Then it was gone. Once again, she was staring at Victor and Jay's dour faces.

Panic set in. "They're coming back," she said frantically.

Victor looked troubled at all of this. His mouth was a tight line, like he wanted to say something. Instead, he ran out the front door in that vamp speed. Celia and Jay followed. By the time they reached the red Infiniti, Victor had already hot-wired it. The engine roared to life.

They climbed in and Victor sped off. Celia was amazed as she stared out the window. Victor was driving at his normal breakneck speed but she could see everything clearly. The trees, the houses, the pedestrians jumping back on the curb as they zoomed by. She wondered if she'd have the ability to run fast and far like Victor.

About two minutes later, Victor wrenched the wheel to the right. Celia and Jay shifted in their seats from the sudden movement. Jay grunted when the seatbelt cut into his throat.

Celia looked around at the deserted area once Victor screeched to a halt. "What's going on?"

Victor glared at Jay through the rear-view mirror. "Get out."

"What?" Celia exclaimed. She looked over the seat at Jay. "You can't just kick him out."

"I can't?" he snapped at her. "I won't go any farther with him."

She was shocked. She could understand Victor's sentiment but she still opened her mouth to argue.

"It's fine," Jay said with an exhausted sigh. He opened the door, which caused the dome light to flick on. It wasn't that bright but the light still hurt her new vision

She squinted at him. "But you don't even know where you are," she protested.

"I'll be alright."

He got out of the car. Victor was off before he could close the door; the force of his speed snapped it shut. Celia sighed, conflicted as usual. She sat silently as he drove onto the expressway. She had no idea where he was headed; she wasn't even thinking about that since she was having more visions.

Milo had picked up a scent inside the warehouse. They followed it, mostly to dead ends. The flashes came and went.

"What is it?" Victor asked, aware of her silence.

"I don't know. They're looking for something."

"It's not common for a human to tap into our minds," he said after a moment. "In fact, I've never heard of such a thing. It's never both ways." She frowned up at him. He stared ahead, looking grim. "When we share blood with a human, we will be able to feel what they are feeling. We'll be able to call them."

She didn't like the sound of that.

"That's also why my vision's clearer? And my hearing?" He nodded. "It's weird."

She couldn't say she liked the feeling entirely. She looked down at her hands, turning them over a few times like she'd only just discovered them. She felt weightless, like she was floating above the seat. And her heart was beating slowly. It thumped hard in her chest at half the speed. There was going to be a crash later. She could tell.

"You said it'll go away after an hour, right?"

He squeezed her knee. *Another flash*: Milo was excited, aroused. He stared into the window of a house. There were three men inside, talking at the kitchen table. The vision turned as Milo nodded to Clarice. She had been standing on the top step of the non-existent porch.

She gave him a lusty smile, then knocked on the door. Milo turned back to the window. The red-haired guy got up with a pained expression from the movement. He tottered across the room to answer the door. The vision dissipated and Celia was staring at the dashboard.

No, she thought. She closed her eyes, willing the vision back. They couldn't get them, she told herself. They would need an invitation inside. The hunters wouldn't be stupid enough to invite her in, right?

Unfortunately, the hunters had never seen Clarice and they didn't have Jay's Vamp-O-Vision. Plus, all she would need to do was touch Colin and he'd do whatever she wished. That's how she had gotten a hold of Celia, catching her when she ran out to her car for her phone. She'd only used her persuasion until she'd pulled her into the Infiniti.

Milo's excitement flared. She waited, expecting another view. None came. She only felt his exhilaration fluttering in her stomach.

"They found the hunters," she reported to Victor.

"Good," he muttered. She was certain she wouldn't have heard that normally but it didn't escape her enhanced hearing this time.

"Victor," she said sternly. "They'll *kill* them or worse."

He jerked his head to her. "Or worse?" he cried, affronted. "Nice to see how you feel about me."

She was baffled by his reaction. Surely he didn't think she was talking about *him*. She had only suggested that they would torture the hunters, like they'd done to her not too long ago. Playing games excited Milo and Clarice.

As she thought about it more, trying to figure out his offense, she guessed their idea of fun could include turning them into nightwalkers. Clarice had threatened to do so much to Jay.

"You thought I was saying being a vampire is worse? That's not what I meant—"

"It's what you said."

She gawked at him. "Why are you so upset? This isn't about you."

"This isn't about *you*," he shot back.

"I wasn't saying that being a vampire was horrible."

"You don't know all the ins and outs of this life. All the things we have to do to survive."

"You mean like drinking blood? I *do* understand."

He shook his head, unhappy with her vehement certitude. "There's more to it than that. There are regulations to follow. Some disregard them because they don't care about keeping our existence secret. But they're important to sustain our livelihood.

"Everything had been going fine for years, and now all of this shit. We've been passive for too long. Ramsey's gotten complacent and look what happened. He lost four of his family!

"Do you even know what your little buddies did? They came right before sunrise and set fire to Ramsey's house. It's destroyed. Uninhabitable. And for what? *We* didn't attack that night."

Her eyes widened. "I . . ." She shook her head, unable to form proper words. "That's terrible."

He was so angry, so cold. He'd never used that tone with her before. Her brows pulled together in concern.

"I understand your anger. And, yeah, maybe I don't get all the rules," she said defiantly. "But there has to be another way. This can't be the only option. And where are we going?"

She caught sight of a green sign that indicated they were headed south. He didn't answer her.

"You're running away?"

"I'm getting you somewhere safe."

"And then what? You're gonna go back and have your turn? Like some kind of monster? Like Milo?"

"I *am* a monster!" he shouted.

Victor once again jerked the car off the road, nearly sideswiping an SUV and a minivan, which was really quite careless. The ingested vampire blood would not save her if they were in a serious accident.

He slammed the car into park. She jolted forward against the seatbelt. He got out in silent rage and flashed into the forest. She stared in astonishment out the window. She couldn't see him, but suddenly a snapping sound penetrated the night. A tall tree swayed and groaned, then fell over. It was so thick and heavy, it made the ground shake.

Four minutes passed before Victor emerged from the forest. She kept her eyes on him as he stalked around the car, brushing dirt and other forest stuff off his hands and shoulders and head. She should've been afraid. But he hadn't taken his pent-up fury out on her, just some poor unsuspecting tree. All that power. As freaky or bizarre as it sounded, it made her tingle.

Maybe it was the vampire blood.

Once he was settled in the car, Victor rubbed his face, like he was exhausted.

"Where are they?" he finally asked.

She'd had a few more flashes while Victor was in the woods, beating up trees. Ha, that sounded like a punk rock, emo band name. Milo had gone through Snipe's wallet, to show him the pictures he kept of his family as a threat. She'd gotten a glimpse of his license.

She told him the South Boston address and he sped off in silence. By the time they reached Snipe's house, it was after three. And there was more company.

Inside, Snipe, Harold, and Colin were at the table. Ramsey, Elizabeth and Annie stood in the kitchen with them. Bryce, Milo, Clarice and Arturo took up space in the living room.

Clarice hissed when Celia entered. She ignored her. She went straight to the kitchen, only glancing at the vamps without recognizing them. The hunters were wounded. Fresh cuts galore. Poor Colin. He looked like he might collapse at any minute. His pain was so clearly etched on his pale, sweaty face—even the freckles were blanched.

Celia shook her head. "This has to stop," she said immediately.

"We weren't actually doing anything," Milo replied snidely. "Ramsey interrupted."

"Quiet," Ramsey said fiercely. Milo's lips pursed together like he'd been sucking on a lemon. Ramsey turned to Celia. "What're you doing here?" He looked past her. "Do you mind?"

Celia was puzzled. She glanced over her shoulder. Victor had stopped short of the front door. His hands were casually tucked in his pockets as he waited for invitation.

The olive-skinned guy, sitting at the head of the table, unhinged his jaw unceremoniously.

"You may enter."

Victor crossed the threshold. He stood at Celia's side, his hand going to her shoulder.

"I came because I want to help," she announced.

She turned to Snipe. He seemed like the one in charge. He stared up at her with callous eyes, as if she was the blame for the vampires crowding his house. The heated glare stung and the urge to run from the house made her stomach clench. Maybe Victor was right. Maybe all of this had nothing to do with her. She could just step aside. Let them hash it out themselves.

Except the last time they all came together, violence had ensued. Obviously a little more violence had occurred before they had arrived. She felt she had to do *something*. Victor was her boyfriend and she didn't want Jay hurt either.

The vampire blood cooled her nerves. She took a deep breath.

"I know that you want to protect this city. But who's to say that the troubles have been coming from Ramsey's group? It could be someone else." The hunters looked doubtful. "Either way, the vampires have their own system; their own way of working things out. If someone's killing people, they'll deal with it."

Harold started to shake his head in protest. "I know," she said before he could interrupt. "It sounds . . . off. They can't help what they are, just like you—" she indicated Colin "—can't help it you have red hair or that you're short," she said, motioning to Harold. His expression turned sour, the *hmph* implied.

"I trust Victor," she continued, without looking at him. She could feel his comforting presence behind her. "And he trusts Ramsey. And I think that if you leave it to them, those types of deaths wouldn't be prominent."

It wasn't quite reassuring, seeing as how she couldn't say for certain the deaths would stop. Victor himself had slipped up. She kept that tidbit to herself though.

"They probably didn't have time to deal with the problem with you guys chasing them. I just feel the vampires can handle their own."

No one was happy when she finished. Someone hissed in the living room.

"Snipe, you can't be considering this," Harold said. Snipe did appear to be considering it.

"This is crazy!" Arturo exclaimed.

Milo was disgusted. "We're listening to *humans* now? Must I remind you they're good for nothing but food and screwing? Why should we have to answer to them?"

"How about to live in peace, maybe," Celia threw over her shoulder. Milo glowered. That rope of entanglement reached out for her. She felt it advance, and was instantly confused because she knew this feeling. She couldn't quite remember the circumstances but her body recognized his magic, which had to mean he'd used it on her before.

There was also the lick of Clarice's power. She'd have to figure out later when he had tried to control her. She turned her back on them, breaking contact. She figured it would be enough to repel Milo. She wasn't sure about Clarice.

It wasn't.

A hot breeze drifted through her, making her sweat. It was so sudden, so uncomfortable that she couldn't think. As if the heat had created a fog in her head. No one spoke at the moment, which she thought was a good thing. She wasn't certain she'd be able to concentrate, she was so hot.

The only cure it seemed . . . was to take off her clothes. The answer came to her so easily. She felt instant relief just from the thought. She knew it was the only way. So she tugged at the hem of her Red Sox shirt. She pulled it over her head, revealing her pink, flowery bra. She wondered briefly why no one else was dying in this heat. Why they were staring at her like she was a crazy person. Those thoughts melted away as soon as they came, as if something told her not to worry about that. She only concerned herself with the heat.

Celia kicked off her sneakers and went to work on her jeans. Victor's snarl made her look up. She only saw him briefly before he lunged at Clarice. Milo stepped in front of her just as she ducked behind Arturo.

Milo shoved Victor, blocking his path. In response, Victor hauled off and punched him in the jaw.

"Enough!" Ramsey bellowed.

Victor stepped back. The maddening heat that had been holding Celia hostage receded. Her face was blank for a second. She looked around.

Harold was staring at her tits like they were speaking to him. Colin was still observing her as if she'd lost her mind and Snipe had at least averted his eyes. The vampires were looking her over, but not with nearly as much interest as Harold.

Confused, she looked down to discover she was holding her jeans open. It took a few seconds for the memory to come back to her: her brilliant idea of removing her clothes to combat the sudden wave of heat. She realized now she had been made a fool.

She quickly closed her jeans. She snatched up her shirt from the floor and pulled it back on, ruffling her hair. Embarrassment flushed her cheeks and neck red, which spiked the curiosity of the vampires. Only Bryce and Milo showed it though. Milo licked his lips indecently to Victor, then smirked.

Celia glared at the vamps in the living room. Clarice stepped from behind Arturo with all the arrogance of someone who hadn't just run like a chicken shit. She blew a kiss at Celia with a wink.

Ramsey was not having it. "I said, enough."

He went very still. Both Milo and Clarice closed their eyes and bowed their heads as if by force while Ramsey did some kind of mental admonishment.

After a few moments where the humans glanced back and forth between Ramsey and the others in confusion, Milo shook his head fiercely. It seemed to take considerate effort.

"Fuck that."

He jerked his eyes to Ramsey. Clarice glanced up cautiously.

"We should've killed these dickheads in the park and been done with it. I can't even stand to be in the same room with this vermin. After all the shit they put us through and you're just gonna let them get away with it. You're a coward, Ramsey. A fucking coward."

With that, he stalked to the front door. He yanked it open with enough force for it to bang against a table. Outside the door, he turned back to the room. Clarice lifted her chin, glaring at Ramsey resentfully. She sashayed out the door in her spike stilettos. The leather of her short skirt squeaked against her firm ass. Arturo sniffed angrily and followed behind them, slamming the door shut. The impact shattered the nearby windows, leaving web-like imprints in the glass.

Their exit left the room disturbingly silent. Celia became aware that the vamps were as still as statutes, not bothering with their human facades in the face of this turn. The hunters looked on edge as well, waiting for what was going to happen next.

Celia's eyes danced from Victor to Ramsey to Snipe. Snipe's dark eyes bored holes into her.

She was still determined. "What's it going to be? Can we call a truce?"

He was quiet for a long time. She was afraid he wasn't going to answer, especially after that little show. Snipe looked at Ramsey for what seemed like the first time. After another long deliberation, Snipe nodded once.

"But only with you," he added firmly, obviously thinking of the new situation now that it appeared his nest was broken up. "We know there're other nests in the area."

He said it as if Ramsey had been trying to deceive them by withholding information. This was news to Celia, though. It hadn't entered her mind that there were more vampires living nearby.

Ramsey hesitated a moment, conflicted. He looked at what was left of his group for a minute. He peered at Victor last as he contemplated. He finally inclined his head in agreement.

You'd think she would be elated. Instead, Celia was a strange combination of wired and burned out. This whole ordeal had taken a lot out of her, believe it or not, and the vampire blood was not helping matters at the moment. Her heart still thumped in her chest so hard it could've knocked her down.

"So, this is settled?" she asked, almost dubiously. "Can you shake on it?"

"You're pushing it, now," Colin piped. There was a tremor throughout the house. They all actually agreed on something.

Celia rolled her eyes. "Fine. Whatever."

She looked to Victor. "I'll take you home," he said, reading her mind.

Seventeen

JAY WANTED NOTHING more than to crawl into his futon and sleep for a week. When he *finally* came across a cab gassing up, though, he directed him to Snipe's. When he got there, everything was still. A light shone in the front window so someone was up.

After paying the cabbie, he shuffled up the walkway. His bones ached all the way down to his pinkie toes. He let out a wistful sigh as he knocked on the door. Even that hurt. Snipe answered, looking as exhausted as Jay felt. He noticed the fresh bruise on Snipe's left cheek, just under his eye. Jay remembered Snipe saying he explained his injuries to his coworkers as results of his rugby meets. Jay wondered if they believed that, especially with his limp.

He stepped aside to let Jay in. Harold was asleep on the fold-up. Colin must've had the spare room.

Snipe had been watching the news. He returned to his recliner. Jay lowered himself onto the sofa, loving the feel of the cushions.

“I could go for a nice massage,” Jay commented. “Happy ending included.”

Snipe didn’t even crack a smile, but he didn’t really laugh at Jay’s jokes anyways. Maybe Jay wasn’t funny. “We’ve come to an agreement with the vampires,” he told him.

Jay raised an eyebrow, surprised. “Oh?”

“It’ll do for now.”

Jay waited but he didn’t say more. “Well, I could’ve just called you ’stead of coming all the way over here.”

“You can have the couch if you want.” He picked up the remote to shut the television off, forestalling any debate. Jay was in no mood to protest or move. Snipe headed off to his room while Jay slowly stretched out on the sofa like an old man.

Harold’s snoring had been covered by the television. Now it filled the entire room. Surprisingly, Jay wasn’t annoyed. What he was was restless. He no longer had a reason to be in Boston. Snipe and the others were set with the vampires, it seemed. He’d already taken care of his vamp.

So why did he not want to leave?

Well, duh, but Jay didn’t want to admit it was Celia. She was tangled with Victor and Jay so did not want to deal with that. The last thing he wanted was for Celia to hate him for axing her vampire boyfriend.

He replayed their kiss a few times, remembering how much she had wanted it, too. He’d never been one to turn away from a challenge. He needed a break anyways. Taking beatings was starting to get to him. Plus, there was no one waiting for him in Dallas. And Colin and the others had started to grow on him.

His mind ticked on a little more until sleep finally overcame him. His thoughts switched to bunnies and oceans and brown-skinned girls with curly, auburn hair.

* * *

After taking Celia home, Victor dropped in on Ramsey. He was there alone, sitting in the dark living room. Victor flipped on the light. Ramsey looked up from the picture frame he was holding in his lap.

Victor glanced down surreptitiously and saw it was a photo of the woman of the house. He was intrigued but decided to err on the side of caution and not mention it.

"Are you okay?" he asked.

Ramsey sighed and a ghost of the smile that used to always lighten his face appeared. "Sure. I mean, this is just the calm right? Before everything goes to hell?"

Victor dropped his gaze. The silence stretched on.

"Don't worry, Victor. I'll find them."

"And then what?" Victor's tone was more challenging than he had intended. But he knew Ramsey would hesitate with killing members of his own seethe, even if they had defected.

Ramsey smiled again. "I guess I'll figure it out then."

* * *

Celia lay on the bed, waiting for Victor to return. Her eyes were closed as sleep tried to tug her under. The power of Milo's blood was weak now; the only trace was a prickly sensation just beneath her skin, like when your foot fell asleep and you shook it to get the blood circulating. Only it was her entire body.

The lamp was on next to her, giving the inside of her eyelids a yellow tint. After a while, she heard soft breathing beside her. She cuddled next to Victor, letting out a contented sigh.

Celia ran her hand under his shirt to caress his chest. "You're cold."

"I guess I'm a little hungry," he said softly. She felt his fingers in her hair, stroking her scalp the way she liked. "You wanted to talk?"

She opened her eyes to stare at his white t-shirt. The request for a conversation seemed so long ago.

"I've been thinking," she said. "About us. And I like what we have. I don't want things to change." She paused. "Do you think we can do this?"

His chest rose and fell under her cheek. It was so weird not hearing a heart or other noises bodies made. She didn't think she'd ever get used to that.

"I can't apologize enough for what I did to you," he said, his voice weary. "I wish that you weren't dragged into this mess but I'm glad it's resolved or whatever we want to call it. You did that." He reached over with his other hand to squeeze her arm.

"Can you forgive me?" he asked.

"Yes," she said without hesitation, which surprised her a little. His cool lips were on her forehead. She lifted her face to his and they kissed on it.

He stared into her eyes for a moment, then grinned. She rubbed his cheek. "You're not a monster," she said firmly. "I don't ever want to hear you say anything like that again." He tensed and she could tell he wanted to protest. So he wouldn't, Celia kissed his lips again.

They held each other for a while before Celia rolled off the bed. "I'm gonna get some water," she told him.

She went to the kitchen where she filled a glass and drank it all in four gulps. As she passed through the living room back to her room, something caught her eye. The streetlight shone through the curtains but they were orange. No, what had drawn her attention was a white light flashing across the curtain, making little swirlies.

Celia.

It was so soft she wasn't sure she had heard correctly. Suddenly, she felt compelled to move closer to the window. Her legs carried her across the room of their own volition. With shaky hands, she parted the curtains. The street was still except for the one dark figure on the opposite building's stoop.

She stared down at the figure, knowing exactly who it was. He looked up and the streetlight illuminated his face.

Milo.

His white-blonde hair looked even whiter tonight. His devious grin was scary. He held her gaze, his power not allowing her to look away, to even move.

No, she thought, which was enough to pry his hold this time. Sensing her resistance, Milo stood. He pursed his lips into a kiss, waved, and then ran at his vampire speed. Though he was gone, Celia stayed by the window, staring at the spot he had occupied.

It had been a warning that chilled her to the bones. She was surprised Victor hadn't come to her side, but she realized it was because her pulse was still the same. Which was crazy, right? Milo was out there. And he knew where she lived. He could feel what she felt. He could even call her to him. It was a creepy connection she despised.

"Celia?" Victor's voice drifted into the room. "So, are we doing Washington?"

She rolled her eyes. The question was just trivial enough to bring her back and make her relax.

Victor was here. He'd help her. He'd protect her.

The thought made her rush to his side, where she clung to him like there was no tomorrow. Tonight, she was safe. And that's what mattered.

New threats . . .

New allies . . .

Read on for an

excerpt from

Sour

Book Two

of the

Bitten Series

Sour

After taking a deep breath, Victor reached out for Celia's right hand. His cold palm pressed against hers. He turned her hand, facing her palm to the ceiling.

Slowly, gently, he brought her wrist to his mouth. His lips were soft against her skin. He paused for only a second before biting. A tiny whimper escaped her lips. His moans were soft though strained because he didn't want to enjoy this. Tonight was definitely not how he had pictured their first time. She felt his moans vibrating up her arm, tingling her sensitive nerves.

Celia told herself to relax. It really was better not to resist. Her lids drooped as she gave into the lovely pulling. He was tugging her from the inside in a rhythmic motion. Her free hand combed through his hair and held on tight. Soon, she was shivering and shuddering like she was having a particularly powerful orgasm. Her breath escaped in ragged gasps.

Victor raised his head after laving her wrist. The marks would flush into a light pink and disappear after a minute or two. He sighed; he hadn't wanted to stop. When he faced her, she saw the color rise in his skin. His eyes lightened as well.

He was in ecstasy. He'd always wanted to taste her; he still remembered the little remnants from her neck that night after Milo's first attack. But when he had asked all those months ago, she had said no and he was forced to refrain. It took years for vampires to gain that kind of self-control, especially with feeding and sex always mingled and muddled together in their world. So, he was pretty much like a Zen master or something. Being allowed to sample her had opened a new door and he wished it didn't have to end. Especially with how sweet her blood was—like pure vanilla. He'd never tasted a human so rich. Just a few drags would've maintained him the entire night, he was certain. Except, if he hadn't stopped, he'd have lost his honey. That's when the Zen master who had allowed him to live amongst humans for a hundred years came into play.

Victor held out his left wrist. She watched as he used the sharp nail of his right index finger to make a horizontal slice along his wrist. The blood bubbled and dripped onto the floor. She'd been contemplating changing the rug, and now it appeared there was a definite need. First the love hole he dug into the cream-colored shag carpet a few weeks ago, and now blood.

She took hold of his arm, gave him one last look—a mixture of fear and conviction—before bringing it to her lips. She closed her eyes as his blood warmed the inside of her mouth. It coated her throat as it made its way to her stomach, filling her up like a medicine she hadn't realized she'd needed.

She noted a hint of tartness to his blood, like how lemonade could have that biting effect. Sweet and sour, bonded together.

Victor was moaning again. His manly grunts, the air seeping from him in slow exhalations were sounds she was not used to hearing. See, her boyfriend was not one for verbal affirmations during lovemaking. He'd been trying lately though, of which she was grateful, but it always seemed artificial. The sighs escaping now were very much authentic and she was the cause. She trembled in happiness.

Ugh, maybe it was all the vampire blood.

Two minutes passed and she was still sucking away. Vampire

blood was like the finest nectar, and she wondered briefly if it tasted differently to other people.

It appeared Celia was not going to let go. Victor had to place a hand on her shoulder, and when she still dragged from him, he gently shoved her back.

Her breathing was erratic and her head spun. She leaned back into the fluffy cushions of the sofa. Her finger traced the corners of her lips, catching the lingering droplets and sucking every bit into her mouth. Her eyes closed while she waited for the calm. It didn't come. Instead, she was wired and tingly all over.

After a few deep breaths, her head cleared. Sharp shivers branched from her lower abdomen, igniting between her thighs. She squeezed her knees together as the flood started.

She peeked over to Victor. His head was bent forward, watching the wound on his wrist slowly mend itself. Celia clutched his hair, though she hadn't intended to be so rough. He looked at her, observed the lust in her face, saw her bite her lower lip. She leaned over and kissed him passionately. A trace of her blood lingered on his tongue. She didn't get the big deal; it tasted metallic to her. She shoved him onto his back with enough force to make him grunt.

Celia was on top of him, grinding her hips between his legs. She didn't bother removing her clothes; her shorts were baggy enough to move aside. She straddled his lap, opened his pants. She took hold of him, stroking until he was ready while laying warm kisses down his neck. As always, she fit around him like a warm glove. Her hips twisted in quick circles. He clasped her waist but she had control.

She teased him, lifting and squeezing until just the head of him remained inside her. She held there, her stomach muscles contracting. Victor's fingers insisted she stopped fucking with him.

"Celia," he groaned. A smirk crossed her face. She let her hips meet his.

She kissed him, not caring that his fangs were out, even when she cut her tongue on one. He took care of that with a little suckling. She flicked the tip of her tongue against his. Her quivering breath was on his face. She felt his soft hands on her neck, massaging the muscles and veins. Then he bit and her breath stuck in her chest.

Fireworks exploded inside of her, in her head and her groin. They sparkled and flamed in a good kind of burning, converging in the pit of her stomach and she was floating on the ceiling. Only Victor's strong arms kept her from drifting out the room, up into the night sky with the stars and the round, full moon.

Celia buried her face in his chest. She didn't know what to do. Whenever she moved, the burning stirred up again, making her breath come in quick gasps. She'd have to wait it out, not that it was unpleasant.

What a new experience. She wondered why he had never told her that would happen if she let him drink from her. She had been denying him the entire time they'd been together—about ten months now; though only during eight of those did Celia know what Victor was. He had explained that sharing blood with a vampire could be addictive for the human. Now she understood why.

Victor could get addicted to this, too.

About the author

The *Bitten* series offers Uzuri a chance to explore the paranormal. It first came to fruition in 2009, and continues to grow in her mind. Uzuri currently resides in Boston, Mass.

Find out more at: www.uzurimwilkerson.com
Follow her at: www.twitter.com/uzuri_iruzu
Friend her on: www.facebook.com/uzuriwilkerson

www.ingramcontent.com/pod-product-compliance
Lightning Source LLC
LaVergne TN
LVHW041111080826
845145LV00007B/1775

* 9 7 8 0 6 9 2 4 9 8 1 9 4 *